CAPTURED & SEDUCED

HOUSE OF THE CAT 1

SHELLEY MUNRO

MUNRO PRESS

Captured & Seduced

Print ISBN: 978-1-99-106329-8
Ebook ISBN: 978-0-473-28365-0

Editor: Evil Eye Editing
Cover: Kim Killion, The Killion Group, Inc.

Munro Press, New Zealand.

First Munro Press electronic publication June 2014
First Munro Press print publication May 2023

DEDICATION

A special thanks to Ravyn Wilde, who helped me during the initial stages of this book. I think Ry and Camryn's story turned out quite well in the end. Thanks so much.

And as always, thanks to Paul, my husband, partner in crime, and fellow adventurer.
Every day is a good day.

INTRODUCTION

A shapeshifter and a wizard slugging it out, an alien world and a hell-horse...

Jockey Camryn O'Sullivan is an alcoholic on a downward spiral after the death of her husband. When aliens kidnap her, she's both terrified and reluctantly fascinated by Ryman Coppersmith. She's positive the weird attraction to her abductor is an anomaly. Something to ignore. She'll train the aliens' horse and they'll return her home. Simple. There's no need for sex or a stubborn male kitty-cat to replace the precious memories of her husband.

Murder. Betrayal. Banishment.

Feline shapeshifter Ry has experienced treachery of the worst kind. When his foster brother—the man who betrayed him—proposes a wager on a hell-horse race, the lure to clear his name is irresistible.

Camryn's arrival triggers a jump in his already overactive sex drive. It's a struggle to keep his hands off his beautiful captive. Something in his mysterious feline background compels him to chase her and the passion firing between them soars out of control. Ry doesn't understand the mechanics of their attraction but knows he can't afford to lose Camryn...despite his promise to return her home.

CHAPTER ONE

"I don't care if Camryn's your sister. She's an alcoholic, and I swear she's overdoing the prescription drugs as well. I don't trust her near our son."

"She loves Luke," Max said.

"Last time Camryn babysat, she let Luke wander onto the racetrack. She was blind drunk."

Her sister-in-law's angry words brought Camryn O'Sullivan to an abrupt stop. She wavered on unsteady legs, not wasted but experiencing a buzz and blissful ignorance of the true state of her life. She smothered a giggle, slapping her hand over her quivering lips. Okay, she'd had drinks. Lots of drinks in pretty colors. Teeny umbrellas to match.

"What do you want me to do? I can't throw her out. She's my twin sister. She doesn't have anyone else."

A hit! Camryn screwed her eyes shut, protecting herself against the onslaught of pain. No, she didn't want to think about Gabriel, about being alone. How much it hurt. Max couldn't make her leave. He wouldn't.

She had nowhere else to go.

"Max, it's almost two years since Gabriel's death. Camryn's not improving. She needs help. More than we can give her."

Silence fell, but Ellen's words throbbed like the harping notes of a badly played violin. They hurt her head and brought forth a wave of indignation. She didn't need help. She needed Gabriel, dammit. Only her husband's presence would belay the paralyzing guilt she carried with her every day.

A rough masculine sigh sounded. "Love, you're right. Camryn needs help, but she doesn't see it. Until she realizes all we can do is be here for her. She has to want change."

"Fine, and meantime, Camryn drags us down with her. I found her smoking inside the stables this afternoon. She reeked of alcohol. Other people have noticed. She won jockey of the year two years running, but she's not getting the rides she was a year ago. Camryn has a real aptitude with horses, the gift you both have, and she's throwing it away."

A direct hit. Ellen's words sliced with precision, ripping open wounds barely scabbed. The agony hit instantaneously, ferocious and heart-stopping. Silent tears ran down Camryn's face, and she staggered against the door. Invisible bands clamped around her ribs. Camryn gasped hoarsely, the last of the drunken buzz bleeding away as she attempted to breathe. She wanted to rock away the pain, the guilt that came from knowing Gabriel would never return.

The wind caught the door, slamming it shut, and the murmur of voices from the kitchen stopped abruptly.

No, not here. She couldn't fall apart here. Camryn fumbled with the handle, increasingly desperate when footsteps neared.

"Camryn? Is that you?" Her twin brother's baritone sounded in the passage not far from where she teetered.

Camryn finally managed to coordinate brain and hands. The door opened. She stumbled into the winter air. The bite of the wind brought a shiver, an increase to her misery. Whiskey. She needed a drink. And maybe one of those little yellow pills the nice doctor had prescribed to help her sleep. Anything to escape the horrid truth. She hadn't meant to leave Luke alone. She loved her nephew. He raced about, so fast on his feet, and the sleepless nights had taken their toll. She'd fallen asleep in Gabriel's favorite chair.

Luke loved horses. No surprise since his father bred and trained racehorses. She and Max had lived and breathed horses since they were Luke's age. Camryn lurched along the muddy track leading to the cottage at the rear of the main house.

Really, she didn't need help. If Gabriel returned things would improve. She could kick the alcohol any time she wanted. A few pills to lift her mood. Camryn didn't need them either. She needed Gabriel.

Camryn burst into her cottage, tracking mud across the tile floor. She staggered through the cluttered kitchen and into the dining room where she'd instructed her brother and his workers to place Gabriel's chair. Camryn slumped into the big, masculine chair and pressed her nose against the cool leather. The faint scent of lavender soap and whiskey filled her senses, and a surge of tears blurred her vision. The chair didn't smell of Gabriel anymore.

It smelled of her.

Camryn crawled onto the chair properly, ignoring the muddy boots on her feet. She curled into a tight ball, her thin shoulders shaking with the force of her sobs. The cruel truth hit then. Gabriel wouldn't be coming home. He would never come home. Gabriel was dead, and it was all her fault.

"This plan will work." Yep pulled on his jacket and fastened it securely against the cold. "I feel it in ma bones."

Kaya smirked at her crewmate, her chin-length blue hair swinging against high cheekbones. She tugged Yep's ponytail. "Your bones are sometimes wrong. My research is, however, correct."

Ryman Coppersmith, captain of the Indefatigable, ignored them both. He'd already made his decision. He intended to win the hell-horse race on Ornum or at least beat his brother Talor and win their private bet. By the time the race ended, Ry hoped he'd be on the way to clearing his name of murder charges. Talor knew the identity of the murderer, but for some reason had never spoken out, preferring to see Ry exiled instead. Ry scowled. He wanted to go home. He wanted to stride through the streets without fear of capture. He wanted to embrace his sisters and visit his mother's grave.

It was time.

After research on Kaya's part, they'd found the stud farm easily enough. They landed the tender in an empty paddock and emerged to the bite of an icy-cool wind and full darkness.

Ry sniffed the air before striding in the direction of the stud farm. Trees. Grass. Mud. Animals. Every breath he took contained a new scent. The needs of the cat jumped to the fore and a low rumble eased from him.

"Go ahead," he muttered to his crew. "I will shift."

He knew he sounded curt, but the urgent need to run thrummed through him, even greater than his desire for a woman, and that was bad enough. Blood surged to his cock, the sharp sensation painful and frustrating. No available woman and he refused to use any of his crew.

Kaya and Yep melted into the darkness while Mogens, who attracted attention because of his changeable skin color, stayed with the tender. Nanu and Jannike presently orbited Earth in the

Indefatigable, hopefully remaining undetected.

After a deep inhalation, Ry ripped off his jacket and shirt and let the feline claim him. Trews and boots melted into his body, replaced by black fur. His bones lengthened and shifted, tendons and muscles reforming to the cat. His color vision faded, his surroundings turning to shades of black and white. Ry dropped to all fours and padded across the moist grass, long tail swishing.

As always, a sense of aggravation followed him. Ry knew nothing of his feline background, had never met another of his species. In one pain-filled evening, when he'd thought he might die, he'd turned into a black feline without warning. He'd yowled his panic so loud his shipmates had come running. Ry grinned at the memory. He'd scared them half to death. Although funny now, his unexpected shift into a powerful black cat had been bloody terrifying.

For all of them.

With help from Mogens, the man who'd become their seer and part of the crew, Ry had finally transformed back, bearing a new cat tattoo on his biceps as a souvenir and his shirt in tatters. Weirdly, his trews had survived the transformation. Talk about a learning experience. And he was still discovering the foibles of his species. The not knowing scared him. It made him wonder if there had been something else inside the bag they'd found with him as a baby. As a child he'd asked, but his foster father had told him the bag contained clothes.

The low voices and footsteps of his crew were clearly audible. Ry twitched his nose and prowled after them, annoyed with their casual approach. A sharp feline yowl reminded them to reduce the noise. Ry broke into a lope, savoring the play of muscles long confined in humanoid form. The wind ruffled his fur while mud splashed his legs and belly.

When he neared the center of the farm where the owners lived, white post and rail fences carved the land into paddocks. Ry leaped over the nearest, his heart pumping with physical exertion. An animal snorted, springing into action and galloping from the spot where Ry had frozen in place.

A horse. The Earth counterpart of a hell-horse.

Ry crept along the fence line not wanting to alarm more animals or attract attention. Once clear, he sped up, muscles moving powerfully, every sense alert. Ry caught the rustle of a small creature in a hedgerow, the tentative neighs of two horses at the far end of a paddock. The chill wind continued to ruffle his fur, the heavy moisture in the air indicating impending rain. Great. Ry hated to get wet. His pace increased to a scamper as he followed the track running between the paddocks.

Ahead, light bled from behind screened windows. According to the information Yep and Kaya had uncovered, the trainer lived with his wife and child. Ry regretted any anguish the trainer's departure would cause and had penned a note, explaining the situation to his family. Hopefully the Earthlings could decipher the universal language. Ry slipped into the shadows and stalked closer, every sense alert for danger.

A cough over to his left grabbed his attention. Ry stilled, whiskers twitching. The sharp tang of sweat and unwashed body caught the back of his throat. The cough sounded again. A figure staggered from a dim-lit porch and wove to the rails of the nearest paddock. Ry's tension eased. The trainer. He recognized the coat the man wore since it appeared in the photo Yep and Kaya had found during their research on the flight to Earth. A lucky break.

Ry padded closer, placing himself near enough to watch without giving away his presence. He needed to wait for the crew to move into position for the snatch to go smoothly. The man appeared short, about Kaya's height, but solid. His reek said he didn't care much for personal hygiene. His stench didn't bother the horses. Two plodded over to him, and one nuzzled his shoulder. The man smoothed his hand over the glossy neck. The other horse nickered. The man stroked it, and the creatures moved away. Soft footsteps dragged his attention from the man.

Yep indicated the man with a jerk of his head. "He waits for us to extract him and take him on the adventure of his life."

Ry stared, unable to see much despite his superior eyesight. The man wore a cover over his head, obscuring his features. Ry's nose twitched at the objectionable odor coming from the man, the air thick with liquor fumes.

Yep seemed to sense Ry's doubts and sought to reassure. "The man's a champion trainer," he whispered. "Nanu and I attended the races two cycles ago. This man trained five of the twelve winners. Several place getters. Man's natural with the four-legged creatures. Hell-horses should respond to him in the same way."

And if they didn't? Grata, he hated this planet. The cold seeped right to his bones, and the promised rain arrived in a slow drizzle. Ry quaked, attempting to shake off the water without audible noise. Didn't work. Miserable, he shivered, ears flicking while irritation built.

"Aw, frag it," Yep swore. "He's moving."

The man intended to seek shelter. Maybe he wasn't as far gone as Ry suspected.

Yep slipped after him. Ry followed with a grumbling sigh, watching the staggering figure with disfavor while he twitched his whiskers. The ground sucked at his paws, the slippery footing making their mission difficult.

The crew moved in, silent signals passing between them until they stood in position. Yep and Kaya converged from opposite sides, springing and disabling the man in well-practiced synchronicity. Kaya pulled the special cloth impregnated with a potion the seer had made from her pocket and pressed it to his nose. The man went limp, and Yep slung the bulky figure over his shoulder before striding in the direction of the tender. Kaya darted up to the shelter and shoved Ry's note under the door before joining Yep.

Ry followed, loping along the muddy track. In a burst of speed, he passed his crew, trying to outrun the returning desire for a woman. It came out of nowhere, unbidden.

Unwanted, the need gripped him with such powerful intensity he stopped in his tracks. Damn, he'd thought he'd manage for a few more weeks.

Ry tried to ignore the craving writhing through his veins. The out-of-control sensation had intensified during the past few months, affecting his sleep. The constant desire for a woman made his temper uncertain, although so far he'd managed to hold things together. Ry knew his need was escalating to dangerous levels. His attempts to manage what he presumed were feline traits and part of his heritage brought a bark of ironic laughter.

The seer saw his turmoil. The others would realize the tenuous hold he had over his feline too if he didn't do something fast. Of course, he'd continue with the search for his people, but meantime, he'd have to break down and find a woman to travel with them during their voyage to take the edge off his sexual needs. Hopefully the woman's presence would slow the downward spiral into the mysterious world of the feline.

The world he didn't understand because he didn't know where he came from or who he was.

Ry raced to the tender and shifted smoothly. His naked chest gleamed with moisture and rivulets of mud, his heart thudded hard and erratic. Inside, Ry ignored his shirt and jacket, preferring to sanitize back on the Indy before he redressed.

"Everything okay?" Mogens asked.

"Yeah." Ry wanted to lash out at the seer's scrutiny, tired of the constant analysis. He growled, a vicious snarl of impatience. Ry wanted to laugh at Mogens' undignified scramble to put distance between them but didn't have it in him. "The crew won't be long. Mission accomplished."

The tension inside ratcheted sharply upward. Ry gritted his teeth, wanting to hit someone. Silently, he calculated the length of the flight to the planet Ornum and how quickly he could find a woman. The idea of sinking into the warmth of a female, of licking her fragrant skin and losing himself in the plain rawness of sex brought an uncontrollable surge of arousal. His cock drew painfully tight, and Ry wheezed through the throbbing ache. He wished he knew what ailed him, why the feline refused to settle even with the suppressant Mogens had made for him.

Footsteps thudded on the tender ramp. Kaya and Yep clattered inside with Yep still carrying the man over his shoulder. He dumped him on the nearest chair and strapped him in for safety. The unconscious human slumped forward, face hidden by the head covering. A noxious smell still emanated from him, the stench compounded in the confined quarters of the tender.

"All aboard." Mogens sealed the entrance. A throaty roar indicated Yep had started up the thrusters, and secs later, they lifted off.

Ry slumped onto his chair and closed his eyes, battling with the compulsion to grab Kaya, who sat next to him. He took a deep breath. A mistake since he almost drowned in her feminine pheromones. He tipped back his head and growled, the catlike yowl full of fury. Kaya's eyes widened, and she jumped to her feet, staring at Ry with something akin to horror.

"Good girl, watch the man for me," Mogens said, pretending nothing out of the ordinary had occurred. "I'll sit there. I want to have a word with Ry."

Ry stirred uneasily. He'd never done that before. Gripping the edges of his chair, he fought for control, despite the air laden with Kaya's scent. If anything, her surge of terror and adrenaline intensified the desire filling his body with savage need. Kaya shifted her weight, drawing his attention. Rich female musk filled every inhalation, along with the stink of the horse trainer. His gaze slid from the slumped figure back to Kaya. An intense shiver racked his body, and Ry closed his eyes, struggling to remain seated. The loss of one sense served to intensify the others, and he hurriedly opened his eyes again.

"Seer, do you have more of the slumber drug?" Ry had to force the words out, past jutting canines. They emerged in a growled hiss, almost unintelligible. He tried again. "Slumber drug." The words were little more than a feral snarl.

Luckily the seer seemed to understand. "I have more." He frowned, a ribbon of black swirling across his bare arms and face. It combined with the white of his skin to darken his complexion.

Good, Ry thought, panting heavily. His chest rose and fell rapidly, the shallow breaths still dragging in too much in the way of sensory input. Mogens knew, as he'd feared, sensed his desperation.

Heat, so intense it seared his body, brought a torturous shudder. He had to rid himself of the inferno inside. Phrull, he needed the release of sex.

So bad.

Ry blinked, sweat pouring down his face. The dampness plastered his black hair to his head until it hung in wet tendrils.

"Dose me. Now. Don't want to hurt." A high-pitched growl erupted, echoing in the tender. He gripped the edges of the seat he sat on even though his fingers had bled to claws. "Kaya." Grata, never forgive himself if he hurt one of his crew. They were his friends. Family. They knew his secrets, were loyal to him, to each other. Ry snarled, trembling on the cusp of a shift to feline. "Mogens," he gritted out.

"I'm not sure how it will react—"

"Do it." An order.

Mogens stood and strode to his satchel. He rummaged through and drew out another of the impregnated cloths they'd used to subdue the human. The seer returned, his face dark black with worry as he glanced at Ry with compassion. "Are you sure?"

The pity made Ry spit with fury. The solid walls of the tender rattled with his bark of anger. In lieu of a reply, Ry reached up and grabbed the cloth. He pressed it to his nose, gagging at the herbal reek. His instinctive reaction was to remove the pad, but Mogens grasped his hand and held it in place. Gradually the world blurred. His arms and legs refused to support his body. Ry slumped over, his world turning black.

Camryn woke to the sensation of the floor shuddering. Her head vibrated in time. Damn whiskey kicked like a mule. A moan escaped, the sound tiny and insignificant. Her eyes flickered, the glare of light intense. A jagged slice of pain cut across her temples. Everything ached, even her eyes. She stopped trying to open them, and her world ceased spinning. Cautiously, she cataloged her body for aches and pains.

Dry.

Her mouth felt like a dusty paddock during the middle of a severe drought. And her tongue—heck, that felt too thick and furry to fit inside her mouth. She moved her arms or attempted to, but they stuck fast against her sides. Her heart thudded, an erratic beat of fear. Her brother. He'd told her—told her yesterday she had to stop drinking. If she didn't...

What had he done?

She struggled, hyperventilating in fear. He wouldn't. He couldn't.

For her own good, he'd said. Yeah, easy for him. He had a wife, a child. They were a family. A unit. She had nothing to live for. Not now.

Camryn forced her eyes open, her heart drumming like the thunder of horses' hooves during a race. Her gaze lit on a large black shape on the floor. Camryn closed her eyes and moved her head in a cautious shake, wincing at the sharp throb. When she opened her eyes again, the object came into focus. A large black cat lay on the floor near her. It stared at her with its green eyes. Its mouth lay open, and sharp white teeth glittered in the bright light. Camryn swallowed. A dream. No, a nightmare. She wasn't awake. Maybe Max was right—she'd started drinking too much alcohol.

The cat stood, stretched just like her mother's used to, extending front legs and sticking its butt in the air. Then it prowled toward her, black tail swishing from side-to-side. A panicked whimper escaped. Camryn wanted to flee but couldn't move.

Not her arms or legs.

Trapped.

The cat stalked closer until she felt the creature's hot breath through the denim of her old jeans where her brother's heavy coat had fallen away. The cat let out a sharp, fierce grunt, raising the hairs on her arms into a distinct prickle. She whimpered, the cry weak and thready. The cat moved nearer still. It opened its huge maw, globules of saliva visible. Oh heck. This was no dream. It intended to eat her. Camryn struggled fiercely, a ripple of pure terror pouring from her parched throat.

The thud of running feet sounded, and two people burst into the room. Camryn's eyes widened, and she screamed again. And again. The black leopard bit her on the leg, the sharp pain silencing her scream abruptly.

They stared at each other before weird jabbers commenced, sounding like Chinese mixed with lots of clicks and guttural sounds too rapid for her to even start to understand.

Camryn moaned when they approached and halted by the leopard. Fear, stark and real, pummeled her body, her mind. She cried out as they moved closer in a collective step.

People. A loose term. Real loose.

One appeared female and had bright electric blue hair and...and pointy ears. Her flashing eyes and rigid jaw brought a warrior to mind. The tight-fitting trousers and brown tunic top, plus the huge number of weapons strapped on her slender yet muscular body confirmed the impression. The other was the palest person she'd ever seen. Everything about him seemed white. Totally colorless. Apart from his eyes. They were the palest violet and focused intently on her. While she gaped at the male—at least the bulge at his groin suggested the masculine gender—he changed color. Streaks of black swirled through the white, mixing to a slate gray. The black kept appearing in long ribbons across the part of his chest she could see until his skin and hair gleamed deep ebony. His eyes remained the same eerie violet.

Camryn's gaze traveled to the black leopard. It sat on its haunches between the warrior and the creepy changing man. Changing Man carried a satchel in his hand. After snapping several clicks at the other beings, he pulled a glass jar from the bag. He opened it and tipped the contents onto the palm of his black hand. He frowned at them, white ribbons of color suddenly swirling across his chest. His head dipped in a satisfied nod, and the things on his hand wriggled like fat scarlet caterpillars.

She whined softly. God, this wasn't a nightmare. These weren't the orderlies at the clinic where Max had threatened to send her.

They were aliens. Aliens.

Her heart pounded, leaping against her breast. Camryn started to struggle. Not even a warning snarl from the leopard stopped her fear escalating into outright panic. With another grunt and three rapid clicks, the warrior approached her. She grasped Camryn's head and held her still. Changing Man picked up one bright red caterpillar between gray fingers and shoved it in her ear.

Sharp pain. Intense. Worse than even the most evil hangover. The caterpillar crawled down her ear canal. She heard the crunching sounds when it attached itself somewhere inside. Her head rang, agony slicing across her temples. She keened, her strength sapped and no contest for the warrior's superior power. The warrior held Camryn's head, forcing it in the opposite direction, baring her other ear for the same abuse. Anguished tears slipped down her face. She sobbed, but that didn't stop Changing Man from forcing a caterpillar inside her ear. Camryn felt every slither when it crawled inside. The pain felt just as intense, the crunching sound deafening while the caterpillar ate into her head.

"Gabriel," she whispered, realizing she'd landed in hell. Gabriel wouldn't be here. Only she had sinned enough to gain entrance to hell.

"Stop crying," the warrior woman snapped, her blue hair flying around her head in a halo. "Can you understand us now?"

She could, but nausea tiptoed through her stomach. Camryn's entire body shuddered with the depths of her misery. She'd heard hell was fiery hot, but ice enclosed her heart, her body. Nothing had changed. She still missed Gabriel.

The woman bent, tipped Camryn's head back and struck her face with the palm of her hand. Camryn jerked back, stopping her crying mid-sob.

"Stop cryin' and hold still while I take the seat harness off you."

"Keep still, child," Changing Man soothed. "We intend you no harm."

Something in his calm violet eyes told her he spoke the truth. Maybe they didn't intend to cut her up for experiments. Camryn cast a quick glance at the leopard and her anxiety ramped up again. The feline looked as if it would devour her in a few bites, gobble her up until nothing remained.

"And him?" she croaked, heart fluttering like the starter's flag in a stiff breeze.

"Ry, back up and leave the woman alone. Shift." The changing man didn't seem frightened of the kitty at all.

Camryn held still while the warrior released the restraints holding her in place. Her attention remained on the black leopard.

She didn't like the way the animal stared at her. The leopard curled its top lip and twitched its whiskers. Then, as she watched, the leopard started to blur. The warrior pulled the harness away. Camryn blinked, her spine slamming against the back of the chair. Tension seeped through her, finding an outlet in clawed hands, gripping the armrests. Under her horrified gaze, the leopard transformed to a man wearing tight black trousers and knee-length black boots. Tall and muscular with a wild mass of black hair falling down to his shoulders. A green gaze pinned her in place, studying her just as intently as she examined him. Her heart did a crazy flip, slowing and suddenly galloping into a frenzied beat. For the first time since she'd met Gabriel, she looked at a man in a sexual way, even if fear tinged the curiosity.

The muscles in his chest rippled when he moved, the skin the color of burnished copper. A tattoo of a cat decorated one biceps, so real Camryn wondered if it might spring to life in the same swift manner the leopard had transformed to a man. The man's trousers clung to his long, muscular legs and slim hips. The bulge at his groin proclaimed his maleness without a shred of doubt.

"You've got clothes on," she blurted. Mortified color spread to her face when she realized what she'd said. In all the books she'd read about shapeshifters they'd ended up naked after their change. When he'd morphed, his lower half remained covered.

"I could always take them off," he said in a husky voice.

They stared at each other, the moment so intense Camryn forgot they weren't alone. Spellbound, she studied his very masculine body, his musculature and his heavily fringed green eyes. She blinked when he stepped closer, and again when he squatted in front of her to cup her cheek with one callused hand.

"You're female." His sigh sounded like a purr, and it dragged every receptor on her body to high alert. Her breasts pulled tight, the hard points dragging across the cotton cups of her bra with every rapid breath. In breathless anticipation, she waited for his next move even as part of her rebelled at the unwanted feelings coursing through her body. This wasn't right. These people had kidnapped her. She shouldn't—she refused—they'd given her something, made her react to this man, this animal.

Camryn sprang to her feet and squeezed past him, fear lending her speed and agility. She bounded for the open doorway and ran down a short passage before coming to an abrupt halt. Whoa. Whoa! This was not happening.

"Where am I?" Camryn stared in stupefied horror at the vast blackness. A man—at least she thought it was a man because he seemed relatively normal with his black ponytail—flew the spacecraft. He'd turned on hearing her question and stared with something akin to shock.

"We're orbiting Earth, waiting to meet up with the Indefatigable," the man said.

"It's a woman," the warrior said in disgust. "You kidnapped the wrong one."

"No crap." The pilot's bushy eyebrows squeezed together in a scowl when he looked over his shoulder again. "No, we kidnapped a man. He wore the same coat as the man in our depictions."

Camryn said nothing, backing away from the fierce man. They'd kidnapped her because she'd taken her brother's coat to ward off the cold? Her head throbbed, and her ears felt tender. At least the caterpillars had ceased their wriggling. She hated to think what they were doing inside her head.

"We seem to have kidnapped a woman masquerading as a man." The warrior glared at the pilot. "You stuffed up."

"We had a depiction of the man in that coat." The pilot pointed at her.

Camryn studied the view through the huge port, thoughts bouncing through her mind. The pilot had taken both hands off the controls. She couldn't see any traffic but surely he should watch for obstacles?

Gabriel...

Tears welled in her eyes. A raging thirst made her swallow, but nothing encouraged saliva. God, she needed a drink. Bad. She stepped back and bumped into a muscular and warm naked chest.

"Turn around," Changing Man said. "We'll take her back and find the right man this time. The real horse trainer."

Belatedly it occurred to Camryn they were talking about Max. "No!" she cried. "No, you can't take Max. He has a wife and a child. They need him." Her heart pounded anew. They couldn't take Max. God, she was such a screw-up. No one would miss her. "Take me instead. I'll do anything. Anything at all."

Without Gabriel, she was nothing. It didn't matter what they did to her. She didn't have a life to wreck while Max...Max had everything to live for. His family. His business. The success starting to come his way. Owners demanded his training skills while they ran in their haste to escape her.

"Take me," she repeated.

"Our goal is to win," the warrior said, her words directed to the half-naked man. "Captain, that's the whole point."

A hand grasped her shoulder. "You're right. Yep, turn back."

"No, wait," Changing Man raised his right hand in a stop gesture. His violet eyes seemed to drill into hers. She trembled under the close attention because it felt as if he stared into her soul. "What if this is fate? I read the night skies while I waited for your return. They spoke of change and opportunity."

The warrior snorted. "Which could mean anything. Things are always changing."

"True," Cat Man said, although he didn't sound as disbelieving as the warrior.

"We'll have to take her back and get the right one," the warrior persisted.

It had become crowded in the front of the ship, and Camryn realized she had nowhere left to run. "Leave my brother alone."

Unfortunately, her order emerged in a scared, girly voice. A fine tremor slid through her body.

"Let's be sensible about this," Changing Man said. "Return to the rear of the tender and let us discuss what can be done."

Camryn saw Cat Man's quick nod of assent.

"Send Jannike a message. Tell her we have a delay. Return to the same landing space," he said.

The pilot nodded and flipped several buttons, taking Cat Man's orders in his stride. Camryn frowned. If Cat Man was in charge she didn't rate her chance of survival. His expression bore such hunger, and the color of his eyes darkened each time he stared at her. The speculation, the sheer lust in his gaze made her nerves shriek. Camryn backed away slowly. She bumped into the changing man and the warrior and at once felt marginally safer.

Changing Man reached for her with his pearly-gray hand. He clasped her forearm in a gentle manner. "This way, my dear."

Camryn couldn't help it. Visions of Red Riding Hood rushed to mind. Wrong fairy tale but the principle remained the same. Sharp teeth were better for eating red meat. They intended to kidnap her brother. God, she couldn't let them.

She turned to Cat Man, took a deep breath. "Please, you can't take my brother. You can't."

"Child, we need him," Changing Man said. "He has expertise we require."

"What expertise?" There must be a way to save Max from the aliens.

"We require a horse trainer," Cat Man said. Once again he'd moved close, and she hadn't noticed until their bodies touched.

Camryn flinched at the electrical surge that zapped the length of her body and edged away with a soft gasp. She forced herself to concentrate. "I can train horses."

"You?" the warrior asked with a sneer.

"Yes," Camryn said, resisting the urge to shuffle her feet. Cat

Man had stepped into her personal space again, leaving her nowhere to move. "I'm a jockey. I ride horses for a living, and I know how to train them. Take me with you. I can do it. Leave my brother with his family. Please."

Ry listened to her impassioned words and wanted to follow her suggestion. Giving in to temptation, he stroked his hand across her cheek. He detested her scent, but her skin felt soft, like the finest, expensive fabrics they'd seized from one of his brother's shipments. He wanted to unwrap the female, toss her in the sanitizer then rub his scent all over her. Mark her as his. The urge thundered through him. His fingers slid across her jawbone, down her neck until he felt the jump of her pulse beneath his fingertips. She was a tiny thing, smaller than Kaya he saw now, with brown or black hair slightly shorter than his. He wasn't entirely sure because it hung in damp, oily clumps around her head. Her eyes were golden brown while her lips...her lips were full and sensual and enticed him to explore at closer quarters. He traced her bottom lip with the pad of his thumb, savoring her quick, ragged intake of air.

"Captain. Ry!" Kaya grasped his arm and shook it, her nails digging into his biceps like talons.

He growled under his breath, and she released him, stepping away, head lowered in submission.

"You weren't listening." Apology coated her voice, but she negated it when she lifted her head to glare. "Have you taken your medicine?"

"Yes."

"When did you take the last vial?" Mogens asked.

"Before I left the tender." Ry forced himself to release the woman, full of resentment at their accusations. He'd taken the medicine. It wasn't his fault the fraggin' stuff didn't work. "How many horses have you trained?" He'd disliked the idea of stealing the man from his family. It hadn't seemed right, even if they needed his help.

"I started training horses when I was fourteen years of age, before I became an apprentice jockey."

The woman refused to look at him. Her reluctance pricked his temper, and he growled. Gasping, she backed away until her body touched the curved wall of the tender. He countered, stepping near enough to smell the layer of enticing femininity beneath the stench of her clothes and alcohol-laden breath. His nostrils flared while his cock reared, thrusting painfully against the placket of his trews.

"Captain. Concentrate," Mogens ordered.

"Get me more medicine."

"I didn't bring any with me. I have more on the Indy."

Ry closed his eyes, attempting to center his mind and push all thoughts of the woman away. It worked until he heard her swallow. His lids opened to see her pink tongue swipe across her lips. They glistened and made him yearn for a taste. A rumble of pure desire rattled his throat, emerging as a barking cough. He didn't want to spend time with a woman who feared him, yet the idea of sending her away disturbed him more.

"If you are lying about your ability, your brother will suffer." He forced strength and a hint of brutality into the announcement.

This race and beating his brother were too important. He wanted his name cleared. They had to do the best they could in the limited time.

"I am a good trainer. I can do the job. You won't be sorry." Her expression appeared open and without deceit. She meant her words. "I'll train your horse, and when I'm finished, return me to Earth."

Ry wasn't so sure.

"Captain, step away from the woman. Let her breathe," Mogens said, tugging at his shoulder. His behavior had agitated the seer because the male's color flickered toward black, the black, white and gray moving in crazy swirls over his skin. The rapid change made Ry dizzy. "Captain."

Ry allowed the seer to pull him away from the woman.

"What's the verdict?" Yep waited for his decision.

It appeared as if they all waited for his assessment. Gut instinct gnawed him again, telling Ry he needed to best his brother and settle the dispute between them for once and all. Ry knew his brother hated him and would do anything to destroy him. He was surprised Talor had even suggested the bet and wasn't about to lose the opportunity to clear his name. The Earth woman could help him gain an edge.

Ry inhaled, his furtive gaze heading once more for the woman. He took half a step forward before he stayed the move. Damn, he was doing it again. The woman called to him on so many levels. Ry prowled across the tender, placing as much distance between them as possible. He flung himself into the chair beside Yep and stared moodily at the woman.

Temptation. Trouble. She presented both.

He sighed. "Set course for rendezvous with the Indefatigable."

Ry hoped like hell he wasn't making a huge mistake taking the woman with them.

Chapter Two

"It went well?" Jannike met them in the transport bay. "Captain?"

Ry didn't answer, brushing past his second-in-command, desperate to escape the woman. This shouldn't be happening. He'd humped himself to exhaustion on Ibrox after learning of his mother's death, and since then he'd taken Mogens' medicine and grabbed every opportunity to bed women during reprovisioning stops.

Aware of his shaky control, he stormed down the corridor, heading for his quarters. Privacy. He wasn't sure what he'd do when he arrived there—more medicine for a start, to bolster his tenuous willpower.

Ry thumped the control to close the door of his cabin and leaned against the rigid surface. Every sense screamed, colors and scents more vivid than they'd ever been before. He stomped to his bunk and sat on the edge to tug off both boots and trews. Naked, he prowled to the sanitizer, desperate to rid himself of the woman's scent, the feel of her silky skin. Ry turned slowly inside the sanitizer. Using the calming exercises the seer had taught him, he attempted to center his mind, let his tension seep away.

Didn't work.

Ten mins later, fully dressed, he strode to the bridge, but before he arrived, the woman halted him in his tracks. In shock, he stared at her. Attraction had simmered in him before, but now...now he saw her true magnificence. One of his crew, probably Kaya, had given her clean clothes and shoved her through the sanitizer. Her dark hair glowed with cleanliness, the color reminding him of a blackbird's wing. Long and smooth it hung down to her shoulders in a dark wave. And her scent. It called him.

With two giant steps, Ry closed the space separating them. He stared down at the human woman, drawing her clean scent deep into his lungs. Unbidden, his hand moved to cup her cheek, and without any thought he dipped his head to press their lips together.

Instantaneous reaction thrummed in his body, nerve endings exploding with the emotions bombarding his mind. The feline pulsed against his skin, battling him for control.

Take her.

The words whispered through his mind, and he drew her against his chest, holding her more securely and taking the kiss deeper. He nibbled her bottom lip, gave her a quick nip when she was slow to respond, and when she opened her mouth in an O of surprise, he slipped his tongue inside.

Sweet. So sweet.

Need and desire pummeled him. He wanted more. So much more. A vision of him thrusting into her wet center gripped him, drove him to run his hands down her back, to explore her curves.

The woman groaned but didn't protest or push him away, and some of his tension lifted. Ry relaxed, fiercely glad of her willingness. He didn't think he could stop, not with ease.

Their tongues stroked together, and soon needy cries came from the woman. She gripped his shoulders and rubbed her breasts against his chest, each of her touches like a remote control on his cock. Ry let his hands slip down her spine to her butt, his breaths hoarse, his knees weak.

He'd never felt this way before. True, the feline became bad-tempered and unpredictable when he neglected feeding his voracious appetite, but this...this...was something different again.

The compulsion he'd labored under since first sighting the woman strengthened, bolstered by her touch and scent. She rubbed against him, seeming to suffer the same throb of urgency. Ry gripped her buttocks and easily lifted her, sliding his erection along the notch between her thighs. Exquisite pleasure roared through him as he smelled her arousal, felt her heat. He shuddered, desperately wanting to touch naked skin, to thrust into her hot pussy.

"Captain. Captain!"

The woman hopped in fright, jamming their bodies closer together. Ry glared over her shoulder at the seer even as he savored the sharp jolt of pleasure soaring to his cock. "What do you want?"

"Unhand the woman, Captain. You can't use her and discard her like the other women," Mogens chided. "We need her."

Ry's hands stilled on her back. The warmth of her skin radiated through the coarse linen of her shirt. She was his. His hands moved down to cup her bottom again.

His.

"Captain." The infinite patience in Mogens' voice finally penetrated the crazed sexual haze gripping him. "Captain, we arrive at Ornum on the morrow. We need a plan of attack." His words also implied Ry could have women tomorrow—as many as he wanted.

Every part of Ry protested when he set the woman on her feet, but he peeled his hands from her shapely arse. He dragged in a breath and watched through narrowed eyes while Mogens led the woman away. Mogens never looked back.

The woman did.

Her brown eyes were wide, full of shock, and he knew exactly how she felt. He'd never experienced such a high or been so driven to claim a woman. His cock throbbed in acknowledgment of the fact. Ry sauntered after them, his gaze fastened on the feminine sway of hips. She wasn't a big woman like Jannike or a warrior like Kaya. Petite, she came up to his chest. Her skin appeared pale and her whole look was one of fragility. Ry recalled the stench on her breath when they'd first found her. She hadn't tasted bad when they'd kissed. No, he'd tasted a hint of one of Mogens' potions. He watched her throw another glance over her shoulder, alarm slamming him when he saw her flash of fear. A rumble of protest vibrated deep in his throat. The woman hadn't acted frightened before.

He knew her mouth intimately, had felt her body tremble against his but had no idea of the woman's name.

Uncomfortable with the direction of his thoughts, Ry stalked in the rear, never shifting his focus from Mogens and the woman. At the age of eighteen, when he'd taken the first steps from law-abiding citizen to thief, he'd decided to avoid romantic entanglements. The life of an outlaw was not conducive to family life. He wasn't partner material because in a society that took pride in tracing their families back generations, he knew nothing, had no official birth papers. Not an attractive proposition for any woman or her family. Even his fiancée Meghan had turned away, preferring Talor instead, meeting him on the sly.

He'd decided to embrace all women instead of one before he'd unexpectedly turned feline. Now his sexual appetites worked better with a variety of women and large numbers. Ry snorted. No female wanted to stand aside while her partner satiated his needs with other women.

Another glance at the woman brought a snarl. The echo bounced back in mockery. They'd reach Ornum soon. He'd take care of things then continue with their cartage and salvage as usual. That had to work. The woman wasn't his and could never be his. He'd promised to return her to Earth. Yeah, hands off while he concentrated on kicking Talor's butt. The need to clear his name was a surefire way of keeping his fascination with the woman at bay.

Camryn let Changing Man lead her away. Her limbs trembled so much she wobbled. Nothing about this seemed real. She'd stepped beyond alcohol-induced dreams and straight into nightmare territory. It was the only explanation for the way she'd let Cat Man paw her. If Changing Man hadn't come along...

Her breath hissed out and alarm took over. The backs of her eyes stung, burning with unshed tears. Gabriel. She hadn't thought of him once while Cat Man had kissed her. Not once. A tear slipped free, and she dashed it away with the back of her right hand. She couldn't do this. She couldn't spend time with a man who...who...

Kissed her as if there were no other available women. Kissed her as if she meant everything.

Her mind shied from the truth—how much she'd enjoyed his touch, encouraged him even. It couldn't happen again. It wouldn't. She'd train the horses for the aliens and follow their instructions, giving them no reason to steal Max from his family. At least she could give her brother and sister-in-law that.

The headache returned with vengeance, pinching at her temples. With a trembling hand, she pressed her fingers against her scalp to massage lightly. The inside of her mouth felt like the compacted dust and dirt of a dry racetrack while her mind screamed for the sweet oblivion only possible with a sip or two of alcohol. God, she wanted a drink in the worst possible way.

Her head continued to thud, woolly and thick, while her limbs trembled in a noticeable way. Embarrassment seeped into her cheeks as she tucked a quaking hand under the tunic top the warrior woman had given her to wear.

Max had pointed out her tendency to shake and shudder during his lecture on drinking. Exhibit two or three. She couldn't quite remember. There'd been a few items. An endless litany. Oh yeah. A snigger broke out, drawing the alien's attention. Loss of memory and unreliability had scored at number six on Max's list. Just went to prove she couldn't be as bad as Max made out if she could remember his stupid list of misdemeanors.

"What is your name, child?" The changing man glimmered an attractive white-gray, reminding Camryn of a lustrous pearl.

"Camryn O'Sullivan."

"My name is Mogens Vere." The changing man halted and gazed deep into her eyes. "Gabriel says it's not your fault."

"What?" A distinct wobble threaded through her voice and shock lashed her body, robbing her mind of humor.

"He was here. He's gone now."

She gaped at Mogens, watched his face bleed from pretty pearl to alarming black. The alien played a cruel trick. Gabriel was beyond reach. Horror built inside until she could contain the pressure no more. It exploded in a scream. Loud. So loud it hurt her head, her ears, set the red caterpillars squirming.

Crazy. Max had missed crazy off his list.

Changing Man's mouth worked, but she couldn't hear his words because her terrified screams drowned out everything. Then hands grasped her from behind, pulling her back against a hard chest. Camryn's scream cut off midway, the throbbing silence almost worse than the high-pitched terror. With a sob, she dragged in a deep breath, struggling for air, battling to control her panic.

How had the changing man known about Gabriel? Had he read her mind? He'd said... Camryn recoiled from the thought.

Arms tightened around her. "What is it? What's wrong?" His seductive voice sent renewed fear through Camryn. She didn't want this, didn't want his touch. She did not.

Camryn struggled fiercely, stomping on his instep with her heavy boots, the only item of apparel that belonged to her. The rest she'd borrowed from the warrior even if they swamped her smaller frame. "Let me go."

The man released her, stepping back when Mogens nodded. Once free, Camryn scrambled away, scuttling like a gangly newborn foal. With wary eyes she waited for the slightest indication they'd jump her. Running footsteps from behind had her whirling about. "Don't come near me," she shrieked. "Stay away."

"Hold." The terse order from Cat Man stopped the aliens. Once his crew froze, he turned his attention to her. Those green chatoyant eyes saw too much. They tempted, made her want to touch. Spooked at the wanton desire swamping her, Camryn retreated when he prowled nearer. "Easy," he crooned. "No one will hurt you."

Camryn's heart thudded. The throb inside her skull marked time. *Wrong*. Nothing easy about this situation. "He said Gabriel was here." She thrust out a trembling finger and pointed at Mogens. "It's a lie. A horrible lie." Changing Man must have read her thoughts to learn of Gabriel's importance to her. "He delved inside my mind...and...and plucked out Gabriel's name. He trespassed on private thoughts."

"I did not." Mogens blazed pure black, violet eyes flashing like beacons in his obsidian face. "I do not read minds." He glanced at Cat Man and his top lip curled. "Others might steal thoughts but not me." Mogens folded his arms across his chest, the action reminding Camryn of a full stop. Changing Man seemed highly insulted at her accusation and quivered with indignation.

"Can we discuss our plan for catching the hell-horse?" the other woman crewmember asked with a trace of impatience. She strode to the control center of the ship. Camryn supposed it was the bridge.

Hell-horse? Catching the hell-horse?

Changing Man stalked past her, following the rest of the crew and leaving her with Cat Man. She pulled up a scowl and aimed it at him. "What did she mean our plan? Isn't it in a yard, ready for me to start breaking in?" *And what the hell is a hell-horse?*

"My name is Ryman. My crew calls me Ry or Captain, not Cat Man."

He slipped his arm around her waist, moving so quickly she didn't have a chance to sidestep and ushered her through the wide doorway to join the others. His muscles flexed against her lower back, the inherent strength of him bringing a tendril of fear. Changing Man mightn't have read her mind, but this man had.

"Damn," he cursed softly. "I didn't mean to frighten you. Usually I can block, but you're broadcasting so loudly it's hard to ignore your thoughts. Once our meeting is over, go to Mogens and ask him to teach you to block thoughts. He's taught my crew. You've met Kaya already. That's Jannike, my second-in-command. Yep over there is our pilot. That's his brother Nanu. Nanu is our engineer, and you know Mogens. This is our hell-horse trainer Camryn."

Camryn swallowed and concentrated on the introductions instead of Ry and the heat emanating from his impressive body. The minute Cat Man touched her all the panic faded. He soothed her ragged edges with his touch. Oh she still craved a drink—badly—but he drove away other concerns. She peeked at him from between lowered lashes, unsure of how to react. Plain weird. He obviously had other rinky-dinky superpowers and did more than read minds and transform to a cat. She shot him a suspicious glance, acknowledging the depth of her unease.

"We will not hurt you." The cat man's green eyes locked on her, magnetic and compelling. With an uneven breath, she ripped her gaze away to stare at her boots.

Take one day at a time, Gabriel had always told her when she'd stressed about an upcoming race meeting or worried about the lack of winning rides. Take each day one at a time and the rest will take care of themselves.

"Welcome, Camryn O'Sullivan." His husky voice stroked across her nerve endings, pulling her body to full alert.

Camryn had trouble suppressing the tremor of awareness. She swallowed, trying to hold her body away from his touch. It didn't work.

He just moved nearer, curving her to his body as if he had every right. "What is it?"

Call her old-fashioned but Camryn wasn't about to tell a stranger, and an alien at that, she wanted to jump his bones, rip off his clothes and rub against him like a cat in heat. *Oh bad, bad comparison.* Her mouth tightened and she shot him a wary glance, hoping like heck he hadn't eavesdropped.

A smirk tugged at his lips, the sexy smile taking her by surprise. Camryn stared, a pulse jumping at her temple.

"I like the way you think."

Camryn gave a gasp of mortified horror, her face flaming. "Get out of my head."

"I—"

The wail of sirens brought a curse. Ry scooped her up like a troublesome parcel and dumped her on a chair. She'd scarcely settled her butt on it when Mogens leaned over and buckled her into a harness. He sat beside her and strapped in, his body tense while he surveyed the blackness outside the ship.

"What is it?" Camryn finally gathered the courage to ask, alarm swooping through her belly when the ship suddenly dropped. Her stomach followed, feeling as if it'd landed on the floor at her feet. "What's happening?"

"Pirates," Mogens said tersely, his attention on the porthole and instruments.

Pirates? Camryn craned her neck, watching the fast-approaching black ship with acute trepidation.

A violent explosion seared her retinas. Their ship tilted. A second explosion tossed the ship in the other direction, forces throwing Camryn against her harness. A squeak squeezed past tight lips. She glared at Ry, casting blame. His fault. All of it.

Hell, she was gonna die.

"Another black ship at Nor-nor-west," the man at the controls said in a tense voice.

"I see him. Three total." The captain sat totally at ease.

Why weren't they firing back?

"Looks like Banio colors," the warrior said, her blue eyes narrowed to angry slits. "How the hell did they know we were in this part of the universe?"

"Get ready to fire," the captain said.

"Ready to fire," the pilot answered.

"Ready to fire," the warrior confirmed.

Camryn grasped the edge of her seat with a white-knuckle grip. Scared rigid, she closed her eyes to shut out the ships firing on them and almost immediately opened them again. A harsh sob jammed halfway up her throat.

"Fire." Cat Man—Ry—finally gave the order.

The ship bucked. Camryn's stomach dive-bombed south again. Yesterday she'd have welcomed a reunion with Gabriel. Now, in the face of death, she learned she wanted to live.

Flashes of light detonated across the black depths of space. Had they hit the other ships? Blind from the bright flares, Camryn couldn't see. A ship returned fire. Their pilot attempted evasive action but wasn't quite quick enough. The ship tilted at an acute angle. Shook wildly. Alarms screeched. One of the aliens cursed.

"Fire in the hold," Ry shouted. "Nanu and Kaya to the hold."

Two of the crew unbuckled and leaped to their feet.

"Come in, *Indefatigable*," a mocking voice transmitted. "We have you, Monsieur Coppersmith. Surrender so we can claim the *très bien* bounty on your pretty head, no?"

"Phrull you, Banio. Fire!" Ry took over Warrior Woman's gun.

Simultaneous shots rang out. A ship exploded in a fireball. Scant seconds later something clipped their ship, sending it into rapid rolls. The other crewwoman flew from her seat, belting into a fixed chair with a sickening crunch. She moaned.

Ry fired his gun again. "Yep, hold steady. Mogens sitrep on Jannike."

Mogens unfastened his harness, grabbed his satchel and scrambled across the bridge to the woman.

"Camryn, man the gun," Ry ordered.

"Me?"

"There's no one else. When I say fire, push the black button."

Camryn fumbled with the harness release. She teetered across the bridge with gangly foal steps.

"Buckle the harness."

Another order. Damn, she didn't want to die. Shaky fingers clicked the harness into place. When she stole a glance at Ry, his green eyes held approval. Calm confidence.

"Ready?"

Camryn licked her lips and nodded, the ball of nerves inside her stomach huge and bigger than any pre-race nerves. This couldn't be any worse than killing aliens on a computer game. Surely? "Yes," she said hoarsely. "Black button. Push on command."

"Line her up, Yep. They'll expect us to go for the stricken ship. Target the other first. Bloody mercenaries." Ry glared out the porthole. "On three, Camryn."

Camryn gave her palms a furtive wipe across her trouser legs. She swallowed, wished for a shot of whiskey. Her knees quaked and she felt strangely disembodied. Just a game, she told herself. A silly kid's game.

"One. Two. Three. Fire!"

Camryn's sweaty finger slid across the black button, depressing it. The ship bucked, a metallic screech grating against her ears.

"A hit! Great shooting," the pilot shouted.

"Once more," Ry ordered.

The pilot lined them up. Ry shouted orders. Camryn fired. When she focused, after a huge explosion of bright light, not a single ship showed in the black vacuum outside.

"We got 'em, Captain," the pilot shouted in jubilation. "They'll think twice before they engage a frigate again. Long-range guns get them every time."

"Don't get too cocky. They managed to inflict some damage. Yep, keep an eye on things. Don't engage autopilot until we're sure we've lost the bad guys."

"Aye, Captain."

"Fire's out," Kaya said, thumping onto the bridge.

"No serious damage," Nanu added, the beads on the end of his braids clacking together as he bounced up and down on his heels. "I'll have it fixed in no time."

The captain unbuckled and strode to Mogens. "How's Jannike?"

"Alive." Jannike sat up with a pained groan. "Damn, my head hurts."

"She has a hard head, Captain," Mogens said, rifling through his satchel and pulling out a jar of salve.

"Maybe next time she'll strap in properly," Ry said. "Then her head won't suffer. Set course to Ornum, Yep."

"Aye, Captain."

Camryn couldn't stop shaking. This was more excitement than she wanted, and they'd just started.

Ornum, Penal Colony.

"This is the planet Ornum." Ry took Camryn's arm in a possessive manner. He noticed the smirks from his crew and knew he'd hear about it later. Not that it was any of their fraggin' business. "Stay close. This is a convict planet and new arrivals are easy pickings." Ry stared at Camryn, trying to impress the need for caution. Part of his mind railed at his stupidity in keeping her with them while the feline wanted petting. He scowled, taking no pleasure in the slight widening of her eyes or the nervous tic pulsing on her smooth jawline. He forced away the tender feelings and concentrated on their real purpose.

A feral smile curled across his lips, replacing his frown. Judgment day neared. Talor would rue the day he'd posted a bounty on him. Almost time to settle the score, and meantime he'd kick his brother's butt and discover why he'd entered a common race on a convict planet, a hot humid place with no luxuries and little society. Talor had an angle. All Ry needed to do was find it.

"I thought Mogens said you had a price on your head. Aren't you in danger here?" Camryn asked, tucking her shaking hand out of his sight. "What about the bounty?"

"I'm wanted on Ibrox. You won't be in danger here, not when the authorities are more interested in the planets willing to pay incarceration fees to house their prisoners." He offered her a cocky grin. "I suppose someone from Ibrox could capture me, take me back to claim the bounty. Haven't had a problem so far. It's been safe enough to use my own name in business dealings. Besides, I'm not the only man here who's on the run. Trust me, you're safe." His brow puckered when he witnessed the way her limbs twitched and shuddered. When he'd asked Mogens about her shakes, the seer had told him alcohol addiction caused the problem. It would pass. Ry hoped so. They needed her fit to train their hell-horse.

"And if that changes? We're together now."

Ry bit back an appreciative snort. Clever woman. "We'll protect you."

He strode along the uneven dirt road, keeping a watchful eye on Camryn and passersby. The main business center reminded him of a border town. The buildings consisted of scrap and cheap prefabricated material shipped in from other planets. Slapped together and patched in places, they weren't pretty but did the job as shelter against the elements. Clouds of black fog screened the view beyond the town, the rays of the hot sun barely piercing the dark blanket. The pungent scent of chemicals filled the air, a byproduct of the ore manufacturing plant, the planet's main source of income. The humidity sent a bead of sweat trickling down his chest.

As they neared the marketplace, the crowd thickened. Beggars scuttled around the fringe, stall holders scrutinizing them with disfavor while shouting about their wares. Flags and banners unfurled in the fickle wind. They announced that the governor of the planet Laurans Swithin was the sponsor of the upcoming race.

"Where do we pay our entrance fee?" Jannike asked. Like him, the tall blonde constantly surveyed the crush of people around them, searching for signs of trouble.

"At Manx manor," Mogens said. "The administrator is taking registrations."

Five mins later they reached the better part of town. Fewer people loitered on the streets. Those who did were part of work parties and under the control of marines. The rattle of chains and shuffling gangs of convicts were a common sight.

"There's the manor over there," Jannike said, pausing to make way for a weird six-legged animal pulling a cart.

"It doesn't look like a manor," Yep said with clear doubt when they stopped to study the squat, dirty-gray building. Different species were here to try their luck. A cacophony of clicks, groans and grunts filled the air as hopeful entrants shouted over each other and attempted to enter the building to plunk down their entry fee.

"Looks like the contest is popular," Jannike added. "Are they limiting entries?"

"No, but we just made it back in time. Entries close tomorrow at dusk." Ry studied the milling men. Some he knew while others he knew by reputation. He couldn't see his brother or any of his staff, but they'd probably completed formalities already. "I'll take care of the entry fee. Why don't you take some personal time? Meet back at the ship at sundown."

"What about the girl?" Jannike asked.

Ry glanced at the wide-eyed Camryn. Easy picking for any rogue, and none of his crew wanted to babysit. "She can stay with me." The sooner they captured their hell-horse and trained it, the quicker they could return the Earthling to her home. Ry ignored the tiny voice of protest. Number two on his list—a willing woman or two. He'd go out later tonight and leave Camryn safe on the ship.

The crew rushed off, leaving them alone. The jostling of the crowd shoved Camryn against his chest, inciting a riot of lust inside him. He breathed shallowly, groping for restraint, mentally slapping his feline into submission.

A team of Red Mumber guards exited the building, pushing the eager entrants into a formal line, using brute force. Weapons gleamed from holsters at their hips, and they brandished silver blades, their red-toned faces bearing a touch of cruelty.

Ry sighed in frustration. "Looks like this might take a while."

"When we've finished here, could we see the hell-horses?"

Not a bad idea. Although Camryn's expression didn't change, she shook violently as if she had palsy. Ry noticed the beings around them stood back, suspecting her of harboring disease. Mogens had assured him the woman was strong enough to train a hell-horse. He hoped so since discussions of the beast's ferociousness fueled conversation at the spaceport and in the city. According to rumor, the animals had killed several contestants already.

"What's the prize?" Camryn whispered.

"Money and the hand of the governor's daughter in marriage."

Her brown eyes widened in astonishment. "You want to marry the governor's daughter?"

Hell no. Life on the run was no picnic. He'd never subject a wife to that. "I have a private bet with my brother. All the rest is unimportant."

"What—?"

"Shush," Ry interrupted. "We're drawing attention."

Camryn gasped when a Red Mumber snarled in her direction. To Ry's relief, she stopped her questions.

Finally they reached the front of the line and paid their currency to the gray-haired administrator who sat behind a bulky desk. The man scrawled on his parchment, his quill scratching loudly.

"Entry fee is one thousand quid." He peered at them, picking up a quizzing glass to study Camryn. "Is she healthy? The ruler is seeking women for his harem. This woman would be to his taste. Give you two thousand quid for her."

"No." Black fury gripped Ry, tightening every muscle in his body. His jaw set hard and he glared at the administrator for his audacity. "She is not for sale." His tone should have ended the matter, but the administrator smiled with smug confidence.

He lifted his quizzing glass to survey Camryn again. "Five thousand quid. That's my final offer."

"My woman is not for sale." Ry gripped Camryn's forearm, willing her to remain silent.

"Very well." The administrator didn't sound happy, and Ry

knew he'd have to guard Camryn well. The administrator's offer was as good as a price on her head to any being who'd eavesdropped. He stared a challenge at the Red Mumber waiting behind the administrator until the guard shifted his attention to his sandaled feet.

They completed formalities, were told the areas they could hunt for their hell-horse, accepted their entry number and a copy of the rule book before leaving. "We'd better return to the ship." Ry didn't release her arm, dragging her from the manor and down the road in the direction of the spaceport.

"I thought we were going to see the hell-horses."

"New plan." Ry stopped abruptly with his back to the nearest building and scanned for trouble. Sensing the Earthling's streak of obstinacy, Ry explained. "A lot of people overheard the administrator make an offer for you, which makes you a liability." A bigger problem than she was already.

"It wasn't my fault." Camryn scowled when she took his meaning. "You mean they'd force me into captivity, to be at a man's whim because of my looks?"

"Yes." *But not if he had his way.* Ry propelled her along the rutted road.

"Don't walk so fast. I can't keep up."

Ry glanced over his shoulder, catching a glimpse of a Red Mumber—the same one who'd stood with the administrator. The back of his neck itched in warning, especially when he caught sight of a second Red Mumber, the muscular beings contrasting with the dingy gray buildings. Damn.

"In here." He didn't give Camryn time to object, dragging her into a tavern. He pushed through the mass of bodies, using his elbows to make his way to the bar. A back door. Ry opened the door a crack and saw a Red Mumber approaching via the alley running between the tavern and the building next door.

"Change of plans." Ry noted a staircase leading to the second floor. "This way." He resisted her struggle and dragged her up the stairs. The flashy interior gave him pause. *A pox on it. A brothel.* He halted before realizing he'd run out of alternatives. Ry smiled at the madam, summoning every measure of charm available. "I know this is an unusual request...could we have a room?"

The madam fluttered her ridiculously long lilac lashes and leaned forward to better display her assets, showcased in a tight ruby-red gown. "We cater for all requests here. Take your choice of my ladies. Would you like two to join you? Maybe more?"

The choked sound from Camryn went straight to his cock. Ry's mouth twisted at the sensual reminder of the woman. Dammit, he'd lied to himself. Another woman wouldn't work. Another woman wouldn't soothe the ache echoing through his body. Another woman wasn't Camryn.

"Just a room," he said in a hoarse voice. A mistake. He sensed his error straightaway. No alternative. *Blast it.* "Some privacy. Some of our crewmembers might stop by to ask if you've seen us..." He let his voice trail off suggestively for the madam to connect the dots.

"I won't say a word." She winked at him, her broad smile indicating a streak of romanticism despite her profession. "My girls know how to keep their lips buttoned. No one will interrupt you." She handed him a key. "The room at the end of the passage."

Ry bent to whisper in Camryn's ear. "Quick." He propelled her down the passage, unlocked the door and shunted her inside. With a final glance and a grateful wave at the madam, Ry entered the room. He locked the door and turned to face temptation.

Camryn glared at him, despite the contradictory tremor of her hands. "I'm tired of you hauling me around."

The flash of anger fascinated him, as did the riot of curses tumbling through her head. He grinned, amusement blooming with full force.

"It's not funny." Her brown eyes narrowed to slits, and when he continued to smirk, she advanced on him, her fists clenched. "I don't like bullies."

"Me neither, but if you're working with us, you'll have to learn to move faster."

"Why? Run away from a lot of thugs, do you?"

Ry stifled his amusement. No mistaking her tone for anything but snide, and here he'd thought the woman lacked backbone. "I'm wanted for murder." He shifted his weight and returned her stare with an intimidating one of his own. "There's smart and there's stupid. I saved your sweet arse, but if you want to live in a harem, fine. The extra quids will come in handy. I can take you straight back and commence negotiations with the administrator."

"Piss off."

A bark of laughter erupted. Not timid at all. The Earthling became more intriguing by the min. "We're stuck here until our pursuers cease their search."

Camryn's dark brows scrunched together. "We could have returned to the ship."

"And attract attention to the Indy? Why do you think we docked our frigate at the old spaceport? It's called keeping a low profile."

She advanced on him, mouth set, eyes flashing. Ry's mouth quivered in the beginnings of a grin. It disappeared smartly when her right hand fisted and she let rip, landing a punch in his stomach. Didn't hurt but he grabbed her hand to avoid a repeat blow.

The instant they touched his control ebbed, the feral cat taking over. Ry struggled to bat him into submission while telling himself he'd saved himself from another blow.

A lie.

Ry ached for her touch, craving her with an intensity he'd never experienced in the past. Despite his misgivings, he went with the feline's desires, hauling Camryn against his chest, holding her squirming body with brute strength.

"Cease." His order brought renewed resistance, and a grunt hissed from him when her boot connected with his ankle. Secs later, his mouth slammed down on hers. Not a gentle kiss but a statement of intent.

A claiming.

After a brief hesitation Camryn's tense body slackened into acquiescence. With a soft sigh, she slid her arms around his neck to cling, lips parting hungrily, her submission taking him by surprise. Her low moan of pleasure dispersed his lingering doubts. Ry relaxed and let the hunger flare out of check.

Hotter.

Brighter.

He ran urgent hands down her back, over her curvy arse and lifted her, cradling her against his chest. The warmth of her body created a series of explosions inside, chipping away the cool voice of reason, the remnants of his restraint.

"You push at my feline," he said in a low growl as he forced himself to pull away a fraction.

"You say it like that's a bad thing," she purred, clinging to him sweetly and baffling the hell out him.

A paradox. The woman was full of them. At first weak and scared, now her fear had eased. Her contradictions fascinated him as much as her exquisite scent and sexy body.

"I need control to keep my feline at bay." The truth, but for the last half cycle his feline had gripped him firmly by the balls. With Camryn's presence, he'd slipped the leash entirely.

"Does it hurt when you change forms?" Camryn stroked his cheek, a frown of concentration on her face. Instantly, power flared beneath his skin, transmitting her touch to every part of his body. The feline arched and purred, and Ry accepted he was in trouble. The woman rubbed wantonly against his burgeoning erection while a smile played on her lips. Seductive. Knowing.

"Not really. The change—it just happens. I picture the cat in my mind and shift." Ry stole another look and knew he had to kiss her again. *A compulsion.* He moved slowly, in an effort to temper his former roughness, not wanting to scare her into telling him to stop.

Their lips touched and he sipped, tasted. Savored. All the time trying to go slow. Yes! To his relief she started to return his kiss, opening her mouth in encouragement to take the kiss deeper. Mogens must have given her some of his mouth fresheners, and she delivered a burst of aniseed along with her enthusiasm. He gloried in the sleek feel of her body, the smooth curve of her top lip and the luscious lower one. A purr rumbled through his mind. Camryn tasted good. Too damn good. And she could kiss, knowing how to tease, to drive him higher, make him crave more. Her sharp nip of pain was soothed with the moist rasp of her tongue. Without stopping his exploration of her mouth, he carried her to the bed, dropping her onto the blue silken covers.

He stared, still trying to do the right thing and ripped his gaze away from her swollen, glistening lips. For a bordello, the room appeared clean and didn't offend his nose with the stench of unclean bodies or the use of scent to disguise offensive smells. Ry removed her boots and set them aside.

"I think I'm dreaming." She lay in the middle of the feather mattress, staring at him with her golden-brown eyes. They glowed like tiger-eye gems while her tongue darted out to moisten the full curve of her lower lip.

"This isn't a dream." A touch of irritation flashed through him, lightning quick and dramatic. He'd never cared overly much about his sexual partners—in the past it had been about appeasing the cat and sating his urges. With Camryn he wanted real and gritty. Hard and furious, but he needed it to be more than just sex. "It's real. My shin aches where you kicked me."

"Does it?" She laughed hard enough to jiggle her breasts, catch his attention. Like an addictive drug, she called him.

Sighing, Ry removed his jacket, unlaced his shirt and yanked it over his head. Without taking his gaze from her, he sat to tug off his boots and foot linings. The softened leather clomped to the wooden floor. Camryn flinched and sat up. Ry stilled, ready to pounce. She wasn't going anywhere. She belonged to him, dammit.

His.

Ry ignored the cat's strident clamor for ownership to watch her closely. He wondered if she was behaving in character, frowned and guessed she probably wasn't. But the knowledge didn't stop him. His body pained him—he had to have her now.

"Every time you touch me all I can think of is sex." Camryn's petite frame arched, reminding him of an agitated feline while her voice held pure frustration and a hint of accusation. "I don't do sex. Not anymore." This time confusion flared in her eyes.

Camryn's bewilderment lightened his tension, bringing a flicker of humor. Part of him wanted to commiserate. It wasn't as if he liked the out-of-control sensations, the driving urge to claim. Ryman Coppersmith walked alone. He'd never take a permanent woman, not when danger lay in every direction.

"You have the same effect on me." Except all he needed was a whiff of her scent to make him crave. He couldn't understand why her presence pushed him so hard, worse than other women.

Her brows lifted, the tone of accusation draining away. "So it's not a drug?"

"No! I've never reacted to another woman like this. *Never*."

"What is it then?" Camryn gritted her teeth and reached out to place a trembling hand on his bare chest. At his harsh rumble, her eyes widened, her expression edging into panic.

The touch, her touch, seared a hot path straight to his balls. He hissed, his lip curling up in part pain, part denial. "Don't stop. Please. Touch me again."

At his plea her fingers flexed, nails biting into his pectoral muscles. A wash of pleasure hit him. He groaned and pounced, trapping Camryn beneath his larger frame. She trembled but didn't protest, merely observed him with wide eyes.

"My mind is screaming at me to move, to run, but I can't." Her tongue darted out to moisten the curve of her bottom lip. "I have never wanted any man as much as I want you right now." A tear leaked from the corner of one eye and trickled toward her ear.

Ry knew. He knew the torment she experienced because he suffered the same sensual plague. "This..." He swallowed thickly, forcing away the urge to claim. "It doesn't mean anything. I can't..." To his great relief, she nodded abruptly.

"Just until I return to Earth. If that's what you want." Her tone and her expressive eyes held a tentative question. Would they return her to Earth?

"Until you return to Earth," he confirmed.

She shivered. "Good. I don't want a relationship. I'm...not good at them," she finished with a rush.

Another tear flowed down her face and this time he surrendered to instinct and leaned over to lap it up with his tongue. The salty taste, laced with her musky scent, pushed harder at his restraint. He trailed kisses across her cheek, leading to her luscious mouth. Ry loosed the tight rein on his control and let the magic flicker freely. Deep inside, the feline purred in anticipation.

Ry slipped his hand inside the neckline of her black tunic. Her skin radiated heat. Smooth, it reminded him of the synsilk so beloved by his sisters. His hand slid across the warm curves of her upper breasts. Almost immediately he wanted more. Ry withdrew his hand and grasped the hem of her tunic. He whisked it over her head and reached down to unfasten the tight black trews. Slowly he tugged them down her legs to reveal a pale pink undergarment that matched the bindings around her breasts.

"Pretty," he murmured, tracing one finger along the fabric around her breasts. Although the garments screened her secrets, they enticed too, bringing a surge of deeper hunger. A groan lodged in his throat when his finger retraced the same path and dipped briefly beneath the fabric. Hurry. Hurry. The word lodged in his brain like one of Mogen's chants.

Ry stood, aware Camryn watched avidly, her attention a massage to his ego. Want, need, pounded him. Urgency. He dragged down his trews, letting his heavy cock spring free. He kicked the garment away and returned to the bed. The feather mattress depressed with his weight, rolling Camryn toward him. She didn't notice, her gaze on his body, his cock. Under her scrutiny, it lengthened, the head flared and glistening.

Silence, thick with tension, throbbed inside the bedroom.

"Do something," Camryn snapped. "Make it go away."

Ry yanked the remaining garments from her body, understanding her exactly. Her bindings confounded him but Camryn flicked a concealed fastening on the front. The fabric fell away, spilling her breasts free until she was completely naked. Beautiful.

Ry stared, a rough purr erupting, vibrating in his throat. His vision flickered from color to black and white before settling in monochrome gray. Didn't matter. He leaned over, drawing in her piquant scent. Rich. Seductive. His tongue dragged across her collarbone, rasping over the delicate dips and curves. He nuzzled her neck, giving her a scrape of teeth.

Camryn squirmed in protest, giggled. "Tickles."

"I don't feel like laughing." His feline strained, pushing against his tight skin. Sharp canine teeth shoved through his gums.

The grin faded, eyes meeting his. Her tongue darted out to moisten her bottom lip. "Don't laugh then."

They stared at one another. Ry moistened a finger and lightly circled the nipple of her right breast. Camryn gasped. Shivered. The scent of her arousal intensified. Ry bit back a feline bark, ran his tongue over his teeth. He shuddered, a full body tremble, and stroked his hand down her body, coming to rest on her smooth hip.

"Part your legs for me."

Camryn splayed her legs without shame, flashing her moist pussy, watching him closely. His patience at an end, he leaned over, slipping his hand between her legs. He'd smelled her arousal but now trailed his fingers over her slick folds, smiling when she sucked in an excited breath. His tongue followed the same path as his fingers, her flavor bursting across his taste buds. Honey and exotic spices. He licked his finger, cleaning it of her juices, watching her the entire time.

"Ry," she whispered, eyes pleading him to touch her.

"Delicious." Ry rose to kiss her, heart hammering. Their lips brushed. Clung. He tunneled his fingers into her hair, gripping the silky strands, holding her head still while he deepened the kiss. *His.* The possessive thought rippled through him yet again. Ry embraced it, loving the way she surrendered to him. His tongue thrust past her lips as he lined up his cock and pushed into her sheath. Hot, clinging flesh gripped his shaft, feeling better than anything he could remember.

Camryn gripped his shoulders, arching up into his stroke and taking him deep. Ry growled his pleasure before dipping his head to thrust his tongue into the corner of her mouth, just as he thrust into her center. Rocking deeper, he squeezed his eyes shut to fully appreciate the warm clasp of her pussy, the hot carnal pleasure of it. Part of him waited for the frenzy to hit, the wildness that always gripped him when he was with a woman. It didn't arrive. Instead, he breathed in her scent, not understanding but ready to savor the unexpected treat of normal sex, like he used to enjoy before the feline appeared.

"Wait!" Camryn screeched. She gripped his shoulders and shook him.

Ry's eyes flicked open in trepidation. "What?"

"You're not wearing a condom. I'm not on the Pill. I can't have an alien child."

The tenseness left his shoulders, even as he registered her fear. "Mogens doses us all with a tonic to prevent offspring and disease. But he suspects I can't produce children. He thinks I must mate with another of my species." Ry glanced away, remembering the woman they'd purchased from the slaver. A cat woman like him. Someone had shot and killed her before they could talk. The loss of the opportunity to interact with another of his species ate at him. "I've never met others of my race."

Camryn frowned. "You're not just saying that?"

"I am not dishonest. You won't have a child with me."

"I'm sorry you don't have family." Camryn reached up to kiss him.

"I have family," Ry snapped, wounded by her sympathy. "The crew is my family, and I am theirs."

"Of course," she whispered, her stroking hands a soothing balm.

Ry let his irritation fade, concentrating on licking and nibbling at her lips, not wanting to discuss his family situation. The kiss deepened. He thrust his cock deeper, gliding in to the root and stilling with a sigh of pleasure before he withdrew again. Camryn gripped his shoulders, moaning softly. Her hips canted upward, changing the angle. Encouraging him. It felt so good. Her internal muscles tightened around his shaft. He growled, savoring the soft whimpers she didn't try to contain. Sparks of pleasure frayed his control, heat rampaging through him. Each rapid plunge into Camryn's tight heat massaged his cock, soothed yet stoked the conflagration building inside him. She felt like a perfect fit, and he didn't want this loving to end.

"Faster," Camryn demanded, her fingernails digging into his shoulders. She arched up into his next stroke. "Yeah, like that."

"Grata." A fine sheen of sweat covered Ry's chest, his back. Muscles flexed and rippled when he drove into her. Faster and faster until the wet sound of arousal filled the room. A primal growl. Clawing tension grew in his balls. With a final hard thrust, he exploded, flooding her with hot spurts of come. Ry slumped against her soft body, groaning with the remnants of sensation spiraling through his veins. Their combined scents filled the air, and the cat purred.

"What about me?" Camryn's brows rose sharply when he grinned and purred even louder. "Is that all you're going to do? Purr?"

Ry chuckled, feeling relaxed and limber. He rolled on his side and tugged at a lock of her silky hair. "No that's not all I'm going to do. I have more planned. Much more." Ry grasped one apricot-colored nipple between forefinger and thumb and tugged. "We have all night—plenty of time for us both to purr."

CHAPTER THREE

TALOR COPPERSMITH'S HOTEL, ORNUM.

Talor had set the trap, knowing Ryman wouldn't be able to resist. The wager, an amusement thought up when he'd happened to see Ryman at the Ornum spaceport. So smug and confident. Now his brother and renegade crew had returned to Ornum after a mysterious departure. A gloating smile bled across his face, satisfaction bringing a buoyant mood. This time he'd outsmart them. They'd feel safe here on the convict planet. Oh, they'd use caution but the frontier feel of the town lent a certain freedom—a place where anything could and did happen. The law only concerned itself with the convicts under their charge. The free men, the alien visitors and the convicts who had worked out their tenure experienced freedom not possible on most planets.

This time he'd destroy Ryman totally, grinding him to dust beneath his heels. First though, he'd toy with his brother and make him realize how puny and vulnerable he was to Talor's wrath.

A knock sounded on the door to his office. Talor grimaced, anger jumping inside and pressing against his temples. He alleviated the ache by loosening his queue, and his long silver hair settled against his shoulders.

"Come."

The door opened gingerly, and his aide peeked inside. "Mr. Coppersmith?"

"Alfredo, I said no interruptions." Even though the door blocked most of his robust body, Talor caught his aide's flinch and took pleasure in it. Stupid fool.

"Ryman Coppersmith has entered the race. You told me you wanted to know when he'd officially entered."

"Thank you, Alfredo. You may go now." The quiet click of the door and the ponderous steps confirmed the man wasn't attempting to eavesdrop for his reaction. Talor flicked his fingers at the candle sconce on the far wall. The candle wicks flared before spluttering out.

A pithy curse emerged at yet another example of his faltering magic. With a deep breath, he centered his mind and tried again. This time the flames burned bright and true.

He leaned back in his chair before jumping restlessly to his feet. He stalked to a sideboard and poured a goblet of plummet wine before returning to his seat. Once seated, he twirled the golden liquid in the goblet, warming it with his hands. The first part of his plan had gone according to expectations. Talor had known Ryman couldn't resist besting him on neutral territory. During his sporadic visits to Ibrox, Ryman usually slipped in and out before Talor became aware of his presence. That was the reason he'd made his intentions to enter the race public. He chuckled, pleased with the way his plan had fallen into place.

Everyone thought he'd entered because he wanted a wife. What would he do with a wife? Oh no. When he won, he wouldn't marry the common creature. The woman always appeared veiled in public. No one had seen her face since childhood, which indicated disfigurement. The race for her hand in marriage backed up the theory. She was a dog. But depending on her looks, he might take her for his harem or sell her onward.

Of course a sale might create problems. A pucker creased his brow but cleared secs later. He'd marry her off to an important statesman. None of the gentry would take her to wife but a statesman would since marriage meant advancement. There—problem solved. When he won, he'd turn the woman over to a suitable candidate and keep the currency part of the prize pot to pay off pressing debts.

And best of all, he'd rid himself of the blight on his life. Ryman Coppersmith—the brat his mother had insisted on fostering and adopting legally despite his mystery background. Bah! His brother was a nobody.

A common thief.

But not a murderer, as everyone presumed. No, Talor had compelled a passing traveler to kill Maxmus whilst setting up his brother. Unfortunately Ryman had escaped the trap.

But this time—ah, this time, Talor would best his brother. With Ryman dead, his luck would turn. Not only would the land his mother had willed to Ryman return to him, but his waning magical powers would recover and flare brighter than ever, the effect rippling down to the family charm business. Soon, the House of the Cat would rule again and he, as its head, would benefit.

Power.

Strength.

Magic.

He'd have it all.

Another tap on the door interrupted his musing. "Enter."

"You have a visitor," Alfredo said. "Ms. Kaya Ignatius."

SHELLEY MUNRO

A crafty smile slid across Talor's lips. The first part of his plan. He'd known the woman would come in handy, and the fact she was good in the sexual department was a bonus. "Ah, the beautiful Kaya. I've been expecting her visit."

Alfredo stood aside and Kaya swept into the room. The aide closed the door, leaving them alone. Talor waved her to a chair and poured her a drink before taking possession of another nearby chair.

"What news?"

"Ry has entered the race."

"And?"

"We leave to hunt for our hell-horse."

Talor sipped his wine. "Where will you hunt?"

"We are flying to the distant hunting ground."

No witnesses when he destroyed their tender. Excellent. "Thank you, Kaya." The news brought triumph. With Ry gone, his troubles would cease. *Kaya, come to me.*

Kaya set down her wine and stood, then glided to him in a sensuous sway, not a hint of hesitation once she'd heard his compelling thoughts.

Disrobe.

To his delight, the blue-haired woman removed her footwear and clothes with unconscious grace. Talor watched the entire time, enjoying the private striptease and reveal of her creamy skin. His shaft twitched and he widened his stance for comfort. Generous breasts. Curvy hips. A pleasant sight to behold, especially with her exotic features and toned musculature.

Hungry to possess her, he stood, kicked off his shoes and rapidly disrobed. Talor reclaimed his seat and beckoned her closer. When Kaya dawdled, he reiterated the demand with silent compulsion. She didn't waver again. Kaya clambered onto his lap and impaled herself slowly on his cock. She was delightfully wet for him. The wench loved his orders. The tight squeeze of her quim brought a shudder of pleasure. He sighed in satisfaction, flexing his hips and leaning closer to take the nipple of one breast into his mouth. He bit down, bringing a sharp protest.

"That hurt."

He soothed the nip with the flat of his tongue and raised his head to nuzzle one pointed ear. "A little pain brings greater pleasure. I promise this will be very good."

"It is always good," Kaya admitted, angling her neck to grant him better access to her ear.

Quite true. Messing with his brother's life always added piquant spice to the mix and the intimate pillow talk with the delightful Kaya gave him an inside edge. Soon—very soon—he'd rid himself of Ryman once and all. To secure his future, he'd do anything.

"Camryn, it's time to go. The Red Mumber has left."

Camryn bolted upright, and the silky bedcovers slivered to her waist, putting her breasts on display for the man across the other side of the bedroom. She blinked in confusion. "Gabriel?"

"Who is Gabriel?"

Not Gabriel.

Sorrow clamped down, a heavy weight on her chest. She grabbed the covers, to conceal her nakedness, her heart pounding as the events of the previous night rushed back. Shit, she'd slept with the alien kitty. She swallowed, the guilt of betrayal pounding her mind.

"Someone I knew. Is it time to leave?" She blinked rapidly and turned away to hide her imminent tears.

"Yes." Fully dressed, Ry prowled to the window and stared down at the street below. Camryn heard the clanking of chains, probably some of the yellow-clad convicts making their way to the factories. She scrambled from bed and yanked on her clothes and footwear.

"Follow me." Ry stopped to hand the woman behind the desk several notes before they left. The rapid walk to the ship passed without incident.

"Where have you been?" Mogens' stern demands grated on her ears and brought more guilt.

Camryn resisted a glance at Ry and let him answer. Mogens' attitude reminded her of her stepfather. The man had meant well but he'd had overprotective down perfectly.

"The administrator wanted to buy Camryn for the governor's harem. He wouldn't take no for an answer. We had to dodge Red Mumbers all night." Ry made it sound as if they'd spent the entire night on the run.

Heat collected in her cheeks when memories of their hot, frantic couplings filled her mind. The pleasure. Next came memories of Gabriel. She'd slept with another man—betrayed Gabriel yet again. Pain clawed her stomach, the wet sting of tears finally falling to cloud her vision. Betrayal. Oh boy. She just kept compounding the errors one after another.

"Did they follow you to the ship?" Jannike demanded.

"I didn't see any, but we'll need to stay alert." Ry turned away to speak to Yep, who wore his hair loose today rather than confined in the normal ponytail. "Any problems?"

"Nope, not a one."

"When do we go to see the horses?" The sooner she started training the better. It wasn't long before the race started, only a matter of months before the big day. "I need to start training, especially if they're as difficult as everyone says."

Ry growled deep in his throat. "You can't leave the ship on your own."

"We could disguise Camryn," Mogens suggested. Today his violet eyes sparkled like amethyst jewels and his skin shone a pearly gray. Camryn had started to think of this as his happy color.

"I can do a disguise," she said.

"You'll have to cut your hair," Jannike said. "The rich black is very distinctive."

"No!" Everyone stared at Ry's strong outburst.

Kaya grinned while Mogens colored to black.

The crew shifted their attention to her. Unable to withstand the close attention, Camryn shuffled her feet and wished she were invisible. Heat collected in her face, kicked along by old-fashioned guilt. She'd slept with another man. Betrayed Gabriel's memory.

"A disguise is a good idea, but it doesn't need to be radical." Ry shrugged from his jacket and tossed it aside. "As for the hell-horses, we'll eat, pack supplies and head out with the tender to one of the outlying locations. The tender is big enough to transport a hell-horse."

"From what we heard at the pub last night we'll need to hunt farther afield. The hunting grounds near the city are almost out of stock," Nanu said, shaking his head and setting the beads on the end of his braids clacking. "The remaining hell-horses are wary and dangerous."

Ry scratched his chest and attempted to reach his back. "Something is biting me."

Mogens reached for his satchel. "Take off your shirt and let me place salve on the bites. Left untreated they'll fester in this tropical heat."

Camryn tried not to look but found her gaze snared by the fluid action of his muscles when he shrugged out of the shirt, the tanned expanse of chest.

"Captain, what have you done?" The horror in Mogens' voice made them all scrutinize Ry. "Look at his back."

"What's wrong with my back? I didn't do anything—"

"Man, I've never seen anything like it before," Jannike said.

"What is it, dammit?"

Camryn circled Ry to stand with the others.

"Look, it's coming out on his chest too."

"This black mark?" Ry rubbed it vigorously, and Camryn watched a black swirl form on his chest in a similar pattern to those on his back. She knew the bruises hadn't been present last night.

"You slept with her." Accusation throbbed in Mogens' words. "Bugger! The blue in yesterday's clouds hinted that might happen. I shouldn't have left you alone."

"Captain, you got horizontal last night," Yep said, smirking. "Way to go."

Mogens pulled a piece of parchment from his satchel along with the old-fashioned quills Camryn had seen the administrator use. "What did you eat last night? Drink? I want details."

Ry grabbed his shirt. "It's none of your damn business what I did last night. Kaya, check the weapons and ammunition. Jannike, check the spaceport for anything that's red and has two legs. Yep and Nanu, verify the ship and the supplies."

"And me?" Mogens asked.

Camryn could have sworn the seer was laughing at Ry.

"Check the medical supplies. From what I hear we're going to need them." He waited for the seer to move out of hearing. "What's wrong with my back?"

"It's covered with blotchy tattoos," Camryn said. "They're black and look like the tribal tattoos we have at home."

"All over my back?"

"Yeah. They're more defined than the one on your chest. Are they still itchy? Should I ask Mogens for some salve?"

"I'll survive."

He might, but the appearance of the tattoos worried him. She could see it in his eyes. Without thinking she reached out to trace the swirl on his pectoral muscle. He flinched, and she jerked her hand from his chest.

"Sorry. Did I hurt you?"

"Touch me again." His voice emerged thick and laden with

need. "Please."

Camryn's hand trembled when she repeated the move, tracing her finger along the blurred lines of the tattoo. His entire frame shuddered and the sound he loosed reminded her of a contented domestic cat. And the heat...the heat coming off his skin spread from her fingertips, down her arm and straight to her breasts. Camryn gasped at the sensation of her tightening nipples and moved closer instead of away. She dipped her head to lick the same path her finger had taken. His skin tasted salty with a tinge of herbs, reminding her of the outdoors. With a lap of her tongue, she traced the vague curving spiral.

"Camryn." His hoarse, needy whisper jerked up her head.

Her body clenched at the desire in his voice, the tension thrumming through him. She stared up at his green eyes. Heavy-lidded, his intent expression seared her. His need pulsed against her own, the emotions a tangible thing.

"The tattoos have darkened on your chest. They're the same as those on your back." Even she heard the wonder in her voice. Unable to resist, she ran a delicate finger across his pectoral muscle, following the curve of the tattoo.

"Aw, hell. Do it again. Touch me." Ry trembled and dragged her against his tense body before she had a chance to obey. The hard ridge of his cock pressed against her belly. The green scent of herbs swirled around them as they rubbed against each other. He dipped his head to claim her lips in a searing kiss, and she did nothing to stop him. Ry plundered, his tongue thrusting forcibly between her parted lips.

She gripped his shoulders, holding tight to anchor herself in the storm of conflicting emotions rampaging through her body. She wanted this. She wanted him with a desperation that shocked her. They'd had sex throughout the night and still she wanted more of this wild, out-of-control feeling because it made her soar, made her forget.

Ry grasped her hips and lifted her, backing her up. Her head clunked against cool metal, but it didn't halt their kiss. Pressed between the hard wall and his muscular body, she couldn't do a thing except yield to his masculinity. Her pussy moistened, throbbing with emptiness. Camryn stroked her hand over his back, and he hissed at her touch. His cock pressed into her, and she felt the throb despite the layers of clothing. She wriggled, trying to get closer. Too hot. Her clothes were in the way.

She gasped, inhaling the pungent herbal scent and musky arousal. More than anything, she wanted to feel her bare breasts dragging against his chest. His mouth on her skin. She smoothed her hand over his shoulder, glorying in his purr of pleasure.

"Camryn." Ry's eyes glittered with lust. "I need you." He gasped, his chest rising and falling rapidly. "I have to...hell, each time you move against my chest or touch my back I can't think. I want to taste. I want to bite and mark your skin. Show that you belong with me."

The thick passion in his voice got to her. Lord help her, but she wanted that too. She couldn't think, couldn't format thoughts. All she could do was feel, crave more. With a shudder, she dipped her head to lick across the fleshy part of his shoulder. Her teeth grazed the fragrant skin, softly at first before she nipped sharply. At Ry's snarl, her head snapped up, but he pushed her mouth right back to where she'd bitten him. Reassured, Camryn lapped across his skin. It felt smooth and silky, his salty taste addictive.

"What are you doing?" The sheer horror in the seer's voice jerked them apart. "Stop right now."

"Go away," Ry snarled.

"I don't think the two of you coupling is a good idea," Mogens said in a stern, fatherlike voice. "The clouds warn it will bring change, things that can't be corrected later."

A thick silence bloomed, and Ry released her. She slipped down his body to stand on her own feet, but still they touched, unwilling to break their connection. Camryn stared at Ry, the heat in his gaze telling her the interruption was a postponement. That's all.

She laughed weakly, giving away her nervousness. After a long pause she finally squirmed from between Ry and the wall. "I thought you were my father for a minute there."

She would have walked across the other side of the room except her legs wobbled. Ry grasped her arm before she fell. He tugged until their sides brushed and clasped her hand in his in silent reassurance. Together they faced Mogens.

"The markings—they're all over your chest." His gaze speared to Camryn. "It's you. You've caused this. Look, the cat tattoo on your arm has disappeared."

"I haven't done anything." The seer's accusation had Camryn pressing against Ry. And she didn't like the rapid shift of the seer's color from pearl gray to thunder black. "It...it's not me," she finished on a firmer note, refusing to let the alien intimidate her.

They needed her help. She was positive they'd do nothing to harm her because they required her to complete their mission. Or at least that was her hope.

"Leave her alone," Ry ordered.

Camryn noticed the crew had returned, attracted by the raised voices.

"They slept together," Jannike said. "They didn't spend the night hiding from Red Mumbers. They spent it horizontal, and she's infected our captain with a disease."

The indignation in the woman's voice brought trepidation. Camryn didn't need an enemy and especially not a large Amazonlike female.

"Butt out." Ry's uncompromising voice held warning.

"She's crew, Ry. She became crew the min we kidnapped her and brought her aboard the Indy. When did you change your rule about sleeping with crew?" Ry's anger didn't cow Jannike, which told her a lot about the man and the way he ran the ship. Despite the outlaw tag, he had honor and integrity.

Camryn let out a soft sigh, realizing she trusted him.

"I refuse to discuss the matter." Ry's voice didn't encourage further debate. "Is everyone ready?"

"All ready, Captain," Jannike said, her stance as rigid as her voice.

The flash of dislike in her eyes sounded a warning to Camryn. She'd trod on the other woman's toes by grabbing Ry's attention. Obviously the other woman considered Ry her property. When she glanced at the others, she saw a similar expression from Kaya. Camryn suppressed a someone-walked-over-my-grave shiver, as her mother would have said.

"Camryn and I will meet you at the tender," Ry said.

"Today," Mogens said.

Ry glowered at the seer. "In five mins. We need to collect clothes and weapons."

"I don't have any clothes," Camryn said.

"I've packed apparel for you." Kaya's tone wasn't any friendlier than Jannike's.

Camryn sighed again, a flash of hurt bringing anguish. This wasn't her world. Her place was... Her thoughts trailed off in uncertainty. Where? Since Gabriel had died, she'd drifted like a riderless horse. She didn't have a place to call home, not with her brother and his family and not here on the Indefatigable.

"Five mins," Ry repeated, his hard gaze slicing each of his crewmembers. After a slight hesitation, they moved, heading to the cargo bay.

Ry took her hand and led her to his private quarters. After a swift, hard kiss on her lips, he turned away to pack a bag. He stowed several sets of clothes plus an assortment of weapons. That done, he grabbed a clean shirt and dragged it over his head. When he looked at her again, his eyes were dark green and full of fire. The heat stole her breath, pinning her in place when he prowled toward her.

"I said five mins, and I mean to keep my promise, but I can't go without marking you," he said in a rough voice. "I need to stake a claim." His bark of laughter held self-derision along with perplexity.

Camryn understood his bewilderment. The need to touch him, to indelibly mark him blazed through her like a compulsion. She didn't understand. Hell, she didn't really want the male, but the sheer desire pulsing through her sex made her wonder if something alien inhabited her body.

Ry nuzzled her neck and shifted aside the fabric of her borrowed shirt to lick her skin. The rough rasp of his tongue sent a tremor straight to her breasts, her clit. Her body throbbed wantonly. Yearned. Ry licked across the same spot in the opposite direction then without warning, he bit down. Sharp teeth sank into her flesh. Fiery pain brought tears to her eyes, and she felt the warmth of blood. Her blood.

A loud groan rumbled deep in Ry's throat. He stroked his tongue across the puncture wounds and immediately the pain receded. Her entire body tingled, her pussy clamping down with hunger. She moaned with pure bliss. He rasped his tongue across the sensitive spot again and pleasure shot the length of her body. Her pussy pulsed with the waves of an unprecedented climax. Camryn gasped, and when he licked across the bite for a third time, she soared. She trembled, her legs crumpling when the waves of acute pleasure became too much.

Ry caught her to his hard chest, a primal snarl of satisfaction emerging from behind his bared teeth. Startled, she stared into his eyes, the waves of pleasure still rippling across her skin and internally. His eyes were still green but the shape...lord, they'd changed shape, becoming more slanted and almost catlike. And the dark pupils, they were thin, black lines. Astonishment froze her in place, her heart galloping in the beginnings of an adrenaline burst. Ry didn't seem to notice. Instead he made a sound like a satisfied purr, reinforcing the catlike image and dipped his head. His tongue dragged across her wound and produced another orgasm so intense she screamed. She arched in his arms as she rode out the waves of fast, furious pleasure. One final lick and she shattered, the world turning dark.

Chapter Four

"What have you done to her?"

"Nothing!" Ry clasped Camryn's petite body closer to his chest and refused to let Mogens inspect her closely. She was breathing, her breasts rising and falling in a steady rhythm. Her color looked good, and he sensed she'd revive when ready. Ry placed her gently in a seat and buckled the harness to keep her safe.

"I need my bag. Be right back." Ry took two steps and stopped, turning back to glare at his crew. "Don't touch her." He waited until they nodded before running along the narrow passage to his quarters. He grabbed his bag and sword and sprinted to the tender, uneasy at the separation from Camryn. He burst through the door of the tender to find Mogens examining her with Kaya hovering at his shoulder.

"Get away from her." Ry shoved Kaya aside, sending her flying across the floor and snarled, flashing sharp canines in warning at

Mogens.

The seer backed away, raising both hands in a signal of surrender. "I didn't touch her. She's all right. Easy, Captain."

Unease filled the main cabin of the tender. Ry eyed each of his crew in turn, waiting for them to acknowledge his status. One by one they looked away, conscious of the danger if they didn't. Ry inhaled, alert for sudden moves. He wasn't sure what ailed him or why his behavior had drifted into aggressive, but he needed to protect Camryn. The need beat at him with primitive urgency.

Camryn gave a small sigh. Her brown eyes flickered and opened. "Hi."

The breathless sound zapped straight to his gut, helped the panic in him disperse.

"Captain?" Kaya asked in a cautious manner. "Are we ready to leave now?"

"Yeah." Ry sank onto the chair beside Camryn. Because he had to, he reached out to touch her hand. She flinched, her gaze wary when she glanced at him. Her fingers rubbed back and forth across the place where he'd bitten her. Hell, he'd bitten her. Ry couldn't believe it. "I'm sorry," he said in a low voice. He didn't want the crew hearing his apology. "I've never done anything like that before. Are you all right?"

He watched, mesmerized, when she ran her fingers over her neck again. "It's okay," she whispered after a nervous look at Kaya then Mogens. "It's not sore." She let her hand drop to her lap and stared out the porthole of the tender.

Ry frowned. The bite had disappeared. No puncture or teeth marks, just soft, silky flesh. He'd tasted her blood, licked the wound clean. What kind of savage was he? He grunted, wondering if he'd ever learn of his heritage and what drove the feline.

Yep powered up the engines, the floor vibrated and they took off, the town mostly engulfed by the black haze. Gradually the gray hovels, smoky chimneys and fog gave way to lush trees in every color imaginable from pale pastel pink to bright red, vast pastures and in the distance chains of bluish gray mountains pushed up to the sky like jagged teeth.

"Are we leaving civilization?" Jannike asked, breaking the silence inside the tender.

"Looks like it," Kaya said with a laugh. "An adventure into unexplored territory."

"At least mercenaries won't chase us into the middle of nowhere," Nanu said.

"Don't be so sure," Ry said. "With the price on my head they'd chase us into the fires of a volcano."

"Maybe that one," Jannike said dryly, pointing at the plume of smoke to their right.

"I still haven't seen a hell-horse," Camryn said.

"Ask and you shall receive." Yep squinted through the porthole. "Check out the porthole to the right."

Camryn leaned forward. "Those black things?"

"Yes, those are hell-horses," Ry said. "Put the tender down in the clearing."

Ry glanced at Camryn, desire flooding him along with a burst of fear. Hopefully they'd catch a hell-horse and be able to start training straightaway, before he unwittingly injured the fragile Earthling.

"How are you going to catch one? You'll need yards to contain the horse so I can train it."

"Yards? Blister it! You didn't think to mention that before?" Kaya asked.

"Someone is hunting a horse down there," Yep said, pointing out a campsite over to their left. "They don't have any yards."

"They don't have me training their horse. I want a yard."

Jannike scowled over her shoulder. "If I wanted to be a builder I'd have attended a skill school."

Camryn glared right back. "I need a yard."

Ry gripped the arms of his chair to stop himself from leaping at Jannike. Anger and rage engulfed him, and luckily, the harness stopped him from an impulsive attack. He breathed rapidly through his mouth, aghast at the violent thoughts aimed at his second-in-command. They were a team, a tight unit who'd together survived diversity. He was fragged if he'd put the crew in jeopardy. Yet his feline compelled him to protect Camryn. Damn! He hoped he didn't hurt anyone trying to balance captain with his urges regarding the Earthling.

Yep landed the tender in a clearing near a river. They disembarked with weapons on their hips in case of trouble.

The hot air folded around Ry, the humidity worse than in town. Within secs his clothes clung to his skin, constricting and moist with sweat. A bright flash of green and red darted through the multicolored treetops, the harsh caw grating to his ears. Lush red and green ferns swayed in the gentle breeze while tall trees brushed the cloud-studded sky. A dull brown bird with a fanlike tail flitted from branch to branch above Ry's head, the high-pitched tweets sounding like a protest at their presence. Over to his right a river rushed past them with white water parting to reveal the sharp teeth of submerged rocks.

They were on the opposite side of the river to the other hell-horse hunters, and hopefully the river would continue to separate them. Ry didn't want to socialize or present a temptation for bounty hunters.

Thick bush and tall trees surrounded the rest of the clearing in a natural barrier, the constant squawk of birds and click of insects indicating a vast amount of life. Hopefully they'd find herds of hell-horses on this side of the river.

"Are the hell-horses pasture grazers or do they forage in the bush?" Camryn asked.

They all stared at each other before turning to Ry. He shrugged. "Hell if I know. What did we do with the information they gave us when we entered the race?"

Camryn snorted. "Do you guys know anything about the horses?"

"We need to find a fast one to win the race," Nanu said.

"We should observe them before we try to catch one," Camryn said. "It will be beneficial to watch their behavior. And I'd better read the literature they gave us."

"How long is this going to take?" Jannike stalked back and forth in front of the tender.

Camryn was right. They needed a plan. Since meeting her, he hadn't been thinking clearly. He had to focus on the important—the opportunity to best his brother and exact revenge would never be better. Here on Ornum, Talor was exposed, and Ry intended to take advantage of his vulnerability.

"Look, they're running them into exhaustion," Nanu said, indicating the competitors over the other side of the river. A group of men ran after a small herd of the hell-horses. The black creatures bounded ahead, easily outrunning the men who weren't used to the stony, uneven ground.

"Are you sure they're the right animals?" Worry furrowed Camryn's forehead and tinged her voice. "They look like overgrown hyenas."

"Don't you think you can train them?" Jannike asked.

"Any animal can be trained, given the right circumstances," Camryn said, continuing to watch their competitor's attempt to capture a hell-horse.

"Will a yard work?" Mogens asked.

"Better than chasing the horse like them," Camryn said dryly.

While they watched, the herd of hell-horses split into two and circled back, surrounding two of the exhausted chasers. Before the other runners could help, the hell-horses attacked, running at the hapless males with teeth barred.

"They're attacking!" Nanu cried.

"Crap." Camryn jerked her gaze from the horses. "I can't watch."

Ry wrapped his arms around Camryn and drew her against his chest, burying her face in his shirt. Horror filled him while he watched the attack. A terrified shriek rippled across the river, raising chill bumps on his arms. Both men fell. The hell-horses kicked and stomped until the men ceased to move. Dead. The beasts yipped and fought amongst themselves, biting and kicking, lashing out until one hell-horse remained, the others driven off. The victor settled to eat his prey, his muzzle covered with blood.

"You told me they were horses," Camryn said faintly, lifting her head to peer across the river. "These animals are predators."

"Hell-horses are scavengers," Kaya stated. "They appear to eat just about anything," she added, her distaste apparent in her pale face.

"I thought the stories were exaggerated," Mogens muttered. The seer had turned ebony black, trauma deepening his skin tone.

They exchanged uneasy glances, and Ry caught several of his crew glancing over their shoulders, peering into the thick bush. Frankly, he didn't blame them. Apprehension prickled across his skin and the new tattoos on his back and chest itched. Ry ran his hand over Camryn's trembling frame, attempting to comfort. The touch eased the irritation in his chest and back, so he repeated the move, holding her tighter.

Jannike spat out a vicious curse and her hand gripped the butt of her weapon, as if she wanted to wade across the river and enter the fracas. Too late, Ry thought, disbelief at the unexpectedness of the attack still reverberating through him. The creatures had moved so fast, acted so ruthlessly in their attack. They were obviously intelligent.

Across the river, a flurry of gunfire rang out. Camryn flinched, and a pained sound escaped Mogens. The hell-horses yipped and snarled, attacking in return. Men shouted. More gunfire filled the air. Both beasts and men fell. When silence fell only a few men remained standing while bodies of beasts littered the ground. The men retreated when another herd of hell-horses arrived.

Scavenger birds arrived to circle overhead, but the hell-horses drove them away from the bodies of the men and horses, squabbling among themselves while they picked over the dead.

Camryn shivered, and a surge of protectiveness filled Ry. He couldn't ask her to face those creatures, to train one. She was so petite—she'd die. They could all die if they pursued this course.

"What do you want to do?" Ry asked, breaking the tense silence. "If anything, the stories we heard were mild. If any of you want to back out of this contest, speak now."

"We'll lose the entrance fee," Yep said.

Ry nodded. "Something to consider."

"I want my share of the currency," Kaya said. "I'm tired of running all the time, drifting from one planet to the next. I want a home, a place to feel safe. If your brother sticks to his word and clears your name we can purchase a home base."

"True," Ry said. "But even if we capture a hell-horse, we still have to qualify and win the final race."

"We're up for the challenge. Besides, we all need a place to call home," Mogens said.

"I am tired of running," Nanu added.

"Oh, come on!" Yep whirled on his brother. "You like the excitement. It's why we joined Ry in the first place. Besides we're still wanted in our homeland."

"It would be good to have a base, a place to repair our ship without looking over our shoulders. We could start a fleet and haul more cargo, enter legitimate trade." Ry glanced at each of his crew in turn and tried to ignore the excited yips echoing across the river. "Camryn." Gently, he pushed her away to survey her face. "What do you want to do?"

"You kidnapped me to train a hell-horse. I'm not here of my own free will." Camryn planted her hands on her hips. "I vote you drop the competition and take me home."

Ry's feline stirred, writhing for freedom. His canines extended inside his mouth, a growl starting to build. The feline didn't want Camryn to leave. He didn't either. Maybe when he'd fully sated himself, maybe then he'd deliver her back to Earth and walk away without regrets.

Jannike snarled. "Don't listen to her. I vote continue with the contest."

"I want to win." Yep stepped up beside Jannike.

"I vote continue," Nanu said.

"And me." Kaya aligned herself with her crewmates.

"Mogens?" Ry prompted.

The seer sighed heavily and went through rapid color changes. "I vote to continue."

Ry expelled a rush of air before nodding. "Good, I think we should keep on with our quest." He would have continued with or without them because he had to best Talor. He wanted to learn why his brother had set him up.

"Do we stick to our plan?" Mogens asked.

"Why don't we split into three groups and scout the area, searching for horses?" Ry said. "We won't try to capture one today. We observe, look for their feeding grounds and learn more about them. After watching the opposition's attempt at capture, I want to study the beasts before we try." Ry searched his crew for agreement. They all nodded, even Camryn. "Camryn, you're with me. Kaya, you too."

Jannike stirred. "Seer, you're with me."

"Make sure you're well armed," Ry warned.

"Look for their droppings," Camryn said. "We might be able to rub them over our clothes to stop them scenting us. If we smell like them they might not attack."

"You mean rub shit over our bodies?" Jannike demanded in icy tones.

Camryn nodded, unfazed by Jannike's hostility. "It's a proven technique used by hunters."

"But we don't have a sanitizer unit on the tender." Yep seemed equally horrified, and judging by the expressions of the others, they didn't want to follow Camryn's suggestion either.

"We can bathe in the river," Camryn said.

"Meet back here before dark. And bring firewood on your way back," Ry added quickly before a fight broke out.

"What? We're staying here overnight?" Jannike stopped in her tracks, her eyes narrowing. "No way are we staying in the middle of this jungle."

"I thought we'd agreed to see this through." Ry worked to keep his tone even. "And if that means staying, then that's what we'll do."

"Aye, Captain." Jannike didn't salute but she might as well have. She checked her weapon and tucked it into the holster she wore strapped to her leg. "Mogens and I will go east." She pointed in the general direction.

"Yep and I will go around the base of the mountains," Nanu said. They checked their weapons and headed out.

"Will the tender be secure?" Camryn's hand shook violently, and she tucked it behind her back.

"It will be once I lock systems," Kaya said.

"Have you shot a weapon before?" Ry knew he was taking a gamble offering her a weapon, but she needed a means of defending herself.

"No."

"I'll give you a simple weapon. All you need to do is flick off the safety, aim and pull the trigger." Ry half expected her to argue but instead she nodded, frowning at Jannike when she departed.

Camryn stared after Jannike until she disappeared into the thick bush. She didn't understand the woman's animosity.

"Camryn."

She turned on hearing Ry's sexy voice. Oh yeah. She had much bigger worries than Jannike's dislike and the capture and training of a hell-horse. There was something wrong with her, something weird about the way she lusted after Ry. Constantly. She had to force herself to recall Gabriel, to picture his face.

"Here's a weapon. Safety catch. Click it off. On. Squeeze this to shoot. Got it?"

"Yeah." As long as the DTs didn't spoil her aim. Camryn glanced across the river at the hell-horses. They were ugly, full of guile and cunning. How would she manage to train one? Her shoulders slumped. There was no other option. She couldn't risk them returning to Earth to kidnap Max.

Ry tossed her a leather holster. "Hook this around your thigh and keep on the safety unless you're drawing your weapon. Kaya, ready to move out?"

"Aye, Captain." She ran down the ramp of the tender and pointed an automatic control at the door. The ramp whirred upward and clunked shut. "Ready to go."

Camryn fell in behind Ry and Kaya when they headed in the opposite direction to the others. The air was so close it felt as if each breath came through a straw. Dots of sweat beaded on her forehead, and her clothes stuck to her skin. They left the sunlight of the clearing and stepped under the canopy of the trees. The tall grasses and leafy yellow ferns gave way to towering trees. The dappled patterns of sunlight played across the ground, gradually disappearing when they made their way deeper into the jungle. Although the trees blocked the sun, the humidity remained. Insects clicked from the leaf canopy in a ceaseless litany that hurt her ears. Others landed on her bare arms and nipped her skin.

Camryn slapped at a large mosquito-like insect and wondered

about diseases. Too late to worry now, and given the habits of the hell-horse, catching an illness from an insect bite was the least of her problems. A bird flitted from a tree branch on her left. It flew so close its wings almost touched her face, and she practically jumped out of her boots.

"Eek!"

Ry whirled so suddenly she screeched again. A feral expression stretched across his face and his weapon cleared his holster in seconds flat. "What is it?" His gaze roved the trees and the narrow path behind them, his stance taut and warrior ready. "Where?"

Heat stained her cheeks. "The bird gave me a fright."

"A bird?" The incredulity in Kaya's voice sent a renewed wash of color to her face.

"I'm sorry." Camryn shrugged, attempting nonchalance but her cheeks flamed with her embarrassment. She wasn't normally such a girl. God, she could do with a stiff drink right now.

Kaya muttered under her breath and continued down the narrow path winding between the trees. The leaves crackled beneath her boots with each confident step.

"You go first. I'll bring up the rear," Ry said.

Camryn nodded, following Kaya. The moist scent of decaying leaves and dampness filled every breath. Camryn shivered, feeling as if hidden eyes watched her. Firm footsteps sounded behind and the sense of someone observing her persisted. Her back prickled beneath the clinging fabric of her tunic, her senses working overtime.

She glanced over her shoulder and stumbled at the heat she saw in Ry's green eyes. Her breath caught and she tripped over a jutting tree root.

"Easy." Ry scooped her up and set her on her feet in one fluid motion. His hands spanned her waist, his touch searing hot.

Camryn bit back a stunned gasp. The desire to throw herself into his arms astonished her. Definitely unwanted, but her dismay didn't stop the yearning. This yearning was worse than craving a shot of whiskey. She forced herself to turn away, to keep walking, one step after another. Her breasts strained against the cups of her bra while her tunic and trews rubbed her sensitized skin. She gulped, confused and irritated at the blast of arousal.

It was Ry. He'd done something alien and tricky to her body while she'd slept. Each step tortured her. Her hands shook while excitement thundered through her in waves. She wanted to turn and throw herself at him so badly, she ached with the desire. But Camryn continued walking, concentrating on taking one step at a time. The attraction and sheer lust for Ry wasn't natural. She must fight. Gabriel. Concentrate on Gabriel—the good times, not the bad.

The track branched off, each fork leading deeper into the bush.

Kaya stopped. "Which way?"

"We need to get into open land," Ry said. "We haven't seen any wildlife apart from birds and insects. Can either of you hear the river?"

Camryn cocked her head to listen and couldn't discern anything apart from the insect and birdsong.

"Nothing," Kaya said.

Ry studied each path before saying, "The river is on our right. I can hear the water. We'll keep going for another two hours before we head to the tender."

Kaya moved off and Camryn followed. Two hours later they halted after forcing their way through heavy undergrowth and tall trees and seeing not a sign of open land or large animals.

"We'd better head back if we want to make it before nightfall." Ry lifted his head, his nostrils flaring. "We don't know if there are other large predators around." He prowled back in the direction they'd come from.

Camryn stumbled after him, so tired she could barely lift her feet. She kept her gaze on his back and pushed her body to keep moving. Sweat dribbled down her face and trickled uncomfortably between her breasts. Her entire body ached with the unaccustomed exertion while her arms and face bore nicks and angry scratches from sharp branches and vines blocking their way.

Despite the approach of nightfall, the humid heat clung stubbornly, and Camryn felt as if a soggy blanket enclosed her body. Her steps started to waver and all she could think of was walking into the river and submerging her sweaty body in the cool water. Maybe a cold bath would make her stop thinking about Ry too.

"Captain!" Kaya hollered from behind her.

Ry stopped and trotted back to them. He took one look at Camryn and his expression tightened with irritation. "Why didn't you say you were struggling?"

"I'll be fine after a bath and a stiff drink."

"Kaya, you go ahead. I'll watch Camryn."

Camryn started to protest but the savage determination on his face snapped her mouth shut. With a militant expression, she stomped after Kaya, her tiredness dissipating in a burst of temper. She didn't need him to watch over her. She needed him to leave her alone.

After what seemed like days, the canopy thinned, and the oppressive gloominess lightened. Weak patches of sunlight left light and shadows on the ground while in the distance she heard the rush of the water.

"Almost there, sweetheart." The husky voice sounded near her ear, and she became aware of a strong hand grasping her right arm, keeping her vertical.

Camryn staggered into the clearing where they'd landed the tender. Up ahead, Kaya started running.

"A blue pox on it! Someone has broken into the tender." She pulled out her weapon and circled their transport before advancing up the ramp.

"Stay here." Ry pushed Camryn behind a tree. She collapsed to the ground, her exhausted legs refusing to hold her weight.

Ry darted forward. Camryn muttered a rude word under her breath and thought longingly of a drink. She couldn't wait to remove her clothes and wash in the river.

"All clear," Kaya snapped. "There's no one here."

"Damage?"

"Looks like they were after parts. Nanu is gonna be pissed. The thieves weren't careful when they removed the parts they wanted."

"Camryn, you can come out now."

Camryn groaned. Fine for him. Quite frankly, she wasn't sure her legs would hold her body up long enough to make the safety of the tender.

No sooner had she thought it than he stood in front of her. With gentle hands, he scooped her up. A protest lodged in her throat, but he bent his head and stopped it with his lips, rubbing them against hers until every thought of dissention faded.

"You did well," he whispered when he lifted his head. He set her down in the middle of their campsite. "Take off your boots and relax. I'm going to check out the damage then change to cat to try and track whoever did this."

"Stop reading my mind." She had to talk to Mogens again about blocking.

"What, you don't want to have a swim in the river?"

Camryn growled low in her throat, copying the same low-pitched sound she'd heard him make when they made love. He had the audacity to laugh, the rich chuckle fading when he entered the tender and vanished. She slumped, the craving for a drink and the comfort of Gabriel's chair so strong she shook with it. The backs of her eyes smarted. She swallowed, her throat so tight it ached. Fatigue weighed her down, dragging her low into familiar despair. A tear trickled free, followed by another and another. A sob tore loose.

Gabriel. She needed him—the touch of his callused hand, his quirky smile, wise counsel, and the way he'd made her feel secure. She hadn't felt safe since he'd died two years ago.

Gabriel.

The rapid approach of footsteps froze her mid-sob. Camryn squeezed her eyes tightly closed.

"You okay?" Jannike's stern demand held compassion.

"Yeah." Camryn forced the answer past the knot in her throat. She sniffed. "I'm fine. Someone broke into the tender. Kaya is pissed."

"Aw phrull." Jannike took off at a run, her boots clomping up the tender ramp.

Camryn wiped her eyes. Staggering, she forced her tired body off the ground and headed to the edge of the river. She kicked off her boots and socks and sat on a rock to dip her feet into the water, sitting for a long time.

The huge sun, or whatever they called it here, dropped below the horizon, bright green and pink streamers coloring the clouds before darkness fell. Across the other side of the river, Camryn heard the growl and mock fighting of animals. They splashed and frolicked in the water while taking an evening drink.

"Camryn, you need to come back to camp now. It's not safe out here." Ry prowled out of the darkness and her heart skipped a beat. His chest was bare, and it was obvious he'd just returned from a run in feline form.

"I need to wash."

"Not on your own." Ry walked up to her and curved an arm around her waist. "If you want to wash do it now." He pulled away and started to tug off his boots. "You have ten mins."

Camryn wanted to tell him to go to hell, but he stepped behind her, smoothed his hand across her shoulder, his fingers drifted across her collarbone. The fight went out of her. Her body softened and she leaned into his strong, bare chest, her trepidation

79

SHELLEY MUNRO

and precious memories of Gabriel fading. His heat warmed her cooling body and suddenly desire writhed through her veins.

"What are you?" she demanded, turning in his arms to glare up at him. The light hit his eyes and they glowed with unearthly brilliance. "What have you done to me?" She took a step back when the glow intensified.

"Camryn, you know what I am. You've seen me in my other form. Know I would never hurt you. Never." Ry closed the distance between them again.

"You kidnapped me from my home." Not that her family would notice. They were probably relieved she wasn't there to embarrass them any longer.

"Business. Everything else is very personal." He trailed his fingers across her cheek.

Camryn gasped the instant he made contact. Heat flashed across her skin. It tugged across her breasts, pulling her nipples tight and zapping straight to her pussy. She gulped at the electric charge when he rubbed his fingers across the same part of her neck he'd bitten earlier. Her knees trembled and buckled. She sagged against him, burying her face against his naked chest.

Ry held her easily. With one hand he removed her thin tunic and tussled with her bra. "How do you get this thing off? Never mind." He tugged the cups aside, revealing tight nipples. With a rumbling purr, he dipped his head and licked across the plump curve of her breast with a decadent stroke of his tongue. He finished with a quick flick across her nipple. Ry lifted his head, studied her reaction. The cool trail left by his mouth tingled. It wasn't enough. She wanted more. She wanted his mouth on her nipple, sucking. Part of Camryn knew she'd regret it later. Right now she didn't care. She hungered.

"Please, Ry. I ache. I need you to make it stop."

"Let me take off your clothes." With economy of movement, he pulled off her bra, trousers and panties, leaving her naked. Ry

80

didn't take his eyes off her while he stripped. His eyes glowed, yet again reminding her of his predator status.

Camryn swallowed, poised at the edge of the water. Gabriel. A picture from their last evening together flitted through her mind, but it dissipated the instant Ry grasped her hand and tugged her into the swirling water. She hesitated when the cool water hit her heated skin. Gooseflesh rose on her arms and legs. The current dragged at her legs, but Ry anchored her with his strength. He pulled her deeper into the river until it covered her breasts.

"Put your hands on my shoulders," he whispered against her ear when he'd directed them into a calmer part of the water. "I don't like getting wet. You make it fun."

Camryn didn't want to like him, but his grin drew her. Slowly she grasped his shoulders and let the current brush their bodies together. She melted into him, rubbing against his groin to gain relief from the ache that had reignited the moment they'd touched. She rubbed fingers across his jaw, the dark stubble rough beneath her fingers. Her lips followed the same path. She nibbled along his jaw before she reached his ear. She licked across the delicate whorls, enjoying the way he offered himself and the soft purrs he made.

"Enough," he growled, and he lifted her, curling her legs around his waist and opening her to his touch. His fingers probed slippery folds, dipped and delved and rubbed across her clit.

Camryn shivered, the contrast of her warm body and the cool water driving her high. Ry captured her mouth, and when she opened to him, he pushed his tongue inside, stroking against hers. Desire, liquid and molten, simmered inside. Quick and fast. Exactly what she needed. She wriggled against him, trying to capture his erection with her hand.

"Now," she demanded. "Ry, now. Please."

He tipped back his head, his eyes sparkling and catlike when they caught the scant light cast by the single moon. He leaned over to capture her lips and pressed into her open body, allowing her to control the pace.

Damn, that felt good. She sank down on his cock, feeling the slow stretch until fully impaled. He throbbed deep inside her channel, and it kindled a fire storm inside her body.

"You feel perfect," he murmured. "Hot and wet and so fraggin' sweet." He nuzzled her neck and bit down on the fleshy part of her shoulder. It should've hurt, but instead intense pleasure filled her. Her pussy flexed around his cock, gripping him hard and making her gasp.

The muscles of his stomach contracted when he lifted her. He let her body sink back onto his shaft. He pinched one nipple, the exquisite pain shooting straight to her core. Why was he so addictive? This was wrong yet she couldn't stop, didn't want to halt.

She leaned into him, kissing his neck, tasting the clean and salty tang of his skin. He thrust, increasing the pace of his strokes until pleasure coursed through her and she clung. She needed to move, she needed to touch and kiss. And some deep instinct bade she make her mark. She licked across his neck, grazed her teeth across the smooth column. Back and forth. Back and forth. Ry groaned. His body tensed when she bit down.

"Yes," he hissed between clenched teeth. "Harder."

Camryn let him feel her teeth. At the same time he pinched and tugged at her nipple. He changed the angle of his strokes, his thrust grazing across her swollen clit. Her hips jerked, the sensations intense.

Too much.

Not enough.

Just right.

Camryn groaned, went limp in his arms and luxuriated in the pulsing aftershocks. She felt his shaft jerk, his raw and guttural shout bringing feminine satisfaction. At the back of her mind she knew she shouldn't feel this pleasure, the drugging contentment.

She didn't deserve a second chance after failing Gabriel.

Ry eased her down and led her from the river. They sat on a large flat stone. She should have felt cold but the hot, intense glow in his eyes warmed her through.

"Tell me about Gabriel." The words made her feel as if he'd immersed her neck-deep in the cool river.

"There's nothing to tell." Camryn studied her hands, noted her fingernails were ragged and ugly. Gabriel had liked her to look after herself. He'd been old-fashioned that way.

"You think about him all the time."

"Of course I think about him. He was my husband."

"He was older than you."

"I loved him. Will you get out of my head?"

"I can't help it. I'm curious."

Camryn snorted. "Curious as a cat, perhaps?"

Ry inclined his head, his green eyes watchful. "How did Gabriel die?"

"I don't want to talk about him." Camryn jumped to her feet and struggled into her clothes. Dressed, she stomped back to camp. She'd get Mogens to give her lessons in blocking and she'd become the best damn blocker ever. No way would she let him fish inside her head again.

"Where are you going?"

"Away from you." She sat by Mogens and asked about blocking. Later when they bedded down, she maintained a distance from Ry. But the man filled her dreams—he and the black cat. She dreamed he chased her. She fled but he captured her, swept her up in his arms and carried her off to his lair.

CHAPTER FIVE

R y's eyes flickered open, and when he inhaled, Camryn's scent hit him. They hadn't bedded down together but, during the night, one of them had moved. His head raised a fraction. Him. Well hell. He smoothed his hand over her back, savoring the warmth, her feminine fragrance. Whenever Camryn left his sight, uneasiness struck him. He didn't understand his urgency, the compulsion to stroke her. When they touched, skin to skin, the contact soothed the cat.

His medicine didn't inhibit the urges he felt when it came to Camryn. Ry hadn't told Mogens he'd stopped taking the medicine. In the past, he'd have jumped Kaya or Jannike without his daily dose. Camryn's presence changed things. She was the only woman he craved.

When he heard the others stirring, he slipped from beneath the all-weather blankets they'd used and rapidly dressed. He walked down to the river edge, the pastures on the other side obscured by mist. The lilac tendrils curled toward them, gradually covering the water. Ry bent to wash his face and returned to camp.

Kaya exited the tender, bearing ration pouches while Mogens brewed kafe.

"Tender will function, but it still needs work." Nanu wiped grease off his hands with a rag.

Jannike stomped over to accept her pouch. "I hope this fog doesn't last for long. I hate waiting around."

"We'll fly to another clearing once it lifts," Ry said. "Since we didn't have much luck here yesterday."

An hour later, the tender set down farther inland in a remote area. They covered their transport with large fern leaves, or as much as they could. Ry hoped the camouflage would deter saboteurs, but they took other precautions, leaving Yep and Nanu on board to guard the ship and finish the repairs to Nanu's satisfaction. Since Nanu's perfectionist tendencies had saved their butts more than once, Ry wasn't about to complain.

"Are we going out in teams again?" Jannike asked.

Ry scented the air for danger. "Not if you don't think it's necessary. We'll cover more ground if we go out singly."

Jannike shrugged. "Apart from the hell-horses, we didn't see any predators."

"I don't know." Kaya surveyed a bite on her arm with a rueful grin. "Some of bugs are big enough to qualify as predators."

Mogens looked up to scan the clouds. "Good tidings in the cloud cover. I will go on my own. Give me a chance to stock my medicine bag. I saw familiar plants yesterday. Maybe I'll run across some ghosts to guide me to the correct path."

Ry shrugged. As long as he didn't start seeing Mogens' specters, he was happy. "We'll meet back here before nightfall. Camryn, you're with me." He refused to let her out of sight. He caught the flattening of her luscious mouth and the militant glint in her brown eyes. Too bad. He didn't intend to suffer alone.

After collecting supplies and water, they left the tender. Camryn walked in the lead, the sheen of perspiration glistening on her skin. His gaze drifted across her shoulders, over the pack she carried on her back to linger on her arse. Curved yet toned, it swayed in an enticing manner. A branch slashed across his face, springing back after Camryn passed. Ry bit back a curse and tried to pay attention to the vegetation. It wasn't easy. The more he sated himself in her body, the more he lusted after her. A disease. It had to be because no other explanation made a scrap of sense.

The bush became denser, and Camryn struggled to forge a path through the mass of undergrowth.

Ry placed a hand on her shoulder, touching her to soothe his raging hunger. "Let me take the lead." He should have done that anyway. No telling what danger lurked in this unexplored land. He'd let his hormones rule him, wanting to watch his woman. Predictably, his cock reared at the thought of taking her. For fleeting secs, a vision of shrugging off their packs and stripping down taunted him. He took half a step closer before common sense hit. They needed to capture a hell-horse. He needed to best his brother. *Concentrate.*

With a soft curse, Ry clasped Camryn's shoulders and shifted her out of his way to take the lead. He set a ferocious pace, pulling out a sharp knife to hack the undergrowth.

The incline gradually increased. His lungs burned and his acute hearing caught Camryn's accelerated breathing and creative thoughts.

If he tries to drive his purple rocket into my parking space again, I'll whack his bag of tricks with river rocks. That will put his kitty out of action. See if he wants to fuck me then.

Ry winced, wanting to protest the threats against his manhood—even though he wasn't sure he understood the Earth terms—but didn't want to halt her fascinating commentary.

The tree canopy gave way to huge patches of blue sky and the leaf litter underfoot changed to rough rock. Ry halted without warning, and Camryn crashed into his back.

"Easy." He grasped her hips and tugged her against his side. "Look."

They stood on the lip of a canyon, a blind canyon as far as he could discern.

"Hell-horses," Camryn whispered. "A herd. There's plenty of water and they're eating those small trees."

Ry scanned the ungainly black creatures. "We need to find the entrance to the canyon."

"A box canyon would work instead of a set of yards. Better since there's feed and water here." Excitement shaded her voice, knocking aside his concerns about her being right for the job. He couldn't afford to let his emotions color the situation. This was a prime opportunity to clear his name, and his feelings for Camryn mustn't interfere.

"Let's go." Ry didn't wait for her assent but started to pick his way down the hill.

Camryn fumed while she followed the infuriating man. She tried to pay attention to their surroundings, the bright flitting butterflies and contrasting dull-colored birds. Most of the ones they'd seen today ran along the ground rather than taking to the sky. Although their surroundings were beautiful, her gaze kept returning to the alien. She kept remembering his urgent touch on her bare breasts, the stroke of his fingers between her legs. Camryn shivered at the memory and was immediately angry at the reaction.

It was good sex. It meant nothing.

Nothing.

But it sullied Gabriel's memory. Each time she had sex with Ry, it became harder to call Gabriel's image to mind, to pretend she made love to her husband.

A sense of helplessness filled her. Her sister-in-law was right. She lacked control. She craved alcohol like most women longed for chocolate. But even worse, since they were in the middle of nowhere without a drop of alcohol in sight, she'd set her sights on Ry instead.

She'd become a sex addict.

With an unhappy grunt, she stomped after Ry. She tore her eyes off his tight, muscular butt and focused on her surroundings. One step at a time.

It took most of the morning to make their way down the side of the hill because of the treacherous footing. Ry had to help her down the steep slopes, his hands lingering for longer than she liked. Even though she hated herself for it, she'd started to long for more mini-cliffs, more hands-on attention. Sick. Damn, she'd lost her mind.

They came to another part where they needed to navigate a short cliff face because there was no alternative detour.

"I'll go first," Ry said.

"I'm not helpless."

"You're a valuable part of our team. We can't afford for you to suffer an injury."

His reasonable tone fueled irritation. "That wouldn't do at all."

"Stop trying to pick a fight with me."

Camryn backed over the cliff and chose a foothold. She scrambled down the cliff face, anger helping her to shove aside thoughts of danger. Luckily she had a good head for heights and her natural balance helped. She reached the bottom before Ry and glared up at him.

"I can do it by myself. You don't need to touch me all the time."

"Do you think I like this? I need to keep a clear head, and all I can think of is having you."

"It's not my fault."

"No?" He'd prowled closer, forcing her to back up until the cliff at her spine prevented her retreat. Ry kept coming. When they were almost touching, he halted and shrugged off his backpack. It hit the ground beside them with a dull thunk. Camryn's heart jumped into a speedy beat. Her tongue snaked out to moisten her dry lips.

"You can run," he whispered, his breath warm against her neck. "But you can't hide from whatever this is between us. My dick is so desperate for you it's like walking with a dagger between my legs. It's getting worse. You have to touch me or I'm going to go mad." He ripped his damp shirt over his head and tossed it aside.

Camryn's gaze roved over his muscular shoulders, over the swirling tattoos that covered his pectoral muscles and stomach. A gasp emerged when she noticed his erection. He hadn't lied about his readiness.

"Of course I didn't lie," he snapped.

She swallowed, her body reacting with speed. Between her legs moistened with a surge of juices and her breasts prickled against her bra. He was doing it again. Reading her mind. She had to practice building walls in her mind as Mogens had taught her.

Ry's mouth slammed down on hers, taking her lips in a rough kiss. Her heart pounded in an erratic manner as his spicy flavor exploded across her taste buds. Wild musk with a trace of aniseed. Addictive. Camryn softened, melting against him, dragging his musky scent deep into her lungs.

Oh boy. She couldn't fight it. She wanted him inside her now. Right now.

"Yes." Ry lifted his head, his eyes a fiery green glow and full of desire. He yanked her tunic, tugging it from her trousers. With urgent hands, he pulled them down and pushed his knee between her legs, forcing her to widen her stance. With one finger he parted her moist folds.

Her chin lowered to her chest, and she sighed, the ripple of pleasure from his touch removing the last vestiges of protest. Ry was right. She wanted him as badly as he craved her.

Ry continued to stroke her clitoris, teasing her needy flesh until pleasure swirled just out of reach. He dragged his trews down and his cock sprang free. Fully extended, the flared head appeared swollen while his sac had drawn tight. She reached out, wanting to stroke the velvet length of him, but he batted her hand away.

"Don't touch." His mouth pulled to a tight line. "I'll explode." He grasped her hips and lifted her effortlessly, piercing her body with his cock, slowly pushing inside. Buried to the hilt, he paused, his eyes screwed shut.

He looked savage, yet despite his scary visage, he'd never hurt her. She sensed this at gut level. She stared down at where they were joined and gripped his shoulders, savoring the stretch and the pulse of his cock against her snug walls. Her gaze lifted to study his features. His chest rose with a deep breath and his eyes opened without warning to stare straight into hers.

"Kiss my neck," he ordered. "Bite me." He released one hip to touch the spot where her fingers curled around his shoulders.

"Yes." Her heart beat faster at his husky order, desire rippling through her core. The weird thing was she wanted to bite him, craved the savage act. Her gaze went to his chest, and she licked her lips. She bent her head to brush a kiss across his neck and nibbled lightly.

Ry growled and started to thrust. Each powerful plunge shoved her against the rough rock at her back, but all she felt was Ry pounding into her pussy. The wet sound of bodies slapping together filled the air, the scent of raw sex and green herbs filling every breath. Camryn licked across his neck, and he groaned, his cock seeming to enlarge until she felt fuller than before. He rocked his pelvis forward, gliding in deep.

"Bite me," he snapped.

Camryn obeyed, sinking her teeth into the fleshy part where shoulder met neck. Fire and chills warred within her body, every nerve ending blazing with pleasure and sensitivity. But it wasn't enough. She hovered on the cusp of orgasm, the sensation verging on painful. Ry kept pounding into her, ratcheting up the heat and pressure rampaging through her body. A sob escaped.

Then he lowered his head and kissed a moist path over her shoulder. The closer he came to the area where he'd bitten her, the more painful her impending orgasm became. He let her feel his teeth, grazing over her flesh. A violent tremble racked her.

"Harder," she said on a long drawn-out groan. God, she couldn't believe the desperate plea in her voice. "Bite down. Please."

Ry hesitated an instant before he bit down. The pain passed in a flash, replaced by pleasure so powerful she didn't think she could bear the intensity. Ry withdrew and pounded back into her pussy. If anything the pleasure increased, pushing her over into climax, sensation pulsing in giant, breath-stealing waves. She gasped, weak and pliant in his arms, still shuddering in post-orgasmic pleasure.

"Camryn." Ry thrust into her again and pushed her head into the crook of his neck. She licked across the base of his neck, and he shuddered, his groan of appreciation making her repeat the move, this time with her teeth. She nipped the skin and he plunged into her with deep, frantic thrusts. He licked her neck, the warm, wet suction driving her higher. The flash of climax seared her again, and she convulsed around his cock, gripping it tightly, gasping for breath.

Incredible. Intense. Unbelievable.

The coppery tang of his blood filled her mouth. It should have repulsed her but didn't. Instead, she held tight while Ry spilled his seed and drifted down through aftershocks to satisfaction.

Ry inhaled deep before lifting her off his cock and letting her slide down his body. "Hell," he said with a rueful laugh. The humor dissipated when he studied her neck. "Are you okay? Did I hurt you?" He ran his fingers across the bite on her neck.

Camryn gasped and tried to jerk away, but he held her fast.

"God, it's bleeding. Let me." He dipped his head and licked the puncture wounds.

The lap of his tongue sent a spasm through her, the brush of his fingers bringing goose bumps. Camryn battled the need to rub against him like a cat in heat. She wanted the sleek thrust of his tongue in her mouth. Her vagina fluttered and he lifted his head, his eyes a deep, mossy green when he stared at her.

"I want to take you again," he murmured, his voice husky and seductive.

"Get out of my head," she protested, but her disapproval came out low and breathy and held not a whit of authority. She tried to build a wall in her mind—one brick at a time—like Mogens had described. The first three rows of bricks were perfect then they crumbled without warning.

Their gazes clashed and while she watched, a slow Cheshire cat smile bloomed across his features. "You like me there," he whispered. "As much as you like me thrusting into your hot little pussy."

Unable to meet his gaze for a second longer, Camryn curled into his embrace. She didn't understand, not any of it, and she hated the out-of-control sensations she experienced when they were together.

It wasn't right.

It felt like betrayal, yet she couldn't stop herself.

"If you think I like this any more than you do, then you're wrong," he gritted out, pulling away from her to glare. He hauled up his trews.

When they no longer touched, she was assailed by a sense of loss. She avoided looking at him and, after righting her clothing, stared at the ground, forcing her mind to concentrate on thoughts of the hell-horses and their training. "We should go."

Ry snorted. "You're right of course. Whatever this is between us can't get in the way of winning the race."

"There's nothing between us. Once the race ends I'm going home."

Ry picked up his pack. "Also correct."

In terse silence, they made their way down the steep incline, and after searching, they found the narrow entrance to the canyon.

"Why don't we block the entrance now?" Camryn wanted to capture the horse and start training. Leaving this strange planet and returning home couldn't happen soon enough. Ry's face had started to replace Gabriel's. She had to concentrate to recall her husband's scent. She needed to depart before Ry stole all her memories.

Darkness had already fallen by the time Camryn and Ry walked into camp.

"Captain, we were starting to worry." Mogens' eyes narrowed. His swift change of color spoke of his true feelings. "Are you hungry?"

Ry could tell Mogens would have plenty to say once he managed to get Ry alone. The seer took too much upon himself. "The terrain was difficult today." He jerked his head in Camryn's direction where she slumped, exhausted, on a nearby rock. "We found a blind canyon containing a large herd of hell-horses and spent a couple of hours blocking the entrance so they can't get out. I don't think they even knew we were there. Anyone else have any luck?"

"I saw herds in the distance, but they sensed my presence," Jannike said. "They ran off."

Mogens shook his head. "No sightings, although I restocked my herbal supplies."

"No surprises here in camp, Captain," Yep said. "The tender is fully functional again, although we'll need to do further repairs once we return to the *Indy*."

Nanu rubbed his face, the smear of grease on his cheek creeping closer to his ear each time he repeated the move. "It's not perfect but it'll do."

"Kaya, how did you get on?" Ry asked.

"I saw a few hell-horses in the distance. You know how we haven't seen any large animal life apart from the horses? Yeah, well, I saw this giant bird that stood taller than me. Nearly crapped myself."

Jannike chuckled. "Have you got a secret stash of ouzotine?"

"I haven't been drinking," Kaya protested, her chin jutting out in combative mode. "I saw a giant bird."

Ry believed her. Kaya wasn't one to make up stories. "Where did you see it?"

"In a lightly forested area, near a big pond," Kaya said. "I'm not making it up."

"We believe you," Mogens said, ever the peacemaker.

Jannike snorted and her lips quirked, however she refrained from further comment when Ry glared at her. The last thing he wanted was squabbling amongst his crew. They needed to pull together, or they'd never have a chance of winning.

"Tomorrow we'll take the tender to the canyon and set up base there. I saw a couple of areas big enough for the tender to land." Ry glanced at each of his crewmates for agreement but didn't expect protests. They were all eager for the training to begin.

Ry glanced at Camryn, his gut hollowing in apprehension. He didn't want her facing the creatures. It was dangerous for a fragile Earthling with slow-healing powers. Forcing down his fear because he had no other option, he turned to Kaya. "Have the rest of you eaten?"

"Yeah. I'll grab pouches for you and Camryn."

"I'm not hungry," Camryn said. "I intend to wash and sleep. And I should study the Dowry Derby rule book again so I know it inside out."

"Child, you must eat," Mogens said. "You must keep up your strength."

In the flickering light of the fire, Ry saw the seeds of protest forming. "I don't need to do anything apart from training the horse," she snapped. "I'm going to wash." She turned her back on them and stalked toward the river.

Ry growled, low and grouchy, and his crew watched him warily. "Pouches?"

Kaya handed him two. Ry prowled into the tender. He grabbed a flask out of his personal gear and stalked back outside. "We leave at daybreak tomorrow. The sooner we capture a hell-horse, the better I'll feel."

"Aye, Captain," Yep said. "We noticed a few tenders flying over today. I don't think we were spotted because of our camouflage."

A thought occurred to Ry. "Any of you see hunting parties on foot?"

"No," Jannike said. The others shook their heads.

"Does that strike you as strange?" Ry demanded. "With the number of people lining up to enter the race, we should have seen more hunters."

"Especially since the hunting fields close to the city are depleted," Mogens said. "You're right, Captain. We should have seen hunting parties."

"There are plenty of tenders flying over," Jannike said after an uneasy silence.

"Yeah, but what does it mean? Are we hunting in the wrong area? Are there easier pickings elsewhere? Or are we being set up?" Ry scanned the faces of his crew, his superior eyesight giving him a good view despite the scant firelight. They all looked uneasy. "We need to beef up security again," Ry said. "I don't like it. My gut is roiling."

"That would be the sex thing," Jannike retorted.

Ry dropped the pouches and flask, moving so quickly she didn't have a chance to avoid him. He grasped her shirt and yanked it, throwing her off balance. "Leave Camryn out of this."

Jannike stilled, not a muscle moving despite the fact he could break her neck at whim. "And maybe you should leave Camryn out of this. She's not gonna be worth a thing as a trainer if you muddy her mind with sex."

Plain speaking. In the past, he'd always valued Jannike's bluntness. Right now he didn't want to hear a repetition of Camryn's opinion. She didn't want his attentions. Ry took a deep breath, consciously wrapping control around him like a cloak. He released his grip on Jannike's shirt and stepped back.

"I'm sorry," he muttered, pissed he'd put himself into a position where an apology was necessary. The knowledge his second-in-command spoke good sense didn't help.

Ry stooped to pick up the pouches and flask and strode from the campsite without another word. Frag it, he knew Jannike was right, but the urge to possess ate at his control. And the moment he touched Camryn he lost any semblance of restraint. All he could think about was having her, taking and giving pleasure.

"Hell," he whispered, the sentiment fierce. Ever since Camryn had walked into his life, his hard-fought discipline had taken a holiday. He'd cut off his right hand before he'd let on how much the loss of humanity scared him. But it did—the ceding of control to the feline happened more often. It terrified him. Other things had changed as well. Physically he'd had to shift on a regular basis, just as he'd needed sex. He'd taken both where and when he could, managing a semblance of discipline.

Ry realized the urge to shift hadn't occurred since he'd met Camryn. The sex thing still happened but only with Camryn. Ry cursed under his breath, knowing he shouldn't go to her but unable to stop. She was a fever in his blood at a time when he needed his wits about him more than ever.

The rush of the water increased as did his inner turmoil. His head told him to stay away. Ry didn't listen. The idea made his gut churn. He spotted her dark silhouette on the edge of the river.

"I brought you something to eat."

"I said I didn't want anything."

"Don't be childish. You need food otherwise you won't be strong enough to train the hell-horse. We need this win, Camryn. I must win."

"Why?" Camryn turned to stare, although he didn't think she could see his expression. "For money and a woman. There must be easier ways."

"Revenge."

She cocked her head. "Against whom?"

"My brother."

"I can't imagine hating my brother that much."

"You don't know my brother," Ry said.

"Are you alike?"

"I was adopted as a baby." His tone discouraged more questions.

"The big, bad face might work on everyone else, but you don't scare me."

Ry's mouth twitched. "I don't know what you're talking about."

"Why don't you get on with your brother?"

"Until I was accused of murder, I thought we got on well. I knew the Coppersmiths adopted me. I knew Talor was the Coppersmith heir, and the business would pass to him. I was fine with that. My father trained him to take over the family business while I didn't do much of anything. I played a lot and caused trouble. I led a charmed life."

"You were a playboy?"

Ry snorted. That pretty much summed up his life on Ibrox.

He'd spent money freely, tupped willing women and acted like an aimless rich kid.

"You need to eat." Ry handed her the pouch. Their fingers touched during the transfer, scorching his nerve endings. Ry gritted his teeth and forced himself to sit on a nearby rock. Her hair hung in wet tendrils around the collar of her tunic, water dripping down to dampen the fabric. She wasn't wearing her Earth bindings. The plump curves of her breasts caught and held his attention. Blast it. He wanted her. Ry shifted uneasily to ease the discomfort.

Camryn glowered until he looked away. He heard the pouch tear open and smelled the spicy meat and plant contents. The murmur of voices carried from their campsite.

"Revenge sounds ominous." Camryn broke the uncomfortable silence between them. "What do you intend to do?"

"My brother and I have come to an agreement. If our hell-horse wins, Talor will clear my name."

"And if you lose?"

"I stop intercepting his shipments and leave the area." And never return. He'd never see his sisters again. Now that he'd had his life ripped from him, he'd come to value the important things—friends and family. He had to beat Talor. Ry opened his pouch and started to eat. When he finished, he set it aside and picked up his flask. He unscrewed the lid and handed it to Camryn.

"What is it?"

"I thought you might want a drink."

Camryn accepted the flask and sniffed before smiling. "It smells like berries." She tipped back her head and drank. "Tastes good." Camryn licked her lips in a slow, seductive move, and a moan formed deep in his chest.

"Easy. It's strong."

Camryn handed the flask back. They sat in a companionable silence, passing the flask back and forth. He felt at ease sitting beside her.

"What is the family business?"

"Magical charms."

"You're kidding."

"No. Coppersmith Magical Charms is well-known and very successful. They sell charms for luck, love and hundreds of other varieties."

Camryn stared at him with wide eyes. "Do they work?"

Ry shrugged because they'd never worked for him. "People believe they work. They keep buying the charms." Uncomfortable talking about his family and past, he changed the subject. "How will we train the hell-horse? What do we do first?" After all, she was the expert, not him. He excelled in thievery and running freight. In truth, he wanted to talk with her, listen to her sexy accent. And the need confused him when all he'd wanted in the past was a quick lay. When he required conversation, he spoke with his crew.

"I guess I'll tackle them like I would an unbroken horse at home. We'll need to choose one and keep it contained. I've been thinking. We'll still need to build a yard even though the hell-horses are contained in the canyon. It will make it simpler. A younger horse would be best since it'll be easier to train. I'll rope it and get it used to my presence."

"We'll have to muzzle it in some manner. I don't want it to attack you or any of the crew."

Camryn shuddered. "I keep thinking about the men who died across the river. I'd hate to have a repeat of that."

Ry recalled the screams from the victims, the savage yips from hell-horses. The carnage. Camryn mustn't die because of his need to best Talor.

The next morning Camryn woke with memories of hangovers past tap-tap-tapping on her brain. Her head pounded with the hoof beats of a dozen horses and...and she was blind! Panic roared through her until she realized her lashes were stuck together. Ow, ow, her eyelashes hurt. One eyelid lifted, then shut immediately in self-defense. So bright. Too bright. She became aware of the warmth scorching her naked back while her bare breasts prickled, icy cool. In desperate need of a drink, she struggled to a sitting position.

"Oh god," she murmured, holding her head between her hands.

"Camryn." The husky voice drew her unwilling attention. Part of her had known she shouldn't touch the drink Ry had offered her, but she'd gone ahead anyway. From the dim recesses of her mind she recalled laughing and kissing and um...quite a bit more as well.

"Camryn."

This time something in his tone made her turn to face him. She gasped. "The tattoo on your chest has changed. It's more defined." Hell, it hurt to speak—no croak—and the sound of her own voice made those horses break into a gallop.

"You have a tattoo on your back." The shock in his voice told her he spoke the truth.

"It doesn't hurt. I mean I don't feel anything. Where is it?" She tried to look at her back and the maneuver speared slivers of pain to her brain.

"On your shoulder." Ry smoothed his hand over her right shoulder blade.

"Don't...don't touch me." Camryn jerked from his touch and the combination of pleasure and pain ceased. The hoof beats in her head were muted now and more in line with a normal hangover. She knew about those, had plenty of experience.

"It's a cat," he whispered, shock lacing his voice. "I don't understand."

The others started to stir. Camryn grabbed her clothes and turned her back on him to dress. Ry watched her the entire time. She felt it, fingers clumsy in her self-consciousness. The spot he'd touched on her shoulder itched beneath her tunic.

Rustling clothes behind her indicated Ry was dressing. The instinct to turn and watch almost got the better of her. Almost.

"Ah, you're awake," Mogens said, coming from inside the tender. Camryn noted his clear disapproval before he lifted his head to scan the angry green clouds low on the horizon. His face darkened rapidly. "Bad tidings in the clouds."

Camryn fidgeted, her shoulder itchy and irritable beneath her clothes, the sullen *trot-trot-trot* in her head adding to her misery.

Tsking, Mogens studied her instead. "What is wrong with you, child? Have you been bitten by an insect?"

"Um no." A weird sort of insect to leave tattoos while a person slept.

"Let me see," Mogens said. "The last thing we need is for our trainer to become ill."

"Show Mogens." Ry's soft voice came from behind. It wasn't a request.

Camryn turned her back and allowed Mogens to lift her shirt. Chill bumps chased across her skin, blown by the cool morning breeze.

A hiss escaped the seer. "Ry, I told you to leave her alone. Too late now." His eyes rolled back in his head and his high-pitched voice danced up and down in a singsong pattern. "The ghost walks beside you still. He has not left and will not leave while you need him. Bad day. Bad tidings."

"What...what are you talking about?" Camryn glanced wildly at Ry, the sudden movement stabbing pain through her temples.

"Mogens, stop. You're scaring her," Ry said.

"You," Mogens hissed, still in a singsong voice. His face bled from gray to inky black, the color of Ry's hair. "You let your basic desires out of your britches."

Ry snorted and snapped his fingers in front of Mogens' face. The seer blinked, his eyes widened.

The sound of slow clapping jolted them all from the trance. "Very nice show," Jannike mocked. "But we have a hell-horse to catch before the tenders flying overhead find the ones you've barricaded in the canyon."

"Good point," Ry said.

The roar of a tender overhead hammered home the need for urgency.

Mogens' hard stare drilled through her. "We'll discuss this later."

Camryn sniffed. No way. They wouldn't discuss anything about ghosts. She'd do the job and they could take her home. Done deal. No discussion required.

Talor's tender, Ornum.

Talor smiled, sweet anticipation bubbling into a smirk. Thanks to the tracking device planted by Kaya, he'd found Ryman without difficulty. His instinct was to crush them, leaving all to rot in this inhospitable land. He resisted, knowing while it might rid him of his immediate problem, it wouldn't yield satisfaction. After the problems his brother had caused during the last ten cycles, Talor wanted Ryman to know who killed him and why. He wanted his precious brother to suffer.

And even better, he'd seen a large black cat in the distance. A leopard. Fate. That's what it was. A sign. His familiar animal had appeared to him. He would succeed now. He'd order his men to capture the creature. A familiar would make his magic strong.

As for his brother, Talor knew the exact pressure to apply

once he'd inflicted the first wound. He concentrated, focusing his thoughts and a slender, red-haired woman walked into the room.

"I have need of you." He pointed to his feet and without a murmur of protest, she knelt before him. Talor smirked at the top of her head, knowing she wouldn't see his pleasure. Nothing more than a shell these days, Meghan's mind blended with his like a well-trained slave. Perfection. Just the way a woman should behave. If it weren't for Ryman, and the fact Meghan had been his brother's lover, he'd have cast her off long ago. No, he kept her around for sentimental reasons.

The woman lifted his silky robes and crawled beneath, letting them lower again over her body. Competent hands grasped his cock and pumped in the precise manner he liked. A warm mouth slipped over his tip and licked delicately at his slit. Talor clenched his hands, a delicious tension swirling through his stomach—a combination of sexual lust and the knowledge he'd soon crush his darling brother. Heady stuff.

The woman's tongue lapped across the flared head of his cock and ran her fingers in delicate strokes over his sac. Gradually his balls tightened, drawing tight beneath his cock while her warm, moist mouth sucked. His robe rustled when her head started to bob.

Talor began to thrust in shallow moves, teasing himself because he knew the gradual build of pleasure would feel better than quick gratification. With almost dreamlike movements, he pumped into the warmth of her mouth. With each thrust he moved deeper until the head of his cock struck the back of her throat. The woman stroked his balls and quickened her pace. Talor closed his eyes and concentrated on the sensations—the scent of her rosegold perfume and the more basic sexual musk, the soft grunts she made each time he drove into her mouth. And the wet slide of her soft lips across his cock. That was best of all—the way the woman swirled her tongue over the underside of his shaft with just the right pressure. Heat rioted through him, and he rocked his pelvis forward. Higher and higher he climbed until the electric feel of orgasm raced up his cock.

"Yes." His guttural shout heralded the rush of exquisite pleasure. Each tight squeeze of her throat lengthened his enjoyment as he ejaculated into her mouth.

Oh yes. The woman who used to belong to his brother was talented. She laved the head of his cock and gradually eased back, letting his softened flesh slide from her hot mouth.

Talor lifted his robes and glanced down at the woman in a dispassionate manner. "You may go now. Make me a carafe of kafe. Go. Go!"

The woman rose and trotted from the luxurious chamber to the small canteen area. Soon the scent of kafe, rich and dark, flowed into his domain. Relaxed, Talor reclined on his bed and pondered the coming days. His stupid brother had no idea of the power he wielded.

True, his own powers had proved unreliable during the last cycles, but the journey to this convict hellhole had produced a delightful change. Suddenly his powers of compulsion worked with precision. His charms sizzled with magic. If he'd known a trip to convict land would create this miracle he'd have visited long ago. He had enough power to cause chaos with Ryman's hunt for a hell-horse.

Unfortunately, Ryman seemed immune to his compulsion, but his crew were not. He'd show Ryman what it meant to butt heads with the head of the House of the Cat.

By the time he finished, only one Coppersmith brother would remain.

Chapter Six

R y skirted a fallen tree and climbed over another. They'd spent the morning building yards to Camryn's specifications. Hastily erected, the yards weren't perfect, but as Camryn pointed out, they didn't know much about hell-horses. If the creatures could jump, they were in trouble.

Heat beat down from overhead, the humidity unpleasant beneath the trees. Ry's shirt clung to his damp flesh. Small biting insects flew in their faces, disturbed when they brushed past clumps of leafy red and pink foliage. Camryn walked behind him, and he could hear her soft breathing, smell her natural musk and the cinnamon of the soap he'd lent her for bathing.

Tension tightened his shoulders, worry for Camryn competing with a vague sense of disquiet. He scanned the odd shaped trees and the clearing to their right. The birds remained silent, a warning, which made him listen to his instincts more closely. Every other time they'd left the tender the sound of birdsong had almost deafened them.

The other crew members were approaching the horses from different directions. They'd planned to drive them into their yards, releasing all but one back into the wild. Several tenders had flown overhead but none had attempted to interfere with their hunt, yet still Ry's gut churned.

"At least the wind has changed in our favor," Camryn murmured behind him.

Ry lifted his head and realized she was right. The robust scent of the hell-horses obliterated every other fragrance. The tang of blood suggested they'd hunted or discovered a fresh carcass. When he cocked his head, he could hear their yaps and squeals of protest while they fought amongst themselves.

They crept closer, Ry's steps becoming cautious as unease deepened. The path between the gnarly trees widened. Camryn halted beside him, her arm brushing his. He steeled himself not to react.

"I see Jannike," Camryn said.

"The others are in position. We can move now."

Camryn grasped his arm to halt him. "How do you know? I can't see them. How do you know they're in position? Oh, you're right. I can see Kaya and Mogens."

"Which hell-horse do you think we should aim for?"

Camryn studied the creatures before replying. "The smaller one on the left, on the edge of the dust bath. It looks younger. It's not too small and moves well." She frowned when a gust of wind brought their scent. "What have they been eating?"

"I'm not sure." One bore a red muzzle, and Ry didn't think the animal wore face paint. "They haven't noticed us yet."

He signaled Yep and Nanu to circle the creatures. They moved closer. A bird burst from the undergrowth and each of the horses lifted their heads and stood at alert.

"Now!" Ry called.

As one they rushed the horses, making loud noises and whacking leafy branches through the air. A big scarred black hesitated. The hell-horse stirred the dust with one front hoof then dashed over the open ground in the direction they'd hoped.

Ry watched the herd go with grim satisfaction. Now all they had to do was capture one. The crew tore after them, hollering to spook them. To Ry's relief, this herd didn't turn on them and attack like the one they'd witnessed across the river.

Camryn raced after the horses in bemusement. They were the ugliest creatures she'd ever seen and didn't smell much better. She had no idea how they'd react to schooling, but they must be trainable if the planet held regular race meetings. Even their gait seemed awkward—an uneven caper with their forequarters appearing higher than their hindquarters.

"Fan out," Ry roared.

Physically fitter than she, the crew worked well together. Camryn tried to keep up, but her sides heaved, her lungs burned. The remnants of the hangover still clung, her temples throbbing from the vicious glare of the sun.

"Faster, Camryn. Faster. You're leaving a gap," Jannike yelled.

The hell-horses seemed to realize this as well. They swung around, galloping at her with a thunder of hooves. Camryn sprinted to plug the opening, her heart pounding in erratic beats. The largest horse charged, and Camryn froze, fearing the creature intended to run her down.

Camryn, dive into the undergrowth. Ry's clear panic rang inside her head. Confused, she glanced around, and when she turned back, the horse was almost on her. With no time to do anything else, she stood her ground and waved her hands, shouting. "Stop!"

The stench from the creatures surrounded her along with clouds of dust. Her pulse rattled inside her ears. The lead horse pulled to an abrupt halt. The shrewd intelligence in the creature's eyes made her push all fear aside. The hell-horse snorted and pawed the ground. Sharp yellow teeth glinted in the bright sun.

Camryn's stomach hollowed, but she shoved aside her dread. Instead, she extended her hand and took a step toward the creature. The herd milled behind the first, uneasiness evident in the way they pranced and yipped.

Camryn advanced another step. "Easy, boy. I'm not going to hurt you. Easy."

No. Don't go any closer. Camryn!

Camryn started on hearing Ry's words in her mind. Imagination. Just another thing to add to a list of weird happenings.

Focus. She had to do a good job for her brother's sake. For Ry's sake.

"That's it. Steady, boy. I won't hurt you."

The horse snorted and held still, watching her intently. Camryn took another step.

"You will not eat me," Camryn said. "I am not edible."

The hell-horse tossed its head and sidled closer, pure curiosity in its eyes.

"I won't hurt you." Camryn took another pace and ran a trembling hand over the shoulder of the creature. The glossy fur felt soft beneath her hands, and if she breathed through her mouth, the smell wasn't too bad.

Camryn sensed rather than heard the crew walk up beside her. Without warning, a tender flew overhead. The rat-a-tat of gunfire sounded, each shot spitting clouds of dust around them.

"Camryn, down!" Ry tackled her, sending her to the ground with a bone-crunching crash.

The hell-horses closed in a circle and milled about in panic. The tender hovered, spitting out shot after shot in rapid succession. Ry rolled into cover, taking Camryn with him. Flares exploded.

Cordite filled the air. A pained shout rang out and Yep collapsed.

"Yep!" Nanu seized his brother and dragged him behind a dark green and red bush.

Jannike and Kaya fired on the tender, but it flew too high for them to hit. Ry fired as well and finally, the vessel disappeared.

Camryn climbed to her feet to survey the carnage. All but one hell-horse lay on the ground, killed in the crossfire. The live one had suffered horrific injuries and swayed, balanced on three legs, coat glossy with blood.

"Is anyone hurt?" Mogens appeared from behind a thorny green tree.

"Yep." Nanu's wail sent shivers down Camryn's spine. The gurgling and harsh sucking from Yep's throat added to her horror.

Mogens rushed past, a dark silhouette against the green and red vegetation. He wrenched his satchel off his shoulder and knelt beside Nanu.

A lump formed in Camryn's throat. She hadn't known Yep well, but he'd always laughed and joked, providing light relief to alleviate stressful moments.

"No, leave him alone."

"Nanu, let me look at Yep. I can't help if I can't see the extent of his injuries."

"Let Mogens look at Yep," Ry said, squeezing Nanu's shoulder in reassurance. When the engineer didn't move, Ry gently drew him out of the way. "Let Mogens do his thing."

Nanu rose, his look of anguish making Camryn's chest ache. "It's too late. He's not gonna make it."

Camryn understood the sense of helplessness assailing the other man. She'd felt it when she'd arrived home to find Gabriel unconscious on the floor of their city apartment. Swallowing the tight knot constricting her throat, Camryn walked over to Nanu and wrapped her arms around him, trying to offer the comfort she'd needed when Gabriel had died.

Ry growled low in his throat when she touched the other man, but she glared over Nanu's shoulder, and his rumbling subsided. After a return scowl, he stomped over to Yep and Mogens.

Camryn couldn't hear what they said but their stiff stances and serious faces confirmed Yep's death.

Mogens rose and walked over to them. "I'm sorry, Nanu. He's gone."

Nanu's keen of grief lifted the hairs at her nape. His torment brought back horrid memories of Gabriel's death, the funeral and the yawning gap in her life afterward. It was like slicing open old wounds. Tears filled her eyes and she swallowed hard.

The thunder of hooves jerked them brutally to the present.

"Where in blue blazes did they come from?" Kaya asked. "The entrance is blocked."

"Someone must have opened the entrance," Jannike said in a tight voice. "Driven another herd into the canyon."

"Run," Ry said.

"I'm not leaving without my brother." Nanu's wild-eyed look told Camryn he'd lose it if they didn't act quickly.

"I'll carry Yep," Ry reassured his engineer. "We are not leaving him behind."

The frantic yips and squabbling between the new arrivals and the vicious, uncontrolled way they attacked the carcasses of the dead hell-horses sent fear dancing down Camryn's backbone. A horse noticed them and charged, teeth bared. Others, attracted by the attack followed the call to charge.

"Run," Ry shouted. "Head for the trees."

Camryn didn't hesitate. Gasping in fear, lungs burning, she forced her legs to pump faster. Jannike and Kaya raced in front of her.

They made the shelter of the trees. Camryn had thought it would slow the hell-horses, but they kept coming.

"I can't go any farther," Camryn gasped.

The tender reappeared and started firing. The gunners in the tender ignored the horses and peppered shots at them, even though the trees obscured their vision and restricted clear shots.

"Grata, behind the tree." Ry cursed when a shot ricocheted off a branch and whisked past his ear. "Here hold on to Yep." He flung Yep at Camryn and Nanu and turned, yanking a gun from his holster in one smooth move. Kaya and Jannike stood shoulder-to-shoulder with him and fired.

The horses went down in a crashing heap but more followed, the beasts determined to attack. Ry fired another round. The scent of blood filled the air, inflaming the hell-horses to a greater frenzy. The ones in the lead tore into the fallen horses.

The tender continued to rain fire down on them, creating confusion among the beasts.

Ry holstered his weapon, breathing hard. "Let's go while the horses are occupied."

They backed away until they reached Camryn and Nanu. Mogens appeared and they all ran into the thicker trees, heading for their tender. Sounds of the carnage faded.

Two hours later they arrived at their campsite, having taken a long route through the bush rather than traveling across open pasture. The intermittent hum of a tender overhead made Camryn glad they'd remained under the cover of the trees.

"What are we going to do now?" Kaya asked with a trace of disgust. "They know we're here, but we can't leave and engage in a dogfight. It's too risky."

"We wait until darkness falls," Ry said.

"Who are they? Why are they shooting at us?" Camryn asked.

"The tender belongs to Coppersmith Enterprises," Ry said in a tight voice.

"Coppersmith?" Camryn asked, her tone one of disbelief.

"Yes." Ry glared up at the hovering tender, hatred disfiguring his face.

Jannike scowled. "Your brother."

"Yes." Ry stalked over to Nanu. The engineer had collapsed to the ground beside his brother. He rocked, mournful keening coming from deep in his throat. He placed his hand on Nanu's shoulder in support. "We will avenge Yep's death."

Camryn watched the way Ry clenched his jaw and the glitter of hate in his green eyes. Granted, she was a screw-up, but her brother had stood by her despite his wife's censure. Camryn sighed, admitting she'd do anything for her brother. She bit her bottom lip in consternation. Why did one brother frame another for murder? How could they hate each other that much?

Chapter Seven

Another hell-horse hunt at a new location. They had to find one today. This was their last chance.

"Take ropes," Ry said to Kaya. "It's dangerous, but you'll have to try to capture a hell-horse. Camryn and I will do the same. We'll meet here before dark falls."

Both Jannike and Kaya nodded, and Ry knew they'd do their best.

"Mogens, you're in charge here." Ry glanced at Nanu with concern and wished there was something he could do or say to help. But nothing would bring back Yep. "If the tender is in danger of discovery, move to a new position. We'll find you."

"Aye, Captain." Mogens glanced at Camryn. "Take care of her, Ry. She is the most vulnerable."

Ry agreed. She was also valuable. Her calm approach yesterday had almost netted them a hell-horse. Hopefully they'd have more luck today. Ry finished packing his supplies and turned to Camryn. He found her watching him and immediately both body and mind changed tack. His heart thundered and his blood rushed south. They hadn't had sex since the previous morning but had bedded down together despite Mogens' dark looks and silent reproach. Seemed the seer had appointed himself Camryn's guardian. At least his verbal remonstrations had diminished, and he now confined his disapproval to facial expressions and swirling skin color.

"Ready?" He walked over to Camryn and slid a hand over her back, finding both comfort and pleasure in the contact.

"Yes." She turned in his arms and stepped back, her expression shuttered. "You promise to take me home once this is finished?"

The feline inside roared in protest at the idea of her departure.

"Ry?"

Her trepidation hit him, and he reacted by offering comfort in the only way he could. "Yes, I'll take you home."

They headed out together, separating from the others when they reached the bush. Ry went first and hacked through the thick vegetation to forge a path, his acute hearing letting him know Camryn followed him. The hum and click of insects surrounded them, the flicker of wings and squawk from a disturbed bird adding to the cacophony.

"When did you discover you were a kitty-cat?"

"Feline."

"That's what I said."

Ry suppressed a grin. "Not long after I turned nineteen cycles. After I left Ibrox to escape the murder charges." He severed a vine with a slash of his knife, pausing to wipe the sweat from his forehead and to scent the air. He caught the rank scent of a carcass and headed in that direction, suspecting hell-horses wouldn't be far away. The terrain grew more difficult to traverse, the trees thick and full of trailing purple vines. The stench of the carcass grew stronger. They were close. He paused to wipe his forehead and pulled a canteen of water from his pack.

"Have a drink. There's water nearby. I can hear it."

Puffing with exertion, Camryn took the canteen and tipped back her head to drink. Her throat worked when she swallowed, attracting Ry's attention. He wanted to lick the smooth column and press his lips to her warm skin. He closed his eyes, fighting the urge. He sucked in a deep breath and regretted it since all he could smell was Camryn. The whiff of cinnamon brought a rush of satisfaction since the scent of his soap clung to her skin.

"I can't hear a thing. Are you sure it's not your imagination?" Not a bit of teasing in her, just quiet determination to get the job done. "Was it scary turning into a kit...?"

Ry growled low in his throat.

"Ah, feline." Camryn flashed a sweet smile, and he had to bite back his answering grin.

"Yeah, it was terrifying." Scary didn't begin to cover the fear and confusion he'd felt, and the blank hole of his past didn't get any better. He rubbed one of his new tattoos before accepting the canteen back. He drank again and savored the faint taste of her on the bottle. What he wouldn't give for a soft bed and clean linens at this very min. With a grunt, Ry replaced the cap and stuffed the canteen in his pack. He slung it over his back, picked up his knife and turned in the direction of the water.

Twenty mins later, they hit the riverbank. A herd of hell-horses grazed on the other side. Three fought over the carcass of an unknown animal while the rest fed on pink vegetation.

"We'll have to cross the river," Camryn said.

"Yeah." Frag it, swimming wasn't his favorite thing.

They both surveyed the wide river. The center ran swift and fast but both sides appeared negotiable, the current more sluggish. Several hell-horses stood in the river to eat the plants hanging from the bank, so the water flow couldn't be dangerous.

"If we want to surprise them we'll need to cross upstream or down."

His thinking exactly. He lifted his nose to test the wind. "Downstream," he said.

The riverbank proved difficult to navigate with trees and vines growing to the waterline. Ry headed back inland and hacked a path parallel to the river. Thorns tore at his face and arms. Insects bit, attracted by the sweat coating his skin. He paused to wipe his face and heard Camryn slapping her arms and legs. The muggy heat brought a dangerous lethargy neither of them could afford. At least the river would cool them off.

The trees thinned and they came to a small creek flowing into the main river. Good enough. "We'll walk down here," he said.

"Okay. So what did you do? The first time you changed to feline, I mean." Camryn flexed her shoulders then slithered down the muddy bank to stand in the shallow water. Ry followed suit and slogged down the stony creek bed to the river. He couldn't see the horses but could smell them. The bottom shelved rapidly, and he cast a worried glance over his shoulder. He waited for Camryn to catch up. The water came up to her chest, the depth didn't seem to daunt her.

Ry turned away, not letting his pride show. He was used to working with Kaya and Jannike. Both women handled anything with aplomb. Camryn wasn't as strong or battle hard, yet she never complained. Most women he'd known in the past would have whined until his ears bled.

He waded farther into the water, the swifter current tugging his body, his pack. Deeper, the water reached his chest. Ry glanced back at Camryn and halted. "Grab my shirt and hang on. I figured out I wasn't gonna die, and the cat thing was something else. The tattoo I used to have on my arm appeared after the first change. I decided to try to change on my own. I'd had a bit to drink before I changed the first time. The second time I had a clear head."

Camryn stopped when the water reached her neck. "Maybe we should have waited to find a shallow ford."

Hell, Camryn was right. His focus on catching a hell-horse had placed her in danger. Again. "We'll go back."

Camryn shook her head. "We're more than halfway. We should keep going. You're braver than me. I would have freaked and gone to the pub. Alcohol is a good way to handle problems." Her tone held self-derision.

Ry took a step, his boot hitting a slippery rock. He went down with a splash, dragging Camryn with him when she didn't let go fast enough. Before he could gain footing, the current swept them downstream. He went under and came up spluttering. Camryn lost her grip on his shirt and bobbed out of reach. The river channel narrowed. Water ran swiftly, white waves churning.

"Camryn!" Ry drifted like a piece of flotsam, swallowed water. Gasped.

The thunder of water and the mist up ahead brought alarm and sheer terror. He wasn't invincible but healed well. Not Camryn. Damn, he couldn't even see her. Where the devil was she? He struggled against the pull of the water, battling to find purchase for his feet. His lungs pumped with exertion. Jutting rocks pummeled his body when he swept past. The boom of the water intensified, the raging torrent swirling into whitewater as the channel narrowed.

Phrull! Waterfall.

"Camryn!" Ry fought the current and bobbed along like a cork. A flash of white caught his attention. There. Hell, he couldn't fail her. He struggled, fighting the suck of the water, the stirring of panic. He bounced off a rock and groaned at the rough gouge of his leg. Gritting his teeth, he grabbed hold of a jutting branch and struggled for footing.

When Camryn passed, he was ready. His hand shot out and seized her arm, gripping it cruelly. She screamed, but he didn't let go, hauling her upward so she could stand and fight the current on her own. When she had her balance, he released her arm and hauled her against him in a tight embrace. Her heart thundered against his chest, each breath coming in shuddery pants. Pale and disheveled, she'd lost her pack, but he'd never felt so thankful in all his life. In that instant Ry knew he was in trouble. Although he'd given his promise, he didn't want to take her back to Earth. He wanted to keep her for himself.

Ry shoved aside the traitorous thought. His brother might have taken everything he valued, but Ry liked to think he'd retained his decency and kept his word. Always.

"I'm ready," Camryn said in a small, unsteady voice. "We should try to get to the riverbank."

"We're on the wrong side." The stark truth.

"If you think I'm going to attempt another crossing you've got rocks in your head. Can't you hear the waterfall?"

And he'd thought he'd done a good job of protecting her. All the time she'd known possible death waited ahead. "Do you need help?"

"The current isn't as strong here." Camryn angled toward the riverbank and Ry followed, ready to grab her should she fall. Guilt hit when he saw the way she favored her arm, but she kept moving until reaching the sluggish water near the riverbank. Progress became quicker after that. They dragged themselves onto the bank, forcing their way through the overgrowing bushes and vines until they lay on dry land, gasping for breath.

Ry placed a cautious hand on Camryn's shoulder and rubbed gently. "You okay?"

"You almost wrenched my shoulder from its socket."

Shame filled him even though he'd do the same again. He'd never hit or brutalized a woman in his life, and it pained him to know he'd hurt her now—a woman he cared for.

"I'm sorry. Let me look."

"I'll get over it. You saved me," she said, sitting up in an awkward position because of the surrounding vegetation. "I don't think I'd have managed to get to the tree on my own. You okay?"

A flash of warmth hit him square in the chest. "Still terrified. Grata, I hate swimming," he said with real feeling.

"Me too." Camryn shivered. "We need to move so our clothes dry. Tell me about Mogens."

The idea of lingering had occurred to him, but he knew she was right. "It's not going to be easy traveling inland."

"Following the river won't be much easier."

"Either we travel inland, or we follow the river until we come to another creek bed. We'll need to go inland to get past the falls."

"Inland it is." Camryn shoved through the bushes and struggled to her feet, favoring her arm. "Which way?"

Ry lifted his head to scent the air and couldn't smell anything apart from vegetation and leaf litter. His senses didn't indicate danger in any direction. "This way. Mogens walked up to me in the middle of a marketplace on Septius. He told me the ghosts of my parents were proud of me. I made a strong, noble cat." He stood and belted his head against a low-hanging branch. "Phrull."

"Poor baby." Camryn leaned close and fingered the spot, tsking when he flinched. "No blood. I think you'll live. Mogens and his ghosts freak me out."

Ry bit back a smile, surprised by a flash of humor. "He doesn't mean any harm. I've learned to listen since his predictions are usually right."

He set off, moving without haste. Although the light didn't pierce the tree canopy, the heat made it feel as if a heavy blanket surrounded them. Sweat trickled down his back and face and ran into his eyes. He swiped his hand over his face and forced his body through a small gap between a tree and a leafy fern. Bloody vines. They were everywhere. Trailing across the ground and winding around trees. Like giant purple webs, they choked the life out of the living to gain a tenuous hold on existence. Unlike insect webs, they weren't easy to sweep aside. They were tough and resilient. His blade had suffered and no longer bore a razor-sharp edge.

"Are you sure you've chosen the right direction?"

"I can smell water."

"Smell it?" Camryn wrinkled her nose in disbelief. "A kitty thing, I suppose. Was the second change to cat as bad?"

Ry ignored her doubt and bent almost double to force his body between two vines. He could hear the water now, a gentle flow across a stony bed. He kept walking, slogging through the undergrowth and hacking the vines with his knife where it was necessary.

"Mogens guided me through the change and asked if my ship required a man skilled in medicine. I decided we did, and he joined the crew. I've never regretted it despite his peculiarities."

They slogged up an incline and scrambled down the other side through a patch of prickly red bushes. At the bottom of the hill, a small creek ran toward the river. "There. What did I tell you?"

With relief, he stepped into the water again and splashed in the opposite direction to the river. Although it was easier to navigate, the trailing vines still created a problem where they stretched across from one tree to another.

Camryn wheezed behind him, laboring without complaint. A new noise—foreign and full of distress—stopped him short. He cocked his head.

"What is it?"

"You hear anything?" Ry asked.

"Yeah." Camryn stepped up beside him and listened. "Sounds like an animal."

Ry started moving again. The distressed cries grew louder. Grunts. Pained groans. Thrashing. Foliage rustling and the rattle of the vines. He could make out a dark shape but couldn't identify the creature. He moved closer with Camryn right behind him.

"It's a baby hell-horse," Camryn whispered.

The creature thrashed in panic on hearing her voice.

"It's caught in the vines." Ry pulled out his knife.

"Ry." Camryn grabbed his arm. "You're not going to kill it."

"Of course not," he snapped, offended. "I'm going to cut it free. We can't leave it there to suffer." He stepped forward cautiously.

Camryn grasped his arm again. "Let me go first. I'll try and keep it calm while you cut the vines." She approached with caution. "Steady, fella. We're not going to hurt you. Easy, boy." She rubbed her hand across the hell-horse's matted coat, murmuring nonsense to the creature. The thrashing ceased but the hell-horse trembled, its eyes rolling in terror. Camryn squatted beside the foal and continued to talk.

Ry hacked through the vines with his knife. The blade bit into the creeper but it didn't give. The vines clacked together, and the terrified hell-horse struggled.

A yip of anger came from behind. A hell-horse attacked, teeth barred.

"Camryn!" Ry grabbed her and thrust her behind him. He whirled to face the hell-horse, knife at the ready.

Camryn tugged his sleeve. "Back up," she whispered. "It's protecting its foal." She continued to yank on his arm until he moved away.

"We can't leave it like that," he said, not taking his eyes off the mother.

"Of course not," Camryn said. "We need to get the mother's trust."

And that wouldn't be easy. The mother approached her foal and nuzzled it with affectionate concern.

Camryn slipped from behind him and approached the hell-horse.

"No." Ry attempted to grab her, and she dodged him, stepping toward the mother. His heart pounded, tensing to leap to her defense. His canines dropped into position and the leopard stirred uneasily, wanting to protect. His eyes bled to feline, his vision flickering between color and black and white.

"Easy," she crooned in a singsong voice. "We're not going to hurt your baby."

The hell-horse pawed the ground, splashing water and throwing small pebbles into the air. It snorted. Ry watched the creature's eyes, scrutinizing the horse's intent. He edged closer and the creature charged. The hell-horse sprang at Camryn with its powerful hindquarters and snapped at her arm, sharp teeth flashing. She leaped out of the way, but the creature snagged her shirtsleeve. The fabric ripped, exposing her flesh.

"Camryn, climb a tree."

She stood her ground. "It's frightened. It will settle."

Ry didn't agree. The creature didn't look as if it would settle until she ripped Camryn apart and ate him for a chaser. "Damn it, back up."

Camryn stood her ground and glared at him. "You might have kidnapped me but that doesn't make you my boss."

"It does if you want to return home."

Her brown eyes narrowed, and he tensed, ashamed of the threat. He mightn't want to let her go but he'd given his word.

"I don't want you injured." Ry wanted to apologize but the words jammed in his throat.

"Because you need a horse trainer." Bitterness coated her words, and she met his authority with defiance.

The hell-horse lined up Camryn for another attack.

"Move. Now!"

Camryn dodged the charge and swung in close to the foal. It bleated in fear, struggling with weak thrashes. The mother yapped and neighed, flashing her teeth in warning.

"Steady." Camryn stroked the foal, attempting to quiet its struggles. The mother released an anxious bark and held her ground. She snorted uneasily through flared nostrils. "Easy, little fella. We're not going to hurt you."

Fear coiled through Ry. He tensed, ready to pounce. If anything happened to Camryn, he'd never forgive himself.

"Easy boy." She stroked the foal's muddy coat and worked her magic. Ry had never seen the like before. "Move closer but slowly. We don't want to panic them again."

Following her instructions, he approached the foal and, without taking his gaze off the mother, he started to hack the vine. The mother stomped her front feet, snorting uneasily even though Camryn continued to stroke the foal. Her soothing voice seemed to placate the mother. Ry severed the vines as fast as he could, but the mother became increasingly agitated. Before she attacked, he cut the vine wrapped around the foal's hindquarters and the foal slid into the water, giving a weak bleat.

The mother yapped, and Camryn cursed, a succinct sound of helplessness and panic. "It's choking. Quick, Ry. The vine around its neck." She struggled to lift the creature so the pressure on its neck wasn't quite as bad. The mother seemed to accept Camryn's presence but didn't like Ry near her foal. She darted in between Camryn and him and snarled, her teeth glinting. No way did she intend to let him get any closer.

"Camryn, can you reach my knife?"

"Yeah, no problem."

"Good." Ry stretched out but Camryn didn't move. "What are you doing?"

"Sarcasm, chump. Of course, I can't reach. I have a sore arm. You'll have to calm the mother because if I move her foal is going to drown."

Ry cursed under his breath, guilt warring with irritation. Smart-mouthed woman needed her arse smacked. He edged back, placing each foot with care so he didn't trip. The tension left the mother and she edged alongside her foal, nuzzling its hindquarters, issuing small chirps of encouragement. Ry let his breath ease out. Closer. No sudden moves. Apprehension lurched inside when he saw a tremor run through Camryn's petite frame. She couldn't keep the foal out of the water for much longer. He approached Camryn along the riverbank, once again moving with caution so he wouldn't alarm the mother. Camryn slipped down to sit in the water, sliding her legs beneath the foal to take some of the strain off her upper body. The foal made wheezing sounds and ceased its struggles.

Without taking his gaze off the mother, Ry advanced. Finally, finally he reached Camryn and hacked at the vines tangled around the foal's neck. His knife sawed back and forward, making little progress.

"Damn it," he muttered. Beads of sweat dotted his forehead and the stench from the foal brought a touch of nausea. He swallowed, cursed and yanked his knife from the vine. He'd try to sever another piece. The next vine was thinner and didn't have the consistency of pliable wood. Yes. He cut another. Poor little bugger. It looked as if he'd been here for days, unable to feed.

"Can you cut this one?" Camryn said, indicating the partially severed one that had given him trouble before.

Ry stood and using brute strength he bent and twisted the vine, pausing to hack a bit deeper. Sweat dripped off him by the time the vine parted.

"Yes. Good job," Camryn said.

The hell-horse mother trumpeted. The shrill cry froze them both in startled shock. Not a call they'd heard before. The hell-horse backed up a fraction, and Ry took the opportunity to lift the foal off Camryn. She scrambled up and, crooning to the foal, started to unwind the vine clinging to his emaciated body. The mother trumpeted again and sidled closer to sniff at her foal. Her body trembled with mistrust, and Ry knew she'd attack if they weren't careful.

"He's too weak to make it out of here on his own. If we leave him, he'll die."

"And his mother will attack if we make a wrong move."

Camryn shrugged. "I won't leave him."

The sole alternative would be for him to carry the foal out. Ry cast a doubtful look at the mother.

"The vines have cut him. The wounds will fester if they're not treated."

Once again a silent statement of intent. Ry scowled. Camryn might not be physically strong, but she bore an inner core of strength that hadn't been apparent earlier. He found it attractive.

"I'll carry him. You calm the mother and make sure she doesn't attack. Here's my knife. I'd give you my gun, but it won't fire until it dries out."

"Which way will we go?"

Ry considered the alternatives. The mare and foal must have come through the trees, but he'd only noticed one overgrown path. Maybe the mare had come here to foal since the foal didn't seem very old. "Our best bet might be straight down the creek bed. Hopefully we'll come to a place where the trees aren't as thick or find a clearing."

"The foal needs to feed."

"We don't have time."

"The foal needs to feed now."

Ry sighed. Her stubborn gene was losing its cuteness. Camryn might be right, but he hated the idea of putting her in more danger. The foal couldn't stand on its own. "Suggestions?"

"I don't have any. It's gonna be trial and error."

Ry dipped his head in a curt nod. Exactly. The Dowry Derby fell into the same territory. They were bumbling from one calamity to the next, and he didn't like the lack of control. He stood, moving without haste so he didn't alarm the mother, and lifted the foal to its feet. It issued a pitiful bleat and collapsed. The mother yapped.

Her nostrils flared and she shifted in agitation.

"Easy now," Camryn said. "Good girl. We're not going to hurt you."

The mare calmed almost straightaway. Although still uneasy, the hell-horse ceased snorting. Ry guessed this was about as serene as she'd get and edged closer, holding the foal up on its feet. The foal gave a sharp yap.

"Good boy," Camryn said. "Everything is going to be okay."

Ry suppressed a grunt. Not anytime soon, not as far as he could see. Without taking his attention off the mother, he moved nearer until the foal nuzzled the mare's hindquarters. At least the foal wanted to feed. He pushed it a fraction nearer and almost cheered when he heard it suckling. The mare stood quietly, although she didn't like him standing so close. Could probably sense the feline. Camryn's presence didn't seem to bother her, which made him happier about her status as their horse trainer.

"Do you think we could train the mother to race?" he asked in a low voice. "The foal is going to need medical attention anyway." Mogens could help in this area. The seer was talented when it came to medicine. It made up for his complexities and periods of strangeness.

Camryn grinned without warning. "My thoughts exactly. It's difficult to tell how old the mare is but she seems strong and in good health. If we show she can trust us with her foal it might make training easier."

"Good." Ry started to feel better about the situation. "If we can find an area big enough for the tender to land, and if the indicator beacons still work after their dousing in the river, we can get the crew to come and pick us up."

"And if you can't?"

Ry scowled, not liking the answer. "I'll need to find the tender while you stay with the hell-horses."

The foal stopped drinking. Ry backed away and eased his arms from beneath the foal. It almost fell. Frag it, he'd have to carry the creature.

"You ready to go?" Camryn asked.

Hell yeah. "If I start walking, maybe the mother will tail us."

"I'll follow."

"Make sure you don't turn your back on the mother," Ry cautioned, glancing over his shoulder. "Or better yet, see if she will follow me and you walk behind her." His gut jolted when he had to turn back to watch his footing. He didn't like leaving Camryn unprotected. If the hell-horse decided to attack, he wouldn't get to her in time.

Ry hoisted the foal into his arms and traversed the middle of the creek. Luckily the water wasn't deep, and the bottom consisted of coarse sand. "Is she following?"

"No."

Ry frowned and kept walking. If the mother rejected her foal due to their intervention they were screwed. A snort and a shrill yap sounded behind him. Water splashed and the hell-horse darted past him with a snort. She trumpeted again, obviously uneasy but resigned. She trotted ahead and stopped to study him before continuing.

Camryn splashed up beside him and Ry felt easier. "Looks like there might be a clearing up ahead."

"Good." Ry didn't like the idea of leaving Camryn alone with night falling. The break in the trees didn't look promising. It certainly wasn't big enough to land the tender. The mother scrambled up the bank and turned to observe.

"Looks like this is the end of the journey," Camryn said.

"The clearing is too small for the tender."

"We're not even sure where we are," Camryn said. "We were swept down the river for quite a way."

Ry climbed the bank and walked to a clear patch. He set the foal down and it licked him before he could move his hand. Surprised at the sense of satisfaction, he scratched the foal behind its long rounded ears. The creature licked his hand again. Ry glanced up to find Camryn grinning. The foal gave a small yip and the mare replied.

He backed away to stand by Camryn, and she leaned against his side. Her clothes were wet like his and her body heat seeped through the fabric. In that moment, he craved her fiercely, but it wasn't the time. Nightfall wasn't far away. He squeezed her upper arm and moved away with regret and a healthy slice of anxiety. The sooner he left the quicker he could return.

"I'd better go now if I want to make it back before dark. Take care." Ry yanked off his pack and shirt and shifted to cat. With a soft growl and one last look at Camryn, he loped away in search of the tender. It was one of the hardest things he'd ever done, and he had to force himself to leave.

CHAPTER EIGHT

TALOR'S TENDER, ORNUM

"Where's Ryman?" Talor Coppersmith paced across the interior of his tender and stared at the other occupant. "He's searching for hell-horses."

"Ah yes. It must be difficult when he's short of crew." Smugness coated his words, but he didn't give a damn. Any means to grind his brother into the dust, to make him suffer. Talor eyed the woman standing a few feet away. The means by which to exact revenge. "I expect you to make things difficult for him."

"It's not easy. I have to be subtle."

"I must have results." Warning threaded his tone and the caution didn't go unheeded. The confusion on her face told Talor she couldn't understand why she was compelled to come to him, that it frightened her.

She swallowed before her tongue flickered out to wet her

bottom lip. "We're staying over by the river, and once we have our hell-horse, we're returning to the city."

Talor nodded. "We have a horse already." He'd managed to get two animals early on and had a team of men to take care of them. Talor was confident one of his hell-horses would win. So far he'd failed to compel the creatures, although he had other strategies in play. Worry didn't keep him awake at night. He scowled. Apart from the pesky debt collectors. They'd get their money once he killed Ryman. Damn man had more lives than a cat.

"What do you want me to do?" Kaya asked, edging toward the exit.

"Keep me informed," Talor ordered. "I want to know my brother's intentions before he acts, where he's going to go and how."

Kaya's chin jutted upward in a show of bravery. "I'm not going to jeopardize my position with Ry."

"It's a little late to worry about your status now. You climbed into bed with me, a willing participant and now you must pay the price." Talor stepped into her personal space to make sure she understood. "You owe me. If you even consider changing sides at this stage, I will make you sorry. Understood?" He sent a compelling thought and the fight visibly seeped from her.

"Yes, sir."

Talor stared an instant longer before turning away in dismissal. He reached for a goblet of vino, the delicate pink liquor from the planet Marseilles, and took a sip. The smooth liquid slid down his throat, tingly tendrils of warmth flowing through his chest.

"You may go." Talor held out his goblet for Meghan to refill and smiled when he heard the retreating footsteps. It was the best thing he'd ever done—hooking up with Kaya. Having a spy in his brother's camp kept him two steps ahead. Oh yes. He wanted Ryman to suffer.

Camryn watched Ry leave with a sinking heart. The idea of being alone scared her silly, but there were no alternatives. And no pub to grab a bolstering drink. She glanced at the mare and foal and smiled when the mother nuzzled her offspring. She couldn't help recalling the hell-horse attack across the river. The screams. The blood. Carnage. She cast another quick look at the creatures. Could she even train the mare to race?

A drink. God, she craved a drink so bad. She wondered if Ry had another flask tucked away. A lock of hair fell into her face, and she swept it away with a trembling hand. She couldn't do this. She'd pretended to Ry and his crew, told them she could, but she hadn't ridden a winning horse past the finish post for ages, not since Gabriel had died. Sure, she'd helped her brother train horses but she'd never schooled one on her own. Knowing the mechanics and putting them into practice were miles apart.

Stress started to crowd in on her, pushing from all directions. Oh yeah. She'd put up a great front—a performance worthy of an award. At least when she was with Ry, her mind focused on other things. Alone, her doubts surfaced.

A sob tore free, and she sank to the ground, curling into a tight ball of misery. When they'd kidnapped her, she had no option. How could she let them return her to Earth, knowing they'd take her brother? No, she'd run out of choices, just as she was out of alternatives now. She had to do this. She had to prove she wasn't a screw-up.

Camryn rocked, tears spilling down her cheeks. These creatures—the hell-horses—were so unlike horses at home. At home, the worst injuries she'd sustained were sly nips when she hadn't paid attention or a kick from a fractious yearling. There'd been spills during training, but she knew how to fall. Nothing life-threatening.

Hell-horses killed.

And enjoyed the bloodbath.

Camryn's thoughts drifted to Ry. The need for his physical presence and his arms wrapped around her body filled her with trepidation. She fingered the place on her neck where he'd bitten her. She'd felt pain before the surfeit of pleasure. If she were an imaginative type of person she'd start to think vampire, but no, he was merely a big pussycat. Another sob shook her shoulders.

Something nudged her shoulder and she unfurled, scrambling backward like a horse shying at a flag. The mare. Oh god. It was gonna eat her.

The hell-horse jumped away with a yelp and cantered in a tight circle before halting to study her. Finally, the mare tossed her head, and trotted back to her foal.

Camryn half sobbed, half laughed, nervous reaction bringing renewed tremors to her hands.

The foal yapped and struggled to rise. Still too weak. Her responsibility. Ry counted on her to keep this foal alive, so the mare stayed around. And right now the foal needed to feed again. Little and often would make it thrive.

She stood, using measured steps so she didn't startle the mare again. Shoving aside her fear, she concentrated on approaching the foal. One thing at a time. That's the only way she'd get through this. If Ry could survive learning he was a feline shifter, she could do this.

"Easy there," she crooned.

The foal gave a small yip, almost like a welcome when she drew close enough to touch him. It tore a smile from her, and she scratched him behind his ears. A sharp yap emerged from the foal and the mare returned the call. Camryn's heart lurched, but this time she reined in her reaction, confining herself to a small eek rather than a full-out screech of terror. The mare had closed the distance between them and stood behind her. Camryn ignored the itch of danger and kept talking nonsense to the foal before she lifted the creature to its feet. A struggle, even though the hell-horse was small and undernourished. Finally, the foal balanced on unsteady legs.

"Come around this side," Camryn pleaded with the mare. "Make it easy for us." To her surprise, the mare trotted around and positioned herself for the foal to drink.

Relieved, Camryn held the foal upright. The high level of intelligence might make training difficult. Somehow, she needed to engage the mare's interest. Make her want to run. Bridles. Saddles. How would this work? From what she understood from reading the rules, they didn't have saddles, bridles or riders. The lack of riders made sense considering the hell-horses liked to snack on each other. Throw in a jockey or two and they'd have a well-rounded, satisfying meal.

Ry said she needed to train the hell-horse to run on command. She considered the mare and knew if she developed a relationship with the creature, a rapport where they trusted each other, her task would be easier.

The mare gave a soft yap, a contented mother sound. Camryn saw the foal had finished drinking and appeared asleep on its feet. She manhandled it over to a clear area and settled him on the ground. Now that the creature had dried off, his appearance edged toward cute. His fur was jet black and, once free of mud and clinging burrs, would feel silky and soft. The black eyes were heavily lashed, and the ears were long like a regular horse but had rounded tips rather than pointy. The tail was shorter and the forequarters and shoulders appeared more powerful than the rear. This meant their backs sloped a fraction and would make balance difficult for a jockey, especially if they didn't have a saddle.

The foal inhaled and released the breath with a shuddery

whisper. As long as the wounds healed and didn't become infected, Camryn thought the creature would recover. Another day and the result might have been different.

She turned her attention to the mother. Although her scent was strong, it wasn't repulsive. Some of the others she'd seen had smelled worse. Burrs matted her mane and coat. Camryn didn't have a brush but perhaps some basic grooming would help to create trust. Holding out her hand, she approached with caution. Hopefully, the mare wouldn't think her hand was a dinner offering because she hadn't noticed the hell-horse eating anything.

"I'm not going to hurt you, girl." Camryn took another two cautious steps. "What am I going to call you? I can't keep calling you 'girl', now can I?" The first name that came to mind was Gabriel, and her vision blurred. Apt. "How would you like Gabriel for your name?" The mare's snort brought a watery grin. "How about Gabby for short? Maybe calling you after my husband will help me keep my mind off that hunky kitty-cat." Her next step brought her hand into contact with the mare. She stroked her hand across the fur, finding it silky. "Good girl, Gabby. Good girl." Camryn tugged at a burr, which was clinging to her coat. The mare snorted and flinched but didn't move. "And how about Luke for your foal?" Calling the foal after her nephew would keep her focused on returning home. "Keep my thoughts off Ry," she whispered.

Something jumped onto her arm and clung, something black and ugly. Camryn flicked it off, but another crawled up her arm and nipped at her. "Ticks!" Camryn ripped it off her arm and blood flowed down her wrist. The mare tensed, her nostrils quivering. Her nicker was one Camryn hadn't heard before.

Food. Oh god. She'd transformed from helpful friend to food. Camryn sucked on the site of the bite and licked the blood away. The metallic taste of blood barely penetrated her dread. She had to stop the bleeding. Now. She clamped her fingers down cruelly, the pressure of her fingers leeching the color from her skin. Backing away, she slipped behind a tree and leaned against the trunk, panting hard. Camryn shook her head and noticed another tick on her arm. Revulsion filled her but she couldn't afford to make the same mistake again. Camryn clambered up a tree out of Gabby's reach and hoped like hell Ry hurried.

"Was it uncomfortable up the tree?" Kaya didn't try to hide her smirk.

At every opportunity the warrior ribbed Camryn about her night spent perched in the tree. Even though it had been three weeks ago, and she'd spent the time since training Gabby and getting her and Luke used to loading onto the tender.

"Old news," Camryn snapped. "I'm going to check on the hell-horses. Gabby wasn't very happy earlier." She stalked away with Kaya's laughter rippling after her and fumed throughout the entire loading process.

The tender finally took off. Camryn and Mogens spent the journey down in the cargo bay with the mare and foal while Ry flew the tender. Mogens gave the animals a mild sedative to calm them, and they seemed relaxed.

They had decided to fly closer to the city and would stay on the outskirts of a mountain village Jannike had heard about during a crew jaunt to a tavern. Sounded good to Camryn. She hadn't liked the city. The convicts and the marines with their easy brutality turned her stomach. Walking down the city streets made her think of a gritty historical novel set in Australia, and the constant black fog was depressing.

The mare whickered and tossed her head. The foal crept closer to Mogens and nudged his arm to urge the seer to scratch behind his ears. Camryn smothered a smile. Luke loved a good scratch behind the ears and became quite aggressive if petting wasn't forthcoming.

Kaya sprinted into the cargo bay. "Ry says to hold tight. We have other tenders in the area."

"His brother?" Mogens asked.

"We're not sure yet. Just be ready for anything." Kaya hurried away.

"Great," Camryn snarled. "If I ever meet his sainted brother I'm going to slap him myself. Ry said Talor set him up for murder." Curiosity tinged her words.

Mogens grunted. "I wasn't with Ry from the start. I understand Talor stole his fiancée. Ry needed currency to escape Ibrox and he cleaned out his brother's safe. He's tried to clear his name. Every trail ran cold. He lives to harass his brother."

"So he steals his brother's cargo shipments? I can't imagine a feud like that with my brother." But she'd disappointed Max. She'd seen it in his eyes each time he looked at her. His disappointment made her desolation worse, and she'd drunk more.

Without warning the tender lurched sideways. Gabby yapped in alarm. Luke practically clambered on top of Mogens, seeking reassurance.

"Okay, Mogens?" Camryn stepped to Gabby's head, murmuring soothing words. Only the tempting scent of a cooked steak had enticed her inside the tender today. Luke had scrambled after Mogens like a friendly puppy.

"We're fine."

The ship lurched again, flinging Camryn against the wall. Off balance, Gabby fell, crushing the breath out of her. Weakly, she pushed. "Move, Gabby. Move." The instant Gabby shifted her weight, Camryn clambered on her back and slid over the other side.

"Impressive acrobatics," Mogens said.

"A childhood dream," Camryn said. "My brother and I gave our parents gray hair with our daring maneuvers while we trained to join the circus."

Gunfire sounded. Gabby growled, eyes rolling and ears flattening to her head. Camryn tensed.

"Pirates." Kaya thumped into the cargo bay. "Ry sent me to warn you. Things are about to get rough. There's a storm coming. We're flying into it." She disappeared at a run.

He wouldn't want to risk the hell-horses. Fair enough. Camryn just hoped they could keep the creatures calm.

"How bad will this get?" she asked Mogens.

Animals sensed things and the hell-horses seemed more intelligent than most. They'd discern their stress, their fear.

She felt the speed of the tender increase. "Do you think the tender following has stopped firing?"

"Hard to say." Mogens skin bled to white then swirled with ribbons of black.

Huh, Mogens feared worse to come. Without warning the ship dropped like a plane hitting turbulence. Camryn gasped, her stomach struggling to catch up. Luke whimpered. Mogens stroked his neck, whispering soothing words.

Camryn wrapped her arm around Gabby's neck. "Steady, girl. It's okay." The mare trembled, rolled her eyes.

The tender's flight path leveled. Camryn's breath eased out in a puff of relief. That hadn't been so bad.

Without warning, they hit more turbulence. A hard bump. The tender dropped again. Camryn's stomach didn't have time to settle before they hit a second bump. Luke yipped, almost crushing Mogens. The seer's skin swirled with changing colors, the pale gray changing to charcoal, the sole clue to his unease.

Camryn pressed against Gabby. Comfort the mare. Keep her calm. The ship jumped, the roar of the engines almost dying before giving another full-throated roar. Gabby squealed, stood on her foot.

A yelp roared from Camryn as pain galloped up to her knee. "Shit!"

The mare was so much bigger. Camryn pushed her withers, struggling to free herself without panicking the mare more.

"Dammit." She choked off her curse. She was collecting bruises faster than an avid gambler collected debt.

"Camryn?"

"I'm okay." Apart from the bruises on top of bruises.

The ship bounced. The mare shuffled sideways, moving off her boot. Camryn winced and didn't have time to check for damage before the ship bucked again like a two-year-old being broke to saddle, each crashing thump sending Camryn off-balance. She lost her footing and fell beneath the mare's feet.

"Camryn," Mogens shouted, but he could do nothing except hold the foal steady.

"Bloody hell!" She scrambled across the slippery floor. Gabby struggled for footing, trying not to stand on her. A hoof clipped her hip. Tears smarted at her eyes.

Her legs were rubbery by the time the buckin' bronco ride ceased. She'd ended up squeezed between the wall and the mare again. Before she could shift, the tender hit more turbulence. Gabby fell, shoving Camryn's arm against the metal wall with such pressure she heard a sharp crack. Pain, agonizing and swift, hit. Tears filled her eyes as she breathed through the agony.

Finally, after what seemed like hours, the ship straightened. Through a haze of pain, Camryn heard Mogens murmuring to Luke. He soothed Gabby, pushing her away from Camryn. The mare's weight had kept her upright and with it gone, she crumpled.

At least there was no blood, she thought before her world faded.

Ry landed the ship on the outskirts of the village near a lake. Set at the base of a mountain with the houses clinging to the slopes, it was a beautiful spot. And best of all, he didn't think there were other visitors in the area, or at least he hadn't spotted any on their radar system. It was a good place to set Yep at rest, if they could persuade Nanu to let him go.

Jannike stood, letting her harness go with a quick yank. "Good flying, Ry."

He grinned. His piloting during the storm had been nothing short of brilliant.

Kaya rose. "Looks pretty out there. Do you think they'll have a tavern?"

Jannike snorted. "Is your hair bright blue?"

"Exactly what I thought," Kaya said, shaking said blue hair.

Ry stretched the tension from his shoulders. A faint whinny from the cargo bay brought a frown along with a rise of tension. Camryn. He took off at a sprint, his boots thudding on the tender floor.

"Captain?" Kaya shouted after him.

Camryn. He cast out his mind, attempting to snatch thoughts from the cargo bay. Nothing. Not unusual when it came to Mogens, but he often caught Camryn's unguarded thoughts from this range. He burst into the cargo bay to find Mogens hunched over her limp body.

The mare bristled, her ears going back as they always did when he went too close. Apart from the first day when she'd let him carry Luke, the mare preferred him to keep a distance. Too bad. He shoved past and crouched beside Mogens. "What happened?"

"The turbulence threw us around. Gabby crushed Camryn against the wall."

"Phrull it." The bloody race was going to be the death of him. His hands tightened to fists and eyes narrowed dangerously. Or his brother...

139

"Gabby didn't mean to do it. It was an accident."

Ry ignored Mogens concern about blame to concentrate on Camryn. Her face looked ashen, and she didn't move. Fear stripped away everything but the need to fix Camryn. So small and defenseless. So still.

"Where's she hurt?" Ry squatted beside her to brush the hair from her face. He couldn't see any blood but sometimes injuries lurked inside a body, unseen. He shuddered, mentally giving thanks for the lack of blood. He'd seen the way the scent whipped the hell-horses into a frenzy. After the tick episode, they'd taken special care to treat small nicks or cuts the sec they occurred. Mogens had also taken the extra precaution of giving the female crew herbal treatments to suppress their normal cycles.

"As far as I can see, it's her shoulder. It's dislocated. Hold her while I put it back."

"Why isn't she conscious?" Ry held her, giving Mogens room to work. She smelled of the herb paste the seer liked to slap on injuries.

"I think the pain was too much," Mogen said, forcing the shoulder back into place with a sharp jolt. "Her body couldn't cope."

Mogens glanced at him as he dipped his head to nuzzle at her neck. Her eyes flickered and she relaxed. Ry nodded at Mogens, and the seer went to work, smoothing more paste on her shoulder. Ry licked her again in the exact place where he'd bitten her neck and nibbled lightly. The contact surged through him, the connection taking him by surprise. He moaned and attempted to rein back his raging desire.

Mogens checked her swollen wrist and smeared herbal paste on that too. "All done."

The clomp of boots announced the arrival of the rest of the crew.

"What's happened? Is she dead?" Jannike asked.

"Unconscious." Ry stood, trusting Mogens to take care of Camryn. He walked away despite the protest of the feline who teased him to linger. A shiver racked his body, and he caught strange looks from both Jannike and Kaya.

"Captain?" Kaya asked, cocking her head like an inquisitive bird.

Ry took a deep breath, determined to act like captain instead of the confused feline shifter who couldn't bear parting from a weak Earthling.

"Where's Nanu?" He wrapped authority around his shoulders like a mantle.

"He's sitting beside Yep's shroud," Kaya said.

Ry nodded, acknowledging they needed to jerk Nanu back into the land of the living. They needed him because they couldn't afford to let the repairs slide. Both the Indy and the tender needed to operate at full capacity. Mechanical difficulties weren't an option. "I need you both to start working on a yard to confine Gabby and Luke. I'll talk to Nanu and come out to help when I'm done with him."

"Aye, Captain," Jannike said.

"Mogens, I need you to make Camryn comfortable and watch Gabby and Luke."

"Gabby will need feeding. We're out of steaks," Mogen warned, reminding him of the hell-horse's need for meat.

Ry nodded. "Once we have the yard constructed, I'll get Kaya and Jannike to go into the village to buy supplies."

"Maybe they'll have more of those large birds we captured at the last campsite. They're easy enough to catch and Gabby seems to like them," Mogens said.

Ry walked away to find Nanu. While he understood the man's grief, he needed to jolt out of his misery. Kaya and Jannike hadn't complained at the extra work, but they couldn't keep it up indefinitely.

"Nanu, I need you to come and help construct the yard for the hell-horses."

Nanu raised his head, eyes bloodshot with huge circles beneath, depicting the man's lack of sleep. "I can't leave Yep."

Ry placed his hand on Nanu's shoulder and squeezed lightly in support. "We need to have the funeral rite here."

Nanu's head jerked upward, the beads adorning his hair clacking with agitation. "No, I must take my brother home. He must burn in the place of my ancestors or his soul will not pass."

Ry forced a harsh tone. "You are outlaws in your home country. The corporation will shoot you on sight."

"No, I must take Yep home." Nanu rocked on the chair without taking his gaze off the shroud covering his brother. "Yep must go home to family."

And sometimes you couldn't go home, no matter how much you wanted it. Ry squeezed his eyes closed for an instant before shoving his sympathy aside.

"I won't let you commit suicide. We will conduct the funeral rite here by the lake. We are your family." Ry grasped his engineer's shoulder again and urged him to stand. He'd use force if he had to because if Nanu didn't snap out of his lethargy someone else would die. With the approach of the race, they needed to focus. Talor had shown he didn't care who got in the way. His brother didn't care who died in their personal war. "Move. Yep is not going anywhere."

Nanu glowered and stood. With a pained look at Yep's shroud, he stalked from the bridge, his back stiff with fury.

The yard construction didn't take long since Camryn had suggested they bring wood from the previous site. Although not big, it allowed the hell-horse and her foal space to move while keeping them confined.

Ry had landed the ship on the far side of the lake in an area away from dwellings and crops. Hopefully their presence wouldn't upset the locals and they'd be welcome to stay until the start of the race.

"All done, Captain." Kaya approached him with a beaming smile. He was grateful for her cheerful presence.

"Why don't you and Jannike head into the village? We need fresh supplies."

"Aye, Captain!" Kaya bound off in Jannike's direction.

"Keep an eye out for my brother or other strangers around the area. We need to watch security." Ry didn't trust Talor. He'd backed off and hadn't followed them into the storm, but that didn't mean they'd given up the chase. For some reason Talor had upped the ante and started to take risks, attacking them whenever opportunity presented itself. Ry didn't understand why Talor's attacks had become so ferocious. He cursed under his breath, wishing he'd had time to do more research when they'd made their last stealthy stop on Ibrox.

Pressure pushed in on Ry. He'd known revenge wouldn't be easy, but he owed it to his friend Maxmus, the friend he had allegedly murdered, according to the law on Ibrox. He owed it to every person crushed beneath Talor's feet. He owed it to himself if he wanted to walk the streets he'd walked as a youth with head held high. He had to prove Talor had murdered Maxmus.

Ry went looking for Camryn and Mogens. He found them where he'd left them, the scent of herbs strong in the air. Luke ambled over and licked his arm. Gabby let out a harsh yap. Ry had come to think of it as her 'return to me' yap. Her foal ignored her and licked Ry again. Luke nuzzled his chest until Ry gave in and scratched him behind the ears. The foal snorted and sneezed, sending spray over Ry's shirt.

"Enough," he said, pushing the animal aside to squat beside Camryn and Mogens. "How is she?"

"I'm awake," Camryn snapped. "I'm not dead."

But she could have been—sucked into the war with his brother like his crew. His gut bucked at the idea, guilt growing. Yep shouldn't have died. His fault.

"She will be sore for a time but should recover well." Relief shone in Mogens' eyes, but his skin color swirled with an uneasy mix of black and white.

Ry scanned Camryn's wan face. She was in pain. "Maybe we should call this off. Take Camryn home to Earth and start up in another universe."

"No! Not after all the trouble we've gone to. We have to see this through for Yep," Camryn said.

"I agree," Mogens said. "We finish for Yep."

Ry wasn't so sure but didn't argue. "Can you stand?"

"It's my shoulder, not my legs." She pushed away from Ry and stood with a grimace. "Are the yards ready?"

Gabby yapped and shook her head so hard her mane flapped.

"She needs to stretch her legs and feed," Camryn said.

"I'll do it," Ry said. "You need to rest."

Camryn slanted him a quick glance before she looked away, a wave of color slashing across her cheeks. "Gabby doesn't like you. I'll have to do it."

Ry acknowledged the truth of her words, although he didn't like it. He stepped back to lean against the wall, well clear of the hell-horses. Camryn shuffled down the ramp and gave a soft whistle. Gabby's head jerked up and she trotted after Camryn. Luke scuttled after his mother, and they clomped down the ramp without the trouble Ry had envisaged. Mogens followed. Luke sidled up to the seer, nudging him for another scratch behind the ears. Ry grinned at the foal's obvious antics—he adored attention from all of them.

"I'm going hunting to feed the hell-horses," Ry said.

"Might I suggest you take Nanu with you? Order him to accompany you," Mogens said. "He needs to keep busy."

Ry agreed. He strode back into the tender to find Nanu beside Yep's shroud. Again.

"Attention!" Ry barked.

Nanu jumped to his feet, startled by Ry's harsh tone.

"Bring your weapon. We hunt now." Ry waited, tapping his foot impatiently. "We will scout a resting spot for your brother."

"No, I take him home."

"You would put us all at risk?"

They stared at each other for a long moment until Nanu shook his head.

Relieved, Ry indicated the engineer should exit first. After a brief hesitation, Nanu exited the tender. He blinked at the fierce brightness of the light and stared about him like a blind man who'd regained his sight.

"Yep would have liked it here."

Across the broad expanse of the lake, snow-topped mountains were visible through the light violet cloud cover. The steep slopes glowed, the bright light casting purple and slate gray shadows. Trees circled most of the lake. The distant sound of voices in song traveled from the village.

"He would," Ry said.

They returned to camp two hours later bearing a brace of birds each. And better, they'd decided on a resting spot for Yep. The funeral pyre would burn on the morrow.

"Feed four birds to Gabby. Mind your hands when you give them to her," Ry said. "I need to check on Camryn."

He strode up the ramp into the tender and found Mogens had fashioned a pallet for her. "How is she?"

"Sleeping. 'Tis the best thing for her. She has been under much stress during recent times."

Ry nodded in silent acknowledgment. "Jannike and Kaya have gone into the village. Why don't you take some free time? I'll watch Camryn. Hopefully she'll recover in time to attend the race meeting the day after tomorrow."

"The clouds have proclaimed it so. You promised to return her to Earth when the racing is done." Mogens' color edged toward black, telling Ry far more than his words.

"I did."

"Do you intend to keep your word, Captain?"

Ry wondered when he'd become so transparent. Holding back his impatience, he lied through his teeth. "I intend to keep my promise."

Mogens scrutinized his face and finally nodded before leaving. Ry felt worse than ever, culpability punching him in the chest. He'd let his feline rule his heart and now it was too late. He couldn't live without Camryn, couldn't imagine life without her. Ry suspected she'd never forgive him.

CHAPTER NINE

RACETRACK, ORNUM TOWNSHIP, TWO DAYS LATER.

The races weren't like any Camryn had witnessed before. Men. They were everywhere. Men who looked like humans and others who were...different. Extra arms. Weird skin colors. Strange protuberances from their heads. Extra heads. And everyone seemed to wear bright clothes. With color everywhere, their group stood out because of their black-on-black color scheme. Of course Mogens flashed between white to gray to black, but since he edged toward pure black now, it was obvious he belonged with them.

Camryn sidled closer to Ry, trying not to let her unease show. The noise levels made her head ache. Bookies—or at least that's what Camryn presumed they were—stood on platforms, screeching out names and odds. Punters thrust quid notes at them and received tickets in exchange.

"Hell Fire! Odds nine to one he won't finish the race. Bat out of Hell! Odds two to one he won't finish!" a bookie cried.

Camryn's mouth dropped open. She tugged on Ry's arm to gain his attention. "They're laying odds on the horses not finishing the race?"

"Yeah. I'd heard they did that."

A blare of trumpets sounded, and a wave of punters hurried into the stadium. Camryn swept along with the tide.

Jannike checked the tickets they'd purchased. "Our seats are this way."

Camryn followed in bemusement. The stadium reminded her of the old Roman amphitheaters. Seating surrounded the dirt racetrack. No grass, greenery or any of the beautiful gardens they had at home. And the smell. After the first whiff of rotten meat and blood, she breathed through her mouth.

The crowd behind jostled her, impatient to find their seats. Ry wrapped his arm around her waist, drawing her against his side to protect her with his greater bulk. She noticed the flair of his nostrils and realized he didn't think much of the stench either.

Eventually they found their seats. Camryn sat between Ry and Mogens, and for once, she didn't protest Ry's possessiveness. He soothed her edginess with his presence and subtle touches. His leg jostled hers, distracting her for an instant. Her eyes closed to focus on the sensations streaking through her—the elevated breathing, the prickle of her breasts and the moistening between her legs. Sighing, she opened her eyes again, no longer surprised but still perturbed by her reaction to this alien man.

Mogens touched her arm, his brows drawn together in a frown. "Is your shoulder giving you pain?"

"It's fine," Camryn whispered, her gaze drawn to the hell-horses parading through an opening in the arena. Her shoulder felt stiff, although the pain had receded. She'd have to take some of Mogens' wondrous salve home with her.

An announcer, hidden somewhere high in the arena, rattled off the horses' names. "That's number six, Little Lucifer, the current champion from Grenfinch stables coming through now. He's won his last ten starts and is a hot favorite for today's premium race."

The horses pranced at the end of leads. Many of them bore obvious scars, white and silver marks peppering their dark coats. Painted entry numbers on the animal's sides aided identification. Camryn noticed the handlers wore protective vests. They sparkled in the sun and reminded her of old-fashioned chain mail. They kept a wide gap between each horse. Not difficult to see why. One hell-horse yanked hard on its lead and lunged at another, dragging its handler across the ground. When the man lost his footing, the crowd cheered. No one rushed to his aid until the distracted hell-horse attacked another with teeth bared.

"Lucky Henry is loose. It looks like Henry is intent on knocking out the opposition before the race starts. If they don't catch him soon he'll be disqualified."

The hell-horse ran a tight circle and bugled at the audience taunting him. He lurched at them, brought up short by a barrier. Camryn had wondered about the metal fence between the track and the public. Obviously for safety reasons.

"Are all the races like this?" she asked in a faint voice.

"This is the first I've seen." Ry watched the proceedings without expression.

"Time has run out. Lucky Henry isn't so lucky today. He's disqualified because he wasn't captured within the allowable time."

An armored cart drove into the arena and sped after the loose hell-horse. When the driver caught up with Lucky Henry, a mechanic arm bearing a noose shot from the side of the vehicle. Lucky Henry slid to an abrupt stop and the vehicle departed the arena, the hell-horse scampering alongside. The crowd jeered.

"We wanna see blood," a man hollered from behind them.

Blood? Camryn didn't like the sound of this race meeting.

The handlers led the horses into starting barriers, one by one. The barriers were similar to the ones used on Earth although solid to avoid the horses seeing each other.

"I can't believe they just let them run on their own," she muttered. "Barbaric."

"Pies. Get your pies here!"

"I'll take four pies," Ry said, signaling the vendor. He handed over two quid notes and selected four pies. He passed them to Camryn to distribute to the others while listening to her mutters. The high fences separating the crowd and hell-horses pointed to one thing—a fight to the death, much like the gladiator arenas on the planet Mykolnos.

He watched while the last horse entered the starting gate. The thumps and trumpets of displeasure coming from the hell-horses were clearly discernable.

Ry reached over to take Camryn's hand. He thought she might reject his touch because she'd avoided him during the last two days even though the attraction burned between them stronger than ever. She didn't. She squeezed his hand and moved closer. The feline purred with pleasure.

"I'm not going to like this, am I?" Camryn didn't take her eyes off the track.

"I don't think it's gonna be pretty," he said, striving for honesty.

"I don't want Gabby to run."

"I know." Ry smoothed his fingers across the back of her hand.

"I'd like to read the rules again. Maybe there's some way we can get creative with the interpretation."

"Not too creative or we'll be disqualified," Ry said.

"And they're off!" the announcer screeched to the crowd's roar.

The hell-horses sprang from the starter's gates but instead of racing to the finish line, the creatures circled each other, searching for openings to attack.

"Oh heck," Camryn said faintly. "This isn't a race, it's carnage."

A loud explosion from behind the starter's gate startled the hell-horses into action. They jumped forward, continuing to snap and snarl at each other. Camryn's hand tightened on his, her fingernails digging into his flesh. Her gaze remained glued to the battle in the arena.

"Looks like Sprightly Teddy is down," the announcer cried. "At the moment it's Hell Frozen Over in the lead. The record race is twenty-five mins, but the pace is off for this one. Looks as if the time will be a slow one. No doubt the creatures were rattled by the early break by Lucky Henry."

"I'm not subjecting Gabby to this." Camryn faced him with defiance. "No way. This is a blood fest."

"Ry," Jannike whispered, leaning past Mogens to peer at him. "Check out the VIP boxes down by the finish post. Talor's arrived."

Ry took his attention off the race to study his brother. His group contained all men apart from Meghan. He still didn't understand why they hadn't married.

"I don't think I want to eat my pie," Camryn said.

"I'll have it," Jannike said. Camryn handed it over.

"Looks like Fiery Heat is out," the announcer called.

From behind them came a large groan and secs later, white betting slips sprinkled over their heads like soft rain.

"Ice Cold has made a break, but Little Devil is chasing hard," the announcer called.

"Go, Little Devil. Run, Little Devil, run," a man two seats away called.

"I can't watch," Camryn said, hiding her face against his chest.

Ry didn't inform her he intended to go ahead no matter her

feelings on the subject. There was too much at stake. He stared at the VIP boxes. Talor held responsibility for two murders. His brother would pay but first he wanted to know why.

"Just look at Little Devil! He's cleaning up. This hell-horse is monstering his way through the rest of the field."

"Go, Little Devil," the crowd chanted. "Attack, Little Devil. Teeth, teeth, teeth!"

"How long until they finish?" Camryn's face still pressed against his chest.

"They're only halfway through. Maybe another ten or fifteen mins," Ry said.

"It's barbarous."

The crowd didn't agree. Men shrieked, waving their hands in the air and stomping their feet in encouragement. Ry could see why the two women had attracted so much attention. Although he'd noticed a few females in the VIP boxes, the main crowd consisted of men.

Ry turned his attention to the racetrack. Another horse went down, and three others converged on it, ripping huge chunks of flesh from its body. The pained and dying shrieks of the downed horse rang through his ears despite the roar of the crowd. Camryn trembled, almost sitting on him rather than her seat. He pulled her onto his lap and held her tight. He wished he could whisper reassurance but didn't want to lie to her any more than he had already.

"Ry, promise me we're not going to put Gabby through this." Camryn gripped his shirt and shook him. "Tell me."

Frag it, he'd hoped to avoid this, especially here. "We'll talk about it later."

Her face froze before anger blazed. "You're going to go ahead with the race, even after seeing this...carnage. You would risk Gabby just to win this race."

"Camryn, there's more at stake here than you realize."

"Make me understand," she whispered, her tone fierce. "Tell me the truth instead of giving me the half-truths you've offered all along."

"If I win, Talor will clear my name, and I'll be free to come and go from Ibrox. I can visit my sisters and my mother's grave." He'd have his family back.

The crowd had grown silent, watching the action on the course.

"And there goes Little Devil with a fast spurt down the rails. Giving chase is Lucifer's Folly. Only four horses left in this race. A slow time today," the announcer screeched. "Brimstone is chasing hard and following in the rear is Satan. Satan is launching a surprise attack. Yes! Brimstone is down. Little Devil is returning to fight off Satan. Looks like Satan is going to surprise everyone. He's attacking Little Devil."

The crowd burst into loud roars, palpable excitement rippling through the arena. The noise made conversation impossible. Camryn pressed closer despite her anger.

Ry's gaze slid from the brutality taking place on the racetrack to the private boxes. His brother sat centerstage, a drink in hand while he watched the action on the track.

The crowd gave a collective groan. "Little Devil is down. Yes, he's gone down. Wait a minute! The race isn't over. He's still fighting. Folks, he's still fighting. Little Devil is struggling to his feet. Satan is attacking but Lucifer's Folly is fighting him off. Little Devil is back on his feet. He's racing away. Not far to go to the finish line. It's still a slow race. Not one for the record books."

"Aw man! Can't believe Brimstone is down," a man shouted from behind them. The crowd roared, alternatively booing and cheering.

Ry watched the three horses join forces to attack Brimstone. The eerie shrieks whipped the crowd into frenzied cheers and catcalls. Camryn trembled in his arms, refusing to look down at the track.

A hell-horse staggered, a deep gash on its shoulder bleeding profusely.

"There goes Lucifer's Folly. Little Devil is chasing hard. Looks like Lucifer's Folly is in trouble. Satan is stomping Brimstone and ripping into him with his teeth."

"Look," Mogens said. "They're bringing in convicts to clear the debris off the track."

"The race is almost over. Satan is feeding. He's forgotten the race. It's a two-horse race. Little Devil and Lucifer's Folly. Lucifer's Folly is weakening. He's staggering. Yes, he's in trouble."

"Go Little Devil," a man shouted.

"Little Devil! Little Devil!" The crowd picked up the chant.

"Lucifer's Folly is down. Little Devil is attacking. We have a run from Satan, but he's left it too late. Little Devil is moving to the finish line. His trainer is roaring encouragement and rattling a feed bucket."

"Look at Little Devil go! You beauty," a man screeched. "Go, you good thing. Go!"

"Satan has noticed his handler. He's scampering after Little Devil. He's left his run too late. It's Little Devil by two lengths. Little Devil wins the Ornum Classic by two lengths with Satan a well-run second."

"Is it over?" Camryn asked. "Can I look now?"

"They're still cleaning up the track," Ry murmured, not in a hurry for her to move. He was quite happy with her in his arms.

"Tell me when I can look," she said.

Ry heard Jannike's snort of disgust and winged a glare in her direction. Camryn was necessary to their plan. They couldn't offend her. With only a month before the heats, they had no option. Luckily Jannike received and understood his silent message.

"The prize-giving ceremony will take place in five minutes," the announcer said.

Some of the people left the stadium to place bets. Others hurried straight for the onsite tavern while others appeared hungry after the exhilarating race. Food stalls dotted around the arena bustled, doing a swift trade in takeaway items.

"You can look now." Unable to resist, Ry placed a swift kiss on her cheek.

Camryn pulled away and blinked like a sleepy bird. She shifted over to her own seat before looking at him with a blank expression. "That was *interesting*."

Ry's heart thumped with recognition, her familiar scent winding through his nostrils and bringing a whisper of temptation.

She frowned. "We might have to go ahead with this race, but we will work out a way so Gabby will win without injury."

"It won't be easy."

"I don't care. You can't sacrifice Gabby just to win your precious race. You can't leave Luke without his mother."

"We'll work something out." Ry leaned forward to confer with Jannike and Mogens. "You seen enough?"

"I'm ready to leave," Mogens said.

Jannike stood. "Let's go."

They filed from the arena, not attempting to speak over the drunken cheers. One of the men they passed tried to grab Camryn, and Ry placed a protective arm around her to stop a reoccurrence. He snarled a warning at the drunk. When a man pinched Jannike's butt, she turned and plowed her fist into his nose. A spurt of blood erupted. The man roared in fury, but Jannike dodged his return punch, much to the amusement of his friends. His threats and his friends' ribald laughter echoed after them.

They exited the gates, declining a pass-out stamp to reenter. The street outside was a different world, a grim reminder of the convict status of the planet. Several sedan chair attendants waited for wealthy patrons to exit while beggars approached each person who left the stadium. Ry waved them off, even though he sympathized with their plight.

"Ah Ryman. Well met!"

Ry turned slowly to face his brother. "Talor."

"How are your race preparations going? I am very happy with my hell-horses."

Ry ignored the males with Talor. "Our preparations are fine, but you'd know that since you're spying on our progress."

Talor ignored the accusation to turn his attention on Camryn. Ry bristled though hid his irritation. "Who is this beautiful woman? I don't believe we've met."

"One of my crew," Ry snapped, failing to hide his emotions.

Talor picked up the monocle hanging from a ribbon around his neck and inspected Camryn. "Ah yes. I've heard you collect waifs and strays."

True, but his crew was loyal. They were more family than Talor had ever been.

"Come with me, my dear," Talor said, his expression intent.

Ry felt Camryn stir at his side, take half a step toward Talor. He grabbed her, drawing her hard to his side. "I don't think so. Goodbye, Talor."

He started walking, dragging Camryn with him, and the others fell in behind until they turned a corner, and the stadium was no longer visible. They hurried down the rutted street, past the piles of rubbish and a rotting carcass of an unidentified animal. A rodent scuttled from an alleyway, spotted them, and disappeared back into the semi-gloom between two leaning buildings.

"Camryn, are you all right?" Mogens asked.

"I don't like that man, but I wanted to go to him." She shivered, her eyes huge and fearful when she turned to him. "Thank you for grabbing me."

"Don't ever trust my brother," Ry said.

"Your brother is a wizard," Mogens said. "I could feel the pulse of power when he focused on Camryn."

A wizard. Damnation, how could he not have known? They'd grown up together.

"He doesn't know you're a shifter," Mogens said, appearing to read his mind. "It's possible his powers developed after you left."

"Or he could have had them all along and used them to murder Maxmus. That would explain the lack of clues and the ease with which I was set up." Ry considered their childhood. "Is wizardry inherited? He and my father were very close and spent a lot of time together."

"It's possible the powers go through the male line. Watch out!" Mogens shouted.

A shower of foul-smelling liquid rained down from above.

"Aw damn." Jannike shook her black boot and muttered a curse. "A bloody chamberpot. These people are so uncivilized."

Ry chuckled. "It's no different from parts of Ibrox."

"Which is why I don't like visiting there either," Jannike shot back.

Camryn stared at the open window and wrinkled her nose. "I'd suggest we hurry. Looks like the woman has more than one to empty." Her warning hastened them and twenty mins later they arrived at the park where they'd left their tender.

Ry paid the tariff to the security booth, and they took off without further mishap, arriving back at their mountain village base soon afterward.

"I'm so glad you're back," Kaya said, sprinting up the ramp of the tender the sec he lowered it. "Luke is missing. Nanu and I have searched everywhere. Gabby is stroppy and if we don't calm her down soon, she's going to destroy the yards.

"I'll go." Camryn unbuckled her harness and sped down the ramp to check on Gabby.

"Where have you searched?" Ry demanded. Surely his brother couldn't inhabit two places at once. Or could he?

"All the spots Luke has played during the last two days. The lakeside, around the campsite, the clearing in the bush. I'm so sorry. He was playing and the next min he'd disappeared. Both Nanu and I have been searching for him for the last hour. He's vanished."

"Split up. Search the areas again, and if we don't find him, we'll widen our hunt."

Mogens tugged at his sleeve. "Do you think he'd go into the village? Do you think someone has stolen him?"

"I don't know." He hoped not. Ry forced confidence into his voice. "Don't worry, we'll find him." The hell-horse foal had become a firm favorite and loved to play with them while Camryn trained his mother. Ry hurried to help Camryn with Gabby.

The mare reared and charged the fence, attempting to escape. Ry started running when he saw Camryn slip into the yard with Gabby. His heart knocked against his ribs in a surge of fear. He choked back the instinctive order that sprang to his lips, knowing any distractions would add to the danger. She'd done this countless times before, but it didn't stop his apprehension. Slowing his pace, he prowled to the rails, his fear turning to anger. Once they found Luke, he intended to take some personal time with Camryn. He'd blister her pert backside for scaring him, if she lived to tell the tale, he thought savagely when Gabby charged with teeth bared.

"Stop it! Gabby, calm down. Let me put your halter on and we can go to find Luke."

Ry clenched his jaw, his worry for Camryn bringing the feline to the surface. A soft growl emerged from deep in his throat. Gabby snorted in alarm and reared again. Ry took a careful step back to give Camryn a better chance of capturing the mare.

From his position outside the yard, he glared at both Gabby and Camryn. Damn, he hoped they found Luke soon. His disappearance would derail their plans. Gabby would have noticed if there were strangers hanging around the camp. Yesterday she'd proved a good addition to their security, alerting them when several village men had arrived to pay their respects.

Camryn approached Gabby, her palm outstretched. Ry heard the soothing tone but not the actual words. His nails bit into his palms, the spiky points close to claws instead of fingernails. He inhaled sharply, shoving the feline back and clinging to his humanoid form. His breath eased out when Camryn stood at Gabby's shoulder and ran her hand over the agitated beast. She slipped on the halter with a minimum of fuss before looking at him.

"Open the gate for me," she said.

"You won't be able to hold her."

"I don't intend to try. Get ready."

Ry moved to the gate, uneasiness tightening his gut.

"Now," Camryn ordered, and she sprang onto Gabby's back, gripping the barrel of the mare's body with her knees.

Sheer black fright swept through him.

"Open the damn gate," Camryn shouted when Gabby reared. "She needs to search for Luke."

Momentary panic gave way to the knowledge Camryn was right. Gabby would find Luke easier than their searches. He dragged the gate open, and Gabby jumped from the yard like a mechanism unfurled without warning. Camryn clung to her back, leaning forward in the manner of the jockeys on Earth. She had the audacity to grin when they galloped past.

"I look forward to blistering your butt, sweetheart." Ry stared after them for an instant longer before whipping off his shirt. That done, he let the change take him. Bones cracked and lengthened. Fur bristled across his chest, arms and legs as he dropped to all fours. Shift completed, he checked the scents, searching through the tangle until he located the foal's pungent scent. He followed slowly, checking for the most recent. It led toward the village, in the same direction Gabby and Camryn had disappeared. Ry increased his pace to a lope, following the scent with ease, tension drumming through him until he realized Luke had wandered off on his own instead of someone snatching him as they'd first suspected.

Ry made good time and reached the village not long after Camryn and Gabby. The village perched on the side of the mountain, a small plateau used as the focal point where they traded goods on market days and hosted feasts. At the far end of the plateau, he spied Luke. Laughter and playful yelps rang out as he cantered after the village youngsters in a mad game of chase. Now and then he let them catch him and the children clambered all over him. Then it hit him. The children were imitating Camryn. They'd obviously come close enough to the yard to spy and had seen Camryn climb onto Gabby. Their exuberant jumping play didn't bother Luke.

Gabby trumpeted, loud and demanding, and Luke's head jerked up. He yapped back and cantered over to her and Camryn, a child still clinging to his back.

Ry shifted and stalked over to them. "You could have told me you'd done that before."

"Where is your shirt?" Camryn's voice was faint, her gaze traveling over his chest and the tight trews that left nothing to imagination.

"I was...hot," Ry said, enjoying the play of color across her cheeks.

"There are children present," she said.

"They don't seem worried about my absent shirt." And it was true since they wore fewer clothes than he did.

"Um, we've found Luke."

"I can see that. I think we've also found a solution to getting Gabby to run fast in the heats. We'll take Luke to the finishing post, and she'll go crazy trying to get to her foal."

"Good idea." Camryn didn't take her attention off his face, and he noticed the clench of her fingers in Gabby's mane while the mare nuzzled her foal.

Ry smothered a satisfied chuckle. "I'll bring Luke." He strode over to the foal and scratched him behind the ears. "Off you get," he said to a grinning child. He noticed several adults had appeared and waved at them before lifting the child from Luke's back. With a tap on the foal's rump, he sent Luke scuttling to Gabby and Camryn. Gabby yapped and, at Camryn's urging, trotted toward their camp with Luke following. Ry strode after them, keeping his gaze on Camryn's straight back. He looked forward to arriving back at camp.

"Dancing practice," Mogens said when they had Gabby and Luke safely back in the pen. "We have to practice before dinner, or we'll run out of time before the ball for the Dowry Derby. Ry said you should all learn to dance so you can interact with the other entrants. Maybe pick up some insider knowledge."

"No way. Not me," Jannike said.

An alarmed expression hit Kaya. "Don't look at me. I'm a fighter not a dancer."

"You're all learning," Ry said. "I need you to charm the opposition, worm info from them. That won't happen if you can't dance. Information is knowledge, and it might help us win the Derby. We need every advantage we can find against my brother."

"Ry, music please," Mogens said. "Where's Nanu? He can help." His robes rustled when he hurried into the tender.

"Do we have to?" Camryn asked.

"Yes." Ry hummed while stepping a square with Camryn.

Soon laughter rippled through the campsite, accompanied by giggles from the village children who turned up to watch them stumble around a pretend dance floor. At last Mogens pronounced himself satisfied with their progress.

"My feet are sore," Kaya said.

"You put them in the wrong place," Nanu said. "Ry is the mindreader. Not me."

"I didn't stand on anyone, and my feet are sore," Jannike muttered. "I'm only doing this because we have to."

"Me too," Camryn said.

Ry smirked at the three females but was wise enough not to comment. "Whose turn is it to cook dinner?"

Mogens frowned at the clouds. Ry noticed they had turned to a delicate gray to match the seer's current skin tone. "The course of action you have chosen is doomed. Someone will die. I will cook," he said in an abrupt change of subject. "Kaya will burn dinner."

They dined on a rabbitlike creature cooked over a spit and fish grilled on the embers of an open fire along with a selection of green leaves and herbs, reminding Camryn of lettuce. Kaya made flat bread to bake on the fire. A meal fit for kings after the endless ration pouches they'd consumed since leaving the Indy. Camryn licked the grease from her fingers and gave a happy sigh until she realized Ry watched her again. Ever since this afternoon when they'd arrived back from the races to find Luke missing, he'd eyed her with the same look. Sort of hungry and determined. It brought nerves to the surface and the cat tattoo that had appeared on her shoulder had started to ache something fierce. Every time she moved, the fabric of her tunic brushed across the leaping cat, igniting nerves and bringing sexual awareness. Jittery, she cursed under her breath, saying a word her brother would've objected to if he'd overheard.

Gabriel wouldn't have liked it much better, but the curse summed up her simmering frustration. The more Ry stared, the edgier she became. Her body tingled in an outrageous manner, her nipples swelled and pulled to achy nubs. Her skin prickled each time she fidgeted, and she suffered for it. She squirmed and glowered at Ry, trying to ignore the heat emanating from her weird tattoo. It didn't make a jot of difference. His wolfish grin brought a rush of arousal. Oops, wrong predator. His big, bad feline grin told her if she didn't run he'd pounce.

Camryn shot to her feet. "I'm tired," she blurted. "I'm going to bed." She bolted, heading to the area where she'd set up her bedding. It wasn't there.

"Looking for something?" Ry prowled from the darkness and damn if he didn't look like he wanted dinner.

"My bedding. I think Luke has dragged it away again."

"For once the foal is innocent." The glint in Ry's eyes didn't diminish. Camryn took a step back, a frisson of alarm trickling down her spine. Mind and instincts warred. She would not touch and give in to her base needs. She would not.

"I don't understand." A lie. She understood all too well.

"I've arranged some privacy for us. I wanted to...talk."

Another quick glance at his face told Camryn he didn't have talking on his mind. "The others will think it's strange. And it's very high-handed of you!"

"No, they won't. Come." He held out his hand and waited patiently for her to decide on a course of action.

Desire tingled through her limbs, despite the lecture she gave herself every morning about Gabriel, about returning home. Camryn pulled memories of Gabriel to mind with difficulty—his twinkling blue eyes, gentle smile and full head of springy gray curls. His dimple that appeared whenever he smiled and the scent of his fragrant citrus aftershave. She tried to hold the image, almost crying when it flickered and faded, overlaid with Ry's dominant face and personality.

And during the entire internal struggle the tattoo throbbed, subtly nudging her to go to him, to beg him to rub his fingers across the achy flesh. She trembled with the need, hating herself for the weakness.

Ry grasped her shoulders with his big hands. "Why the frown? You like being with me." His fingers caressed and upped the temptation, increasing her inner battle.

Camryn yanked from his seductive touch and edged away, her pulse galloping. To her shame he spoke the truth. Somehow he'd turned into her drug of choice, her crutch to use instead of alcohol. His presence and his touch...

The damn tattoo! She'd never felt this intense hunger until the cat had appeared on her shoulder. There was something dreadfully wrong with her, to let the kitty overwrite the special memories she held of Gabriel, the special ones she held close to her heart.

"I shouldn't. You're not good for me." Well! Her weak tone certainly told him, put him in his place. Not.

"Ah, but together we're perfect." His husky voice brought another surge of sensual awareness. Her heart did a little change up in gear, and although her head told her to run, she remained rooted to the spot. He reached her side, before her mind overruled her needy body, and cupped her face with one hand. Ry traced her lips with his thumb, eliciting a shudder of desire. She gasped and his thumb slipped inside her mouth. "Separately we're misfits, you and I. Together we're right. Just perfect."

Camryn attempted to deny, her tongue flicking across his thumb. Ry froze. His eyes glowed in a supernatural way, and her resolve weakened even further. He removed his thumb from her mouth, started on her clothes, one item at a time.

She stood passive, shivering at the lazy trail of kisses across her collarbone, the stroke of fingers across the curve of one cheek. He nibbled at the cords of her neck and peeled away her tunic. His large hands cupped her breasts, lifted them to his mouth. Suckled. Camryn sighed at the warm tug of his lips. She'd stop him soon.

In a minute.

But it didn't happen. Her need rose to urgency. She shuddered, swallowing while heat suffused her body. It emanated from the cat tattoo on her back, drawing her to him.

"I'm going to take you, taste your sweet juices then fill you with my cock."

She found herself naked, stretched out on her bedding and on the verge of begging him to hurry, to fuck her. She didn't need any preliminaries. Ry stripped off his shirt, leaving his chest bare and loomed over her. Her pulse raced and she reached up to stroke his back, savoring his hiss of pleasure when she ran her fingers across the swirling black marks covering his back and chest.

"Please," she murmured, the begging in her voice stark and clear.

"I intend to please you, sweet," he purred.

And he set about proving it. Each touch, each brush of his fingers teased her higher, made her want him more. A small voice at the back of her mind reminded her this was wrong. Gabriel. But her husband drifted away when Ry smoothed his hand over her tattoo. She sought his mouth, luxuriating in his lips against hers, hard and demanding a response.

"Please touch me." Camryn stirred restlessly, wanting more. Needing it. An addict for his touch.

"I want to take my time and savor you."

"Ry." She packed every bit of desire she felt into his name, thrumming with urgency, the need to possess and be possessed. "Please touch me *now*."

"Part your legs for me, Camryn." He slid one leg between hers and pushed, thankfully understanding her urgent need.

"Yes," she whispered, obeying immediately.

He lifted her bottom with his hands and kissed a trail of kisses over her inner thigh, drawing closer to her wet core. She tensed at the stroke of his tongue, sucked in a breath and released it on a moan. Chills raced across her flesh, a direct contrast to the fire whipping from every spot he caressed with his fingers and mouth. And her tattoo. That strange spot on her back felt as if it were on fire.

"Do that again," she begged, feeling the liquid arousal of her body.

He repeated the move, a loud purr erupting. The feline sound jerked her to reality. Heck, what was she doing?

"When did Jannike join the crew?" she blurted. Yeah, that was it. Fight the feelings coursing through her body with small talk.

"We met during a bar fight. Ended up fighting on the same side." His green eyes glowed when he glanced up at her. "You can ask me anything you want, but don't you prefer me to pleasure you instead?"

His smile tugged deep in her belly, and breathless, she blinked at him. She didn't know how he managed it. When they were together, all she could think of was making love—sex. Yeah, sex. That's all it could be between them.

Ry dipped his head and made a slow pass with his tongue across her swollen flesh. He ran a finger down her slit and pushed it into her channel. "I know you want me as badly as I want you. It's as sexy as hell."

His dark voice unfurled a lick of heat despite his smug tone. She wriggled and the abrasion of her tattoo against the bedding brought a startled gasp.

"Ry." She relaxed in silent permission for him to continue. Camryn couldn't fight the escalating desire any longer. "Now. I need you inside me right now."

He licked and sucked swollen folds and nerve endings, drove her high and hard. Quick flicks of his tongue. Seductive and lingering strokes. Either way it added up to pleasure.

"Ry," she gasped, her climax crashing over her.

"You look so beautiful when you come, I just want to do it over again." Ry shucked his remaining attire and moved up her body, thrusting inside her entrance even as the ripples contracted her vagina. He pistoned his hips, going deep while his lips and tongue invaded her mouth. He pushed her with each plunging stroke, their sweat-sheened chests sticking together until they both exploded, their cries of pleasure loud enough for the crew to hear.

Languid and relaxed they held each other, hands idly stroking.

He purred, and damn if she didn't want to purr as well. Great sex. Stupendous sex. But with the thought came a return to reality.

"Gabriel," she whispered. She felt Ry tense and closed her eyes, realizing what she'd done. Guilt hit her hard, for leading Ry on and for sullying Gabriel's memory.

"I'm not Gabriel. Look at me."

She opened her eyes to stare at him in defiance.

"This is just sex," she snapped, the anguish leaving only raw pride. "Nothing more. And when the racing is over, I'm going home. You promised."

Ry glared, pulling away from her. He stood and moved his bedding.

"I love Gabriel." Even though she said it in clear defiance, something made her want to take it back. Stubbornly, she kept her mouth shut. It was for the best. They had no future. Camryn tugged her bedding up to her chin, turned over and pretended to sleep. It was just sex. That's all.

CHAPTER TEN

After the previous night's argument, Camryn didn't want to attend the ball. Ry insisted, despite the icy atmosphere between them. He'd also insisted that Kaya and Jannike attend, purchasing gowns for each of them. Exquisite gowns of the sort Camryn had read about in books set during the Regency period on Earth. The gowns were the same style although different colors to suit their complexions. They required a base garment beneath to yank in their waists and force their breasts upward.

"What was Ry thinking?" Jannike wheezed. "I can't breathe. How the devil do I fight in this?"

"I don't believe you're meant to fight," Mogens said in his dry way. "It's a ball. You're meant to dance."

"We can always poke out eyes with our fingernails," Kaya said cheerfully.

"Or stomp on people's feet," Camryn added. "Although maybe

one look at our hands will do the trick." She held them up for inspection. "I scrubbed for half an hour and couldn't remove the dirt."

"True. My fingernails might work." Jannike lifted the skirts of her long hunter green gown to inspect one shoe. "The shoes don't look robust enough for kicking. I'll need to stick to stomping." She scratched the back of her neck, unused to the ornate hairstyle as much as the unaccustomed finery.

"This is a dance," Ry said sternly from the doorway of the hotel room they'd rented. "There won't be any need to fight."

Camryn scowled on hearing his voice, her mouth dropping into a distinct gape on seeing him. Dressed in black, he wore a fitted jacket with breeches and stockings. The only relief was the sparkling silver design on his waistcoat. When Camryn scrutinized the pattern, she recognized the spirals and whorls as those of his tattoo. On his feet, he wore highly polished shoes with shiny buckles. He grasped an ornate walking stick with a silver cat head in his right hand while a black ribbon tied back his dark hair in a queue.

"Huh! Tell that to my gut," Jannike said. "It's bouncing fast enough to spin thread."

"Because you haven't attended a dance before," Mogens said. "You'll enjoy it. I've shown you how to dance and know you will acquit yourselves with decorum."

Kaya shrieked with laughter. "Mogens, you sound like my stepfather."

"Fine," Jannike said, reaching behind her back to unfasten her gown. She scowled at Mogens. "You go in my place if you think it will be so much fun. I'd like to see you decked out in this cage thing. I can't breathe!"

Mogens drew himself up tall. "I do not wish to attend the ball. It is your destiny, not mine."

"What! Don't tell me," Jannike said, holding her right hand to her forehead. "You read the clouds and they said my attendance is necessary."

"Quite so," Mogens replied, unruffled by Jannike's sarcasm.

"Think of it as an assignment," Ry suggested. "I need you to circulate. Dance with as many of the other contestants as possible. Smile. Bat your eyes and ask questions. Do not leave the ballroom, and don't eat or drink anything unless it comes from a plate or bottle everyone else eats or drinks from."

He handed them gloves to match their dresses and waited for them to draw them on before nodding with satisfaction. "Perfect. We need to collect information tonight. Information is knowledge."

"This ball is a wicked waste of currency," Jannike grumbled, tugging at the bodice of her green dress.

"Perhaps," Ry said, "but necessary. I want to know what my brother is up to."

The marker tolled eight.

"It is time," Mogens said.

"Are you all set for your mission?" Ry asked.

"I am," Mogens said. "I have arranged a job in the cloak room."

"Camryn, a word? We'll be with you in a few mins," he added to Mogens.

The seer's color flickered, edging toward black as he ushered Jannike and Kaya from the hotel room.

"My brother will be in attendance tonight. Don't let him get you alone." Ry brushed his thumb across her bottom lip. Her mind told her to step away. Her body disobeyed. She shivered under his delicate touch. "Talor hates me." His expression hinted at pain, but all he said was, "You know what he's capable of."

"Your brother gives me the creeps. I hated the way he made me feel at the races, the urge to do what he wanted even though I didn't want to obey. Believe me—I intend to stay away."

Ry nodded with satisfaction. "Good." He dipped his head to

steal a kiss, caressing her lips and demanding her response. Camryn fought the desire that burst to life inside, fought to hold on to her anger, fought to remain impassive. She called up Gabriel's image, and again the memory blurred, overlaid with Ry's vitality. He refused to let her hold back or hide. His lips dominated while he gently cradled her head. With his tongue, he traced her bottom lip. Her heart thundered and a mew of need escaped, her nipples tender against the stiff bodice of her gown. She inhaled through her nose as much as her corset would allow and quickly wished she hadn't attempted to breathe. His scent, so seductive and full of memories, hurled temptation her way.

"Mine," he whispered before he opened the door and stood back to let her exit the hotel room.

Camryn forced her feet to move, sweeping past him like an imperious duchess. She was not his, would never be his no matter what he said. Soon she'd return to New Zealand and life would revert to normal. She'd return to her job and live a quiet life, avoiding alcohol and yellow pills, content in the knowledge she'd known love with Gabriel. Another man wasn't necessary. As long as she kept busy, she wouldn't fall back into the abyss of despair she'd inhabited before her kidnapping. Her time spent with the aliens had taught her that at least.

They caught up with Mogens and Camryn walked beside the seer, her agitation lessening with movement. Ry had no right to treat her like a possession. A frown formed. No touching, since that's where she seemed to go wrong, since she lost every vestige of willpower with skin contact.

When they reached the foyer of the hotel, they found it full of men and women waiting to enter the ballroom. Crystal chandeliers sparkled overhead, sending shards of fragmented light from the candles across the room and its occupants.

The gowns of the women attracted Camryn's attention. Many were daring and some edged close to scandalous. The women reminded her of colorful butterflies while the men dressed similarly to Ry in black or white or a combination of the two.

"Where do these women hide during the day?" Jannike asked.

Camryn wondered the same thing. They seldom saw women out on the streets unless they were convicts. What did they do with themselves?

The line of people waiting to enter the ballroom moved at a steady pace, and soon Ry handed his invitation to the majordomo.

"Mr. Ryman Coppersmith and companions," the man intoned.

Ry strode into the ballroom as if he owned it, ignoring stares and whispered conversations taking place behind gloved hands. Taking her cue from Ry, Camryn sashayed inside with head held high. Kaya and Jannike followed their example. A footman handed the three women a dance card each.

The ballroom stole her breath and heightened the perception of walking into a Jane Austen novel. Although she'd been a tomboy in her youth, she'd still read the classics and the odd romance while recuperating from a fall from her pony. A sad crush, they'd have termed this ball. Although early, dancers crammed onto the dance floor dipping and whirling to the music of a string band.

Five huge chandeliers, filled with glowing candles, lit the room. Plants and strategically potted palms offered both decoration and privacy. The ballroom opened out onto a balcony for those who wanted to take the air. The combination of perfumes, tallow candles and unwashed bodies made her nose twitch and her eyes water.

"I see a free table over by the balcony," Ry said, nodding at a plump matron who gaped at him in consternation.

Camryn noticed other men and women with the same reaction. She nudged Kaya and they shared a grin.

The string band launched into a new set of dances and the couples on the floor commenced the series of intricate moves Mogens had taught them.

"I say, I know this is forward of me since we haven't been introduced, but may I sign your dance card?"

Camryn turned to face the man with the suave voice, and mindful of Ry's instructions to mingle, she beamed at him. "My name is Camryn O'Sullivan." She offered the man her gloved hand. He raised it to his lips and brushed his mouth across her knuckles. "I would be honored to dance with you." Camryn handed over her dance card and realized things were less formal here than they would've been on Earth during the early nineteenth century.

Encouraged by her friendliness, other men arrived and took possession of her dance card, scrawling their names against dances. Finally, Camryn slipped the dance card over her wrist and waited for the commencement of the next dance. Feeling a gaze, she shifted a fraction, angling her body. Ry stared at her, his expression one of irritation before he gave a clipped nod and strode from sight. A sense of rejection filled her despite her earlier resolution. Her stomach hollowed. Silly really. This ball was business. She had no right to feel anything toward Ry.

Ry had known Camryn would attract attention. It worried him, but he'd had to let her attend. Whenever she was out of his sight, he felt physically ill. The symptoms, mild at first, had grown more acute. Ry needed to speak to Mogens but had put it off because he knew the seer would issue dire predictions along with disapproval. He knew he should stay away from Camryn O'Sullivan. Try telling his feline, the reason he kept failing. Mogens had warned him earlier, yet compulsion made him keep her close. The impulse had increased until now he craved her presence, her touch and taste. He watched her chatting to several males and had to quash his surge of jealousy.

Aware he needed to mingle, he approached two women and signed their dance cards.

"Mr. Talor Coppersmith, House of the Cat," the major domo

droned.

His brother. Of course they'd bump into each other straightaway.

"Ryman, how are you?" A private smile twisted Talor's lips, as if he knew how much Ry wanted to wring his neck.

"I'm very well." But he'd be better once he exacted revenge and discovered why Talor hated him so much. He felt subtle probing of his mind. Damn, Mogens had been right about his brother. Shoving the intrusion away, he held his brother's gaze. The debonair demeanor didn't fool him. Smugness accompanied the charm, putting Ry on notice. His brother had a plan, just as he had one. "How are Edrea and Cody?"

"Our sisters are well. Where is Camryn, Ryman? I must claim a dance." Talor picked up his bejeweled quizzing glass and surveyed the ballroom then zoomed in on the dance floor.

Ry bit out a curse. He'd known Talor had taken a liking to her and hated the idea. The min he'd involved Camryn and his crew, their lives were at risk. One of the Coppersmith brothers would die, and even if his gut hadn't told him this, Mogens had yesterday after reading the clouds.

"Ah, there she is, dancing with one of my friends." Talor beckoned, his manner imperious, and Ry saw the man dancing with Camryn stop to whisper in her ear. She glanced over at them with a frown. Ry knew she had little option, saw the fierce grasp the man had on her arm. He'd better not leave bruises.

"How convenient. They're coming over." Talor sounded smug and sure of himself.

"Talor, I believe you've met Camryn O'Sullivan already," the man said after bowing from the waist.

"Enchanted, my dear." Talor took Camryn's hand and lifted it to kiss the back. Instead of kissing her gloved hand, he pressed a kiss to the bare skin of her wrist above the line of pale lilac fabric.

Ry forced himself not to react.

"Talor," Camryn said in a hoity-toity voice.

"A woman as pretty as you must be used to men making fools of themselves in her presence," Talor said smoothly.

"I don't go out much. I'm a widow," Camryn said. "I loved my husband very much and I'm not intending to replace him."

"I am sorry to hear that," Talor said, patting her hand with familiarity again. "I understand since I lost my mother not long ago. Her passing still hurts."

Ry snorted. "A pity you didn't see fit to inform me."

"I didn't think the news would interest an outlaw."

A stunned silence fell. It pained Ry to know the woman he'd known as mother had died and he hadn't said goodbye. Grief bloomed at the knowledge she'd died thinking him a thief and a liar. Katia Coppersmith had possessed a heart of solid gold and he had loved her.

"The death of a loved one always brings great pain," Camryn murmured.

Anguish twisted inside Ry. Camryn still loved her husband, or so she said. It had been the other man's name she'd whispered last night, not his.

How did one fight a dead man?

The music trailed off and the dancers dispersed from the floor.

"I believe the next dance is mine," Talor said, smiling at Camryn.

Camryn's brows arched in a delicate manner. "Really?" She glanced down at her dance card before turning her attention back on him. "Are you HOC?"

"I am indeed, my dear. I'm head of the House of the Cat." He offered his arm with a smug grin and after a brief hesitation, Camryn placed her gloved fingers on the crook. "I believe the music will start shortly."

Ry wanted to grab Camryn from his brother. He caught a quick flash of her thoughts, her irritation at Talor's presumptuous behavior, and attempted to quell his jealousy. The amusement flitting across his brother's face told him he'd failed. Ry watched her to measure possible distress and saw a woman in complete control. Mogens had told him to trust Camryn and it seemed he was right.

With stealth, he attempted to read his brother's thoughts. He caught the flash of anger before the emotions shut down abruptly. A mind block. Ry's hands clenched and his smile never wavered.

"Ah, here's Meghan," Talor said, his expression sly. "You're old friends. Why don't you say hello while we're dancing?"

Ry froze for a sec, staring at the beautiful redhead. Her betrayal with his brother had changed his life.

"Hello, Ryman." Her throaty voice remained the same, and it was like stepping back in time.

"Meghan." Ry sensed Camryn's interest. When he gave in to temptation and scanned the dance floor, he witnessed her anxiety, the way her teeth raked her bottom lip.

"Aren't you going to kiss me, Ryman? For old time's sake." Meghan pressed her full breasts against his chest. She smiled up at him, her blue eyes sparkling with humor and a tinge of lust.

Ry didn't feel a thing and pushed her away without regret.

"Look at that strumpet," an elderly woman said to her companion in a loud, carrying whisper.

"Crumpets? Funny thing to serve at a ball." Her companion's confusion was clear.

"Millicent, I told you to bring your hearing trumpet," the woman scolded. "Strumpet, not crumpet."

Ry turned back to Meghan, acknowledging the woman was correct. Meghan wore a sheer dress and she'd dampened the fabric, so it clung to every curve, leaving nothing for a male to imagine. She cozied up to him again.

Take your hands off that woman.

Ry stilled. Me?

Yes, you great lummox. You're making a spectacle of yourself, came the tart and very familiar voice.

Camryn?

Who did you expect? The abominable snowman?

Ry separated their bodies to create a gap between him and Meghan. He'd no idea what an abominable snowman was but it didn't sound good.

Thank you.

Ry narrowed his eyes and watched Camryn complete an elegant sashay before smiling at her partner. Their hands touched and she twirled gracefully, her lilac skirts flaring outward to display a flash of ankle and a deeper purple underskirt. His breath caught. With her black hair piled on top of her head, she was stunning. The lilac gown suited her perfectly, showcasing her slim waist and gorgeous breasts. He didn't want any of the other women, wasn't even interested in looking. Ry wondered if he was sick since this had never happened before. He loved sex, though since meeting Camryn he only craved her. No, not sex. They made love. And now she'd started communicating with him telepathically. Satisfaction at the intimacy chased away astonishment until Camryn rejoined with Talor. He watched their hands make contact and scowled at his brother's smug countenance. He wanted to rip his woman from Talor's arms. Pushing aside every shred of inner protest, he concentrated on Meghan.

"Would you like to dance?" Frankly, he'd rather not, but he could act as a civilized gentleman if necessary.

The relief in her expressive eyes suggested Talor had requested her to entertain him, perhaps distract him. Talor would have a plan, just as he did. He hated involving the women and dragging them into the middle of their personal battle.

When the band started their next number, Ry and Meghan joined a new set forming on the dance floor. From the corner of his eye, he noticed Camryn with another man and relaxed until he recognized him as another of Talor's friends. It was obvious Talor knew what Camryn meant to him and intended to capitalize on the weakness.

"Why are you still with Talor?" Ry asked.

Meghan tripped before collecting herself. "You are a murderer."

"No, I'm not. If you think that, why are you dancing with me?"

"Talor said I must," she whispered with another glance at Talor.

"Talor is a liar." Ry completed the prancing steps around Meghan before turning to face her. "You should leave him."

Her shoulders slumped. "I can't. I want...I can't leave Talor."

Ry wondered if Talor was strong enough to compel her all the time. He caught a glimpse of Camryn. *Camryn, be careful. Your partner is one of my brother's friends.*

Camryn didn't react, but he caught her surprise. She smiled at her partner as they joined a set of dancers. *Do you think all the names on my card are your brother's friends?*

I'd assume they were. Don't tell them you are our trainer.

Camryn laughed at something her partner said. Ry's admiration rose. *They think we are lovers?*

She sounded curious rather than upset. Ry smiled at Meghan and minced into the next set pattern of the dance. He caught a flash of Camryn's thoughts. *Gabriel.* Ry's smile died and jealousy took grip. Envious of a dead man. He snorted and attempted to concentrate on both the dance and Meghan.

Camryn whirled along the line to face another partner. This man kept his eyes on her face instead of scanning her breasts or attempting to grab her butt like her last one. Reassured, her gaze drifted to Ry. She'd talked to him telepathically. Confusion and a touch of fear gripped her mind.

More woo-woo for her to cope with.

She hated that woman's hands crawling over Ry, the familiarity of her touch. Camryn flashed a smile at her partner and continued to sashay through the steps of the dance. She extended her hand and clasped her partner's, prancing around him like a high-stepping horse, her attention still on Ry.

The woman—his partner—was shameless. Camryn's jaw locked into place while she worked to control her seesaw emotions—her possessive feelings for Ry Coppersmith. Weird, she'd argued with him yet still hated him touching another woman. She had to focus on returning home.

The thought of home soothed her—her brother, her nephew, even her sister-in-law and Gabriel. He'd have loved to see her in this balldress and dancing. She'd always joked he'd been born in the wrong era, making Gabriel laugh about his cradle-snatcher status.

Her new partner's fingers slid across her inner wrist in a stroke of intimacy. Suddenly, she heard the man's thoughts, just as she'd communicated with Ry.

Bet she's hot between the sheets. Talor wouldn't want her if she wasn't. He cast a speculative look at her before thinking, I wonder if he'd share. He does owe me a favor.

Camryn spun away, following the steps while shock reverberated inside her. Did they think her a whore for sale? Yes, she slept with Ry, but she didn't intend to share her body with another man. Or two. A favor? Huh! Camryn fumed. Talor Coppersmith was a slimeball sleaze. And his friends weren't much better.

What is it? What's wrong?

Camryn's head jerked up and she almost tripped before recovering the rhythm. Nothing's wrong, she snapped. Apart from you talking inside my head. It's disconcerting and rude!

I'm not talking alone, Ry said dryly. I can do disconcerting, if you want. Imagine this, he said, his thought throbbing with pure seduction. Imagine we're by the lake. The sun is shining and it's so hot the crew is relaxing on the ship. We're alone.

Alone? Camryn curtsied to her partner.

Yes, alone. I undress you. Slowly. I take off your tunic first to reveal your silky skin. I kiss the curves of your breasts, your shoulders and neck and lick across your collarbone. I trace my tongue around the outline of the tattoo on your shoulder.

Camryn shuddered, her stomach clenching with desire, her tattoo starting to burn beneath the fabric of her pale lilac dress. He couldn't do this to her. He couldn't. You're supposed to reconnoiter, to help us win the race. The race is the reason we're here. Remember?

You don't like sex? You don't like me stroking your nub until you scream your pleasure? You don't like the way I plunge my cock deep into your core and stroke you inside while my fingers brush across the cat on your shoulder?

I need a drink. Ry's soft chuckle echoed inside her head.

You don't need a drink. You need me. Ditch the man. Tell him you're tired and send him for refreshments. I'll meet you on the balcony.

It's not polite.

I want you, Camryn.

Camryn's breath exited in a slow hiss. She shouldn't. It set a bad precedent—jumping when Ry said jump. After this dance, stressing her thought with firmness.

He chuckled again, the pleasure and male satisfaction sending a tickle of heat through her veins. I'll bring you a drink. We'll go out to the garden for privacy.

After this dance, Camryn repeated. The dance passed in a whirr of indecision. This was wrong. She knew it. She was undisciplined according to her sister-in-law.

But despite knowing she should discourage Ry, Camryn found herself in the garden, the cool air a balm to her aroused body.

I'm over by the fishpond, to your left.

Cocky kitty-cat.

His rich laugh filled her mind. I love your insults, sweetheart. They make me hot.

Camryn rounded a hedge and found him in the secluded shadows. "I need to work on my insults."

"I intend to keep both your mind and mouth so busy you won't have time to utter them," he whispered before he drew her into the gloom and claimed her mouth.

She felt the thick ridge of his cock against her belly, felt the firm muscles bunching beneath her hands. When she ran her hands over his back, he voiced a hoarse curse. Her hand faltered until she realized she'd caressed the tattoos on his back. From experience, she knew how sensitive they became during lovemaking. Camryn shuddered at the thought of him tracing the outline of the cat on her shoulder and moisture pooled between her legs. "Touch me." Her voice held a note of pleading.

He lifted his head to laugh at her. "I am touching you."

Camryn swallowed, part of her still horrified at the alien tattoo. "My tattoo." She wondered if it would disappear when she returned to Earth.

"When I'm inside you," he promised, his eyes gleaming with sensual promise.

Her heart fluttered, the subtle quiver echoing in her womb.

Ry unfastened the placket of his breeches and bent to lift the hem of her dress. Camryn felt the cool air on her nether region. No panties. The lack of underwear was disconcerting but convenient.

His fingers slid across her moist folds. A purr rumbled deep in his chest. "You want me." He stroked her flesh, trailing fingers back and forth in a determined assault until pleasure spiraled just out of reach. "Admit it," he added. "Tell me."

"I want you." God help her, but it was true. Ryman Coppersmith—drug of choice.

Ry guided his cock to her entrance and impaled her, lifting her with ease while he plundered her mouth. "Yes." No mistaking his reply for anything but satisfied.

Their clothes rustled with each move. The faint tinkle of music poured from the ballroom along with soft voices, but Camryn concentrated on Ry, the way he surrounded her with his strength and protection, how he made her soar. He made good on his promise, stroking his fingers across her tattoo. Even with the fabric between her skin and his hands, the sensation overwhelmed her, made her gasp and her pussy clench hungrily. Anyone could discover them at any time, but she didn't care. All she wanted was Ry. He lifted her and let her sink down on his shaft. A moan fell from her lips at the sweet contact. She shuddered. They'd scarcely started yet the familiar low pressure gathered between her thighs.

"Come for me, Camryn." He teased her sensitive nub while catching her gaze.

His chatoyant eyes—they glowed full of mystery. Passion. Promise. Camryn ran her hand down his back, felt the buck of his cock in her warm channel, and suddenly her body convulsed with the force of her release. She cried out and Ry sealed her shout with his mouth. He thrust once. Twice. And stilled, panting while his cock jerked deep inside her. For an instant he squeezed her tight before separating their bodies and refastening his breeches. Once Camryn had righted her gown, he drew her into his arms and kissed her, lingering over the task. With each touch he cherished her, making her feel precious. Important.

Masculine voices dragged them apart.

"Go inside," Ry murmured. "I'll make sure no one follows you."

Camryn fled, her heart pounding. Ry made her feel things she didn't want. She climbed the stairs into the ballroom, determined to find a drink just as soon as she tidied up her appearance. Surely one drink wouldn't hurt?

The interior of the retiring room was luxurious like the ballroom. Candles flickered in wall sconces and several chairs were available for the ladies to rest. An ornate mirror filled most of one wall. Camryn checked her appearance and apart from the slight flush in her cheeks appeared normal. Amazing since her life raced out of control. She tucked an errant curl behind her ear and sank onto a chair. This relationship with Ry didn't have a future.

It couldn't.

Two women entered the retirement room. One wore a gold-jeweled mask, covering most of her face. Two rounded holes allowed her to see.

"Do not mind me," the masked woman said to her companion. "I will keep company with this lady while you are occupied."

"But your father...you won't take off your mask, will you?"

Camryn heard the apprehension in the woman's voice and curiosity jumped to the fore. Why did the woman wear a mask? Was she scarred or injured?

"Of course you may join me." Camryn scoffed inside at the formal words. The ball and these fancy clothes were going to her head. Soon she'd start acting like the lady of the manor. She thought about Ry and what they'd done in the garden.

Nope, not lady material. To her eternal shame, after Gabriel's death she had slept with several men to ease the pain. It hadn't worked and she'd found alcohol did a better job of hiding the pain. "I'm Camryn," she added.

The masked lady smiled, or at least Camryn thought she did because of the movement of her jaw.

"I am Gweneth Swithin. The governor's daughter," she added.

"Oh!" Camryn said, shocked. "The dowry bride. Aren't you worried about the identity of your future husband?" Camryn felt anger on the woman's behalf, especially since some of the men who had entered the race were horrid. She'd hate an arranged marriage.

"It is my chance to leave this world, to start over," Gweneth answered with an unconcerned shrug.

Camryn knew she'd never feel so blasé about marriage. "But what if you hate the man who wins the race?"

"You must be a visitor to Ornum," Gweneth said. "Surely you've noticed the shortage of marriageable men here on the planet? Most are convicts who have committed crimes on Ibrox. Serious crimes. Every man who has entered the race has money and some are of high status. My father is doing as he thinks best."

"But what if you don't like the winner?"

The woman laughed. "Marriage is too important to leave to karma. We must take control and direct fate. As time passes, my new husband and I will grow to like one another. My father has promised this."

"Oh," Camryn said, battling to hide doubt. "That's nice." But she didn't pay attention to the woman's explanation. Her mind had grabbed hold of a salient fact. The woman expected to marry the winner. Marry him. After seeing the hell-horse races, she knew Gabby had a good chance of winning if she ignored the other horses in the field.

The woman's companion returned and with a polite nod, both departed the retirement rooms, leaving Camryn frozen in her chair. The thought of another woman in Ry's bed made her stomach roil. She... No!

Camryn forced herself to push aside her personal opinions. She would help Ry and his crew to win the race. They would return her home. Her growing feelings for Ry had no future.

CHAPTER ELEVEN

Relief filled Ry when they returned to their campsite after the ball. Although conditions were basic, it felt like home. He sensed the crew was pleased to return as well, out of the sight of Talor, his spies and the pre-race excitement.

"Any problems?" he asked Nanu.

"Apart from Luke being constantly underfoot, it was very quiet."

"No problems with Gabby?" Camryn asked.

Nanu shook his head. "I've been grooming her just like you showed me. She's eating well, but I think she missed you. I'm about to feed her. Are you coming?"

"Try and stop me." Camryn jogged from the tender and fell into step with Nanu.

"The responsibility was good for him," Jannike said. "Nanu looks better."

"I fancy fish for dinner," Kaya said. "Anyone feel like fishing?"

"I'm up for fishing," Jannike said. "Care to wager on who catches the biggest fish?"

"I will cook it," Mogens offered.

When the seer walked past, Ry stopped him with a raised hand. "Mogens, a word?" Today he was ebony, which alarmed Ry.

"I thought to walk along the lakeside to the berry patch. Will you walk with me?"

Ry accepted the bucket Mogens held out and followed the seer. For a time they walked in companionable silence. A white and scarlet bird cawed from the branches of a dead tree, and the shrieks of children playing in the village carried on the wind. They reached the berry patch, and Ry started picking the juicy orange berries, dropping them into his bucket.

"You wished to speak to me?" Mogens prompted.

"Since Camryn has joined us I haven't wanted or needed another woman." Ry glanced at his feet, feeling like a child confessing to his parent. "I haven't taken any medicine since we left the Indefatigable."

The look Mogens sent him dissected like a sharp knife. "No medicine at all?"

"No."

"And your sexual lust and cravings have gone?"

"For every woman except Camryn."

Mogens dropped a berry in his bucket and straightened with a frown. "Since Camryn's arrival the black tattoo blotches have come out on your back and chest."

Ry nodded. "And a black cat appeared on Camryn's back."

Mogens scratched his chin. His skin swirled from black to white and back again. "Anything else?"

"We can communicate telepathically."

Mogens shot him another piercing glance and rubbed his chin again. "Hmmm."

"What does it mean?" Ry snapped, starting to feel like one of Mogens' plant specimens.

"I'll need to consult the clouds, but I think you and Camryn have mated."

"Mated?" Ry shook his head. "Impossible."

"How do you know?" Mogens asked. "You don't know anything of your species. In all our traveling and searching we haven't found anyone like you."

"Apart from the slave we rescued."

"Yes, it was unfortunate we couldn't speak with her before she died. Still, I believe the two of you are mated."

"I can't have a mate," Ry said, shock reverberating through him.

"But you don't know for sure," Mogens pointed out with irrefutable logic.

"We can't be mates. I promised Camryn we'll take her back to Earth once the race is over."

"That might prove a problem if you're mated to her."

Grim-faced, Ry continued to pick berries until Mogens decided they'd harvested enough. They ambled back to camp in silence, Ry's mind circling like a spaceship orbiting a planet. Damnation, he'd promised her.

Mogens set the buckets of berries aside and prepared to consult the heavens while Ry decided to indulge his feline in a run. Maybe he could outrun his problems...

Four days later, steel gray and violet clouds skittered across the sky, cloaking the landscape with dowdiness. Although early in the day, it seemed like dusk. Mogens clucked under his breath and muttered a chant in a strange language of clicks and grunts.

Despite the strangeness, the vernacular had a lyrical quality.

Camryn stroked her hand over Gabby's glossy neck and laughed when the mare curled her top lip up in pleasure to display her sharp teeth. Without warning her head jerked upward, her ears swiveling forward. She turned her head to stare at the trees on the far side of the lake near the village.

"Someone is watching us train," Camryn said, her stomach contracting with foreboding.

"It's probably the village children," Nanu said, looking up from where he worked on creating a set of blinkers for Gabby to wear, made to Camryn's specifications.

"No, the children come here to watch and play with Luke. Where's Ry?" Camryn asked, but she knew where to find Ry. She just hated to admit every sense told her the man wandered through the bush on the lake edge.

"I don't know," Nanu said. "He was checking supplies on the ship."

"Never mind. I'll find him." Damn, how could she smell him? Imagination? Camryn turned to face the tender and inhaled. She smelled metal, a whiff of sweat and heard a soft curse. Jannike. The soft murmur of a feminine voice told her of Kaya's presence in the hull of the tender as well. When she inhaled again, she smelled cooking. Her eyes narrowed. Impossible. Unless...disbelief drew her up tall. How could she smell the cooking pots from the village? Camryn turned and drew in the air. Nanu, Gabby, Luke and the seer. She smelled all of them. Ry too. When she turned in the direction Gabby stared, she smelled gun oil, unwashed male bodies.

"Mogens. Nanu. Take Gabby and Luke to the tender. Now," she said, wishing they'd hurry instead of staring at her like one of the pouty fish that swam in the lake.

Mogens shimmered to deep black but instead of flickering back to gray, he remained the color of soot. He muttered, the guttural clicks making the hair on her arms and legs lift.

Nanu tugged on the collar with the bell they'd made for Luke, so it was easy to find him and the foal trotted after the engineer. Gabby gave an inquiring whicker and after hesitating, her ears flickering in the direction of the strangers, she followed Nanu and her foal.

Camryn strode toward the bush where she thought to find Ry.

Mogens grasped her arm when she passed, pulling her to a stop. "The ghost cries for you. He mourns."

Camryn wrenched her arm free. "I don't know what you're talking about."

"You do," Mogens said, his eyes rolling in the peculiar manner that told her he was in the middle of one of his weird turns. "He mourns. He cries."

"I need to find Ry."

"Ry is the problem," Mogens said, waving his hand in front of his chest. "You must move on."

"I am moving on," Camryn said sharply. "I'm going to find Ry."

"Something is wrong," Mogens intoned. "Wrong. Very, very wrong."

Urgency pounding through her veins, she ignored the chant Mogens started even though it scared her. Camryn ran through the trees, her gut telling her something bad was about to happen. They needed to leave. They needed to get to safety.

Now.

Something was wrong. Ry didn't know what or how he knew. One moment he enjoyed the play of muscles and the feel of the damp earth beneath his paws and the next sec dread filled him. He skidded to a rustling stop, sliding in the leaf litter to listen. Silence. No birds. No small rodents digging for food.

Ry wheeled around and hastened toward the tender, instinct telling him he needed to hurry.

"Ry!"

Camryn. Panic roared through him. He skidded to a halt, calling up his human form even before he stopped. Panting and out of breath, he almost ran into a tree. He twisted his body and collided with Camryn. They toppled to the ground.

Blood pooled in his groin when her scent washed over him, and he pressed an open-mouthed kiss to her neck. His tongue slid across the fleshy part of her neck and as always, he had the urge to bite. Camryn shuddered and gasped aloud.

"No," she said. "There's someone spying on us. I felt danger. I sent the others to the tender."

"What about Gabby and Luke?"

"Them too. They're waiting for us."

Ry rose in a smooth movement, offering Camryn a hand to help her to stand. He started through the bush at a jog with Camryn racing behind him.

"Aren't you going to tell me I'm imagining things?"

"Nope." His quick glance showed him Camryn ogled his butt despite her clear worry. He grinned, the desire to preen offset by his apprehension. "Mogens has scanned the clouds all week. He's black most of the time. I've only ever seen him like that once before, not long after I first met him. He saved me from an attack by a rival captain."

They burst from the trees. Camryn ran beside him, breathing hard but keeping up.

A gunshot rang out. Secs later pain lashed across his pectoral muscle and one shoulder. "Faster," he roared, forcing aside the throbbing threatening to send him to his knees.

"You're hurt," Camryn cried.

Another shot rang out. This one missed, hitting the ground and sending shards of stone flying.

"Zigzag," Ry ordered, pain threading his voice. "Run zigzags so they can't keep you in their sights."

A third shot fired. Ry's steps faltered. Agony washed through him, and when he glanced down, he saw a furrow through his trews. Hell and damnation.

Camryn slowed to slip her arm around his waist. "We're almost back at the tender. Keep going."

Hell, his leg stung. He didn't think they'd done much damage. Blood trickled down his leg with each step though.

The tender engines started when they neared. The ramp slid down and Jannike sprinted out to help. He wanted to shout at her to stay on board but knew he was putting Camryn in danger. They needed Jannike's help. When another shot sounded, someone in the tender returned fire.

Jannike and Camryn shouldered most of his weight as they struggled up the ramp into the tender. Ry collapsed onto the floor with a groan. Mogens rushed over with his satchel.

"Have we got everything on board?" Ry demanded. It was difficult getting the words out, tough focusing.

He felt the tender take off. "Who's flying?"

"Nanu is quite capable," Mogens said. "Besides, he has Jannike to help."

"Not if someone is firing on us. I must help. They probably have ships. They need me." Ry pushed up with his arms, collapsing when his injured leg refused to work. He cursed as the tender shot upward, the flight path not as level as usual. Ry heard the whine of another shot. An explosion. The tender lurched, sending Camryn off-balance. Ry yanked from Mogens' touch, attempting to grab her before she hurt herself. The abrupt movement jarred his leg, a sharp shard of pain making him curse. At least he caught Camryn and slipped her against his side, her presence calming him.

"Let me look." Mogens made a tsking sound. "The chest wound doesn't look bad." Using a knife, he cut Ry's trews from his leg. "Hold still." He grabbed a wad of absorbent cloth, wiped away the worst of the blood. "The shot is still in your leg. It's deep." He found a pair of pullers, designed to extract splinters or shot, before looking him directly in the eye. "You'll have to shift."

Ry glanced at Camryn. "It will upset Gabby. We can't have her panicking mid-flight."

"As you will." Mogens probed the wound.

Ry hissed and squeezed Camryn's hand tight. "A pox on it."

"Won't take long." He probed again and yanked out blood-covered lead ball. "It's out."

The tender bucked, tilting in a precarious manner. Ry slid across the floor and Camryn slithered with him. A gun fired.

"What's happening?" Mogens shouted so the others could hear.

"They're firing on us. Everyone strap in. Aim," Jannike hollered to Kaya. "Fire!"

The two women worked together while Nanu did a good job of piloting in combat conditions.

"I need to get to the bridge." Ry dragged himself through the tender.

Mogens and Camryn followed. "Ry, I need to bandage your leg now. You can't afford to lose more blood."

"Dammit, there's another tender bearing down on us," Jannike snapped.

"What about Gabby and Luke?" Ry asked.

"We've strapped them in, so they won't hurt themselves and padded the stalls just like Camryn told us," Nanu shouted over his shoulder. "Dammit, Ry. Hurry up. I'm not a pilot. I'm an engineer."

"Fire!" Jannike shouted.

Their tender shuddered when Nanu evaded.

"Shot!" Kaya roared, pumping her fist in the air with jubilation. "It's crashing."

Camryn peered out the porthole and saw the plume of smoke and the fireball when it crashed in the middle of thick bush.

"The other tender is breaking off. They're leaving."

"Great job," Ry said.

"Where should we head to?" Nanu asked, breaking the tension on the bridge.

"We need to find somewhere else to train," Camryn said. "I don't want to upset Gabby and Luke by moving them into the racing stables. She starts to nip when she gets anxious."

"We can do without that," Ry said. "Hell, this leg hurts."

"Why does a little nip matter to you? You can just turn into a kitty-cat and heal your wounds," Camryn said.

"Meow," Jannike said after the silence stretched.

"Braver than me," Nanu muttered.

"Stop whispering about me," Camryn snapped.

"You heard?" Ry demanded.

"Why wouldn't I?"

"Mogens, can you tell me what they were talking about?" Ry asked.

The seer shook his head.

"Oh come on. You must have heard them." Camryn stalked closer to Ry and poked in him the middle of his chest with her finger. "This is some sort of game. Make fun of the poor Earthling, right." Poke. Poke. Poke.

"Why doesn't she just pull his tail?" Jannike asked.

"Because he conveniently doesn't have one at the moment," Camryn snapped.

Ry and Mogens exchanged glances.

"What? What?" Camryn dropped her hands to her sides and glared at Ry, her hands curling to tight fists. "What secret alien stuff are you talking about now?"

"How is your sense of smell?" Mogens asked, his black head tipping to the side like an inquisitive bird.

"There's nothing wrong with my sense of smell. I can tell Luke has been rolling on his food again or burying it and digging it back up. He really needs a bath."

"Huh, I'm not going to bathe him again." Kaya jumped into the conversation, with a rueful glance at her forearm. The white scar tissue glowed against the tan of her skin.

"I told you not to force him. You can lead a horse to water and that's all," Jannike said.

Camryn rolled her eyes and turned to Ry. He had a peculiar expression on his face.

"Perhaps we'll talk about it later," he said with a glance at his crew.

"Oh no. You're not putting this off. No more secrets. If there's any alien mumbo-jumbo going on I want to know."

"She has a right to know." Mogens padded the wound and wrapped a pale gray bandage around Ry's leg. His skin swirled gray for an instant before turning back to solid black.

"Aha! Alien crap again," Camryn said in triumph.

Ry's jaw worked. His eyes flashed and the bottom seemed to fall from Camryn's stomach. His anger alarmed her, but not enough to let him brush off her questions.

"I told him he shouldn't have touched you," Mogens said.

The rest of the crew tried to look busy. They didn't speak to each other, but it didn't matter. Their expressions spoke volumes.

"What do you mean?" Camryn fought to keep calm. They wouldn't drag her sex life into the conversation.

"Your vision is good, your hearing is extraordinary, and you can communicate telepathically with Ry," Mogens said.

"Wow!" Kaya blurted. "You guys have private conversations?"

Camryn slashed a glare in her direction. "You'd better believe it."

Kaya paled at her aggressive tone and subsided as if Camryn had slapped her. "Sorry," she muttered. "I didn't mean to butt into private stuff."

"And Camryn has a tattoo on her back," Jannike said. "I saw it when you were swimming in the lake."

"Ry doesn't need his medicine anymore," Mogens said.

The entire crew turned to stare at Camryn.

"Don't you have to watch the road or something?" she asked Nanu, pointing at the sky outside the porthole with a wave of her hand.

"Nope, traffic's clear. I have time to listen."

Kaya giggled, and the crew's gazes ping-ponged from her to Ry and back again.

"Don't treat me like a specimen," Camryn snapped. "Spit it out. What the hell are you talking about?"

"You and Ry have mated," Mogens said. "That's what we're trying to say."

Chapter Twelve

"Rubbish," Camryn said.

Ry's gut churned. At least she hadn't run screaming from the bridge, but she hadn't exactly jumped up and down with excitement. Apart from clear irritation, Ry couldn't fathom her thoughts. Mogens had taught her to block well.

"The tender will alert me if we're going to crash into another object," Nanu said.

"Collision in ten secs," Kaya droned in a metallic nonhuman voice.

Nanu spun back to the controls so fast he almost got whiplash. "There's nothing on the radarscope. What's wrong with this stupid ship?"

"This is a trial to test your speed," Kaya said in the same robotic voice.

"Dammit, that wasn't funny," Nanu said.

"Yes it was," Kaya droned.

Although glad his crew was in high spirits, Ry studied Camryn with concern. Her senses, her new abilities. The mysterious tattoo. He'd done something to her when he'd bitten her on the neck. It was the only explanation.

"Since everything is under control here, I'm going to check on Gabby and Luke," Camryn said.

"You'd better hurry," Nanu snapped out, his gaze on the radarscope. "I thought we'd lost them, but we've got company again."

"Want me to take over?" Ry asked.

"No, I can do this." Confidence radiated in his voice.

"Strap in up here, Camryn. I don't want you injured."

She didn't say a word, but simply dropped into the empty seat beside the seer and clicked the harness into place.

Ry peered over Nanu's shoulder at the scope. "It's a cruiser."

"That's what I thought," Jannike said, frowning out the port at the distance ship.

"What are they doing near a convict planet? It's not a place for tourists. They're more likely to get their throats slit than find souvenirs to take home."

"Maybe they're lost," Kaya said.

No, they weren't lost. Ry narrowed his eyes and gauged his inner instincts. Not a thing sprang out to disturb him. "Maintain course," he said, and flicked several buttons on the console. "May we offer assistance?"

Ry waited but there was no reply.

"Strange. No life forms registering on board," Jannike said.

Kaya cocked her head. "Can we salvage?"

"Not without the Indy." Ry's gut started prickling.

What is it? Camryn's alarm sliced through his head.

I'm not sure. Do you feel anything strange about that ship?

You're asking me?

197

Yeah. He trusted Camryn. They hadn't known each other long yet he'd trust her with his life.

"I say detour," Kaya said.

"But what if there are life forms on board?" Mogens asked.

Nanu spoke up. "Captain, I'm picking up another tender. The ship masked its presence. In full sight now."

"They're leaving," Jannike said.

"Veer off," Ry said. "Now."

Without warning, the cruiser exploded in fiery fireball, searing his eyes.

"Fire ship." Jannike hissed in distaste.

Their tender bucked before Nanu steadied their trajectory and guided the vessel from danger in time to avoid the backlash from a second explosion.

"Hailing." The mocking sound of his brother's voice floated through their communications system.

"Talor, what do you want?"

"You have more lives than a damn cat," his brother snarled.

Doesn't he know? Camryn sent the thought to him along with a mocking grin.

Ry couldn't help a return grin despite another example of his brother's determination.

"Flight path direct to the city," Ry said to Nanu.

"What if they come after us?" Mogens flashed an unhappy gray before whitening.

"I don't think Talor wants to kill me yet," Ry said with a calm shrug. "He wants to taunt us."

Camryn peered at the instruments. "Is the tender following?"

"Doesn't look like it," Jannike said.

"The sooner this race is over and I can go home the better," Camryn said with real feeling. "I wish you'd never heard of my brother." After a final look at him, she muttered under her breath and stomped down to the freight deck.

"When are you going to tell her?" Mogens asked.

"Tell her what?" Kaya asked.

"Nothing." Ry attempted to glare the seer into submission. Mogens shook his head, the stubborn clench of his jaw telling Ry the seer had much more to say. Ry wasn't gonna tell Camryn a thing. Although he liked his new ability to control his body, the constant craving for Camryn felt worse because he knew there was no future for them. No way did Ry want to confess he couldn't live without her.

Heats, Race Day, Ornum.

"The crowd isn't going to like our style of racing," Ry warned.

Camryn chuckled to hide her nerves and the fear galloping through her gut. "There's nothing against it in the rules. I've read them from page one through to the end. You've all read and interpreted the rules the same way I did. The winner is the first hell-horse past the finishing post."

"Yeah, well. It might work once, but it won't for the second race."

"So I'll think up another plan. When we make the final race, we'll have an edge no one else has."

They led Gabby into the stalls, keeping her away from the other hell-horses. Luke followed between Mogens and Jannike. He dawdled, wanting to sniff and check out everything. Kaya had to walk behind to prod him. Nanu carried a bag of special treats for Gabby.

Gabby's calm manner and the way she handled the frenzied yelps and grunts of the other hell-horses pleased Camryn. If they could keep her relaxed and Luke out of trouble, they'd make it through to the finals.

"The variables we can't control worry me." Camryn wished like hell they didn't have to put Gabby through this carnage.

The noise from the arena beat at her head like thundering hooves, even out in the stable area. One variable they hadn't thought about.

"How is Gabby going to hear us or know where the finish line is?" Jannike asked.

"Camryn has a plan for that," Ry said.

"I'm hoping that for once Ry's scent will help. She's come to recognize it and especially if Luke's scent is coming from the same direction." Camryn crossed her fingers.

"Handlers, suit up in protective gear and prepare to lead your hell-horse to the starter gates," a voice droned.

"Our cue to get to the finish line." Ry hesitated. "I'll lead out Gabby."

"No, I'll be fine."

Ry scowled before kissing her once, hard and fast. "Take care." He strode away with Jannike.

Still tingling from the kiss—nerves, she told herself—Camryn pulled the protective garment over her head and clipped on Gabby's lead. The number ten was painted in bold white paint on Gabby's flanks. "This is it, girl. Everything we've trained for. I need you to run like the wind straight to Luke." She ran her hand over Gabby's glossy coat, no longer worried the mare would injure her. Despite her odd looks and dangerous nature, Camryn had come to love both Gabby and Luke. They all had. Hopefully they'd beat Talor's beast in this race, rubbing his aristocratic nose in the Ornum dust. And she could go home soon.

Camryn led Gabby out to the roars of the crowd. Several other hell-horses were loaded in the starting gate already, the stench enough to make Camryn breathe through her mouth. Gabby walked into the starter's gate without hesitation. The other hell-horses loaded, snapping and snarling even though they couldn't see each other. Gabby quivered, her ears pricked. The starter's flag went up. Tension thrummed through the arena. Then the gates burst open with a metallic screech. Gabby bounded out and galloped toward the finish line, leaving the other horses squabbling behind her.

"Gabriel shoots from the starter's gate," the commentator shouted. "Dante, Jase's Luck, Bob and Bloody Hell converge in a herd. They're attacking one another."

The crowd roared and Gabby kept running. "Go, Gabby," Camryn cried, sprinting to the finish post via the handler's walkway.

"Max's Dream is down. Dante is attacking. Look at the blood," the commentator roared. "Paul's Gold and Demon Lad are attacking Dante, fighting for the spoils."

Camryn blanked out the commentary, concentrating instead on pushing through the crowds thronging the rails to watch the race. She arrived at the finish post and Ry's side just in time to see Gabby shoot over the line. The mare ran straight for Camryn and Luke. With an anxious whinny, she sniffed her foal before she deigned to accept a treat.

Mogens stood with Luke while Camryn affixed a halter to Gabby. Camryn frowned at the blood on the mare's right shoulder. "We should get them to the stables before the other horses finish. She must have cut herself leaving the starting gate."

"Good idea," Mogens said, giving the slight cut on Gabby's shoulder a cursory glance. "I don't think it's bad, but the blood will only invite attack. We need to get to safety."

Camryn saw Ry hovering by the gates, gesturing for them to hurry. The thunder of hooves behind them hurried her along.

They jogged away from the finish line. A shower of bottles and food rained down on them, the crowd booing and hissing because they'd wanted to see bloodshed.

"I've never seen a race like it before," the announcer said.

"Cheat. Cheat. Cheat." The chant went up around the arena.

"We have the judge's decision," the announcer said. "The winner of this heat is Gabriel. All relevant rules were adhered to."

"Cheat. Cheat." A rotten vegetable splattered the ground in front of Luke. He started, his yelp of fear drawing Gabby's protective instincts. The mare trumpeted a warning, baring her teeth at the nearest bystanders. The men shrunk back with shouts of fear, scuttling over each other in their panic despite the protective barrier.

"Quick." Ry raced from behind the gate and hurried over to Luke, soothing him. "We need to get them inside."

With a steady voice, Camryn urged Gabby to move faster. An angry yip made her pulse race and not in a good way. She glanced over her shoulder and saw a huge solid mass of black bearing down on them. Gabby pushed in front and shrieked, barring her teeth.

Ry opened the pen gate and shoved Luke instead. Mogens darted inside to open the stall and encouraged Luke to enter. He whinnied anxiously at his mother.

Gabby attacked, raked her teeth across the flanks of the first horse and spun away before he could attack again. He leaped at Camryn but overran, missing her by inches. She wrinkled her nose at the stink of rotten meat and the distinctive reek of hell-horse.

"God, Camryn," Ry muttered. He swept her up and lifted her into the safety of the pen then grabbed for Gabby's halter. Luckily for him, Luke let out an anxious yap and attracted his mother's attention. She darted into the special reinforced pen, and Ry slammed the gate shut, barely managing to fasten it before the other hell-horse charged.

"Quick," Mogens grunted. "Give her a treat."

Outside the reinforced pen, they heard the hell-horse kicking and yelping in fury at missing his prey.

"I'm glad we're in here," Camryn said, "But how are we going to get out?"

"I'm sure the hell-horse will become distracted by the others finishing the race." Mogens didn't seem worried.

Camryn glanced at Ry. "We've qualified for the final."

"So has Talor's horse since he crossed second."

With a cautious glance at Gabby, Ry circled the hell-horse as much as the confines of the crowded stall allowed. He slipped an arm around Camryn's waist, staring at her with a clear challenge. Camryn thought of Gabriel and sighed. Why did this have to be so difficult?

Outside the stall, they heard the shout of male voices, the furious yelp of a hell-horse. Then silence fell.

Time to move.

Warmth seared her side where she touched Ry. Comfortable, she didn't want to move but knew it was time. One final race and she'd return home, move on and learn to live without Gabriel. Somehow.

"We should leave," Ry said. "I thought we'd get Gabby and Luke bedded down for the night and go out for dinner and a few drinks."

"What about a guard for Gabby?"

"I'll stay behind." Gray swirled across Mogens skin before blending into the black and fading away. "I have much to think on tonight."

"Are you sure?" Camryn asked. "You watched over Gabby and Luke last night."

"The ghost is here," he said in a low whisper, pointing behind them. "Look."

Ry stiffened, not enough for anyone else to see but Camryn felt his unease. The same disquiet flickered through her, and she had to force herself not to glance behind them.

Jannike snorted. "I can't see anything." She opened the stall door and stalked into the pen. "They're getting ready for the next heat. We should leave now."

"We should watch the other races to form a strategy," Camryn said without enthusiasm. It was a smart, clever thing to do—go into a race with knowledge of the other horses' abilities and strengths.

At her side, Ry nodded. "Camryn's right. We'll help you load Gabby and Luke into the tender and meet you at the King's Head later tonight."

Ten mins later the tender took off and Camryn walked at Ry's side. They slipped into the owners' section of the arena. The other owners fell silent despite the parade of hell-horses to the starting gates for the next heat. Camryn saw disgust, envy and open curiosity on the men's faces. All of them bore the stamp of determination. They wanted to win this race—the same way Ry wanted to win. They wanted marriage to the governor's daughter and the dowry that came with her.

Ry slipped into an empty seat, and Camryn took the one beside him. A hell-horse reared, refusing to enter the gate and a convict prodded it with a long, sharp stick. With a pained yelp, it sprang into the gate. The convict slammed the exit shut to prevent the hell-horse from backing out. Camryn worried while she watched. They'd gone through the heat almost unscathed, but the other owners wouldn't let Gabby win the final race so easily.

"Any ideas," Ry asked in a low voice.

"None I care to discuss here."

Silence fell between them while they waited for the start of the fifth heat. The starting gate clattered open, and the hell-horses sprang out.

"And they're off," the commentator roared.

The crowd burst into cheers and roared encouragement to their favorites. Some of the owners had managed to purchase previous winners and these animals knew the process. The inexperienced hell-horses floundered, unused to the brutality and the excited roar of the crowd. A hell-horse stumbled. Camryn reached for Ry's hand.

Feeling the weight of a stare, Camryn glanced to her left. Ry's brother gawked at her, hatred blazing. When he saw he'd snared her attention, he winked. Camryn turned away, a sense of dirtiness creeping over her skin like a rash. Talor Coppersmith was a handsome man. Although not as tall or muscular as Ry, he bore classic good looks, highlighted by his striking long silver hair, and charm. According to Kaya, he had money and prestige. A good catch yet she wasn't interested in anything he had to offer. He gave her the creeps. His brother on the other hand...if it weren't for Gabriel...

Maybe we should pattern our race on the Earth model. It's still first past the post takes the prize in the final race, right?

As long as they don't change the rules, Ry broadcast his thoughts to her without taking his gaze off the carnage down on the track.

Can they change the rules?

I don't know. They might try since the crowd wasn't happy with the way we won.

Camryn turned to glare at Ry, putting all her anger into her thoughts. I don't care how much you want to win this race. I will not have Gabby put at risk.

Ry's gaze flickered to his brother and away. "I want to win this race."

"And what do you intend to do with a wife?" Camryn snapped. "No one has mentioned her. Are you going to set up home and live happily ever after?" Her stomach tightened to a tense knot.

Jealousy.

She heard it simmering in her voice and her thoughts jarred to a halt. No, it couldn't be. She wasn't jealous. It was sex. Good sex and nothing else.

"People are staring," Ry said, his voice neutral.

Irritated, Camryn focused on the track. It started raining with dusk approaching. Around them owners ignored the downpour to shout on their hell-horses. Some groaned. A pale green alien spat out a salty curse before storming off. A serious business. These men wanted to win and not one of them cared what the woman looked like. They wanted her dowry and the prestige that came with the win.

She shouldn't worry. Soon she'd be back home. Her life would go on, and she'd forget about Ry, forget about hell-horses and forget about everything else. She didn't care what he did with the woman. A fine sheen of sweat sprang out on her forehead. Her right hand trembled. Camryn hid it beneath her jacket and admitted to herself she was a big, fat liar. She cared. Big-time.

Without seeing, she gazed at the track and the race wound to a conclusion. Four hell-horses finished, the last staggering and on the verge of collapse. Blood dripped down its side. Sensing weakness, the hell-horses turned to attack. Camryn couldn't bear to watch and hid her face against Ry's chest. Treating animals like this was obscene.

Ry disliked Camryn's silence after their departure. Ever since her outburst about the governor's daughter in the race arena they'd spoken in single syllables. His gut churned. He wanted to crush his lips against hers, pin her in place and thrust into her until they both exploded with pleasure. Then he wanted to do it all over again but slowly this time, building Camryn's passion until her eyes fogged with hunger and she sobbed out his name. His name. He wanted to push into her dew-slicked flesh and ride the waves of pleasure with her throughout the long night and every night.

His name.

His woman.

He wasn't going to take her back to Earth. He couldn't since living without her wasn't an option.

A mess, but he'd taken heart from the jealousy he'd heard in her voice when she'd spoken of the governor's daughter. Camryn still thought of her husband. She'd named their hell-horse after him, for grata's sake. A scowl twisted his lips. Bloody difficult to compete with a dead man. A saint. He shot a glance in her direction and found her watching him. He smiled, knowing she was as torn as he was.

"Hungry?"

"Yes."

But not for him. Obvious when he plucked a hazy picture of Gabriel from her mind. An older man, a ghost, and impossible to fight.

Pissed, Ry scanned the street they walked instead of demanding she give him a chance. Lamps lit the way, allowing them to pick their way past refuse and dodge the puddles of water left from the unexpected squall that had hit the city during the early evening. At least the rain had tamped down some of the stench clinging to the buildings and streets. A couple of prostitutes stood in a doorway, their tight red dresses displaying ample breasts while their bragging and winks encouraged the men passing by to enter and pay for unprecedented pleasure.

The three men in front of them walked into the Tasty Tart Tavern, the tinny sounds of a battered pianoforte carrying outside when the door opened.

They continued, heading for the King's Head Tavern. The lights from the King's Head shone like a welcoming beacon. Part of Ry welcomed the noise and gaiety they'd find inside while the other part of him wanted to spend precious time with Camryn. There had to be a way to persuade her to stay with him. Besides, if Mogens was correct, it was too late. According to Mogens, they'd mated.

Fear gripped him at the thought of her leaving. His hands clenched and he wished he knew something about his background, his real parents. All he knew were the bits his adopted mother had told him—of how she'd gone for a walk, trying to outrun black depression after the death of her baby boy. She'd seen the ship, the blaze of flames when it flew overhead, the explosive crash not long after it landed. Katia Coppersmith had refused to give him up, saying he'd arrived at her doorstep for a reason, and she intended to keep him. She'd named him Ryman after her father and treated him like a son.

He'd been too young to recall the rejoicing when Katia Coppersmith had fallen pregnant again and delivered a healthy son and heir for the House of the Cat. All he remembered was the way she'd treated him—like a member of the family. She'd been firm with discipline and generous with praise and love for all her children. After her husband had died, she'd held everyone together while Talor had taken over at age sixteen cycles. Not long after, Ry's life had changed radically. Labeled a murderer, Talor had literally handed him to the law. His escape from incarceration had been pure luck, and revenge had set him on the road to thievery.

They reached the King's Head. Ry stood aside to open the door for Camryn, wishing things were different and Camryn wasn't part of his plan for revenge.

Too damn late. And in truth, he wouldn't change the way he'd done things.

The crew spotted them and waved to attract their attention. Ry escorted Camryn over to their corner table before signaling a barmaid to take their order. Part of him was glad Mogens had chosen to stay at camp to watch over Gabby and Luke because he couldn't take another night of suspicious looks and swirls of gray within solid black. He wished the happy white Mogens would return instead of the gloomy seer who saw ghosts and spouted of dire things to come each time he read the clouds and weather patterns.

The drinks arrived, and Ry shunted them around the table. He took a sip, savoring the taste of hops and stronger flavor of flyss, an additive used to give the mild ale a kick. He glanced at Camryn, saw her blink at her first swallow from the tankard and drink some more. For a brief instant he considered warning her about the strength of the drink. No, it didn't matter. He'd watch over her. A few drinks wouldn't hurt.

In the predominantly male tavern, the women attracted attention. Both Jannike and Kaya ignored it, Camryn appeared discomforted. Ry slid closer and slung an arm around her shoulders to signal ownership. His move didn't go unnoticed. Camryn didn't object. She didn't cuddle closer either. Ry's feline pushed at his skin, a snarl sounding inside his head. Camryn jerked in surprise, her gaze flying to his, eyes widening.

What? he asked, pretending innocence while shock rippled through him. She'd heard his feline's displeasure. Ry concentrated on Camryn, his heart thundering while need poured through him. Muscles tensed and energy coiled low in his belly. His cock pulsed and thickened, and all he could think about was getting her alone and naked. Nothing else mattered, not his brother, his blotted reputation or the desire for revenge. Camryn was the one.

"Buy ya a drink, love," a man shouted over the din.

Ry glanced up to see his crew watching them both. Not good, both from a security standpoint and the gossip they'd take back to Mogens. Damn, he needed an excuse to get her alone. He needed to make her understand they were a team. A unit. They really were mates, just as Mogens had said.

"A drink?" the man hollered again. A dark beard covered most of his lower face, and he'd pulled his long black hair into a greasy queue. He shook Jannike's shoulder, smiling to reveal missing front teeth.

"No." Jannike shrugged off the beefy hand and slid closer to Kaya. "I'm with her." Jannike ignored Kaya's curse to plant a sloppy kiss on her cheek.

The man cast a considering glance at Kaya, grinning again. "No problem. I'll entertain you both. Have you fixed in no time."

Kaya jumped to her feet. "I don't need fixing."

"Aw no," Nanu said with dismay, showing some of his old self. "Don't start a fight. I'm comfortable here. I've ordered food. Please don't start a fight."

Kaya punched the man's gut when he sidled close enough to pinch her butt. Off balance, he knocked a pitcher of ale over several of the occupants at the next table. Cursing they sprang to their feet. Tables crashed to the ground. A man cussed. He bumped into a barmaid, and she dropped her tray of drinks.

"Hell." Ry stood and glanced at Camryn. "If anyone touches you hit them."

"But—"

"Hit first and save the questions for later. Crew, let's move it. Meet up at the Nag's Head if we get separated."

Ry grasped Camryn's hand and grinned. "Let's go." He circled the worst of the fighting and used his bulk to plow through the combatants. Camryn used her elbows like weapons, beating off anyone who tried to touch or grab. They emerged from the tavern with Camryn laughing.

"I knew having to stand up for myself with all those jockeys would come in handy. You can't play by the book during a fight."

The book. Hell, he hadn't thought of it for ages and maybe he should have. Maybe it held answers, but he'd have to return to the Indy to check.

Camryn paused on the corner and waited for a sedan chair to pass. "What book?"

Nanu rushed out of a side door and Kaya and Jannike followed on his heels. A crash sounded. "Cease fighting," the landlord hollered. "I'm calling the watch."

"Just got out in time," Kaya said with satisfaction, jerking her head in the direction of the approaching marines.

"Keep your fists to yourself next time." Nanu's angry gaze slid to Jannike then Kaya. "I'm hungry. I wanted to eat my meal before I left."

"Pooh, males have no sense of fun," Kaya said.

"They're governed by their stomachs," Jannike said.

"Or their libidos," Camryn added with a sly look at Ry.

Ry snorted. "I haven't heard you complain about my libido before." His crew turned to watch in fascination, their heads swiveling back and forth in intense interest.

Behave, Ry thought sternly.

Or else?

Or else I'll put you over my knee and paddle your backside.

Promises, promises. Camryn stuck her nose in the air and sashayed down the street to the Nag's Head, her backside swaying in a seductive manner. A stumble spoiled her perfect exit.

The imperfection brought a crooked grin. Hot damn, his mate was something. But together they could be better, if only Camryn would listen. The book, he decided. He'd return to the Indy and take Camryn. They had a couple of easy days. The crew could cope without them, and it would be an ideal opportunity to spend time alone with Camryn. Mogens might object, but Ry refused to listen to the seer.

"Camryn and I are going back to camp," he said.

"All right." Jannike's lips quivered, as if she wanted to laugh.

"I need to return to the Indy to collect something," he said. "You're in charge while I'm gone. Protect Gabby and Luke and look after Mogens."

Jannike snorted. "He's seeing more ghosts than usual."

"He hasn't been himself since Camryn arrived."

"I'll watch him. How long will you be gone?"

"Two nights. Thanks. I owe you." With a nod, he hurried to catch up to Camryn. Now all he needed to do was persuade her to go off with him.

"Camryn, you ready to go back to camp?"

"I don't wanna go," she said with an enticing pout.

"You don't always get what you want." Wasn't that a fact? He hadn't gone looking for a mate. It had happened anyway. He frowned before deciding on a different tack. "I need your help."

"What help?" Her words slurred a little and she hiccupped.

"When my brother set me up to look like a thief, I evaded capture, broke into Talor's estate, the House of the Cat, and removed several items. I think some of those things might hold answers to the things happening between us." It was worth a shot and gave them a good excuse to spend time alone. "I need to collect them off the Indy."

"You don't need me to travel to the Indy."

Clever girl, but not exactly the truth. They hadn't been apart before. Ry suspected a separation might present a problem. Damn, how did he get her to change her mind? "If you don't want to come with me that's fine," he said, attempting casual.

Jannike stepped up beside him. "You coming with us, Camryn?"

"Yes."

Ry willed himself not to react even though his feline roared with displeasure. "I'll see you in two days." He walked away. He caught Jannike's soft murmur when she queried Camryn's decision. Camryn's reply came instantly. She didn't want to go with him.

Pain weighed down his chest. Hard to breathe. His stomach clenched, and he had to force himself to keep walking. Disbelief flitted through him. How could she let him walk away? How could she not feel the same? Ry fought his need to grab Camryn and depart with her over his shoulder, but pride bade she come to him of her own volition. He kept walking. The streetlamps gave way to darkness, his excellent vision canceling out the handicap. He continued to their camp, his mind on what to do with his mate. Hell, Mogens had mentioned it so many times he'd started to believe. Camryn felt like his mate.

Uneasiness assailed him without warning. He paused, trying to decide what had alerted him to danger. Two men stepped from the shadows, their dark clothes blending to conceal. An echo of footsteps told him at least one person followed behind him. Ry grunted, his hands clenching to fists. He was in the mood to hit someone or something. Bring it on.

CHAPTER THIRTEEN

Camryn slouched on the wooden bench, wishing she'd gone with Ry instead of staying with the others. But he'd annoyed her with his assumption she'd run after him like a pet lamb. She clenched her tankard of ale, took a minute sip and set it down again. She'd drunk too much already. For a change, she didn't want more.

A sense of foreboding hit her without warning. Her spine hit the wall behind her, and she gasped, jumping to her feet.

"What is it?" Jannike demanded.

"Ry's in trouble. We have to help him."

"Are you sure?" Kaya asked with disinterest.

Jannike stood. "Let's go."

"Aw damn," Nanu said with a longing look toward the kitchen. "I'm not going to get my dinner here either." With another sigh and a scowl at the kitchen, he followed.

Camryn burst through the door onto the street with Jannike hard on her heels.

Jannike grasped her arm to halt her panicked headlong sprint. "Wait. What is it?"

"Ry. Trouble." Camryn struggled to free herself.

"How do you know?"

"I...I don't know. I just do." Camryn saw Jannike's frown despite the poor lighting. A spaceship flew overhead, a jet of flame spurting from the rear of the craft. A rumble of thunder resounded in the distance, the heaviness and humidity promising more tropical showers to come.

"I hope you're going to feed me back at camp," Nanu said. "I'm going to fade away."

"This is stupid," Kaya said. "She doesn't know anything. Let's go back inside and eat our dinner."

"She has a name," Camryn snapped, lifting her head to inhale. Ry. Without questioning her instincts, she started to run. It wasn't the same way they'd walked to the tavern, but her gut told her Ry had walked this road.

"Wait, dammit," Jannike called.

Camryn heard the thud of boots when Jannike raced after her. She never slowed and splashed through puddles, heedless of the wet, cold water. Ry. His name echoed through her mind, desperation to get to him reverberating through her. She kept running, Jannike and the others following.

A battlelike cry up ahead made her put on a spurt of speed. Damn, she'd known he was in trouble. Four men on one. They were just about to even the odds.

Stay back, Camryn.

And miss all the fun?

You distract me.

One of the attackers planted a solid fist in his middle. Camryn heard the air hiss from Ry, his pained groan. With a battle cry, she launched herself at his attacker. Jannike, Kaya and Nanu arrived and waded into the fight. A curse sounded. The crunch of fist hitting bone. One attacker fled while the other three continued with dogged determination.

Camryn seized a man's shirt. He tried to throw her off to attack Ry again. Laughing, she clung. Let him try to throw her off. Better animals than he had tried.

Get ready to jump. Ry's thoughts shot through her head, and she tensed, waiting for his signal.

Now.

Camryn let go and pushed herself away from the man. She landed hard in the middle of a pile of smelly bovine dung. Ry clipped his jaw, and the man went airborne. He hit the mud and didn't move. The remaining two took off, leaving their friend to his fate. Jannike crouched beside him to go through his pockets.

"Are you okay?" Ry hauled her into his arms, his hands running over her body to check for injury. Heat suffused Camryn, her sexual response instantaneous. She shivered and let out a soft moan. "Where does it hurt?"

"Stop touching me," Camryn hissed. "I'm not hurt. I...I..." She groaned again, the sensation of his hands brushing across her nipples shooting desire straight to her core. All Camryn could think was how much better it would feel if there were no clothes between them and if his mouth drew on her nipple.

"No identification. Nothing to say who sent him. Are we done here?" Jannike asked.

"I'm hungry," Nanu said in a plaintive voice. "I need food."

Jannike's brows rose when she saw where Ry's hand rested. "Do you need us anymore?"

"No, we're good." He glanced at her. "I take it you're coming with me?"

Camryn swallowed, fought a brief inner battle and finally nodded. "Yes." She had to accept it. There was something wrong

216

with the way she craved sex with Ry all the time. Her skin burned and she throbbed with desire. And her heightened senses. It wasn't right. Heck, it scared her because she was starting to behave like him.

"We'll go back to the pub," Jannike said.

Nanu nodded enthusiastically. "Maybe I'll get to eat my dinner this time."

They left to head back into the center of town, leaving Camryn with Ry.

"How do we know there aren't more people lying in wait for us?"

Ry wiped a spot of blood from the corner of his mouth. "We don't, but I don't sense anything. Do you?"

Camryn lifted her head and opened her senses. She couldn't feel anyone lurking in the shadows or hear the elevated breathing of an assassin hiding in the shadows. "No."

Ry chuckled, the rough edge sending another wave of arousal through her sensitized body.

"Kiss me," she whispered, standing on tiptoe with her lips pursed.

"No, not now."

"Why not?" Camryn could feel the tension in him.

"Because if I kiss you I'll need more, and I don't want to take you in the middle of this dirty street. I want privacy for what I have in mind. Besides, you need to sanitize."

"No argument about that." Camryn shivered and nodded, her head feeling strangely heavy. Every inch of her body tingled and craved him, the strange tattoo on her shoulder feeling scorching hot. She shrugged, part of her uneasy but the rest excited and eager. The hot expression in his green eyes increased her tension, and without another word, Ry took her hand, setting a fast pace and practically dragging her down the rutted street. He snarled at a beggar who approached them and ignored a pair of prostitutes offering sensual delights.

"We'll do a foursome, love," one shouted after them. "Discount prices for a handsome gent like you."

"They all want you," Camryn said. "Even Jannike and Kaya look at you, but you never look back."

Ry stopped walking and frowned at her. "I'm not a saint. I used to take any handy woman who wanted me." He swallowed, his eyes glowing when he looked down at her. "I had to—it was a compulsion inside and the medicine Mogens gave me only helped between spaceports. Since you've arrived I haven't been with anyone except you. I haven't wanted anyone else."

"Is that good?"

"I don't know." Ry's powerful shoulders moved in a helpless shrug, and he started walking again. They skirted a group of men standing outside a crowded tavern and another group of men standing in a tight circle. They cheered and shouted, offering encouragement to something Camryn couldn't see.

"What are they doing?"

"Bird fight. The birds fight to the death and the men bet on them."

Camryn hurried past, glad Ry was at her side. Many of the men staggered, drunk on the local ale, and she witnessed three fights during their hurried trek down the center of the street. She shot a glance at Ry and found him scowling. It wasn't difficult to pick up the tension. A different tension from before, but Camryn didn't understand. They'd talked about sex and women...

Shit, what would happen when she left to go home?

She shot him another uneasy look while her mind grappled with the problem. If they won the race, Ry would have a wife and money. He wouldn't need her. So why did she hate that idea?

They walked in silence. Camryn noticed they were both scanning the street for signs of danger until they reached their campsite.

"Anything wrong?" Mogens called from his seat beside the small campfire.

"Something's come up," Ry said. "Camryn and I are making a quick trip to the Indy. We'll be back before the final race."

Camryn smiled at Mogens. "Can you make sure Gabby gets plenty of exercise? We need to keep up her fitness levels for the race."

Mogens' mouth firmed to a slash of disapproval. "Do you want me to ride Gabby?"

"If she'll let you," Camryn said.

"We were ambushed on the road tonight. Jannike will tell you about it when they get back to camp. Take extra care with security."

Mogens dipped his head in acknowledgment. "Someone tried to steal Gabby. I scared them off and will continue to keep watch. I can't sleep anyway," he said. "The restless ghosts whisper."

"Will you be all right here alone?" Camryn asked with a quick glance at Ry.

"The clouds said so. The men ran off screaming. They will not return."

Ry nodded. "If you're sure. Do you need anything from the tender?"

"Bring me my spare satchel of medical supplies," Mogens said. "I will have need of it. When do you leave?"

"We'll go as soon as we unload the necessary supplies off the tender."

"I did it earlier," Mogens said. "The clouds foretold of a journey, so I prepared."

A shiver went through Camryn. Sometimes the seer was damn creepy.

They flew the tender to the private spaceport on the other side of the planet where they'd left the Indy. After a while Ry couldn't take the silence anymore. It throbbed between them, reminding him they were alone. He ached for her, but along with desire came guilt. She'd asked about other women. Camryn had all the information, but he didn't think she'd put it together yet.

He wasn't going to let her go.

He couldn't.

The self-reproach played with his mind, and Mogens wasn't helping with his attitude. He understood Ry wouldn't let her leave. Ry knew he hadn't acted wisely with Camryn, letting his libido rule his actions. In his defense, he hadn't known the consequences until too late. Now he'd trapped both of them. Ry wanted Camryn, needed her for survival.

"Are you going to let me know how we're going to win the final race?" He didn't want to fill the silence with tortured thoughts any longer.

"I think we should treat this race like the ones we have at home. I'm going to ride Gabby."

"No!" A sick sensation churned his stomach. "Some of the hell-horses are veterans. They're man-eaters and have grown used to the taste of flesh."

Her chin lifted in firm challenge. "Do you have a better idea?"

"No." He'd thought long and hard about the race and Talor. "I could ride Gabby."

"Yeah, that would work," she mocked. "Gabby tolerates you at best and you're big, too big. Your extra weight will slow her down."

Ry exhaled in irritation. She was right, dammit. Admitting defeat, he said, "We need to keep this quiet. We don't want anyone else knowing beforehand because we'll lose our edge."

"What if someone has seen me riding Gabby and preparing her for the race?"

"Hopefully they'll think you have a death wish and not consider other possibilities."

Camryn snorted. "How much longer before we reach the spaceport?"

"Fifteen mins."

"Perhaps you should go faster." Camryn smoothed back a lock of her long hair and he caught the furtive way she licked her lips, leaving them glistening.

Ry clenched his fists to stop reaching for her and did as she suggested, pushing the tender to greater speed.

They made it in ten, slipping into Indy's bay. If they kept a low profile no one would realize they were there.

Ry turned to Camryn. She swallowed, the smooth line of her throat attracting his avid gaze. The desire to see her black hair loose and flowing around her shoulders was like one of Talor's compulsions. He slipped his hands behind her head to remove the leather tie Mogens had given her, and with great satisfaction, he watched the fragrant locks fall free. Leaning down, he buried his nose in the scented strands, breathing deep. He'd never, never tire of her spicy, piquant scent.

"We need to get you in the sanitizer unit." The street dirt and dung clung to her clothes, smelly but not lessening his need of her.

A snooty gasp escaped her. "Are you telling me I stink? Such gratitude. And after I saved you too."

Ry suppressed his amusement and didn't bite back. Bite. Devil take it, he'd love to take a bite or two. His cock swelled to press insistently against his trews, and impatient to get to his berth, he swept her into his arms, exiting the tender with rapid steps. His boots thudded on the metallic floor of the frigate, beating in time with his heart. It was a quick trip to his cabin. He shouldered his way inside and kicked the door shut with his boot before setting Camryn on his bed.

Without moving his gaze from her, he tugged off his boots and made short work of removing hers as well. Their clothes landed haphazardly on the floor. He switched on the sanitizer unit and pushed Camryn inside. She sat on his bed while he took his turn to refresh.

Then his stingy store of patience gave out. He crawled onto the bed, crushing her into the firm mattress and claiming her mouth while he cuffed her wrists above her head with his hands. It had been too long since they'd been together. Way too long.

He tried to take it slow. He really did. With his tongue he outlined her mouth. He pressed his lips to hers, savoring the tart spiciness and softness, the way she pressed as close as possible. His heart thudded, pounding against his ribs, and he was lost in a wash of sensations.

Heat. Scents. Her quick breathing.

His skin itched, his back and chest prickling enough to make him uncomfortable.

"Oh," she gasped, wriggling to free her hands so she could explore his body. "I have to touch you."

"Soon." Yes. He needed her touch. Desperately. Her fingers kneaded his pectoral muscles, clutched his biceps and he shivered, the pleasure more intense than it had ever been. He stroked one breast, and he took pleasure in the way her nipple tightened at his touch. The scent of their arousal filled the air, pushing him even higher.

It was hot. Fast. Scary even.

His mouth fastened around her nipple, and he sucked hard in the way she liked. She bucked against him, her cry of pleasure echoing through his chamber.

He needed to taste her. Now. Urgency propelled Ry down the bed. Roughly, he parted her legs and lifted her to his mouth. His tongue raked the length of her slit, gathering her cream. Camryn moaned, her brown eyes closing while soft color suffused her cheeks. He lapped at her entrance, the rasp of his tongue making her quiver. The taste of her rushed across his taste buds. The rough sound that escaped Camryn spurred him on, and he trembled when his tongue slid across her swollen bud.

"I think about this, about being with you all the time. With you

I'm powerless," he confessed, sharing what was in his heart. He loved making her sigh and groan and shudder with desire. It made him feel powerful and important. Escalated need clawed him, and he realized how much he ached for her, ached for this. His tongue stabbed inside her core while his fingers teased her higher.

"No more, Ry. Please," she begged. "Inside me. Now."

"I live to please you, sweet." Instinct guided Ry. He flipped her over so she rested on her stomach and arranged her until she balanced on all fours. A pleasurable shudder racked him, the ache in his balls one of savage demand. Ry smoothed his hand over the rounded cheeks of her arse then pushed into her. Watching his cock disappear into her hot, wet flesh was the sexiest thing. The grip of her flesh and the way she gloved him so tight was miraculous. His growl of pleasure reverberated between them.

"Camryn, I wish you could see this, our flesh joining."

"Describe it for me. Make me see."

"First, I watched my cock disappear as I impaled you. When I pushed inside, I started to feel your flesh parting to let me inside then the way you pulse around me, squeezing and massaging my shaft. It feels amazing."

"What else?" she whispered.

Ry wished he could see her face. This position felt too good to move though, and he leaned over, brushed the dark hair from her shoulder to press his lips to the leopard tattoo on her back. Her sheath spasmed around his cock, squeezing him rhythmically. It felt damn good so he repeated the move, scraping his teeth across the sensitive skin and rasping the sting away with a lap of his tongue.

"Each time I pull out, I can see my cock shiny with your juices. It's sexy knowing you want me, that you're welcoming me into your body. I like the easy glide into your body. I want to go slow, but the massage of your channel against my shaft feels so damn good. I want to do it again and again. Faster and faster," he whispered into her ear.

Camryn pushed against him, taking each gliding thrust and demanding more, as if his words made her hot. Voicing his feelings sure made him hot. Ry withdrew, moving back enough to see his glistening cock and pushed back into her, the firm slide of her flesh against his bringing exquisite pleasure. Unable to help himself, he quickened his strokes. Pleasure roared through him with each hard thrust, each touch.

The liquid sound of arousal competed with Camryn's ragged sighs and the roar building in his throat. He gripped her hips and thrust, each smooth glide of his cock driving him toward climax. Ry slipped one finger between her legs, stroking across slippery folds and teasing the small knot of nerves that gave her pleasure.

"Yes," she whispered, her breathing shallow, labored. "Keep talking."

"Your sighs and the demands of your body drive me to speed. I start thinking about biting your flesh to give you greater pleasure." Giving in to temptation Ry leaned over to scrape his teeth over the crook of her shoulder and neck. He felt the convulsive clutch of her inner muscles, the shiver and tensing, heard her sweet moan of pleasure. With her flesh gripping and releasing him so exquisitely, he shafted her hard and fast. The electrifying sensation of orgasm rushed up from his balls and he exploded, the velvet heat of her quim milking his cock.

Chest heaving, his nostrils flared, their combined scents pleased him. Without haste he pulled away, separating their clammy bodies. The feline part of him snarled in displeasure when their bodies parted. Sighing, he tugged Camryn's petite frame against his chest. Pushing the silken curtain of hair from her neck, he licked the area where he'd bitten her.

Camryn stiffened against him, her breath catching. "Oh heck."

Ry stilled, the human part of him appalled at the red mark he'd made on her delicate skin. "I'm sorry I hurt you," he said, regret throbbing in his low voice.

"No." Camryn turned in his arms and peered earnestly into his face. "No, you didn't hurt me." She brushed the hair from his face. "Lick me again."

He lapped across the reddened flesh, across the slight indentation where his teeth had sunk deep. There was no blood. No angry wound.

"Ooh," she whispered, and he watched in amazement as pleasure deepened the brown of her eyes. A delicate flush colored her cheeks.

Her enjoyment ignited desire in him again. He dipped his head to kiss her, pushing his tongue between her parted lips, tasting her, and collecting her soft, breathy sigh before it gained substance. With one hand, he tugged at a nipple and pinched it between his fingers, wanting to drag another sweet sigh from her. No sigh this time, but she clutched him, stroking her hand over his back. The score of her fingernails went straight to his balls. His cock pulled tight, urgency pushing him again.

But this time he didn't want to risk hurting her. He wanted Camryn to set the pace, or as much as he could cede control to her. This thing between them burned out of control. He couldn't talk to Mogens anymore. Instead, he took each day one at a time and tried to work things out as he went—the way he'd handled things since his feline had materialized and thrown his life into turmoil.

One day at a time.

He flipped over to his back and took Camryn with him, surprising a yelp out of her.

"What?" Her black hair fell forward to screen her expression.

"Your move."

Camryn laughed and tucked her hair behind her ears, baring her neck to his gaze. "I know how to ride."

The need to see her rising above him, the delightful thrust of her breasts while she pleasured them both rippled through him.

SHELLEY MUNRO

"Prove it."

Without hesitation, she straddled his legs. He thought she'd sink onto his cock, but she leaned over him and nipped his chest. He jumped, relaxing only when she soothed where she'd bitten him with her tongue. Her touch, the scrape of fingernails across his nipple and the graze of teeth drove him high, tightening his balls and lengthening his cock. He trembled, needing her to hurry but contrarily enjoying the care she took with him. In the past, sex had always been quick. Necessary. Furtive even because the loss of control to the feline had shamed him. It had been a means to an end—something to soothe his hormones and allow him to function in a semi-normal manner.

This was different. More. Much better.

Joy wrapped up with teasing and lazy satisfaction. With Camryn he savored sex. It meant something more than appeasing his feline. He felt a connection.

Camryn moved down his body, touching and petting him until purrs of pleasure erupted. Another new thing that had arrived with Camryn. He'd never purred before. She took his cock into her mouth, and his breath caught, the heat unbearably good. Quick flicks of her tongue kindled an inferno. His belly quivered and drops of pre-cum leaked from his slit. She licked them away, tormenting another bout of purrs from him. Laughter filled her, the sound reverberating through his cock and propelling him toward pleasure.

"Enough," he complained.

Aw, poor kitty. Can't cope with the teasing.

Ry growled and she just laughed. The wet rasp of her tongue teased the sensitive underside of his swollen shaft. Her fingers stroked his tight sac while she sucked and drove him into a frenzy of need. A rough rumble vibrated in his chest as he attempted to hold himself in check.

To his relief she stopped persecuting him, the heat of arousal in her cheeks telling Ry it was twin-edged torture. Lifting above him, she guided his cock to her and sank down, enveloping him with her heat. His heart skipped a beat as he concentrated on sensations, the moment.

"That feels good. Real good." Ry let his fingers drift across her knee. She looked so beautiful, rising and falling above him, her head tossed back, black hair flowing across her naked shoulders.

"Feels pretty good on my end too."

He caught the blaze of happiness simmering in her eyes before she closed them, before his gaze drifted to her breasts. They bounced lightly with every move, her apricot-colored nipples drawing his attention. He reached up to pinch one and she swayed toward him with a slow, purposeful move that smoked his insides. Gradually she increased her pace, her breathing harsh. Her skin glowed with perspiration, a rough sound of animal enjoyment slipping from her throat.

"I thought I was the kitty," he murmured.

Her brown eyes opened and narrowed, the shifting light making her appear feline. Ry blinked and the impression receded. Camryn moved rapidly, distracting him from the thought as flesh slapped flesh in a sensual dance.

"Ry," she sobbed out his name, slumping forward and coming apart in his arms.

Ry held her for an instant before flipping her onto her back. He thrust hard until his climax neared. The soothing stroke of her hand across the swirling tattoos on his back finished him off, shooting him into an intense orgasm. With his eyes squeezed shut, he relished the clinging feminine flesh, the glide of her fingers across his back and her seductive scent. He nuzzled her neck, breathing her spicy aroma deep into his lungs. His nostrils flared and he dipped his head to brush a kiss across her mouth.

His woman. He knew they belonged—now all he had to do was convince her.

"So where's this book you mentioned?" Camryn asked, twirling her fingers through his dark hair. She tugged to emphasize her question.

With a sigh, Ry reached into the hidden alcove below his bed. He pulled out two cloth-covered parcels. Even though he couldn't read the contents of the book or open the mystery container, he'd kept them, instinct telling him they were important. He unwrapped the first and studied the leather-bound notebook with new eyes.

"The last time I opened this to read, the ink disappeared. After three pages disappeared, I decided to stop reading. I haven't opened it since."

Ry smoothed his hand over the cover, noticing the fine tremor with a faint frown. The unease he'd felt on holding the book last time had disappeared. Either that or his memory was faulty. Holding the book brought a rush of other memories—of Talor's betrayal. And Meghan—her perfidy had hurt most of all.

"Are you worried about the words disappearing again?"

"I...no. Just thinking about Talor."

"He's not worth the time or energy." Her dark eyes glowed and answering heat flared to life inside Ry. "Look at the book."

Although Talor hadn't mentioned the book, he must have suspected Ry had taken it along with the currency. Nervous tension thrummed through him, and he wiped his palms on his bare legs, took a deep breath and started to open to the middle of the book.

"Wait!" Camryn slapped his hand away. "Shouldn't you open the book at the first page? Didn't you say the words disappeared? The start of a book is the introduction. The important stuff is in the middle and toward the end."

"I knew there was a good reason for bringing you along." Besides the fact he couldn't bear being parted from her.

"Because I'm smart," she shot back. "You detest stupid people."

Ry blinked. He'd chosen his crew because they were all capable of thinking on their feet.

"The first page," he said, uneasy with the way she saw through him. It had taken his crew time to adjust when he'd suddenly shifted to feline. Camryn teased him, referring to him as a kitty whenever she wanted to irritate him.

"The first page." She squeezed his hand in encouragement. "Go on. The worst thing that can happen is for more words to vanish. Personally the idea is a bit of a stretch for me, but what do I know? I didn't believe in aliens. Or kitty-cats," she added, pure devilry lurking in her eyes.

Ry snarled because she expected the reaction, but silent humor flickered through him, and he had trouble restraining his grin. After sucking in a quick breath, he opened the cover of the book to the first page.

House of the Cat. Ornate decoration surrounded the words. His breath caught as he stared at them. They didn't vanish but remained clear.

"Have they disappeared?" Camryn's nose wrinkled in a cute manner.

"It's the title page. It's still visible." The last time the writing had vanished too quickly to decipher a word. Still, he hesitated to turn the page in case this was a one-off.

"Do you think I could see?"

Ry nodded. It was the title, and it didn't matter if it faded. "Come and sit," he said, patting his knee and leering at her. Part of him wondered at his playful manner. He'd never felt this way before—relaxed and at ease.

Camryn wrinkled her nose again, and giving in to temptation, he leaned closer to kiss the tip of her nose before rubbing his lips over hers. Camryn dived right into the kiss, opening her mouth to allow him entrance to the moist heat beyond. The taste of her crawled across his senses, sweet and spicy, and he tangled his hand

SHELLEY MUNRO

in her hair, holding her prisoner so he could slake his thirst. Ry didn't think he'd ever tire of the taste of her, the velvety-soft feel of her lips moving against his.

When he lifted his head, their breathing was labored, and Camryn sat on his knee. Smiling, he scooped the book from the floor where it had fallen, turned it up the right way and opened to the first page.

"House of the Cat," Camryn whispered, her thumb brushing across the decorative scroll surrounding the words.

They both stared in heavy silence, waiting for something to happen.

"Turn the page."

A smile formed at her clear impatience. Ry glanced at the next page, his breath catching until he realized the words weren't fading.

"It's a diary."

"Yes." And not an interesting one, judging by the entry on the first page. Someone had planted trees in the grounds of the clan house, detailing the exact locations and type of tree planted.

"Whose diary?"

Ry flicked to another page and a second.

"It's different writing. Joseph wanted to keep this book about the new House of the Cat and say nothing of the old life. Although I came with him, disgusted with the way our brother acted, I cannot ignore the past. It shapes us..." Camryn stopped reading. "Do you have any idea what this person is talking about?"

"No."

"Are you sure the words disappeared?" Camryn asked. "Maybe they came back."

"I opened the book toward the middle and flipped over a couple of pages." Ry turned the pages without reading. "There. Look. Two blank pages. This page starts halfway through a sentence."

"I don't understand. Why aren't the words disappearing now?"

"I don't know. This page mentions a ball and lists the guests who attended. Not noteworthy for anyone but the owner of the diary." Ry idly scratched at his back before setting the book aside. He reached for the other fabric-wrapped parcel and peeled it away to reveal the oblong copper box. The instant he touched it, the jewels encrusting the top changed from colorless to a dazzling array of red, green and blue. The largest rich blue jewel in the center sparkled. Giving in to an urge, he stroked it with his finger. A tingle shot down his arm and he jerked his finger away in surprise.

"Wow," Camryn whispered, her eyes wide with wonder.

Ry turned the container over, searching for a concealed button or catch to open it. He pressed the stone in the center, but nothing happened. "I don't know how to open it." He turned it over again and noticed the stones lining the side of the container remained clear and translucent with no apparent color.

"Can I try?"

Ry handed her the box and watched her inquisitive expression. An indulgent smile curled across his lips, and he pressed a kiss to her shoulder.

"There's no noticeable joint." The frown in her voice was clear. She didn't enjoy puzzles. "I wonder why the stones on top glow a different color when I touch it."

Ry took a closer look. The blue of the center stone wasn't quite as deep. He touched it and the color darkened to a rich, vibrant blue. He removed his hand and when Camryn touched the stone, it lightened to an attractive steel blue. "I've no idea. Maybe there's something in the diary." He stood, his abruptness making Camryn slide from his knee.

"You're lucky I had a firm hold on the box."

Ry shrugged. "I've tried dropping it. Nothing happened."

Camryn chuckled. "I would have liked to have seen that."

"I jumped on it too," he confessed, wanting to make her laugh to witness the way joy took hold of her entire face, her eyes sparkling, all demons chased away. She didn't think about the other man—Gabriel—when she laughed.

"It survived the ordeal all right," she said with another laugh. It warmed his insides. Camryn set the box aside and turned to him, arching her eyebrows with a teasing glance. "Are you going to feed me? We missed dinner. And a bath. I need to wash again."

"We could go out," he said. "We'd have to wear a disguise, but we can go to a bathhouse."

"A communal one?"

"No." Not bloody likely. His eyes only. He'd pay more and hire a private bath. It would be safer anyway. "They have private rooms for hire. There's a chophouse nearby with good food."

"Sold," she said. "But don't you want to read the diary first?"

"I can read about gardening and balls when we get back." He sighed. "I thought I might find a clue this time. Seems I was wrong."

Chapter Fourteen

Talor's Hotel, Ornum

"Where is he? Where's my brother?" Talor focused on Kaya, not bothering to hold back his anger. Power swirled through the air, making the woman's blue hair rise and crackle. She had the good sense to study her feet instead of holding his gaze. She'd made the mistake before and paid for her impertinence. "Where?" he thundered.

Kaya winced when the glasses on the sideboard rattled. "He went to the Indy with Camryn. He said he had to collect something. I don't know what."

He didn't require a charm or compulsion to know she spoke the truth, not when it trembled in her voice.

Talor paced across the floor of the hotel room, impatience simmering through him. His brother had more luck than anyone he knew. The mercenaries he'd hired had failed in their mission.

Every time he tried to shoot Ryman and his crew out of the sky, his brother escaped. He'd attempted to steal their hell-horse so at least he'd win the final race, but the seer had scared his men so much that two of them still weren't speaking in coherent sentences. There had to be some way—some weakness he could exploit.

Ryman must die. Soon. He couldn't hold his creditors at bay for much longer. He needed the inheritance to revert to him.

He whirled back to glare at the woman. "Seduce him. Slip a knife in his ribs while he's sleeping."

The woman's face paled. "No."

"No?"

"He's only interested in Camryn." She couldn't quite conceal her irritation, and this piqued Talor's interest.

"The woman. Where did she come from? Who is she?"

"She comes from Earth. She looks after the hell-horse."

"Hmmm." Talor scratched his chin and paced the length of the reception room again, circling the plain wooden table and mismatched chairs. Bah! He hated this place, the necessity of soiling his hands. But the bad run of luck at cards and failing powers over the last two cycles had left him desperate, willing to try anything. Especially since his creditors were starting to cry foul and demand their money.

Talor snarled under his breath, tension thrumming in time with his pulse. None of this would have happened if his mother hadn't given Ryman a slice of the Coppersmith fortune. She'd always been blind to Ryman's faults, even when he'd left, stealing away in the dead of the night with heirlooms and cash. Currency that belonged to Talor.

Luckily no one outside of the family lawyer knew of the inheritance, not even Ryman, but Talor couldn't sell the property his mother had left to his brother or mortgage the place. Damn, he had to get rid of Ryman and the property would return to him since his brother didn't have children. There had to be a way.

"Tell me everything you know."

"I have to go," the woman said. "I can't delay any longer or they'll ask questions. Besides, I've told you everything I know."

Talor acknowledged she could leave, aware she remained his sole link to his brother's activities. He needed her help. "When will they return?"

"Tomorrow, I believe. We haven't heard otherwise."

"You will meet with me as soon as they return."

"It's not easy."

The woman grew braver. Fury washed through him, sending her hair swirling again. She gasped at a charge of electricity and backed away, wariness etched into her expression. She was right to feel apprehension, right to worry because as soon as his brother died he wouldn't need her aid.

"You will meet me every day until the start of the race," he instructed. "Or else."

Talor watched her leave and continued to fret during the long night. Although his powers had gained in strength, he felt as if his life ran out of control. And his men still hadn't captured the elusive black leopard, although they'd reported seeing the creature running near the village in the mountains. He needed the animal to ensure luck for House of the Cat.

The next afternoon, he waited for Kaya to meet him in the village tavern. She didn't come. Another day passed, and he waited inside the tavern. Exhausted. Tense.

Finally he saw her. He jumped to his feet and stalked over to confront her about her tardiness.

"I told you to meet me yesterday," Talor snarled.

Kaya didn't flinch. "I couldn't get away."

"You didn't want to sneak away," Meghan corrected from behind him.

"Is that true?"

"Yes," Kaya said. "I won't be coming to see you again."

"Ryman will cast you out when he learns of your treachery."

The color bled from her cheeks. "Maybe, but at least I'll have my self-respect." She turned away and Talor grasped her arm, hauling her to a stop.

"What does my brother intend to do today? How does he attempt to win the race?" He backed up the questions with a blast of compulsion, his grip tightening cruelly on her forearm.

Kaya's eyes rolled while she fought an inner battle. His compulsion won.

"Camryn intends to ride our hell-horse to victory." The unwilling words squeezed past her lips.

"Ride?" Talor's eyes widened at the news. "Impossible. The other horses will rip her to shreds."

"They'll have to catch her first," Kaya said and walked away without looking back.

Dowry Derby Race Day, Ornum.

The crowd roared. Sumptuously clad musicians entertained along with jugglers and tumblers. Palpable excitement pulsed through the cram-packed arena.

"Welcome to the Dowry Derby." The announcer's screech boomed through the loudspeakers.

Camryn walked away from her viewing position to slip into the stall. Gabby tossed her head and danced on the spot, just missing her foot.

"Easy, girl. It's me. Remember me?"

Gabby settled but issued a troubled whicker. Luke squeezed past his mother to nudge Camryn on the leg, unruffled by whatever disturbed Gabby. Chuckling, she scratched him behind the ear and placed her hand on the mare's quivering shoulder. Gabby suffered the same nerves as she. The mare had always been uneasy in Ry's presence and recently had started reacting the same way with her. Camryn hoped they'd both make it through the race without mishaps. Just thinking about the carnage she'd witnessed whenever hell-horses attacked sliced fear through her gut. But this was it—her mission.

They had to win for Ry, for the crew. She could not screw this up. A desperate need to talk to her brother struck her then. He was her best friend in the world, the only person besides Gabriel she could always count on in a fix. Even if he had threatened to book her into a clinic for treatment.

But what about Ry?

The words jumped into her mind. She stared into the depths of the stall, her heart thudding in loud, solid beats. Breathe. Breathe through the panic. She inhaled, concentrating on her goal, visualizing riding past the winning post with the other hell-horses behind them. Her positive thoughts skidded to a halt. What would happen if she failed? If she didn't win the race? If something happened to Gabby and she was injured?

"Camryn, are you in there?"

Her pulse rate lurched into a crazy beat before a deep inhalation calmed her pre-race nerves. "I'm in here, Ry." Competently, she placed the makeshift saddle on Gabby's back and fastened the girth strap.

The door to the stall opened. Gabby snorted but Luke never hesitated. With a welcoming squeal, he charged, almost knocking Ry over. Ry laughed and petted the creature, rubbing him behind the ears until Luke trembled with pleasure.

"They're starting to lead the horses out. I...hell, Camryn. Stay safe." He hauled her into his arms and held her so tight she felt his heartbeat. His familiar scent wound through her senses, calming her in a way her deep breathing exercises hadn't. With gentle fingers he tilted her head up and kissed her—an unhurried kiss that brought a surge of need yet made her feel treasured. Their tongues tangled in an easy rhythm, each thrust and surge echoing in her sex. When they finally pulled apart, her legs trembled, and her entire body hummed.

The sharp thud of a fist rattled the stable door next to them. Ry released Camryn and stepped away.

"Are you sure?" he asked.

"We've discussed the race. This is the only way."

Ry pinched the bridge of his nose and gave a sharp nod. "Do you have your protective hat?"

"Yes. And the protective vest should help if I have trouble." She handed the hat to him, and he pushed the stall door open. Camryn blinked at the brighter light and amplified noise.

Mogens stood outside and for once his skin edged closer to white than black. He smiled, but the crease between his eyes told of his concern. Instead of trying to talk her out of riding, he strapped on Luke's halter. Before leading the foal off to the finish line, Mogens fumbled in the pocket of his trews and pulled out a colorful collection of twigs and flowers and a bright yellow feather bound together with strong red grasses. He tied the charm in Gabby's black mane and Camryn heard a series of rhythmical clicks when he whispered a chant. With a final pat on Gabby's glossy neck, he bowed to Camryn.

"Stay safe." Mogens led Luke away.

To Camryn's relief Gabby remained calm, unworried by the separation from her foal. Ry and Camryn led her through the crowds of people lining the railings from the stable into the arena. A security man objected to two handlers entering the track, but a higher-ranked official waved them through the fortified gate. A loud cheer echoed in the stands. Gabby danced on tiptoe and tossed her head.

"Steady, girl," Camryn whispered, stroking her hand across the mare's neck. "Steady."

A herd of butterflies took flight inside Camryn's stomach, and it felt as if they bumped and crashed into each other.

You can do this, Camryn. The crew has confidence in you. They've placed a heavy bet on Gabby to win.

Camryn snorted. Up the pressure, why don't you?

They glanced at each other, and she laughed. "What if we fail? What if we don't win?"

"I have faith in you."

A hell-horse snarled. Another yelped. The barrier gates rattled, and the waiting horses stirred in restless reaction.

Camryn swallowed. "I want to go home." Tears shaded her voice and she blinked hard to stop them spilling free.

"Everything will turn out all right." He kissed her quickly and drew away. "You'll have to get on now."

"Don't forget to take the bucket of treats to the finish post." Camryn secured her protective hat on her head.

"I won't." He gave Camryn a leg up and she landed astride Gabby's back.

The roar of the crowd died an abrupt death. Gabby flinched at the pulsing silence while the butterflies inside Camryn's stomach stirred, knocking into each other in panic.

"What are they doing this time?" the announcer demanded. "Are we looking at something extraordinary here today? You'll remember last time this hell-horse named Gabby ran straight to the finish line without stopping to fight. She ran a record time."

The crowd burst into excited chatter. This time Gabby remained calm. She walked into the starting barrier and stood quietly despite the increased noise.

Camryn sighed in relief at the ease of this maneuver, pleased they'd practiced so many times in training. The rancid smell of the other hell-horses permeated every breath she took. Camryn started to breathe through her mouth, her eyes watering.

SHELLEY MUNRO

Another horse loaded beside them, growling low and mean even though the creature couldn't see Gabby. The gates rattled again.

"Three more," a rough voice said.

Camryn tensed, fear and anticipation colliding in the pit of her stomach. So much rode on this race.

They loaded the other horses with efficiency, but to Camryn a lifetime passed, one slow sec at a time. She wiped clammy palms on her black trews. The final horse entered the gate, creating more racket than all the other horses combined, kicking and lashing at the barrier.

"Another hell-horse with a rider," the commentator shouted with excitement. "This race will go down in history."

Another rider? What the hell? Camryn craned her neck, attempting to look over the barrier. Unfortunately the design meant she couldn't see the other hell-horses. She couldn't see a damn thing.

Ry? What's going on?

Camryn, you okay?

Yes. What's happening? Who is the other rider?

He didn't answer and apprehension seared her. Gabby caught her unease and started to stomp restlessly while Camryn bit her lip, her mind racing with reasons as to why Ry hadn't answered.

The gate rattled, and suddenly Camryn could see the track stretching out before them, the finish line like a welcoming beacon.

"And they're off!"

Gabby hesitated. The other horses sprang from the gates. Camryn nudged Gabby, squeezing the barrel of her body with her thighs. The mare jumped from the starting gate. Camryn leaned low, urging her on with hands and heels. Over to their left a horse squealed and reared in the gates. Camryn heard a man shout.

A hell-horse appeared beside them, neck extended, and teeth bared. Gabby frog-hopped out of the way, the abrupt sideway move throwing Camryn off balance. Only instinct, honed from

240

years of experience, allowed her to stay on Gabby. She kicked her mount hard, surprising a grunt from the mare. Gabby wasn't used to vigorous kicks. She leaped forward, thankfully heading in the right direction.

"Run, girl. Run. Come on. Please. We need to find Luke."

Something crashed into Gabby, knocking her offstride. Again, experience allowed Camryn to keep her seat. Gabby whirled to attack the hell-horse behind. Bigger than she, it was an aggressive male with a scar-covered hide. Terror gripped Camryn as she hauled on Gabby's head and wished they'd been able to fashion a bit and bridle to give her more control. This halter wasn't the best.

"Gabby. Turn!" Camryn applied the signal she'd taught the mare, squeezing her thighs tightly and leaning her weight forward. Too late. The mare had caught the bloodlust of the others. She charged the stallion without a shred of fear or hesitation. The clash almost unseated Camryn. She lurched sideways. With desperation, she grasped Gabby's mane and clung. If she fell... God!

"Look at the rider," the commentator shrieked. "I've never witnessed the like before. Watch out! Hell and Back is returning for another go!"

The stallion reared before charging. Gabby spun and kicked out with her rear feet.

"Gabby!" Hell! The finish line looked so far away. Her spine jarred from the series of quick rabbit hops Gabby completed before she lashed out at the stallion again. With an indignant yelp, the stallion backed away to concentrate his attack on another hell-horse.

"Yeah! Score one for the girl's team." At least Gabby faced the right direction now. She dug her in the ribs and urged the mare on with both heels and voice.

"Go, Gabby. Run! Don't you want to see Luke?" Please, please want to see your foal.

Another hell-horse jostled her. Gabby yelped and spun to face the danger, her ears flat against her head.

"Food, Gabby!" Camryn leaned forward to holler in the mare's ear. "Food." Damn, she'd known this wouldn't be easy, but she hadn't expected this much trouble either. She had to exert control instead of letting Gabby do whatever she wanted. Camryn jerked hard on the halter and gave the signal for run. She almost cried when Gabby obeyed her command, even though the mare ran in the wrong direction.

"Gabriel is running the wrong way," the commentator shrieked. "This is history in the making. Look at the hell-horse move."

Camryn noticed the other rider appeared terrified. He rode on Talor Coppersmith's mount Dante, and he had his arms wrapped around the hell-horse's neck. It bucked and zigged, trying to throw the rider off, but without success. The rider's shrieks of fear were audible even above the thunder of hooves and the yapping, snarling and loud whinnies from the other hell-horses. Not her problem. He screamed when another hell-horse attacked and bit his leg. The crowd roared then a deathly hush fell.

Camryn let Gabby canter in a circular pattern until she faced the right way and applied her hands and heels, urging her to gallop straight past the fighting hell-horses. When they came abreast of the stallion, Gabby hesitated. Camryn was ready for her refusal. She kicked with her heels, a sharp dig, mentally apologizing but determined. To her relief Gabby responded. Camryn leaned forward, balancing to take account of the uneven gait of the mare.

The crowd cheered, a change from the jeers of the last race. Camryn heard the thunder of hooves behind but didn't look back. The finish line beckoned. They rounded the bend, and the finish post came into their view. Beyond the finish, Mogens and Ry stood with Luke. She knew the exact moment Gabby spotted her foal and the white bucket of treats held by Ry. Gabby sped up, her attention on the end of the track. The thunder of hooves continued behind her, if anything becoming louder. The crowd roared encouragement.

"And Gabby is leading. Dante has tossed his rider and is hot on her tail. Little Diablo is gaining, placed handy on the rails. Hot as Hades is down. Black Hell is stopping to take a look."

Camryn urged Gabby on, concentrating on finishing rather than the fate of Dante's rider. Dante galloped behind, gaining. She heard the snap of teeth, smelled the fetid breath.

"Keep going, Gabby. Keep going."

The hell-horse kept gaining. Frantically, she drove the mare toward the finish post. Gabby stretched her neck, and they were over, winning by half a body length.

"And the winner of the Dowry Derby is Gabriel, owned by Ryman Coppersmith. Second is Dante."

Exhilarated, Camryn let Gabby slow. They'd done it! They'd beaten Talor Coppersmith.

"Watch out, Camryn," Ry roared, starting to run.

Before she had a chance to react, the hell-horse clamped its teeth on Gabby's rump. Then Dante let go and lunged at Camryn.

Attendants scurried from hiding, hesitating to get too close.

Ry grabbed up the bucket of treats and started to toss them at the horses. He barked orders at Mogens while he tossed the smelly treats at the over-excited horses. "Take Luke and get Gabby to follow."

Dante snapped at Camryn's leg again and ripped away part of her trews, slashing her leg before getting the scent of the treats. Ry chucked more at him and sprinted toward Gabby with the open bucket.

To Camryn's relief Gabby trotted after him. Her glance behind confirmed the other hell-horses were busy scrambling for treats and squabbling amongst each other.

Her leg didn't seem too bad. A bit of blood but not bad enough to cause the other horses to attack. Up ahead, Mogens opened the stall and stood aside after Luke entered. Ry placed the bucket in the stall and jumped back out to give Gabby plenty of room. When she ran into the stall, he reached over and dragged Camryn free.

"Are you all right?" he demanded. His heart pounded beneath her touch, and he held her so tight she had trouble drawing a breath.

"We won."

He pushed away to glower at her. "Blast it! I thought I'd lost you." Then a slow grin bloomed on his handsome face. "But yeah, you won the race for us."

"I can go home."

His smile faded, his expression growing impassive. "You don't need to go straightaway. We must attend to formalities first."

"Let me treat your leg." Mogens pulled out his satchel and moved closer to Camryn. "Ah, it doesn't look bad. A mere scratch, although with the carrion some of these hell-horses eat it might become infected." He busied himself with mixing a smelly paste of green herbs and soothed them on the jagged scratch.

Now that the adrenaline rush had faded, her leg started to throb. With a drooping head, she sat on the ground, letting Mogens tend her injury. Inside the stall, Gabby and Luke grunted and yelped while they ate the last of the treats.

Camryn noticed Ry's scrutiny. The instant he caught her glance he turned away, but a flutter of fear hit her. She wanted to go home and yet she didn't. Unhappily, she concentrated on Mogens and tried not to think about never seeing Ry again.

Later that night, The Celebration Ball, Ornum.

The governor insisted Camryn honor them with her presence at the celebration ball. And she had to wear a dress. She'd tried telling the man who arrived with the engraved invitation she had nothing to wear. Heck, she wasn't a circus chimp the governor could trot out to entertain the locals. Camryn scowled down at the elegant white dress and snorted in derision. This garment exposed a great deal of her chest.

Yeah, a circus chimp in a dress.

A novelty to entertain the guests.

From the moment she walked into the ballroom at Ry's side, people mobbed her, wanting to bask in her spotlight of sudden fame.

A tall, wiry man halted her progress. He swallowed and tugged at his starched cravat. "How did you do it? How did you manage to ride your hell-horse without getting eaten?"

Others crowded around, separating her from Ry. Camryn forced a smile. *Ry? Where are you?* She couldn't sense him behind her any longer.

Over the other side of the room. His thoughts held clear disgust. *These bloody women are like forest leeches.*

Camryn's smile became more natural. *I'm sure you'll cope.*

Oh hell. I'm heading outside to the gardens. Ry blocked his thoughts and when she turned to check, she caught a flash of his dark hair before he disappeared outdoors. She wished she could vanish.

"I want to know the answer to his question," an elegant man said and pressed a kiss to her hand with practiced ease.

Camryn tugged when his mouth lingered. What was wrong with the men here?

An elderly gent held up his quizzing glass and peered at her. "Yes, it's becoming difficult to obtain replacement hell-horses when they are killed during a race. Please give us a few hints. It's an expensive business."

Camryn took a step backward, their zealous expectation making her nervous, and promptly bumped into yet another eager hell-horse owner. This must be how a goldfish felt. She loathed the commotion. Where were the others? Maybe she could make a run for it and hide out with Mogens or Kaya. Or Jannike.

"I want to hire you to train my hell-horses," the elegant one said.

The man with a golden quizzing glass puffed up with indignation. "I say, Griggins. Not sporting! I want to hire her."

"There are two types—the quick and the dead," the handsome Griggins said.

"And I thought that was our hell-horses," a wit from the rear of the circle retorted.

General laughter ensued but the comment put the focus on her again. "I'd be happy to answer your questions, but I must...um...retire to the ladies' room." Before they could protest, she pushed between two of the men and darted away, intent on escape. The ladies' retiring room looked good.

"Excuse me," she muttered when a man would have stopped her. Ah Kaya. Safety in numbers. Camryn darted around a large, heavily bejeweled woman before coming to an abrupt stop. Kaya stood with Ry's brother, Talor. Something in the way they whispered together hinted at more than a casual meeting.

Camryn stared in suspicion. Had she told Talor about the way they intended to run their race? The reason Talor's horse also had a rider? Talor's hand rested on Kaya's shoulder. Kaya wrenched from his touch, but Talor grabbed her arm and instinct told Camryn they were arguing. Lovers? It looked that way, which meant Kaya had probably given Talor information about their strategies, had informed him of their locations.

Kaya's gaze met hers and even across the ballroom floor, Camryn saw the other woman stiffen. When Talor touched her shoulder again, she said something and stalked away. Talor met Camryn's gaze and smiled a predatory grin. He headed straight for her. Camryn spun away and bumped into a small man.

"I'm so sorry."

"It is of no import," he said with a charming bow. He stood with several others. Hell-horse owners she'd guess, judging by the predatory light in their eyes.

The owners, of course, were all men. They circled her like a shark circles its prey, beady eyes fixed on her. But instead of attacking, they fired questions at her.

"How can you control a hell-horse? You're so little." The huge, towering man had the effrontery to grasp her upper arm and test her biceps for strength.

"Sir!" Camryn jerked away. When she managed to get her hands on Ry she'd commit murder. A tingle sprang to life low in her belly. Perhaps not murder but sensual torture might not go astray.

And Kaya...Kaya would face the consequences of her actions. If she were guilty, Camryn would make sure she paid.

"Were you not fearful?" a woman asked, giving a theatrical shiver. The jiggle of her bountiful breasts diverted attention from Camryn.

"How did you train the creature? What is your secret? What are you going to do now? Will you work for me?"

"No! Work for me. I will pay you well and make you rich." The questions kept coming thick and fast until Camryn's head spun, and still Ry didn't come to her rescue.

But then why would he?

He had what he wanted. He'd won the race and beat his brother. He had the woman and her huge dowry. Ry had his brother's promise to clear his name, although Camryn didn't believe Talor would follow through with his pledge. She wasn't sure Ry believed it either.

The dramatic blare of trumpetlike instruments blasted through the chatter, bringing a halt to questions. Someone tugged on her dress, and she turned, ready to deck them.

"What do you want?" she snarled at the skinny man who had touched her arm.

"The governor wishes you to sit at the head table," the man said in a pleasant voice, clearly expecting her to answer in the affirmative.

Sighing, Camryn accepted the inevitable. Hero of the hour or the oddity, depending upon which person discussed her ride. "Thank you. I would be honored."

The man offered his arm to escort her to the large double doors at the far end of the room. People stood aside to let them pass.

She wished everyone would stop treating her like a heroine because she'd had no choice but to help Ry. Now with her mission accomplished, it was time to return home—no matter how much leaving hurt.

The governor sat at the head of the table. Ry sat beside him with the governor's daughter sitting on Ry's other side.

Camryn marched beside the courtier, each step rife with anger. She wanted to return home—she really did, but Ry had sneaked under her guard. At first it had been physical then their relationship and her feelings had grown. She'd miss him. A cold knot formed in her throat and no amount of swallowing would dislodge the obstruction.

Forgetting Ry would prove difficult, but she could do it without sliding into depression again. She'd go home and begin over. A fresh start. Hopefully her brother would forgive her past behavior.

A woman's soft laughter drew her attention. The governor's daughter. The woman wore her mask. Nice, but not good enough for Ry.

Jealousy flared inside her. Resentment.

When she heard the husky rumble of Ry's voice, his laughter, Camryn wrenched her gaze away to concentrate on the courtier. He seated her in the empty seat beside the governor.

"Hello," the governor said. "I've wanted to meet you."

The governor reminded her of a plump frog. He was an ugly man, squat and rounded, but he had beautiful brown eyes. They sparkled full of life. His voice didn't fit his appearance, the smooth and sexy tones almost mesmerizing and calming. She summoned a smile, attempting to put Ry and his new woman from her mind. Home. Soon she'd arrive home, and everything would return to normal.

"It's a pleasure to meet you," Camryn said.

"The pleasure is all mine," the man said in his chocolate-smooth voice.

Camryn suppressed a shiver. She'd bet this man could make a race commentary sound sexy.

"I know this is a celebration," the man said. "But I wondered if I could set up a meeting with you tomorrow?"

"What sort of meeting?"

The governor covered her hand with his. "We can discuss details then. I'd love to hear about your training methods in greater detail."

"Of course," she said.

"Wine?" a waiter asked.

"Yes, please." Camryn bobbed her head with alacrity. A drink sounded perfect. The waiter poured ruby-red liquid into a jeweled goblet. Before she could take a sip, the musicians stalked to the center of the room and blasted out a short, vigorous blast of music. Latecomers hurried to their seats while others ceased their chatter.

The governor stood, reinforcing Camryn's thoughts of an amphibian. "Ladies and gentlemen. Welcome to the Dowry Derby celebration. Those of you who witnessed the race will have relished the wonderful spectacle." He paused and turned to Ry, a broad grin of self-congratulation on his face. "I give you the winner of the race and of my daughter's hand in marriage, Ryman Coppersmith!"

Applause and cheers rang out. Camryn's stomach clenched in protest.

Ry stood, aware of Camryn's distress. Her anguish battered him even though she'd blocked her thoughts. Mogens, Kaya, Nanu and Jannike sat together, their grins wide and happy. They trusted him to stay true to his word and to split the dowry between them. The currency was easy, but the woman—that's where things became tricky. The governor expected him to wed his daughter. He couldn't. He felt nothing for the daughter except sympathy. Not even her attractive scent tempted him. Devil take it, he didn't even know what she looked like. No one did. If she took after her sire, no wonder she wore a mask in public.

Camryn. She, alone, made his blood burn, his cock harden. All along he'd focused on two things—winning the race and clearing his name. His brother had set him up, and he wanted to know why. He wanted to discover why his brother wanted him dead instead of merely banished from Ibrox. At the thought of his brother, Ry sought him out amongst those at the ball. Talor wasn't present. Ry swore as a thought occurred. He'd probably gone, trying to wriggle out of his bet.

"Gweneth, would you please stand?"

The governor's rich voice held the attention of everyone in the room without difficulty, despite his appearance. Ry's eyes narrowed, wondering if the ruler came from one of the magical races. He was small enough to be a Regit gnome. He turned to the daughter, searching for a clue as to race of origin.

"Please take Ryman's hand."

Ry bit back a protest, even as his flesh crawled, but he extended his hand, his gaze going to Camryn. His, the feline snarled through his mind. Not this woman.

Gweneth placed her gloved hand on his.

"The marriage will take place in three days," the governor said with great satisfaction. He picked up his goblet and lifted it. "A toast. To the happy couple."

Goblets rose. Shouts of congratulation and ribald laughter

rippled across the room. Ry kept a careful smile on his face despite the horror piercing his heart.

"I am pleased you won the race," Gweneth said in a gentle and biddable voice. "You were my favorite. I believe we will suit each other very well."

Ry railed at fate. The governor would expect the marriage to go ahead. Beating his brother had been everything, the clearing of his name—if his brother kept his word—but perhaps he should have considered the consequences. How the blue blazes did he fix this? He picked up his goblet to find it empty and set it back down.

An instant later a waiter arrived with a pitcher. "I believe you wanted a refill, my lord," Gweneth said.

"Thank you."

Gweneth leaned over until her breast brushed his arm and placed her hand on his thigh. "I will be a good wife."

Ry forced himself not to jerk away. Her scent—she smelled of delicate flowers instead of the sweet, exotic spice he'd become used to with Camryn. The thought of touching her brought no pleasure, no erotic expectation.

He acknowledged the truth to himself. He couldn't marry this woman, not when he craved Camryn. No, he couldn't marry Gweneth when he loved Camryn.

Camryn was his future. They belonged together.

CHAPTER FIFTEEN

AFTER THE BALL, ORNUM HOTEL

"Looks like we're gonna celebrate a wedding, captain," Jannike said.

Ry ripped off his cravat and stomped across the hotel room they'd hired for the night. "I am not marrying the woman."

"Why not? She seems lovely," Camryn said.

"I don't want to marry her," Ry growled, anger making him want to shake Camryn. Hell and damnation, he didn't want anyone except her.

"You should have thought about the woman before you entered the race," Camryn said, her tone flippant.

"I entered the race to irritate my brother," Ry snapped, taking two giant steps to bring them face-to-face. They glowered at each other, emotions crackling like the whistle of a whip. "According to my sources, the bastard has left Ornum. If I want to clear my name

I'll need to confront him on Ibrox."

"Well now you have a wife." Camryn turned away, igniting his temper further. He pounced, grasped her arm and yanked her against his chest. With a testy snarl, he lowered his head to claim a kiss. Exerting ownership.

His.

At first she fought him. He used his greater strength and his lips to woo her to his way of thinking. He heard the others whispering and their hasty retreat, the creak of the door when it opened and closed. Ry wrapped his arms around her in a possessive manner. Camryn was his mate and he refused to let her go.

When he pulled away, they were both breathing hard.

"I don't want to lose you."

"But I'm going home," she said, her gaze narrowing as realization set in. "You're not taking me home." The statement came out flat. Cool and furious.

Ry winced, knowing he deserved her fury. "I can't let you leave," he whispered, his emotions torn.

Camryn jerked away, spitting like a feline in her wrath. "Don't touch me."

He held up his hands and backed away, heart pounding while guilt stabbed him. "I need you. I love you."

"Love." A choked laugh escaped her. "You don't understand. I want to see my brother, get my life back to normal. I...I want to sit in Gabriel's chair, to have my things around me and return to a routine. It's taken me a long time to realize it, but I need normality, people around who love me. I need stability. Gabriel gave me strength. I need to find it again."

"You can have all that with me," Ry said in desperation. Ironic. He'd never had to fight for a woman before. Never. They fell over themselves, battling amongst each other to win his favor, all except the woman he really wanted.

"The governor intends for you to marry his daughter. She wants to marry you. You're obligated to follow through. You signed an agreement when you entered the contest."

After talking to the governor and his daughter, Ry knew Camryn was right. "We'll leave. If I'm not here to marry Gweneth—"

"Run away?" The scornful note brought a rush of unaccustomed color to his cheeks.

He'd spent almost his entire life running away, labeled with the tag of murderer and thief. He was sick of running. Ry maintained eye contact despite his discomfort and went with the truth. "I don't want to lose you."

"You can't have everything you want" Camryn stalked to the door and slipped from the hotel room, leaving him alone.

Ry stared at the stout wooden door before a snarl erupted. He reached for the doorknob and threw it open before prowling the hall, intent on following Camryn's scent. Walking away wasn't an option. Not now. The thought of separation from Camryn brought him out in a cold sweat. Ry snorted. Damn if he didn't believe Mogens.

A mated pair.

Camryn mightn't agree, but they were in this together. Together they could make this work. All they needed was compromise.

Camryn hovered in the reception area of the hotel, obviously realizing she'd be a target for thieves because her dress glowed like flickering candlelight. The crew stood watching her, straightening when they registered his presence.

"Don't go outside, Camryn. Come back with me to the room," Ry said. "We'll talk."

"I've completed my mission. You need to keep your end of the bargain. If you don't, I'll find another ship to return me to Earth. Kaya, can I borrow your cape?"

"Sure." Kaya handed it over.

Camryn swung the black fabric over her shoulders and fastened the toggles on the front.

Ry planted himself in front of her, at a loss as to how to make this right. "Don't go."

"I can't stay." Camryn stepped around him and darted into the night.

Jannike placed her hand on his shoulder. "Captain, you—"

"I know," he snarled, and strode after her.

"Touchy," Jannike muttered.

"I don't know about you, but I'm going too," Kaya said. "I'm not going to miss this."

"Me neither," Nanu said.

Ry heard his crew and his scowl deepened. Of course they had opinions. He increased his pace. He would not let her go.

The crowd thickened and he lost sight of her. Her scent mingled with the other pedestrians and panic beat at him. It wasn't safe on the streets at this time of night. He pushed past men, frantically searching for a glimpse of Camryn.

The furious squawk of birds told him of yet another bird fight. Cheers and booing made his ears ring. Where the blue blazes was she?

Camryn. He shoved through a gap and caught a flash of her pale face. Ry lunged through another gap, saw a man wearing a red jacket grab her and drag her into a narrow alley.

A marine?

He sprinted after them. The people milled around, slowing him down. Cursing, he pushed and shoved, desperate to get to Camryn. A large man with a bald head took exception to his use of force and swung with his fist. Ry dodged the punch. He raced into the alley just as Camryn and the marine disappeared. Before he had time to rush after her, someone thumped him over the head from behind.

Camryn fought to return to Ry for naught as the marines hustled her away. Terrified, she had problems forming her thoughts, trying to communicate telepathically.

"Where are we going?" she demanded.

The marines ignored her, instead increasing their pace. There were so many of them. It didn't make sense.

Camryn attempted to dig in her heels, but they dragged her off despite her protests, hauling her down the street and leaving one shoe behind.

"Where are you taking me?" Ry! Ry? Can you hear me?

She focused, emptying her mind of everything apart from Ry. For once she crashed through the barriers she normally kept intact. Nothing. No white noise or flashes of seductive thoughts. Just silence. Five minutes ago she would have cheered, and now she missed Ry's presence. Worry and fear slithered down her backbone. "Where?"

"To a safe place," one said.

Several sniggered and nudged each other. Apprehension lurched inside Camryn on seeing their faces. Something wasn't right.

"Am I arrested? What have I done?"

The jail came into sight at the end of the street. They marched toward the fortified building, the lanterns on the main thoroughfare much brighter than the street they'd just traversed.

In front of them two men staggered along the edge of the road, holding each other upright. One burst out with a dirty ditty about a curvy trollop with a mole above her lip. Evidently she was infamous for pleasuring two men at once.

The marines marched her past a kafe shop, a pie shop and another tavern.

"I haven't done anything. You've snatched the wrong person."

Even though they hadn't spent much time in the city, she'd heard stories about the jail. She'd seen the way they treated the convicts, the methods they used to rob them of dignity, their humanity. Just the idea of entering the place brought shivers of horror. The smell battered her when they reached the courthouse, an indescribable stench with a hint of toilets and sweat, along with things she didn't want to ponder. She steeled herself and breathed in a last gasp of semifresh air, prepared for the worst.

But the marines kept marching. They didn't stop at the jail.

Her mouth dropped open in sheer surprise.

"Best shut your mouth, girlie," the marine walking beside her said. "No telling what might glide inside." He winked at another marine and they burst into crude guffaws.

Camryn ignored their hilarity, her mind busily working on the why of this matter. Ry? She tried again. No response. Hard pressure forced down on her chest, fear taking its toll. He'd lied to her about taking her home, intending to keep her like...like some sort of love slave.

A snort escaped. Love slave didn't come into her job description. She had to admit Ry had a way about him that made her want to offer her body every time they were alone. Yeah, she was a willing participant when it came to Ry.

The marines quick-marched and Camryn decided she'd better pay attention instead of daydreaming about Ry and his sexual prowess. If she wanted to escape, she needed to concentrate. Collect information.

They turned into a better part of the city where the men who held office lived. Halfway along the street they halted at a townhouse. One of the marines pounded the doorknocker. A loud clatter sounded when the lock slid back. The marines waited until the door creaked open.

"They're waiting inside for you," the marine standing beside her said. "In you go." He gave her a nudge in the middle of the back.

Camryn staggered forward before skidding to a halt. The last thing she saw before the door shut were the smirks of the marines. Their sniggers were audible even after she could no longer see them.

A single lamp lit the entranceway. Camryn gained the impression of dark wood and a tiled floor. She shivered at the cool air, a direct contrast to the humidity outside. The tiles were cold on her bare foot.

"This way, if you please." A slender woman with her bright orange, red and gold hair piled on top of her head appeared from the shadows and the large man who had opened the door stepped away to sit on a spindly chair, a gleaming cutlass at his side.

Camryn hesitated, glancing at the stout door and the silent man guarding the escape route. She wouldn't be leaving via this door. She turned to the emotionless woman and followed, her curiosity aroused. What was this place and why had the marines acted so amused? It didn't smell like a jail despite the security.

Once they left the gloomy entrance hall and headed down a narrow passage, myriad scents bombarded her, so many her nose twitched. She sneezed. Sandalwood. Patchouli. Citrus. Floral, floor polish and a faint tinge of something antiseptic.

A buzz of feminine chatter pelted her when the woman led her into a huge reception room. Velvetlike red fabric screened the windows. The white tiles were still cold beneath her feet, and it was a relief to step onto the large red and black carpet, which concealed all but the outer tiles around the edges. A table laden with beverages and plates of pretty iced cupcakes stood to her right.

About thirty women occupied the room, chatting and laughing with each other. Their gowns were sumptuous synsilk and lace. Decadent. In different colors, they showcased the women's figures to perfection. Camryn had never seen so many beautiful women in the same place at one time. Some were obviously alien with delicate pastel coloring or slanted eyes, but all appeared humanoid in appearance.

Confusion didn't begin to cover Camryn's emotions.

Her female escort glided into the middle of the room and clapped her hands. Silence fell.

The woman gestured in an imperious manner to Camryn, indicating she should join her. Slowly Camryn obeyed, halting at her side. Every woman seemed to focus on her then, their quick summations and conclusions clear on their faces. Her muddy appearance and disheveled hair amused them. Some tittered when they noticed her single shoe.

"This is Camryn O'Sullivan. She is joining us."

Camryn didn't understand. A guard stood at the door, yet these women lived in apparent luxury. Not one of them appeared unhappy. What kind of jail was this?

"You may go back to your tea now," the woman said, and the gay chatter recommenced. "Come," she said to Camryn. "I will show you to your room and arrange for new clothes and a bath."

"But—" Before Camryn could ask questions the authoritative woman swept away with a rustle of skirts. Camryn ran after her. Her breath came in pants by the time she caught up at the top of a flight of steps. "Wait," she gasped. "I don't understand. What is this place? Why am I here?" She tugged on the woman's scarlet bell sleeve in a demand for answers.

The woman frowned at Camryn's hand, her displeasure clear. Camryn released the woman's creased sleeve and stood defiant. She wanted answers. Now.

The woman smiled, although it never reached her eyes. Camryn's instincts urged her to step away since the woman reminded her of a tiger about to pounce. "You are at the governor's house. This is where he quarters his harem. And you, my dear, are his latest addition."

"Hell, is that Ry?" Jannike raced down the narrow alley to where Ry lay on the ground.

Kaya sprinted after her. "Is he dead?"

"He's not moving," Nanu said.

Jannike snarled, sending the trio of scavenging males fleeing. She castigated herself for letting Ry and Camryn leave ahead of them. Although she hadn't liked the woman at first, she'd come to admire her courage and tenacity. The way she'd trained the hell-horse despite the great danger to her personal safety.

Jannike's long legs took her to Ry's side quicker than the others. She squatted beside him. Blood matted his hair at his nape. With her fingers, she touched his neck. A strong pulse.

Air whooshed from her lungs with relief. Turning his head gently, she checked for further damage. Although his head wound still bled, already the flesh knitted together. Thanks to his feline genes, Ry healed fast.

"Is he okay?" Kaya demanded.

"Let me see," Mogens said.

"Yeah, his hard head saved him." The panic in Kaya's voice made Jannike look closely, made her question. As part of the crew, Kaya lived with the danger and accepted they were on the run and might die. "Why?"

"Jannike, I've...um...done something bad, something stupid."

After studying Kaya's guilty face, Jannike took a wild guess. "You're the informer."

"I don't know what happened. I didn't mean to tell Talor a thing then suddenly I'm spilling my guts." Her head drooped, glossy blue hair sweeping over her cheek.

"Mogens thinks Talor has magical powers."

"That's it," Kaya said, slashing her hand through the air with a hint of passion. "He asked me a question. I didn't want to answer and the next min I'm babbling every secret without hesitation. I'm so sorry!"

"We'll talk about it once we're back at the hotel room."

Kaya nodded. "I guess I need to confess to Ry once he recovers. Do we carry him?"

"Unless Mogens has any ideas." Jannike stood aside to let the seer check Ry. "Mogens? How is he?"

"His head is healing. He will recover." Mogens grimaced. "It might take time for him to wake."

Nanu gestured at Ry. "How will we get him to the hotel? We'll attract attention."

"Hire a sedan chair," Mogens suggested.

Jannike frowned. "We'll have to pretend he's drunk. If they think he's sick, they'll suspect the plague and refuse to take him."

"We'll need to get him to the main street. None of the chairmen will come down the back streets. They'll think we're going to rob them," Kaya said.

"We'll drag him if we have to." Jannike went to his shoulders and lifted while Kaya took his feet. She held back a grunt, knowing this wouldn't be easy and would take time and much exertion. But Jannike did it because Ry was a friend. And she knew he'd do much more to save any of them.

Mogens grasped Ry's middle, easing the weight. Moving slowly, Nanu led the way, watching for trouble with weapon drawn. They splashed through a deep puddle, the rank water leaking over the top of her boots. Jannike grimaced but didn't complain. Instead, she worried about Camryn.

"Ry is going on short rations once he's better," Kaya said with a grunt.

"He's all muscle," Mogens said. "Nothing wrong with him."

"Try telling that to my back." Jannike didn't think the entrance to the alleyway appeared any closer than when they'd started. "What do you suppose the squishy things are underfoot? I can't see but they're slippery."

Nanu's laugh held humor. "There's a tannery shop next door."

"Eew," Kaya said.

They passed a pile of furry debris, which backed up Nanu's statement.

"Not much farther," Jannike said. A lie. The distance hadn't reduced but she figured encouragement would help.

"Ry didn't want to get his boots dirty," Kaya grumbled.

"Bloody oath," Ry said in agreement.

Startled, Mogens released his middle, and Jannike staggered under the extra weight. He almost hit the ground before she caught him.

"How long have you been awake?" she demanded.

"The smell woke me."

"Can you stand?"

"No idea." Ry groaned. "What hit me? My head feels as if it might explode."

"Damn, Ry. You weight a ton," Jannike said. "New plan. Kaya's gonna let go of your feet. I'll help you balance."

He staggered but to Jannike's relief, managed to stay on his feet. With her help, along with Kaya's, they shuffled to the end of the alley.

"I'll get a sedan chair." Mogens disappeared around the corner.

"Did you see Camryn?" Ry asked. "I saw a marine grab her."

Jannike frowned. "Marines? If that's true they'd take her to jail."

Ry winced. "What? Why?" He closed his eyes. "I can't contact her."

"Telepathically?" Kaya asked.

"Which means she's not in the vicinity," Jannike said. "We will find her, but first we need to get you to safety."

"No. I have to find Camryn." He attempted to stand on his own.

Kaya lost her grip, and Ry toppled to the ground, dragging Jannike with him.

"Damn it, Ry. Get off me." Jannike struggled to her feet, mud soaking her jacket. With Kaya's help, she managed to haul Ry to his feet again. Ignoring the snickers from Nanu who ambled behind them, they made it to the main road where Mogens had waved down a sedan chair.

An hour later Jannike let herself out of the hotel room again. Ry had wanted to search for Camryn, despite being in no condition to leave his bed. With her help, Mogens had managed to force a sleeping draft down him and he'd fallen silent. But only after extracting a promise from her to go to the jail to learn what she could. Jannike snorted as she made her way down the rear hotel stairs to the street outside. Her back ached from dragging Ry around and her shirt clung to her back and chest. She could smell herself and it wasn't pretty. A yawn slipped out. It had been a long day and was about to get longer.

Twin lamps burned outside the gateway, but nothing could make the place feel welcoming. Jannike scowled at the nervous anxiety in the pit of her stomach. She could do this. Forcing aside memories of months spent rotting in a similar place on another planet, she strode to the sturdy gate and pounded on it with her fist. A guard slid a viewing slot open and peered through.

"Whatcha' want?" He spat a wad of chewing tobacco at her feet.

"Did a woman prisoner arrive earlier?"

"Don't give info for free."

Jannike stilled. "What did you have in mind?"

The tall lanky male looked her up and down. "Kiss and a feel of ya tits for starters."

"All right."

The guard opened the gate and sauntered out. Face expressionless, Jannike leaned over and kissed his mouth. She winced at the hands that gripped her breasts and willed herself not to react. After allowing the groping for thirty secs, she pulled away.

"No prisoners due until tomorrow." The guard spat again, this time hitting her boot. Her mouth tightened. "New shipment from the hulks on Ibrox due then."

"So you haven't received any new prisoners this evening, either male or female?"

"Nah, could do with a little female company though. Liked the feel of ya tits. Don't suppose you wanna let me dip my wick?"

"No." Jannike had promised herself she'd never use her body as a bargaining tool again. She had her limits. "Thanks for the info."

Jannike hurried back to the hotel. When she slipped inside, Ry was still asleep. Nanu and Kaya had claimed floor space, and both sat up when she entered. Mogens' skin glowed an eerie black, almost blending into the darkness. She should have been used to it but seeing him this way always brought discomfort.

"Did you find her?" Kaya asked.

"No." Jannike wiped the back of her hand across her mouth. "Do we have anything to drink?" She could still feel the guard's moist mouth on hers, his grubby hands groping her breasts. Shuddering, she accepted the bottle of grog from Nanu. Tipping back her head, she took a long draft. "I don't know where Camryn is because they didn't take her to the jail."

"What do we do?" Kaya asked. "Where is she?"

"Nothing can be done now," Mogens said. "We should rest. Tomorrow, we hunt."

"Ry is meant to go to the governor's house tomorrow to talk with Gweneth and collect the winner's purse." Nanu said what they were all thinking.

"He won't marry her," Jannike said.

Not one of the crew disagreed with her.

CHAPTER SIXTEEN

Ry woke and bolted upright in bed to see his crew sleeping on the floor. Apart from Camryn. Hazy memories returned—winning the race, the ball. Talor departing without making good on his promise. His fight with Camryn.

She'd left.

"Jannike," he barked, recoiling at the pain slicing through his head. He probed a sore spot with his fingers and winced.

"Aye, Captain." Jannike woke alert and ready to take action.

"Where's Camryn?"

"We don't know. She's not at the jail."

"Talor?"

Jannike frowned. "I'm not sure."

Kaya stood and switched her weight from one foot to the other. She stared at her feet before blurting, "I told Talor about our plans."

"What?" Nanu howled, springing to his feet. "Yep died because of you!" He launched himself at Kaya, attacking with his fists. She didn't try to fight back. Blood spurted from her nose. Her head snapped back, hitting the wall before Jannike dragged Nanu away.

"Let her talk," Mogens said.

"I met Talor during one of our trips to Ibrox. I didn't know who he was since I hadn't been on the Indy for long and he doesn't look like Ry. We spent time together. I liked him," she mumbled, heightened color in her cheeks.

"Go on," Ry said, his stomach tight with tension. Where the blue blazes was Camryn? Was this Kaya's fault?

"When I found out who he was, I tried to stay away. I couldn't. He'd tell me to meet with him again and I would. I couldn't stop myself."

"Compulsion," Mogens said. "It's obvious your brother has the power to coerce. Just as I said before."

"Did you tell him anything about Camryn?" Ry stood and concentrated on Kaya even though his head ached. Although he wanted to blame her, he couldn't. He knew his brother.

Kaya shook her head. "No...well, I did. But there wasn't much to tell Talor, apart from the details of our hell-horse and what we intended to do. Thankfully, he didn't always ask the right questions."

"Ah, Captain, you might want to put on some clothes," Jannike said.

"No point dressing fully," Ry said, grabbing his trousers. "I'm going to shift and search for Camryn."

"But someone will see you," Jannike protested. "You'll cause a riot."

"Too bad. It's the easiest way for me to search for Camryn."

Mogens faded into gray before seeping back to black. "You'll heal better in feline form."

"What about the wedding?" Nanu asked.

Ry growled. "I don't want to marry the governor's daughter."

His crew all looked at one another before Jannike spoke. "But, Ry, what about the currency? If you refuse to marry the woman the governor won't hand it over."

"I know. Let's find Camryn first then we'll worry about the wedding and dowry." Picturing his feline, he shifted, fur rippling across his skin, the magic of the change reshaping bones and limbs until he stood on all fours, waiting for his crew. When they stared, he growled and followed up with a warning bark. They erupted into action, all dressed in secs flat.

Jannike opened the door and peered outside before standing aside to let him out. Frankly he didn't care if anyone saw him. All he wanted was Camryn.

Ry prowled down the stairs and heard his crew clomping behind him. Impatiently he waited for them to open the door leading to the street. He burst outside, the hurried footsteps behind telling him his crew followed where he led.

Camryn stalked the perimeter of the luxurious bedroom. Her prison. Behind the sumptuous velvetlike curtains, stout bars blocked an exit via the window. The thick door remained locked despite her vehement protests. She had no idea of the time but the scant light entering the small, barred window told her it was still dark. She paced the confines once again and opened her mind, searching for Ry. Nothing.

"Damn and blast," she muttered, kicking the door when she passed. "Shit." Camryn limped a few steps when pain radiated from her toes and up her leg. At least it wasn't the same leg the hell-horse had bitten during the race. That was still a little tender. She had no idea what Mogens put in his green paste, but it was a wonder, promoting rapid healing. She limped over to the bed and flexed her toes. A double bed, she noted with a healthy dose of unease. They'd have to hold her down before she'd have sex with that short tub of lard.

Tiredness pulled at her as she tried to connect with Ry again. Like an unwelcome rash, he appeared whenever she didn't want him. Right now she'd give just about anything to see him walking through the door. Because she felt pissed and bore the stubborn gene, she stood and limped around the room once more, the thick floor covering muting her footsteps. The lap of luxury and she wanted out.

"Camryn," the whispery sound floated from the corner of the room.

She froze, rooted to the spot, every sense working to relay information to her doubting brain. No one was present. She was alone.

"Camryn." This time the voice was familiar.

"Ga-Gabriel?"

A faint form shimmered before her, and she blinked to clear her vision. "Trust your instincts, Camryn," he whispered. "Love the cat."

"But I...I l-love you." Shock made her stutter.

The form glided across the floor and hovered, a little scary but also mesmerizing. "You have a huge heart. Room for another."

"No!" Camryn blurted. "I failed you."

"Never," he said. "Go with love sweet, Camryn." Gabriel's form started to fade.

"No, don't go." Her heart drummed in choppy, audible beats. She reached out, trying to grasp him, stop him, but her fingers groped air. And then there was nothing.

She blinked. Had she imagined him? Blast it, she had to leave before she went mad.

Another survey of the room confirmed her findings. There was no way out, and depressed, she slumped on the bed.

Camryn woke suddenly, at a loss to explain what had disturbed her slumber. A click directed her attention to the door. It opened before she had a chance to hide.

"Hello, my dear," the governor said.

The woman with the orange, yellow and red hair stood aside to let the tubby man enter.

"It's very early. I didn't think you'd be awake."

"So why did you come here?" Camryn demanded, moving away from the bed. The gleam in the man's eyes made her uneasy. Surely he didn't expect her to welcome him? "I need my beauty sleep."

"Enough," the woman snapped, her gaze hard. "You will not speak to the governor in that manner. Some respect please."

"When he earns it," Camryn gritted out.

The governor ignored her outburst and surveyed her as if she was a new purchase and unfamiliar. "She smells. Arrange a bath and the usual grooming. Clothes—I'll leave to your discretion."

"Don't I have a say in this?" Camryn asked snidely.

The governor chuckled. "No, my dear. No choice whatsoever."

"Very well," the woman said, and her nose wrinkled as if she didn't relish the chore. "It will be done."

"I will visit tomorrow night," the governor said with a lingering look at Camryn.

Camryn suppressed her shudder. She knew what thoughts ran through the pervert's mind. At least Ry had given her a choice and hadn't forced himself on her. She'd taken one look at the hunky alien and hadn't been able to take her eyes off him.

"Sweet dreams, my dear," the governor said. "I look forward to tomorrow night." He walked out with the woman following two steps behind. The door closed and the lock clicked into place.

Camryn closed her eyes, despair creeping up on her. No! Ry and his crew would find her. She knew they would.

Ten minutes passed. No longer tired, Camryn paced. The lock

slid back again, and the door opened. The boss woman entered along with two men bearing a large tub. Several other ladies followed, carrying buckets of steaming water. The men set the tub down and moved back against the wall while the ladies poured the water into the tub and left the room.

"Strip," the woman in charge said.

Camryn glanced at the two silent men and frowned before returning her attention to the woman.

"If you do not strip the men will do it for you." Amusement colored her voice and Camryn sighed.

Slowly she let her cape drop away. "I will need help with the buttons."

"Georges, help her with her buttons," the woman directed.

Camryn could tell by the curl of her lips the woman expected an argument. A glance at the two men told Camryn there was no point offering resistance. Better to pick her fights.

Georges walked over to her, and Camryn offered her back. His big fingers fumbled the buttons and soon her gown gaped, only held up by her hands at her breast.

"Continue," the woman said.

Camryn let the dress slip to the ground. She stepped out of the pool of fabric and rolled down her stockings.

The ladies arrived again with more water. One added a vial of oil to the bath and soon a floral scent reminiscent of lavender filled the room. Another placed a small container of something on the lip of the bath while another carried towels.

Showtime, Camryn thought with a wry twist of lips. She unfastened her stays and chemise, tossing both aside. Her nose rose in the air when she glanced at the woman in charge. "I presume the bath is for me?"

"What is that on your back?" The woman grabbed her shoulder and roughly turned her to face to door. A gasp of horror escaped. "Out," she ordered. "Everyone out. You, take her dirty clothes with you."

The two men halted their perusal of her breasts and snapped to attention, marching from the room at the order. After gathering her soiled clothes, the ladies with the buckets followed. The door shut, leaving Camryn alone with the agitated woman.

"You wear the mark of the cat." Accusation shaded her words and her brow creased in a mighty frown.

Camryn didn't understand her acute about-face. What did the tattoo mean? Ry didn't know. His strange tattoo puzzled him. Mogens knew nothing, or if he did, he wasn't saying while the rest of the crew hadn't seen the tattoo. Mogens thought it related to Ry's race. Lately he kept muttering about mates.

After a long pause, Camryn decided to follow gut instinct. She lifted her chin. "Yes, I do."

"This changes everything. Take your bath. A maid will bring you clean clothes and food." Then she strode from the room.

Camryn waited for her to lock the door but didn't hear the click announcing her imprisonment. She darted forward to test the door and found it open when she twisted the handle. Whatever the mark of the cat meant, it had rattled the woman. She shut the door, frowning. Difficult to go anywhere without clothes. Camryn walked to the bath, deciding to take advantage of the warm water. The water splashed when she climbed in. Warm and fragrant, it came up to her breasts. She leaned back with a soft groan of pleasure. She scrubbed the dried mud off her feet and washed her entire body. Although tempted to linger, she climbed out. Heedless of the puddles she left, Camryn marched over to the bed and dried herself, wincing at the tender spot on her back. The mysterious tattoo. She wished she could see it properly. The tender didn't have mirrors, and she'd had to rely on Ry and Mogens to describe it—a leaping black feline, according to them.

The door opened and a woman entered bearing a set of clothes. A second bore a tray of food. They stared at her back, their gazes full of curiosity.

Camryn accepted the clothes and yanked on the chemise, frowning at the lace and silky fabric. Fine and transparent, meant to attract a man. Her scowl intensified. No way did she want to entice the fat tub of lard. Every time she looked at him, she pictured a frog.

The woman handed her the stays and dress that went on the top. Bother, no panties again. Going around naked beneath her clothes made her nervous. It made her worry about a reversion to childhood clumsiness.

Camryn pulled on the stays—this one laced from the back—and silently presented her back so the woman could lace them. The dress went on next. White stockings secured with lacy garters. She stepped into the matching slippers. Once dressed, the women left her alone without locking the door.

When the woman's footsteps receded, Camryn sneaked from the room to start her clandestine exploring. There had to be some way out. She smiled. Her brother would never believe this when she told him. Her sister-in-law would probably want to sign her up for rehab.

"Ry, slow down," Jannike called.

Ry grunted and slowed his lope to a trot. The trail smelled faint. He wanted to hurry before people started pouring from their houses to complete their morning business and obliterated the trail. He trotted down the street, slowing when he neared the jail to scent again. Relief filtered through Ry when he located her scent continuing past. Stories and gossip indicated harsh treatment at this jail. He scurried onward, footsteps behind indicating his crew still following.

The trail took them into a better part of town, through a marketplace—empty now—and into streets of imposing houses built by the rich merchants who made Ornum their home. The trail petered out at the doorway of a smart townhouse. Ry halted, flicked his tail.

Camryn?

Ry? Is that you?

Ry bared his teeth in a feline smile when he heard the excitement in her voice. Who else were you expecting?

The governor. This is where he houses his harem.

Ry growled, low and fierce, making his crew stiffen in alarm. If he's touched you—

No, he intends to come back tonight night after the wedding celebrations.

A snarl rumbled up Ry's throat and his top lip curled to display fangs. There's not going to be a wedding. Not when you're my mate.

Whatever, Camryn thought with impatience. When you're ready, I want to leave.

How many guards?

One on the door. I've seen two other men. The woman who runs the place brought them with her to encourage me to undress when she wanted me to take a bath. We need to look at the diary and the gold box again. They freaked out when they saw my tattoo. The woman called it the mark of the cat. It meant something to her. She said she'd need to talk to the governor.

If they're worried about the tattoo, the real thing will upset them, Ry told her. Where are you now?

Upstairs. I've sneaked out of my bedroom. I'll creep downstairs.

Stay where you are. I'll come to you.

Ry blocked Camryn's protests and stood back to give Jannike access to the door. A bark of impatient demand escaped. He wanted to touch Camryn, to hold her. He wanted to mark her with his scent and exert his ownership. No matter what Camryn thought, what she said, she belonged to him. Time she acknowledged the fact. When Jannike stopped beside him, he stalked up behind her and gave her an impatient nudge.

"Don't you think we should stake out the place first?" Kaya asked.

Ry let out another impatient bark. They needed to work out a better system of communication. When Jannike still hesitated, he nipped her leg.

"Ow! Dammit, Ry. There's no need to bite," she snapped. "What do you want me to do? Knock at the door?"

He grunted and gave her a sharp push with his paw.

"You've put a hole in my trews," Jannike protested.

His growl grew impatient, and with a scowl in Ry's direction, Jannike pounded on the door.

"Nobody is home," a voice said through the door.

"There must be a rear entrance, a servant's entrance," Nanu said. "We should enter that way."

Ry didn't think much of the idea. He wanted Camryn. A sharp snarl gave his opinion.

"I think we're going in the main entrance," Nanu said dryly.

Jannike pulled out her gun and fired at the lock. She fired again before the door flew open. Ry lunged inside, following the scent trail direct to Camryn, leaving his crew to deal with the man at the entrance.

Camryn met them at the top of the stairs. "About time. What kept you?"

"Where's the rest of the staff?" Jannike asked, pushing the guard into his chair.

"They're frightened of the woman," the guard said, his eyes bulging. "Nothing frightens Madam Riches. Apart from her." He pointed at Camryn. "The staff take their cue from Madam."

"I don't know why," Camryn said. "I didn't bite. Not once."

Ry barked and prowled over to her to rub against her legs. A loud, happy purr rumbled from him.

"Keep the cat away from me," the man said when Ry's tail slapped him across the face.

Ry scrutinized Camryn, mesmerized by the blinding smile that spread across her face. She clicked her fingers at him. "Come, Kitty."

Jannike smothered a chuckle. Nanu laughed outright.

Camryn sashayed out the front door, her backside swaying in a sexy manner. A low grumble sounded deep in Ry's throat when he stalked after her. He'd see how brave his mate was when he faced her man to woman.

"I don't know why you're insisting on my presence." Camryn's eyes narrowed. They'd returned to the hotel to change before heading to the governor's mansion. "Is this a punishment because I called you 'Kitty'?"

Ry glared back. "You are the most stubborn, infuriating woman I've ever met."

"So why do you want to keep me? Why won't you take me home?"

"Because I need you."

Camryn fell silent, thinking about his words, remembering the panic and anxiety she'd felt while locked in the harem. Okay, she conceded. He might have a point about them being mates, but she didn't have to embrace the fact. "I'll change clothes first. And we should study the diary."

Ry's gaze raked across her, his eyes darkening with clear interest. "No, you look beautiful. We'll check the diary when we return."

"I stand out like a traffic light. I don't want to attract attention."

"We might need you to distract the governor," Jannike pointed out.

Camryn exhaled noisily, feeling half naked in the dress even though she knew they were right.

"Ready?" Ry asked, taking in his crew.

At their nod, he moved.

"The ghost has gone," Mogens said to her in an undertone. "He has passed on his message and is at rest."

Camryn stared at the seer, chill bumps prickling on her arms and legs. "Gabriel?"

"Yes," Mogens said. "He knows you're safe now." The seer strolled away, leaving Camryn staring after him in consternation.

"Camryn, is something wrong?" Ry's brow furrowed as he reached out to cup her cheek.

"I'm fine." She ambled after the crew, trying to sort out her thoughts. That had really been Gabriel. She'd loved him so much. Still loved him, but now she felt at peace and the sense of blame for his death had lifted. Camryn didn't understand what had happened and decided not to mention it to the others, to embrace the serenity instead and just be. Yeah, it was weird but in a list of bizarre occurrences, a ghost didn't stand out any more than aliens. Snorting softly she hastened to catch up with Ry.

It took them half an hour to walk to the governor's house. Camryn wondered about the bride, if she'd be disappointed. Gweneth looked forward to marriage, even though she didn't know a thing about her prospective husband. What sort of a father gave his daughter away to a man neither of them knew?

A chain gang of prisoners jogged to the manufacturing plant for their day of work, guards snarling at any male or female they thought moved too slowly.

A woman stood on a street corner, selling pastries. "Meat pasties for sale. Get your meat pasties here."

Other men and women were setting up their produce.

Ry stopped a few houses away from the governor's mansion. "Remember, this time we'll enter via the rear."

"We know the plan," Nanu said.

They slipped down an alley and found the gate of the governor's mansion open to receive a delivery. They were inside before the servants realized anything was amiss. Jannike and the others held the servants while Ry and Camryn hurried off in search of the prospective bride.

"Which way?" Camryn asked. "The next floor?"

Ry paused to sniff. "Yeah, up the stairs."

Camryn followed him up the curving staircase and to the right. She heard voices coming from a room about halfway along the passage.

Ry pressed his finger to his lips. They crept closer, pausing outside the doorway.

"Do not take your mask off, girl. I do not care to see your face." The governor's distinctive tones.

Camryn and Ry exchanged a glance and by common consent waited.

"It's not my fault I take after my mother," a woman said in a pained voice. "Don't you think my bridegroom will want to see my face when we are married?"

"You are nothing like your mother. Not with the abominable mark on your face. It's the mark of the damned. You will marry with your face veiled. I do not care to see you."

The cool dismissal in the governor's voice was in direct contrast to the pain in his daughter's voice. No wonder she wanted to leave.

You can't leave her with that abominable man.

I'm not going to marry her when all I can think about is you.

Tough decision, Camryn mocked.

No decision at all. Ry strode through the door, indicating she should follow. "Hello," he said in a hearty voice.

"You!" the governor said in clear shock on seeing her standing beside Ry. His gaze slid down Camryn's body and back up to linger on her shoulder. He backed away until the wall halted his retreat.

"Did you think I'd stay in the harem and wait for you?" Camryn asked in a sweet voice.

"Guards!" The color had bleached from the governor's ruddy face, leaving him looking as pale as Mogens on a good day.

"They won't come," Ry said. "My crew is downstairs. Besides, Camryn is my woman. I don't like stealing."

"Your woman," the daughter said.

"My woman," Ry confirmed with conviction.

"My daughter belongs to you now," the governor said. "If you don't take her I won't give you the dowry."

"Go and get the currency," Ry said to the governor. "Come straight back or I'll make you sorry."

"You and whose army?" the governor asked with a sneer.

A standoff. Camryn knew Ry and his crew needed the currency. They'd talked about setting up a base—a real home to return to at the end of a long journey. A spike of pain hit her then. A shock of truth. She loved the annoying kitty. But she also wanted to return home.

Ry, she thought. *Shift to cat. The tattoo of the cat on my back scared them. Maybe a feline in his face will switch his thinking about this matter.*

Maybe, he answered.

"The currency," Ry said.

"As long as you stick to your end of the deal," the governor said. "My daughter goes with the currency. You must take both."

"Why don't you just send her away?" Camryn tilted her head to stare at the tubby man. "If she offends you so much."

The governor seemed to shrink at her words.

"He can't," Gweneth said. "He promised my mother he would see me safely married. He promised her on her deathbed and fears bringing a curse on himself."

"What curse?" Camryn asked.

Gweneth glanced at her father before speaking. "The cat will stalk through the land. It will wreak havoc and destroy all those who stand in its way."

Did you hear that, Ry? Is she talking about you? It would explain why the woman in the harem quarters panicked on seeing my tattoo.

"I won't marry you," Ry said, turning back to Gweneth. "I am already mated. But you can come with us as part of the crew."

Gweneth turned a searching gaze on Camryn. "I remember speaking with you at the ball. Is he an honorable man? Or would I suffer if I join his crew?"

"He is honorable," Camryn said. It was nothing less than the truth.

"Father, would that be acceptable?" Gweneth asked. "You would be rid of me."

"No, you won't be married."

Ry stalked closer and loomed over the governor to growl at him.

"Yes, yes," he said hastily, sweat beading on his forehead. "On the condition you never return to Ornum again."

Ry stretched out his hand without hesitation. "I agree. Give me the currency now."

The governor practically ran from the room.

"Go with him," Gweneth suggested, her voice heavy with hurt. "Do not trust him until you have the currency in your hands."

Ry nodded and slipped out to follow the governor. I think it might be time for the cat to make an appearance.

"Would you like me to help pack your clothes?" Camryn asked. "I can help you choose what to take with you."

"Thank you." Gweneth pulled a soft bag from a wardrobe.

A loud shriek sounded, fear echoing throughout the mansion. Ry?

Merely pulled out my party trick. No problems.

279

Camryn smiled and calmly continued.

A maidservant hurried into the room. "What is happening? Who is she?"

"Never fear, Amme. I am leaving the mansion, just as my father arranged."

"Before your wedding?"

"I won't be getting married."

"But the curse. Where will you go? What will you do? Never mind," the maidservant said. "I will go with you."

"I'm leaving now," Gweneth said. "Besides, I do not believe the so-called curse. I have never seen black cats on our planet."

Huh, little did they know, Camryn thought.

The maid considered her mistress and nodded. "I will pack also."

Camryn wondered what Ry would think of an extra woman on his crew and decided it didn't matter.

They finished packing and made their way down to the servants' entrance where the crew waited.

Ry, we're ready to leave.

On my way.

Ry slipped into the room to join them, wearing a grin. "Most profitable. He paid me to leave and gave me a bonus for his daughter as well." He noticed the maid. "Who's she?"

"Another crewmember," Camryn said.

"The tender will be crowded." Ry winked. "We'll have to share quarters."

Camryn suppressed a growl at his smug expression.

It took them some time to make their way to the tender after stopping at the hotel. Mogens and Nanu left to collect Gabby and Luke from the stables while the others stopped via the hotel to collect their gear. Once they were all on board, they took off, leaving for the spaceport.

"You can take your mask off now," Camryn said, curiosity getting the better of her. "You don't need to wear it anymore."

"You might change your mind when you see my face." Fear, stark and vivid, glittered in Gweneth's eyes, and she backed away from both Camryn and Mogens.

"Take it off," Mogens said. "You're among friends. None of us will judge you." His voice sounded huskier than normal, his color a glittering white. It didn't seem to faze Gweneth, which made Camryn think more of her. Mogens made most people uneasy.

Gweneth fumbled with the strings holding the mask in place because her hands trembled so much. Feeling pity, Camryn walked up behind and took over.

She peeled the mask away, a gasp escaping when she caught a glimpse of her face. "Bloody hell. Ry!"

Attracted by her shout, the crew came running. They stopped and stared.

"Nanu, take the controls," Ry said in a strained voice.

He walked up to her and reached out to trace the tiny cat tattoo on her right cheek. The same tattoo had marked the woman they'd purchased from the slaver. Gweneth trembled under his touch but didn't move.

"Madam," Ry said finally. "Where do you come from? Are we related?"

Chapter Seventeen

"Do you know anything about your mother?" Both excitement and trepidation collided in Ry. Another clue to his background. The mystery ate at him just as badly as the desire to clear his name.

He needed answers for himself and for Camryn. His mate.

"I don't know much," Gweneth said. "She died from complications, not long after my birth."

"You must know something. Where did she come from? Which planet?" Desperation tore his gut. She must have some knowledge. He grasped her shoulders and shook her. "Were you born with the mark on your face?"

"Ry, let her go." Mogens yanked his arm, and when Ry turned his attention from Gweneth, he saw the swirls of black unfurling on the seer's face. "You're frightening the women."

"But—"

"Back off," Mogens snarled. A puff of magical power shimmered around him without warning, sending an abrupt shock through Ry. He released Gweneth and stepped back with a sense of astonishment. Silence filled the bridge, and they all shifted uneasily. Camryn stared at him with a silent question.

"I'm sorry," Ry apologized. "I didn't mean to frighten you. Please tell me everything you know about your mother."

"Gweneth is telling you the truth," the maidservant said. "She knows nothing of her mother or her mother's family. Her father refused to discuss the matter and blamed Gweneth for her mother's death."

"But what about her face?" Camryn asked.

"The mark appeared during my thirteenth cycle. Faint at first, it looked like dirt. With each passing cycle the mark deepened and became more defined. During my fifteenth cycle my father made me wear a mask."

"You will never wear a mask again," Mogens said.

"No," Ry agreed, attempting to conceal his disappointment even as his gaze swept to the leaping black cat on her cheek. How could he not have known? He'd smelled the woman with the slaver as soon as she entered the tavern where they were drinking. He'd liked Gweneth's scent but hadn't felt an attraction to her. "We're going back to Ornum to question the governor."

"No," Camryn said. "Quite frankly I want to go home. I don't want to go back."

"No," Mogens said. "Gweneth will not be safe. I have seen it in the clouds."

"Kaya, contact the governor via the comms unit as soon as we reach the spaceport. Privacy mode. We journey to Ibrox. Once Talor clears my name, we'll decide on our next move."

"Aye, Captain."

"And you will take me home," Camryn said.

Ry nodded, unable to bring himself to say the words. Fear

flickered through his veins as truth whispered. He didn't want to go on without Camryn. When they landed on Ibrox, he would take her to the House of the Cat with him, and once he'd met with his sisters and Talor, they would talk. His jaw tensed at the thought of separation. That couldn't happen. He didn't think he could settle on Earth, not when he still had to search for his people.

He bowed to Gweneth. "Please comb your memories for anything relating to your mother and her people. I am of the cat," he said, his manner formal. "I search for our people."

Gweneth stared, her mouth dropping open in surprise. "When I sleep I dream of cats. Big black cats lounging in the sun and playing together in a clearing. Is it possible I dream of our people?"

"Wow," Kaya said. "When I dream it's of battles. Blood. I want the dreams you're having."

"I have had the same dreams, but I thought it happened because I wasn't shifting to my feline form enough," Ry said. "Mogens?"

"Dreams are powerful things. They hold truth."

Which didn't help much, but hope surged inside him anyway. "Can you shift into cat form?"

The maidservant gasped and pulled a talisman from her pocket. "Blasphemy."

"It's all right, Amme. I sense no evil in him."

"He hides it behind his human guise," the maidservant said. She stood her ground, yet her eyes rolled in fear.

Gweneth closed the distance between them, ignoring the maidservant's squawk of protest. She placed her hand on Ry's chest. Ry took satisfaction from Camryn's harsh inhalation before turning his full attention to Gweneth. "I can feel the power beneath your skin." She stroked her hand across his chest and a purr erupted from deep in his throat.

"That's enough," Camryn snapped, and she squeezed her slight frame between him and the taller woman, pushing her away.

"Have no fear. I'm not interested in your man." She stepped

away and Camryn relaxed a fraction, curling into his chest. Ry nuzzled her neck, savoring her feminine scent and wrapped his arm around her waist, needing closer contact. Inside he gloated, although he knew better than to show his triumph.

"No, I have magic inside me, but I cannot change forms. If I touch a person I can tell if they speak the truth."

"Maybe she is still coming into her powers," Camryn said. "It took you a while to gain your powers."

"Have you always lived on Ornum?" Jannike asked.

"Yes," Gweneth said. "My father took up the position of governor before my mother died. We've lived there ever since."

They landed at the spaceport, and after settling Gabby and Luke aboard the Indy, they moved to the bridge.

"Comms connected, Captain."

"Thank you, Kaya." Ry walked into the privacy unit and prepared to interrogate the governor.

"You promised not to contact me again," the governor protested, his long white nightshirt and nightcap emphasizing his pallor.

"That was before I discovered the cat etched into your daughter's cheek." Ry didn't feel guilty about waking the man from his slumber.

"You can't bring her back," the governor blurted.

"I don't intend to," Ry said, struggling to keep his voice even. "Tell me where your wife came from."

"A planet in the Western sector. She lived with her aunt and uncle and never bore the cursed mark on her cheek or on her back like the other woman. Never."

"Which planet?"

"Tagorn."

"Is there anything else I should know?"

The governor shook his head.

"Thank you for speaking with me." Ry disconnected the call

and left the privacy unit. He'd never visited the Western sector before. He intended to play tourist very soon.

The trip back to Ibrox took seven days, days filled with tension and short tempers. Ry throbbed with it and was relieved to arrive at their destination. It was past time for him to face Talor.

"Ready to land, Captain." Nanu went through landing procedures and soon they moored in the Ibrox spaceport.

Ry grabbed a knife from his chamber and shoved it into his boot. At the last min he also collected the diary and box, shoving them into a small pack. It was possible one of his sisters remembered them and could help with the mystery. When he left the Indy, the entire crew waited for him outside. "Are you all coming?"

"Yes." Nanu scowled. "We want to make sure you get there in one piece and—"

"We're nosy," Kaya added.

"I'm still a wanted criminal. It's dangerous keeping company with me."

Nanu snorted. "What's new? Besides, I want to confront your cowardly brother. It's his fault Yep is dead."

Ry sobered, aware Nanu still grieved for Yep. "I'm sorry." Nothing could bring Yep back.

Jannike tapped him on the shoulder. "In other words we're going with you. You can't trust Talor. This is probably a trap."

"All of you?" Ry's gaze slid over Gweneth and her maidservant, ignoring Jannike's words. He didn't trust Talor farther than he could kick him, but he was tired of running.

"I wish to see the city and your House of the Cat," Gweneth said, lifting her chin to boldly meet his gaze. She didn't duck her head, her determination shunting aside self-consciousness. "It is strange you bear a cat and also used to live at House of the Cat, no?"

"Yes." The coincidence hadn't escaped Ry.

"Where the mistress goes, I go," the maidservant said.

"Looks as if we're all going to the House of the Cat," Camryn said.

Ry had timed their arrival for morn since most of society kept late hours. The workers had risen for the day, but they took one look at their weapons before melting into the shadows.

"This is where you were raised?" Jannike asked when they paused in front of metal gates bearing the crest of a cat.

Ry grinned at the disbelief on her face. "Yeah. Home sweet home."

"I wouldn't have wanted to leave," Kaya said. "And all we've seen is the fancy gate."

"I didn't have much choice," Ry said, recalling the hurt from his brother's betrayal—the way everyone had believed his brother rather than him. He pounded on the gates to the mansion and waited for a footman to answer the summons.

"Yes?" The man wore House of the Cat livery. Ry didn't recognize him.

"We are here to see Talor Coppersmith."

The man went away, returning after several mins. The gates opened. Ry stalked through, his crew following. The subtle magic emanating from the mansion welcomed him. A smile of wonder curled across his lips. This place, the House of the Cat, felt like his home. He wondered if the authorities would be quite as welcoming once they realized he'd returned. Hopefully with Talor's support, the authorities would drop the charges. He was tired of running.

Ry halted at the bottom of the stairs leading to the front door. The imposing entranceway looked the same with two trees bearing bright yellow fruit, one on either side of the black shiny door and a golden cat-shaped knocker.

"Take a walk around the gardens," he said. "Follow the path." When his crew stared at him, he gestured with his hand. "Go. I don't need you spying on my reunion with my sisters."

"Spoilsport," Kaya said.

"Give the man some peace." Gweneth placed her hand on Mogens' arm.

Camryn shrugged and turned away to explore the gardens with the others.

Ry reached out and snagged an arm around her waist. "Not you. You're with me."

The door flew open, and his sisters stood there, both slim and silver-haired like Talor. For an instant he stared then he sprinted up the steps to gather his older sister, Edrea, in his arms. After embracing her, he grabbed Cody for a hug too. He felt their pleasure in seeing him and it warmed him through, erasing fears they might reject him because Talor had poisoned their minds.

"Oh Ry. It's so good to see you," Edrea said, her silver hair in an elegant updo as befitted her married status. "Talor said he'd seen you and you'd probably come home."

"Where's Talor?" Ry wanted this settled.

Cody smiled and tossed her head, setting her loose silver locks in motion. "We expect Talor later."

Ry turned to escort Camryn and found not even one of his crew had moved. "My crew," he said. "This is Camryn, my mate."

"His lover," Camryn corrected, bringing a spurt of irritation to Ry. Why couldn't she accept the truth? "He's taking me home soon."

Ry could hear his sisters' thoughts and blocked them despite his fascination.

Edrea offered a gracious smile, reminding Ry of their mother. "You'd better come inside. All of you."

Ry followed his sisters inside and heard his crew trample after him. Memories crowded him—running through the house with Talor and his sisters while playing hide-and-seek, his mother's hugs and kisses when he'd fallen and hurt himself, their father's stern lectures when they misbehaved and his mother's tears when his father died.

Camryn reached for his hand and squeezed in silent comfort, aware of the thoughts rioting through his mind.

"Ah Ryman." Talor strolled into the large and sunny reception room. He was dressed in black trews and a billowy white shirt, his long silver hair tied back in a tail. "You've arrived." Ry noticed his double take on seeing the cat on Gweneth's cheek. Instead of appearing discomforted as most people would, he seemed intrigued. "And your lovely bride. I believe congratulations are in order."

Ry stilled not liking his brother's tone or the sword belted to his side. Instinct told him Talor intended to go back on his word. Hell, he'd suspected he would right from the start. "Gweneth and I have agreed not to marry since I am already mated to Camryn." His sharp glance at Camryn dared her to contradict him. When she sat on a two-seater, he claimed the space beside her. The touch of their thighs soothed his roiling gut. *A pity we aren't alone*, he thought.

Camryn stiffened at his side. *Look at Talor, his body language. He's up to something. See the way he keeps touching the hilt of his sword? Do you think he has notified the authorities?*

"Ryman, I need to talk to you about our business dealings. Perhaps we could take a turn around the garden? Alone."

"Really, Talor. I think we can have drinks before you conduct business. Everyone sit. Please make yourselves comfortable," Cody said, with a chiding glance at her brother.

"Uh, what if we dirty something?" Jannike asked, her gaze flickering over a delicate cream-colored chair.

"Then we'll clean it," Edrea said, picking up a small golden handbell. She shook it vigorously.

"Where are you from, Camryn?" Cody asked, settling on a chair, and fluffing her full skirts.

"I come from Earth, and your brother is returning me there very soon."

"For a short visit," Ry said. "We can spend longer next time." He witnessed the surprise in her brown eyes, the slight narrowing of them while she considered.

"That sounds interesting," Edrea said.

"We haven't seen our brother look so happy since Meghan—" Cody placed her fingers to her lips in clear consternation. "Oops."

"I must insist we discuss our business. Now," Talor said in a hard voice.

Ry felt a sharp tug in his mind. He batted it away before glancing at his sisters and his crew. *Camryn, do you feel that?*

Yes. Something he's doing makes me want to stay seated.

Can you stand?

Yes, I think so—if I block hard.

Ry stood and immediately Camryn followed suit.

Stay here with the crew.

A rude snort escaped Camryn. *Look here, buster. You can't have it both ways. If I'm your mate that gives me rights. I get to watch your back. Besides, I don't trust Talor.*

Ry offered his arm to Camryn before turning his attention to Talor. "Out in the garden?"

Talor's eyes glittered. "She can stay with our sisters." He followed the words with a mental push to obey.

Camryn smiled sweetly, holding her blocks in place. "I believe I'm in need of some fresh air."

"Very well," Talor snarled in clear frustration.

The thick carpet muted their footsteps until they reached the tiled entranceway. Instead of exiting via the front door, Talor wheeled to the left and led them outside through a door leading onto a verandah and into a garden. A fountain tinkled and the scent of flowers wafted from the gardens.

Cool air tugged Ry's queue as he watched his brother, experience telling him to fear the worst.

Shift to cat, Camryn suggested. Give him a fright and take the upper hand.

Nodding, Ry smirked. He'd learned of his brother's powers. Some of them, at any rate. It only seemed fair that Talor had the same advantage. Without haste he unfastened his shirt and removed it. With his gaze on Talor, he called up the cat and shifted to his alternative form.

Talor's mouth opened and snapped shut. "You! You're the cat. That's why my magic—"

"What about your magic?" Camryn scowled at Talor. "Do you enjoy forcing people to act against their will? Do you like setting innocent people up for murder?"

Ry snarled and Talor's hand snapped to the hilt of his sword.

"He isn't a Coppersmith," Talor snapped. "Bloody ironic. My parents adopted a cat. No wonder the business prospered while you were here. We had our very own familiar right at hand, all the talisman we needed for good luck and success. I bet you laughed the entire time."

Ry shifted smoothly back to humanoid form. "I didn't know until I left Ibrox."

"Too bad you have to die," Talor sneered. He yanked his sword free of its scabbard and slashed at Ry. "I'll use the woman as my familiar. I presume the cat on her cheek indicates her feline nature."

Ry jumped back. He heard hurried footsteps behind him but didn't take his eyes off Talor.

"Mogens read the clouds. He told me I'd need to bring you a sword because he wouldn't be able to move," Gweneth said.

From the corner of his eye, Ry saw her hand the sword to Camryn. Interesting. Neither Camryn nor Gweneth seemed susceptible to Talor's powers. Ry accepted the sword from Camryn and dodged a frenzied slash from Talor. Temper. Temper. It would be the death of his brother, if he didn't rein it in.

Talor cackled, the hint of crazy sending a chill down Ry's spine. "Bastard. No matter what I do, you're there like a damn disease. Always interfering. I had to get rid of you." He lunged, the sword whistling through the air. "But you managed to escape, even when I set you up for murder. And you're still screwing with my life. A cat! I should have killed you outright rather than trusting other people to do the job for me."

"Who murdered Maxmus?"

"A passing beggar," Talor snapped. "I compelled him to kill Maximus and planted your name in the redcoat's minds. Pitifully easy, except you escaped."

"What do you want?" Ry stood out of range, watchful and alert.

"What do I want? Your bloody head on a serving platter!" Talor advanced on Ry, murder in his eyes. He attacked, temper reined, replaced with determination.

Swords clashed with a metallic clang. They thrust and parried. The blades flashed, striking with arm-jarring blows. Ry circled his brother warily. Both breathed hard, chests rising and falling from exertion. Sweat beaded their faces.

"I never wanted anything to do with the Coppersmith fortune," Ry said.

"So you stole from me instead."

"You stole my fiancée, the one person I thought I could trust. I heard the two of you planning to turn me in to the authorities. I was desperate and took money from your safe to get off the planet, to stay alive." Ry felt the insistent pressure on his mind, the compulsion emanating from his brother. He forced it away. "You're in debt," he taunted.

"No thanks to you," Talor retorted, attacking with aggressive thrusts of his sword.

"Your debt has nothing to do with me," Ry said, parrying the blows.

Talor attacked, driving forward in a determined attack. Ry felt a prick of pain on his right biceps. He jerked back, glanced down at the bloom of blood. Talor lunged again. Ry held his ground, parrying the strike. Blocking, he waited for an opening. Talor stumbled, and Ry took advantage, forcing his brother back with a rapid surge. Immense satisfaction filled him when he connected with Talor's shoulder. He eased back, giving Talor a chance to recover, but his brother snarled and struck. The swords whistled through the air, clashing violently.

"If one of us has to die at least let me know why."

Talor attacked, the ferocious metallic clang filling the air. Sweat, a tinge of fear filled Ry's senses. Blood colored his brother's shirt red, the scarlet patch obscene against the white syncotton. Ry retreated, gasping with exertion.

"Frightened to strike the killing blow," Talor sneered.

"Mother wouldn't want this."

"This is all her fault." Talor circled and sprang. Their swords collided in a furious assault. Ry blocked and dodged an unexpected kick. Pain radiated from his kneecap, and he staggered, allowing his brother an opening. Talor darted at him, Camryn's scream giving Ry the impetus to roll. Talor's sword speared the ground, right where Ry had stumbled.

"Grata. Mother willed land to you—land I needed to expand so I could pay off my creditors." Talor cursed, fumbling to free his sword. "She left land I'd been promised to you—a worthless murderer."

Furious, Ry shoved him from behind. Talor sprawled facefirst on the lawn. He rolled, scrambling to his feet and grabbing up his sword. Chest heaving, Ry attacked.

"Bastard." Talor recovered, pounced, sword brandished. Steel met steel. Swords slashed together. They surged. Retreated. Talor tripped and Ry capitalized, thrusting his sword into Talor's chest. Talor dropped to the ground and didn't move.

Camryn rushed forward. "Ry, are you all right? Is he dead?"

"I'm fine." Still breathing hard, Ry staggered to his brother's side. "Talor?" Blood seeped from his brother's chest, his breathing harsh and labored.

"Not dead yet," Talor gasped.

Ry cradled his brother's head, desperately needing answers. "Why? Why do you hate me so much?"

"Jealous." Talor coughed, the liquid sound indicating a fatal wound.

"But you're the heir. I've never disputed the fact."

Talor gave a sickening gurgle.

Camryn ripped the bottom of her tunic, holding the pad of fabric to the wound to staunch the blood flow. "The sword—can I take it out?"

Ry leaned over his brother to remove the sword, but a groan slipped free when pain hit his shoulder. He needed to shift to speed healing.

Camryn handed him another piece of tunic. "Change so you'll start to heal."

"I can't," Ry mumbled. "No matter what happens he's my brother. I have to stay."

"Hold his hand. Talk to him while I take the sword out."

The thunder of feet announced his crew's arrival. Ry noticed his sisters as well. He ignored everyone to clasp his brother's hand.

"I wouldn't stay with you." Talor gasped for breath. "You win again." His lips moved, his words scarcely audible.

Ry dipped his head to catch everything his brother said. "Don't talk. Mogens will look at the wound for you."

"Always win. Mother loved you. I needed the land and all the money." Another horrifying gurgle bubbled up his throat and his eyes fluttered. His labored breathing ceased.

"Talor!" Ry grasped his shoulder and shook. "Dammit, what about Mother? Did she believe I was a murderer? Talor?"

Mogens pushed him aside. "Ry, he's dead. You can't do anything now."

"He forced a beggar to kill Maxmus and used compulsion to make the authorities believe I'd done it," Ry said. "How will I clear my name now that Talor is dead?"

"It's possible his death has freed everyone he compelled," Mogens said. "We were able to move again a few mins ago—I presume it was when Talor fell. It's an old crime and perhaps they'll forget you were a suspect."

"Or we could blame Talor," Cody said in a hard voice. "I can't believe..." She trailed off with a shake of her head, unable to voice her thoughts.

"He mentioned Mother's will. I presumed Talor would inherit the bulk of the estate since he was heir. What was in the will?" Ry asked Edrea.

"I don't know. We didn't attend the reading at the lawyer's office because Talor said it wasn't relevant to us," Cody said.

"There's something in it for Ry," Camryn stated. "I could hear it in his voice. He was hiding the truth."

"He was hiding a lot," Ry said. "What do we do now?"

"I suppose we'll need to call the authorities. Oh dear. The scandal!" Edrea flapped her hand in distress. "Talor—I had no idea he felt like that about you."

"Did you know Talor was a wizard?" Camryn asked.

"Mother told us when we were younger that the oldest male in the family inherits powers, and that they're handed down from oldest son to oldest son. She told us we weren't to discuss it with our brothers or father and if we had any questions we had to promise to ask her," Cody said.

"We kept our promise," Edrea added. "Because she was so adamant. But truly, we didn't know Talor had framed you, Ry. We never guessed. We presumed the powers related to the items sold in the Coppersmith business. The charms Father and Talor designed and made to sell."

"He was very charismatic." Kaya's expression was harsh as she stared at Talor's body. "He fooled a lot of people, concealing his true self beneath the charm."

"Ry, please shift so you'll heal," Camryn ordered. "Your brother is a feline shifter," she said to Ry's sisters. "There, no secrets now so you can shift."

With a wry smile, Ry shifted. He heard his sisters' twin gasps, and Camryn's soft laugh.

"Good, Kitty," she said.

Chapter Eighteen

Later That Night, House of the Cat

Ry pulled the box from the canvas covering and reclined against the pillows, his shoulder touching Camryn's. An emotion he identified as happiness filled him to bursting.

"The stone in the top of the box is glowing a different color. It's a deeper blue than before."

Ry lifted the box to study it closely. "I'd hoped Edrea or Cody knew something about the origin or who wrote the diary."

Camryn yawned, stretching her naked body and raising her arms above her head. "It must belong to your natural parents rather than the Coppersmiths, especially with the cat engraving. You should show it to Gweneth. Maybe she'll know what it is. You know, even if you never find your people, you shouldn't worry. The crew is your family." She chuckled, the corners of her eyes crinkling. "You collect them."

"Maybe I'll ask Gweneth." Ry leaned over to nuzzle the soft skin of her neck. He sucked and bit lightly, still in awe of her trust. No way did he intend to give her up. Maybe Camryn was right about his family. At the rate, he was going they'd need a bigger ship. "I've collected you, and I'm not giving you back," he said with a soft growl.

"You promised."

"I suggested a visit. What if I took you home for a visit whenever you wanted?" he countered.

Camryn pulled away from him, her eyes narrowed. "We'd stay together as lovers?"

"My mate," he said simply. He took her hand, tracing his fingers across the calluses she'd received from riding Gabby. A wave of tenderness swept him. His mate. "I keep telling you we belong together."

"I'm not good with relationships." Camryn swallowed, her eyes darkening as her thoughts drifted to the past.

"We could learn together." What did he say to Camryn to make her want to stay?

"Gabriel died because of me. The ambulance officers said if he'd received help sooner he would have survived."

"They don't know that for sure," Ry said, anger at the unseen men filtering into his voice. "Besides, according to Mogens, I'm very fit and healthy."

Camryn sighed. "I've had fun, but I need to stand on my own. Before you came, I was sinking. I've learned a lot about myself since leaving Earth. I need a purpose and I need love."

Ry stared at her as shock punched a hole in his gut. "You have love. Mine," he snapped. "I've told you before. I thought you believed me. I can't imagine spending my time with anyone except you. I love you." The last came out with a growl. He hadn't imagined telling a woman he loved her. Once his feline genes had appeared along with his intense sexual needs, he hadn't let himself think of the future, hadn't thought a life with one woman would be possible. It hadn't seemed likely.

"You love me?" A small frown marred the smooth skin of her brow.

"Yes." He set the box aside and gathered her close to claim a kiss. It started out gently, a mere brushing of lips, before the kiss took a decided carnal slant. He pushed his tongue past her lips and explored the softness beyond. Mine, he thought. My love. My woman. He pulled away to stare at her. "Do you think I'd let anyone else call me Kitty?"

"Dammit, I didn't want to love you." Camryn wrapped her arms around his shoulders, holding him tight. Without warning, the magic of the house seemed to pulse and surround them. It tickled across his back and when he lifted his head, he noticed a soft blue glow. The glow surrounded them both.

"Camryn, do you see it?"

"Yeah." Wonder shaded her answer. "It's amazing, but what does it mean?"

The skin of his chest and back prickled, the sensation deepening to almost painful. Ry tensed against the cramplike ache arcing through his chest and back.

"Eek!" Camryn said. "Something's moving beneath your skin." She pulled away to stare at his chest.

While they both watched, the inky black swirls gathered to form a solid mass.

"Still love me?" Ry gritted out. "With all the weird stuff that keeps happening?"

"Being around you makes life interesting," Camryn said, but her nose wrinkled in a combination of fascination and horror.

"You'll stay with me?" Ry demanded, something inside insisting on her commitment. He'd do anything for her, except let her walk away.

"Yes," Camryn snapped. "I thought men avoided talking about

this stuff. I love you, okay? But that doesn't mean this is a good idea. I told you I'm not relationship material."

Ry grinned. He'd known she loved him, but the words brought intense satisfaction and a sense of rightness. The pain eased off and when he glanced down at his chest he saw the marks had disappeared as mysteriously as they'd appeared. "Have the marks disappeared on my back?" The blue glow continued to surround them, caressing Camryn's curves.

"Roll over a bit more so I can see."

Ry obeyed, presenting his back for viewing.

"Amazing," she muttered.

"What?"

"You have a huge cat springing across your back. It's a bit like mine but bigger." She traced her fingers over his back, and he shivered, the skin sensitive in much the same way as Camryn's.

He rolled back to stare up at her.

"The black has faded from your chest." Camryn ran her fingers across his pectoral muscles, eliciting a completely different feeling. Heat roared through his body, and he tugged her onto his chest, aligning their bodies to perfection. He reached up to kiss her, freezing when an expression of agony creased her face. "Camryn?"

"Hurts," she gasped.

"Where? What hurts?"

"Every...where." Camryn's body twitched, her arms and legs jerking while she writhed against him. She moaned and crawled off him to curl into a fetal ball.

Ry moved closer, alarm filling him. There was no blood. The blue glow had left him and only highlighted Camryn. As he watched the blue turned to bright red. Camryn screamed, her pained shriek lifting the hairs on his arms and legs. Ry reached out to soothe her. His hand brushed her tattoo and she stilled. The glow danced across his arm and gathered in a ball until it covered Camryn's tattoo in red fire and seemed to seep into the skin. Camryn quivered and lay quietly, apart from her harsh pants of breath.

"Camryn. You okay?"

"Yeah. It felt like my insides were turning inside out." She moved gingerly, straightening her body until she lay on her back.

Ry stilled on hearing her description. Swallowing, he stared at her with foreboding. "Ah, I've felt the same thing before." He shuddered, even now remembering the pain when his feline powers had kicked in.

They shared an intense look, Camryn scowling at him. "When?"

"After I left home, when I discovered I was a feline shifter," he said with a trace of caution.

"What?" she shrieked. "I've turned into a kitty-cat?"

Ry winced, understanding her reaction because he'd gone through the same thing. In his case he hadn't had someone to help him with the sheer terror and disorientation of the change. "Let's find out." Ry stood and waited for her to climb off the bed.

Camryn glowered at him. She knew he wanted to help but this was beyond anything she'd experienced before. "I don't want to be a cat."

"I'm sorry."

Camryn knew he meant it, but his concern didn't help. She sucked in a deep breath and smelled dozens of scents. Her hearing—she could hear the rattle of decanter against glass in the library on the floor below. Nanu was still drinking porter. Uneasily, she glanced at the oil painting on the far wall. She could read the signature of the artist without difficulty. Fear licked through her veins. A kitty. Part of her accepted it even though her mind railed against the idea.

"How? How did this happen?"

"I don't know." He shrugged and she felt his clear frustration. "I wish I could tell you."

"To change I picture the cat in my mind, right?" She'd asked about how he changed forms before and knew the drill. A tremor shook her hand, and she hid it behind her back. With a deep inhalation, she thought of Ry in his cat form.

It hurt. Pain speared through her for an instant before she felt her body changing shape. Panicked, she tried to stop but Ry's deep voice calmed her, pulled her through and suddenly she dropped to all fours.

"Camryn," Ry said, smoothing his hand over her head, ruffling her fur.

Her fur. Camryn sneezed, and her tail flicked, lashing across her hindquarters. Camryn started in fright, bringing an abrupt bark of laughter from Ry.

Stop laughing at me, dammit. I'm not used to this.

"Do you want to go outside and run around the garden?"

Are you going to change too?

"Try and stop me." He strode to the door before turning back to grab a robe and shrug it on. "Better not shock the footman on duty."

She padded after Ry, mind busy cataloging scents and tactile sensations. And the things she could see. Incredible, even though her vision was black and white.

"Quiet," Ry said, but Camryn had already heard the low tones of men talking near the front door. They detoured to another room and Ry opened a set of double doors leading into the garden.

Camryn squeezed past him, assailed by myriad scents. Flowers. Coal smoke. Lingering food aromas from dinner. The sharp stones on the footpath gave way to grass beneath the pads of her paws. Behind her she heard Ry's robe whisper to the ground and the sharp cracks his bones made when he shifted to feline. Then he lunged at her in a mock charge. Laughing inwardly Camryn darted away from him, enjoying the play of muscles and the pure rush of speed.

This is amazing.

Are you okay? Ry loped beside her while they ran a circle of the rear garden.

I'm stuck this way. Half woman, half kitty.

It's not so bad. You have me. Ry sounded uncertain, making her realize how difficult it must be not knowing his background.

A rush of tenderness swelled inside her. She loved this man. Without another thought, she pictured her human form and managed to shift. A bit disorientated, her heart still pumping from the rush, she sashayed to the doors they'd exited.

"After you take me home to visit my brother and family, we can start searching for yours. We'll go to the planet Gweneth's mother came from and investigate from there."

Ry fell into step beside her, stooping to pick up the robe he'd worn before he shifted. "Are you sure?"

"Yeah. I'm positive." She'd miss Gabriel as much as she always did, but not everyone gained a second chance at love like this.

They made it to the bedroom without discovery and locked the door to ensure privacy.

Ry smiled and ran his hand over her naked shoulder. He kissed her gently, sliding his lips across hers. "I love you."

"I know," Camryn said with a trace of smugness. "And now you're stuck with me."

Ry chuckled. "Count on it." He tugged her onto the four-poster bed and kissed her neck.

"The box is glowing a weird blue color," Camryn said. "Look." She reached over to pluck it from the dresser and handed it to him. The stone set in the center is a different color. Push it and see what happens."

Ry picked up the box. Camryn could tell it was with little hope since they'd tried to open it before. He ran his fingers across the bright shining blue stone in the middle. With a soft click, the box sprang open.

"Phrull!" Ry muttered. "I've pushed that stone a hundred times and nothing has happened."

Camryn crowded closer. "What's inside?" There had to be something. Her breath eased out when she saw the aged parchment inside—more than one sheet.

Ry opened the first one and scanned the contents. "It's a letter."

Son,

This is the traditional letter written by a father to his son and is bespelled to open only when a mate is found, and the bond formed. Congratulations on finding your mate. I'm sure she's very beautiful and a valiant warrior, willing to fight at your side.

Ry stopped reading. "Do you think this letter is for me?"

"We couldn't open the box and now we can. Of course the letter is intended for you."

Ry's eyes held wonder and he blinked before he started reading again.

I'm going to mention family history, although I'm sure this is old news. It doesn't hurt to emphasize how foolish rifts are amongst kinfolk, especially if they are the result of a stupid argument. My grandfather and his brother argued over policy and the way the House of the Cat should run. Richard left our home planet of Viros and settled on Ibrox many galaxies away. Contact between the Coppersmith brothers ceased. For a time life continued without problem until my grandfather argued with the House of the Cawdor. They hired a wizard to place a curse on the Cat and our luck suffered. Our crops failed and sickness came to our people and loyal followers. You were born during the middle of a great famine. I realized our bad luck started when the two brothers fought. It was time to repair the rift. I decided to travel to Ibrox and attempt to mend the hurt between our families. Surely two cousins can reconcile? The lives of my family and our people depend on it.

If you are reading this letter, I know my journey has been a success and once again the House of the Cat is restored to its former glory—a harmonious clan who pull together to face the good and the bad.

Ry looked up from the letter. "Talor and I are related."

"That's weird. You didn't look alike at all."

"I don't understand why I've never heard anything about this."

"But if your parents crashed maybe there was no reconciliation. Maybe your great-grandfather never spoke of the matter again. Maybe he wiped his hands and started afresh."

"I wonder if Talor had a box like this," Ry said.

"He didn't appear to have a mate. He might have possessed a box and not been able to open it or perhaps your great-grandfather departed from tradition. And from what Talor said the family prospered because you acted as a familiar for them, even though your powers hadn't manifested."

Something slipped from between the pages of the letter and fluttered to the ground. Camryn plucked it from the floor and handed it to Ry. A sense of contentment flooded her when she touched it.

Ry smiled. "It bears a leaping cat."

Camryn crowded closer to him. "It's the same as our tattoos." She glanced up at his face and read his mind with ease. "We're going to my home first, to visit my brother. You promised. I want to spend at least a month there and return often." Camryn held her breath, waiting for his reply. She thought he'd hold to his promise, but if he didn't she'd have to test the bonds between them. Anxiety at possible separation made her bite her bottom lip. No matter what, he couldn't use this mate stuff to force her to act against her wishes. She had a creative imagination when it came to payback.

Ry leaned over to kiss her. "I made a promise and intend to keep it. My family hasn't returned to their home planet for many cycles. An extra month won't make any difference. Besides, we'll need to do some research first."

"I love you."

"I'm counting on it because Mogens informed me the rest of the crew wish to visit your home with us."

"But...but I thought they'd want to have some rest. Recreation." Camryn tried to imagine her brother's reaction and failed.

"You are right. They're my family," Ry said. "Our family. I couldn't say no."

"I guess it would be all right," Camryn said with clear doubt. "My brother has an open mind." And he'd need it. "What about Gabby and Luke?"

"I didn't think another space voyage would be fair on them. I thought we'd stop by the Coppersmith estates and leave them there. Cody is great with animals. She'll make sure they're cared for. Sound okay?"

"Yeah." It sounded great. An adventure. With no doubt a few trials along the way. "I can't think of anyone I'd rather have at my side," she said, and smiled because words were inadequate to describe her happiness and satisfaction. An adventure indeed. "My very own kitty-cat."

"Who are you calling Kitty?" Ry stroked his hand across her back, rubbing her tattoo. A purr erupted and she arched against him with real pleasure.

Camryn chuckled, biting back a groan when his busy hands cupped her breasts. "I guess it takes one to know one," she said. "Two kitty-cats together."

An indignant snort emerged from Ry, but Camryn held the idea for a little longer. Although she was teasing him, she knew it was true. They had so much in common. Yeah, they belonged. Camryn purred and turned in his arms so their lips met. Their bodies strained together, whispering love with every touch and caress.

Camryn parted her legs and Ry slipped inside, the sensual stroking making her groan out loud. It felt so good, so right. Perfect. Like a dance, they glided together, stoking the passion and cementing their love.

They belonged.

Two felines together.

Want to know what happens when Ry, Camryn, and their crew visit Earth? Read **Merry & Seduced** (www.shelleymunro.com/books/merry-seduced).

Or maybe you'd like a glimpse of Ry before he became the captain of the *Indefatigable*? Join my newsletter to receive a free deleted scene from Captured & Seduced. (www.BookHip.com/XKKTDRT)

Turn the page for a glimpse of **Claimed & Seduced**, the next book in the *House of the Cat* series.

Happy reading,

Shelley xx

EXCERPT – CLAIMED & SEDUCED

"You will *choose a wife and marry before this cycle ends. You must follow tradition and do your duty."*

Prince Jarlath Leandros of the planet Viros scowled, loathing the demand in his memory as much as he'd disliked hearing the command from his parents in person. A blur of activity in his peripheral vision jolted him, and he signaled Black, his cambeest to halt.

"Halt, beest." Impatient with the order, Black danced on the spot, the broad leathery pads of his feet thumping the ground. Jarlath curled the fingers of his left hand into the shaggy fur of the beest's hump, just in front of his padded saddle to calm him. Glad of the distraction from his militant thoughts and memories of his mother's piercing voice, he peered through the maze of black tree trunks and the tangle of green-and-pink undergrowth.

Brigands or something more innocent?

"Prince? Is something wrong?" Ellard Tetsu, his security guard, pulled up beside him, a heap of dried pink leaves from the overhead trees crackling beneath his beest's feet. Dubbed the feline shifter with a face only a mother could love, he possessed steadiness and competence. Others might poke fun at his large nose and the ears that protruded a fraction too much, but Jarlath spent much of his time with this man he called best friend. Ellard's tan cambeest snorted a protest and shook his shaggy head at the delay to their normal routine.

"I thought I saw something." Jarlath scanned the scrubby bushes a second time. Rather than alarm, unusual curiosity poked at him. Him—the man his younger brother insisted was laughably predictable and always, always did the right thing.

I bet you fiddle your women in the same position, at the same time of night, on the same mark of the week-cycle.

Lynx's mocking words still stung like a bumble-wasp. Truth—his brother had the right of the situation. He lived in a deep, dark rut. *Grata fire!* He and Ellard were riding the exact path they followed each day.

Ellard narrowed his bright green eyes and perused the vicinity with his usual stoic confidence. "I don't see anything." He shifted his huge frame to study the path they'd already traversed.

"Where does this track go?" Jarlath demanded, his tone abrupt as he pointed to a fork in the trail.

"No idea, my prince."

"We'll go that way for a change," Jarlath said and urged his cambeest into motion by squeezing his legs against the barrel body of the creature.

"Wait! Jarlath, that's not a good idea—" His friend broke off with a curse, and Jarlath heard Ellard's cambeest crashing after him. "At least let me go first," Ellard called.

He found himself grinning. Ellard had called him Jarlath, and his friend didn't do that often, which told him the departure from norm was overdue. Maybe this was the reason he'd felt dissatisfaction, the reason his resentment of his younger brother had swelled and festered, the reason his temper stirred with little prodding.

"Jarlath! You should let me go first."

He ignored Ellard, examining their surroundings instead. Ah, there *was* someone on the path. The disturbance wasn't his imagination. He signaled his mount to slow but the cambeest increased his speed.

"Halt, beest!" Jarlath shifted his weight and hauled on the harness reins. Black ignored the command and bolted, the cool air whistling against Jarlath's face. His cambeest shot past a tree. Too close! Jarlath gritted his teeth at the friction of leg and coarse trunk. Pain reverberated down his limb. He gripped Black's shaggy hump with pincher fingers to right his balance. "Stop, you cantankerous beest!"

Without warning, Black screeched to a halt. Jarlath shot forward, flipping over his beest's head. His world slowed, lurching back into place when he struck the ground. Packed earth and gravel punched his head, his shoulder, smacked the breath from his lungs. Fire burned along his cheek. He struggled, wheezed to get air. A groan rippled up his throat as he lay there. Then a familiar snort had him attempting to move. Pain streaked along his arm, and he realized he still held the reins.

"Oh, dear," a soft, feminine voice said. "Are you injured?"

A murky shadow obscured his vision. Jarlath squinted, desperate to see the source of the musical accent. Another breath sawed down his throat. The roar in his head subsided to a dull throb that sat behind his right eye. Flowers. He could smell flowers. Something cool stroked his cheek, wiped across one eyelid and the darkness lifted. He blinked. Once. Twice, and his world came into sharper focus. A woman? A third blink brought the shimmer into one unwavering vision.

A beautiful, exotic woman.

Her skin was pale and bore a tinge of pastel green while her sable-brown hair hung in loose waves around her shoulders. He dragged in a breath, his mouth dropping open. She was no figment of imagination. Not with the soft ends of her hair tickling his cheek. Black trews constructed of synleather covered her legs and a white tunic clung to the swells of her breasts. A black vest and knee-high black boots completed her masculine attire. The scent of berries and sugary sweetness, greenery and female filled his nostrils. An enticing combination.

Fascinated, he continued staring. Rude, of course, yet his mind cataloged the differences between her and the women he interacted with at the castle. This one wore a blaster strapped to her thigh. The hilt of a knife peeked from the top of one boot. No doubt, her means of protection against wild animals or the brigands who sometimes frequented the forest. His rapt gaze returned to her face, her berry-stained lips and higher to stare into green eyes flecked with gold.

"Have you addled your head? Beest, shift out of the way, so I can tend to your master. You have blood on your face."

"No," Jarlath cried, panic overtaking the pain hammering his shoulder and eye. Black would hurt her. His cambeest disliked contact with strangers and several stable hands bore the scars from his beest's uncertain temper. He'd raised Black from a youngster, and like all cambeests, Black had bonded with one person and one person only—him.

"Out of the way, beest." To his amazement, the woman scolded Black and shouldered him away so she could crouch on his other side. Black behaved like an inside pet and nuzzled the pockets of her vest. His cambeest rumbled—the equivalent of a feline purr—and Jarlath felt his mouth go slack.

"Jarlath, my prince." Ellard thundered into the clearing and was off his cambeest in secs. His weapon cleared his holster, his homely face set in ferocious lines. "Take your hands off him."

"I'm checking him for wounds," the woman retorted and brushed Jarlath's hair from his forehead. Her fingers were soft and stained from picking berries. "Hush your prattle, man. It's undignified."

Ellard spluttered, and the chuckle that escaped Jarlath would have shocked his brother. Blood and liver pills, even he was a bit stunned at his amusement.

"Ah," the woman said in satisfaction. "You were winded. Let me help you sit up. The cut above your eye is still bleeding. I'll fix it in a thrice."

Her full breasts brushed his shoulder as she slipped an arm around him to lend him aid. Something bright and unexpected flared in him then that stole his breath, something inconvenient since his father was discussing alliances with *him* as a bargaining chip.

Jarlath dragged in her scent again and his cock saluted her proximity, but even more astonishing, his slumbering feline stretched beneath his skin. He hissed, gawking at her in shock.

"Prince Jarlath, it's my honor to assist you." She pulled a clean handkerchief from her tunic pocket and pressed it to his eye.

Something about her husky voice tickled his memory. "Have we met?"

"Keira Cloud," she said. "I've attended several of the court gatherings with my husband." She lifted the handkerchief. "Ah, I think the bleeding has stopped, although you might get a black eye after a bump like that. Can you stand on your own?"

"Yes. Thanks." She was married. Some of the excitement fizzling in his gut dispersed in a swell of disappointment. Unusual and exotic. Beautiful. A smart man would have snapped her up at the first opportunity.

"Marcus Cloud?" Ellard shoved his blaster back in his holster without taking his gaze off her.

Something in his friend's attitude made Jarlath study her more closely. As he pushed to his feet, he watched every hint of bright expression drain from her features.

"That's right." She drew herself up to her full height and her chin lifted a fraction before she stomped over to a nearby container of berries. The crackle of dried leaves beneath her booted feet signaled her irritation. Black nudged her arm and she absently scratched behind his long rounded ears before scooping up her container.

Ellard scowled and fingered the onyx cat he always wore around his neck. "We should go, my prince. We have the formal ball to prepare for tonight."

"Everything is in hand," he said with a sharp glare at his friend. "There's no reason for haste."

"I think it would be best," Ellard persisted.

"I apologize for my friend's rudeness." Jarlath plucked several dried leaves off his shirtsleeves and patted the worst of the dirt from his trews. "Do you and your husband live nearby?"

"My husband died several cycles ago," she said. "I run the farm on my own now."

"I'm sorry."

"Thank you," she said.

No tears. No wailing or angling for favors. She plucked several berries off a bush and dropped them into her basket.

"Can I help?" Jarlath wasn't sure who was more surprised. Him, Ellard, or Keira.

"The man first in line to the throne wishes to pick berries?" Her expression held suspicion.

Jarlath's lips curled upward, humor and a trace of awe doing a number on his normal serious mien. Most people treated him like a dangerous animal and practically tiptoed around him in case they caused upset. This woman attracted his attention with her refreshing attitude.

"Of course he doesn't," Ellard scoffed. "You dishonor the prince. Apologize."

"Enough," Jarlath said. "It was my idea, not Mrs. Cloud's."

"Call me Keira," she said.

"Are you unwell, my prince?" Ellard asked, his scowl doing nothing to enhance his plain face. "Your manner is odd today. Perhaps we should seek the opinion of a court physician."

Jarlath ignored his friend. "Do you have another receptacle?"

"Have you picked berries before, Prince Jarlath?"

"Today, I am Jarlath," he said. "No. Show me." Even he heard the trace of arrogance in his voice. "Please," he added to soften the demand.

After a searching look, she turned away to retrieve a container made of a thin transparent material, the like of which he'd never seen. "Pick the dark red berries. They are the ripe ones. And watch out for the thorns. The berries are delicious, but the plants fight to keep their fruit intact."

He picked one and popped it in his mouth. The tart juices exploded across his taste buds. The berry was so delicious he ate another two.

"My prince," Ellard said. "I require a private word."

"It can wait until we return to the castle." Jarlath trotted over to the nearest scrubby bramble bush and scanned for dark red berries. Ah! There was one. He plucked it from the bush. "I have one."

"Good," Keira said. "I need to fill all my containers before I return home."

Jarlath glanced at Keira. Black was following her and kept nuzzling and butting her for attention. He caught Keira's low chuckle and saw her hand flash out to pet his cambeest on its shaggy shoulder. The big creature dwarfed her, yet she didn't show fear. Black let out another throaty rumble of content, and Jarlath shook his head. Extraordinary.

"Jarlath, will you listen?" Ellard demanded. "This isn't right.

Keira Cloud is not a suitable person to honor with your presence."

Jarlath glared at the berry bushes. His fingers clenched his container harder, and it buckled under the force. The berries ran to one side before he regained control and leveled it. A quick breath later, he trusted himself to speak. "I do my duty. I serve the House of the Cat and never falter from doing what is right. Once, just once, I'd like to do something for fun instead of sticking to my rigid schedule."

His friend's jaw went slack. "Fun?"

"My life is like the marks of a timepiece," Jarlath snapped. "Monotonous and boring. I'm tired of the continuous schedule and wish for a change."

"Fine." Ellard's voice grated like claws against a fibreblack floor. "But not with *her*."

Jarlath shot a swift glance at Keira then placed his attention squarely on Ellard. "I'm picking berries, experiencing something new. What is your problem?"

"She's a murderess," Ellard said.

"Suspected murderess," Keira called. "I was never charged."

Ellard narrowed his gaze and aimed a fake smile in her direction. "Eavesdroppers never hear well of themselves."

"Gossips are old women with nothing better to fill their day." Keira reached for a berry and added it to her container as if she hadn't insulted the prince's bodyguard, a dangerous and powerful man.

Jarlath laughed, the sound rusty and harsh, but amusement none-the-less.

"Prince, you can't afford to associate with her. Marcus Cloud's son and daughter still accuse her of murder. They say she poisoned her husband to gain possession of his estate."

"And again, I was never charged. The judge threw the case from the circuit court. Oh, flying stars," she said. "Believe what you want. Help or not. I don't care."

Jarlath observed her stiff back as she marched to the berry bushes on the far side of the clearing. Black ambled after her, and Jarlath whistled out a breath of amazement. "I am staying to pick berries."

"This is a bad idea. They say she put a spell on Marcus Cloud, that his marriage to her was most irregular. You are behaving oddly."

"You worry overmuch." Jarlath plucked more berries, his mind on the woman as he completed his task. An accused murderess. Interesting. It took a strong woman to stand up for herself. A thorn scratched the back of his hand as he reached for a berry. He winced, freed himself and let his mind wander back to Keira. So beautiful. Different from the women he met. He tried to imagine one of them picking berries and failed.

Every woman of his acquaintance spent their days socializing and shopping, never once lifting a finger when servants could work for them. Soon, he'd have one of those women as his wife. The idea chafed like an ill-fitting formal suit, as did Ellard's hostile attitude. A woman of Keira's station was fine to bed, but not to place in his life on a permanent basis.

His feline stirred again, stretching beneath his skin in a lazy yawn. Jarlath froze, stunned by the sensation, excited and yet apprehensive in case he was imagining things. He'd thought he'd lost his feline, thought he'd suffered the same tragedy as many of their subjects.

A sad truth.

The people of the House of the Cat clan were losing the ability to shift. Their scientists were working on the problem, but a cure for the strange malady eluded them. So far, they'd kept this failure a secret from outsiders, but at some point, their problems would become public knowledge. The kingdom would grow more vulnerable since slowly their fighting force was losing an important weapon in their fighting arsenal.

Jarlath held his breath and focused inward. A flicker, like the sleepy stretch of someone awakening, caressed beneath his skin. Another burst of excitement shot through his veins. He hadn't felt his feline stir for three cycles now. Something to experiment with in the privacy of his chamber. He missed running in feline form, the explosion of sensory details that came with a shift. Yes, the sec he reached his bedchamber, he'd attempt a shift.

"Prince, please don't do this." Ellard resorted to begging, and the emotion didn't set well on his craggy countenance. His broad fingers dwarfed his onyx cat pendant as he rubbed back and forth—a sure sign of his agitation. "They say she comes from the planet Gramite..."

Jump into this adventure today. Purchase **Claimed & Seduced** at your favorite online retailer. (www.shelleymunro.com/books/claimed-seduced/)

ABOUT SHELLEY

USA Today bestselling author Shelley Munro lives in Auckland, the City of Sails, with her husband and a cheeky Jack Russell/mystery breed dog.

Typical New Zealanders, Shelley and her husband left home for their big OE soon after they married (translation of New Zealand speak - big overseas experience). A twelve-month-long adventure lengthened to six years of roaming the world. Enduring memories include being almost sat on by a mountain gorilla in Rwanda, lazing on white sandy beaches in India, whale watching in Alaska, searching for leprechauns in Ireland, and dealing with ghosts in an English pub.

While travel is still a big attraction, these days Shelley is most likely found in front of her computer following another love - that of writing stories of contemporary and paranormal romance and adventure. Other interests include watching rugby (strictly for research purposes), cycling, playing croquet and the ukelele, and curling up with an enjoyable book.

Visit Shelley at her Website

https://shelleymunro.com

Join Shelley's Newsletter

https://shelleymunro.com/newsletter

Also By Shelley

House of the Cat
Captured & Seduced
Claimed & Seduced
Merry & Seduced
Stranded & Seduced
Seized & Seduced
Hunted & Seduced
Festive & Seduced
Betrayed & Seduced
Enticed & Seduced

Middlemarch Capture
Snared by Saber
Favored by Felix
Lost with Leo
Spellbound with Sly
Journey with Joe
Star-Crossed with Scarlett